Paul Kilduff's first novel was **SQUARE MILE:**

'A slick, punchy thriller by a banking insider, full of financial know-how'

Daily Mail

'An entertaining debut with an all-too-believable ending'
Sunday Telegraph

'A rattling good yarn'

Irish Independent

'An insider's account of the pleasure and pain associated with playing with vast amounts of other people's money ... Kilduff writes with authority ... He handles the world of high finance and soft-top BMWs with aplomb'

Irish Times

'An attractively written first novel, whose strength lies in the creation of the bank's atmosphere, and the detailed analysis of financial jiggery-pockery'

Evening Standard

'Set in the world of high finance and high flyers in the City, Paul Kilduff paints a detailed and intriguing picture of the players and their environment ... The most gut-tightening, enthralling tale I have read for a long time'
Dublin Commuting Timesa

By the same author

Square Mile

About the author

Born and educated in Dublin, Paul Kilduff moved to London where he spent six years working with a US securities house and an international banking group. Paul returned to live and work in Dublin in 1995. *The Dealer* is his second novel.

The Dealer

Paul Kilduff

CORONET BOOKS

Hodder & Stoughton

First published in Great Britain in 2000
by Hodder and Stoughton
First published in paperback in 2000
by Hodder and Stoughton
A division of Hodder Headline

A Coronet Paperback

10 9 8 7 6 5 4 3 2 1

British Library Cataloguing in Publication Data
Kilduff, Paul
    The dealer
        1. Financial institutions – England –
        London – Fiction
        2. Suspense fiction
        I. Title
    823.9′14[F]

ISBN 0 340 73875 8

Printed and bound in Great Britain by
Mackays of Chatham PLC, Chatham, Kent

Hodder and Stoughton
A division of Hodder Headline
338 Euston Road
London NW1 3BH

To Gerry and Joan

*'You are the bows from which your
children as living arrows are sent forth.'*

Kahlil Gibran
Poet and philosopher, 1883–1931

PROLOGUE

MORE THAN SEVEN BILLION POUNDS was added to share values in the City today as dealers celebrated London's FTSE-100 hitting another all-time high. Cheers went up in dealing rooms as the Footsie closed up 71 points on the day. The strong bullish sentiment is attributed to a combination of excellent company results and hopes of further mega-takeovers to follow before the end of the year.

SHARES IN PROVIDENT BANK rose a further twenty-five pence following the agreed six billion-pound takeover by British Commercial Bank. Barbara Ashby, head of UK equity research at investment bank Blake Brothers & Co., said that the price rise indicated investors thought another bidder, possibly a large European bank, might top the current offer on the table.

POLICE HAVE CONFIRMED the body found in the River Thames near Greenwich is that of missing bank executive Alexander Soames. Mr Soames, 49, was Finance Director of Provident Bank. He was last seen alive at a secret company board meeting in the Dorchester Hotel where the terms of the surprise takeover deal were finalised. DI Edward Hammond from the Metropolitan Police said the circumstances of Soames' death are suspicious and are currently under investigation.

Business Day
Evening Standard
www.thisislondon.co.uk

SOMETHING IN THE CITY

If the City of London were an independent country, it would be ranked as the 20th richest in the world, just ahead of Belgium, Austria and Sweden. A single square mile stretching from the Law Courts in the west to the Tower of London in the east is billed as the world's leading international financial centre. And why not?

The City's foreign exchange market handles five hundred billion dollars every working day. The City produces total annual wealth of one hundred and fifty billion pounds, almost twenty per cent of the UK's entire earnings. Twenty billion of this comes from overseas earnings. There are six hundred foreign banks in London, more than anywhere else in the world; there are more American banks than in New York, more German banks than in Frankfurt. It is the largest global market for foreign equity trading, Eurobond dealing, fund management, insurance and maritime services.

Consequently, it is commonly believed that everyone in the City receives immense salaries, supplemented by generous bonuses, profit sharing and corporate perks. By and large, this appears to be true. The Government's official national earnings survey shows that the average City salary is £40K, twice the national average. Ten per cent of City staff earn more than £70K. At the top end of the scale there is a small elite of dealers, salesmen, fund managers, research analysts, directors, partners, lawyers and corporate financiers who earn in excess of one million pounds a year.

But as Chris Tarrant is prone to utter on his Capital FM breakfast show when Texans win millions of bucks on their State Lottery: are they really happy?

ES Magazine

CHAPTER ONE

BISHOPSGATE, LONDON EC2

Greg M. Schneider had a plan that always worked. There was a right way and a wrong way to buy ten million quids' worth of paper and he knew the difference. This damn deal had to be done so that no one else in the City knew that the ex-pat they feared of late was in the market in such size. Greg never paid top dollar for what he so desperately needed. He spoke to no one in particular, but every other equity dealer in the vicinity heard his distinct transatlantic drawl above the pulsing buzz of the first floor.

'We need to make some serious loot today, guys.'

No reply. A bead or two of sweat formed on his temple in anticipation of the market action to follow. The air con really sucked in this frenetic dealing room. Never as good as back in the States or in the Merc. Greg was a long way from Long Island but even after four years of hell in the City he still looked like a New Yorker on a short-term posting overseas. If only it were that simple.

He rolled up the sleeves of his white button-down Brooks Brothers shirt. His cotton vest, or undershirt as his countrymen quaintly referred to it, was clearly visible below. An essential garment for all his former colleagues in Mitchells on Wall

Street but never worn here in the City. His internet-ordered Barneys Fifth Avenue silk tie with the minuscule dollar logos hung from the undone top button of his shirt. He hadn't been home in years. Pity. The loose tie was the signal to his peers that he meant business today. He was about to go play with the big boys on the street. Slam dunk, hopefully. He spoke to his team without averting his steady gaze from the flashing real time prices.

'Anyone got any good ideas for me?'

Still no brave volunteers. The pressure on them to perform was constant. They were only as good as their last deal. It was always a zero-sum game. What they might make today in Blakes, some other unfortunate less-experienced punter in Goldmans, Deutsche, Morgans or Salomon would lose. They all needed a successful year of dealing.

Greg flexed his taut shoulders as he sat looking at the SEAQ screens arrayed before him. He rolled his chair nearer to the row of dazzling neon and ran his hands through his dark wiry hair that never needed a comb. He searched for early stubble on his square jaw. A sallow face, good skin, blue eyes and the reassuring evidence of a close shave; all apparently went down well with the opposite sex. He had Blakes' money to spend and it was burning a hole in his deep pocket. It was definitely time for stage one of the master plan. He directed a follow-up question at a colleague.

'Any stellar ideas for me today, Chas?'

Charles Wilson looked uneasy as he stretched his sartorial trademarks, those badly needed braces with humorous designs of fast cars and faster women. His chair creaked with the effort. Chas always claimed that he was the perfect weight for his height. True enough if he had been six foot four instead of the more average five foot ten. Seventeen stone was a lot of finely honed muscle for a guy in his late thirties to carry around in between smoking cancer sticks and downing pints of real ale in the Bull & Bear. Chas went to the gym, but not to pump iron

4

with competing beefcake or trot miles on machines in front of overhead CNN screens. He preferred watching the perspiring talent in micro leotards. His idea of outdoor exercise consisted of an evening in a beer garden. Chas had recently discovered that his nickname was an anagram of cash. They assured him that this was a mere coincidence.

'I don't know, Greg. I only work here.'

Jesus, Chas, get with the program. Greg's team had made a solid six-million pounds dealing profit last year and were up to three million by the June half-year end. It was simply not enough for Old Nick in the corner office. Crosswaithe's target for Greg and the other three was seven million for the entire twelve months. This could be done if Greg's luck continued in this bullish yet volatile market. He did after all have an edge over other players sitting at far more influential dealing desks throughout the City: the closely guarded secret of his amazing run of success. Greg pushed his senior dealer.

'So what's happening in the market today? Who's in the news?'

Chas was still floundering. He wished he had done more digging around in the newspapers this morning.

'Speak to me, buddy. We need a play on some stocks. Some short-term punting for some fast bucks, keep Old Nick over there happy for a while. He's getting some serious heat from the Directors upstairs.'

Over time they'd got used to all this transatlantic jargon. It was never shares, always stocks; never companies, always corporates; never pounds, always bucks; never pressure, always heat. And everything was goddamn this and goddamn that. Or fucking this. Never the Queen's English. Old Nick detested bad language on his personal dealing floor. This wasn't Wall Street after all. It was Blakes.

'What's on the SEAQ announcements page? Any corporates with results out today?'

Chas keyed in the page numbers to the SEAQ screen,

bringing up a list of company names. Greg stood beside him and glanced down the alphabetical list of FTSE and Mid-250 stocks that would be announcing final and interim results. Difficult to see exactly with Chas's beer belly partly obscuring the view. It was Chas who dared to have the first idea.

'Midland Engineering are announcing full year profits. What about them? Worth a punt?'

Chas keyed in their stock code and Greg looked at a chart of their share price trend for the past six months.

'The stock price never goddamn moves. No volatility there for us. Even if they announce mega profits, the stock price won't react much.'

They went through other names but soon reached a stalemate. Greg had another idea.

'What about companies with AGMs today?'

Chas displayed a shorter list of those companies holding annual general meetings, that rare occasion when the Directors actually faced their shareholders and made carefully calibrated trading statements about company performance. Sometimes good news emanated and had a favourable effect on a share price. It might be an opportunity for a crack dealing team to make a fast few hundred grand or more.

Chas suggested a few likely names but Greg didn't seem interested. He was about to invest millions of pounds in a single stock for twenty-four hours and he had to be right. He needed a special corporate. His eyes came to rest on a stock in the middle of the list.

'What about County Beverages? Their AGM is at three o'clock today in the Dorchester Hotel. What do you think?'

Chas was senior enough to disagree with his boss whenever he had the inclination. But only just.

'No. Poor management. No strategy for the future. Ancient production facilities. No way.'

Wrong attitude, thought Greg. Although the investment bank of Blake Brothers & Co was not the biggest in the City, he had a growing reputation as head of their Special Situations dealing desk. At thirty-two he was future Director material in the bank and they all knew it on the first floor. In the meantime he had the hundred thousand basic salary, the German roll-top SLK coupe and the overly generous bonus every year courtesy of Old Nick. Again he had to remind Chas of why their desk existed.

'We're not investing for the long term. We want some good news at the AGM shortly after three o'clock. Then we will cash in our chips as soon as we can.'

Chas printed a six-month price chart for County Beverages from the humming laser printer.

'Look at the figures, Greg. The price trend is downwards. It's too bad to bet our precious money on.'

The star dealer had other ideas. 'I think it's perfect. The stock is out of favour. It's cheap. The bad news is already discounted in today's price. It can't go much lower.'

'Watch it.' Chas was still unconvinced.

They walked back to the dealing desk, knowing there was no going back once they piled into County.

'It can't be as simple as that, Greg.'

'Why not? Let's not try to complicate matters here.'

Chas still wasn't won over. 'It's a hell of a gamble.'

'Chas, I hate to tell you this but that's why we are here. It's our job.'

'OK. How much will we buy?'

In for a penny, in for ten million quid.

'Let's do ten. That's all we can do now or we'll blow our thirty million position limit and the guys in Risk upstairs will be all over us.'

Chas exhaled audibly. The desk only dealt in millions of pounds. Ten million quid on County Beverages for one day was a high roller bet.

They had picked the stock. Time now for stage two of the

master plan. To spend. 'Where's the team when you need them? Where's Jules?'

Chas stood up to improve his view. Well worth it.

'She's over at the coffee machine. Here she comes now.'

When Jules walked through the first floor the volume of conversation noticeably dropped as eyes followed her weaving path between the rows of desks. She was a sight to behold; all their attention was still focused on her as she reached Greg's desk, took off her navy jacket and hung it on the back of her chair. They were visibly impressed as she revealed a partially see-through cream silk blouse that allowed a tantalising glimpse of a lace-edged bra. She had blown Greg out years ago in the Bull & Bear. Shame.

'Right, boys, what's on the agenda today?'

Julia Anson was ready for work. Which left the fourth team member; the Hon. Henry Smythe arrived.

'Morning gentlemen. How goes it today?'

Late as usual. A well-thumbed *Times* under his arm. Cufflinks yet to be inserted in a badly creased shirt. Smythe was a real Hooray Henry all right. He had passed his six months probationary period. Just. But a public school education and wealthy parents wouldn't protect him from the real world forever.

Time for work. Greg spoke to the troops.

'We're getting into County Beverages in size. Let's do this carefully and quickly. Don't spook the market makers until we are all done.'

The SEAQ screen quote page showed twelve investment banks that were ready to deal immediately in County Beverages in decent volume. The bigger text at the top of the screen showed the current best buying price and selling price. The numbers that mattered were 498 and 503: 498 pence if you wanted to sell and 503 if you were buying in normal size lots of twenty-five thousand shares.

Greg never bought small amounts of shares; that was for the man in the street. The market makers out there had a spread of five pence. Greg wondered how anyone could be happy making a one per cent profit. He wanted, and needed, so much more today. The mathematics were simple; even Henry didn't need a calculator this time. Ten million quid to buy. A fiver a share. Two million shares. And four eager people at the dealing desk.

'We'll do five hundred each.' The five hundred thousand was implicit and they knew it. 'Do two fifty each with two different houses, and call them one after the other without putting the phone down. Chas, you do Mitchells and HSBC.'

Chas nodded and wrote the bank names on the corner of his dealing blotter. As if he would forget them in a moment like this.

'Jules, you call Salomon and Goldman.'

She could use her charms down the telephone line to keep these market makers sweet. Greg had deliberately given her Goldmans. She knew Todd, the market maker cum movie star, well. Rather too well if office gossip was to be believed.

'Hooray, you take Nomura and ABN.'

Hooray nodded his agreement as he leant forward in his reclining chair. For the first time that morning he focused on the work in hand, rather than on the society pages of his newspaper. He wrote the names down carefully. He needed to or he would forget them.

'I'll take the Germans.' Greg would call Deutsche and Dresdner KB. Crunch time. It was easy to buy large lines of FTSE constituent stocks; they were all dealt on LORDS, the automatic dealing system. Greg just keyed in the number of shares and his order flowed automatically and simultaneously to the market makers. County Beverages, however, was only a Mid-250 stock and was dealt over the telephone. Personal contact was a risk. Market makers were continually looking for clues in the intonation of the buyer's voice, their sense of urgency. Anything to avoid being legged over by their peers. Even by Jules.

The telephones were poised in damp hands. Greg glanced at the international wall clocks: 8.42 a.m. in London. The offer price of County Beverages was steady on the SEAQ screen at 503 pence. They would not fill an order of this magnitude at that single execution price. When the market surmised what they were doing then the price would definitely rise. Time would tell how much. There was no reason why this should not work right …

'… now!'

They hit the direct line dealing boards and were instantly through to the relevant market maker in the bigger houses in the City. They each had their own individual patter to disguise what they really meant. 'I'm looking for a line of County Bev. Say about two hundred and fifty.' *Well, two hundred and fifty thousand to be exact.*

'What's your best price on two fifty County Bev?' *I am buying them at any price right now.*

'Might be keen on some County Bev stock, if there's some going?' *I hope you're a seller in size.*

'Any chance of an excellent price in County Bev, Todd?' *Any chance of another excellent date, Todd?*

It took thirty seconds and two telephone calls each. When they were done, each signalled to Greg with thumbs raised. It made a pleasant change from raised middle index fingers in times of stress. He was now the proud owner of two million County Bev shares at approximately five quid each. They shouted out their execution prices. Greg wrote them on his dealing blotter where he recorded everything that mattered.

'504 with Mitchells and 505 with HSBC.'

'503 Salomon. 507 Goldman.'

Chas couldn't resist a jibe. 'You were well and truly shafted by Goldmans, and not for the first time, eh, Jules?'

'504 pence with Nomura and 504 ABN.'

Greg had dealt 505 with Deutsche and 504 with KB. He averaged the prices. It came to 504.5 pence. They had done well. The prices in the screens had hardly moved. One or two ticked up a penny but nothing to get excited about. It didn't constitute a significant trend. Yet.

They knew the drill. Time to move the market unilaterally, build up the creamy froth like that on a pint of County Beverages premium special brew. Greg gave the instructions.

'Chas, do Morgans. Ask for two fifty more and drop out. Don't buy a single goddamn share. Jules, call Lehmans. Hooray, call CSFB. I'll do UBS. Now.'

They were back on the telephones immediately.

'What's the best on two fifty County Bev? How much? Too high. I'll go elsewhere.'

'I'm looking for two hundred and fifty County Bev. I'll pay tops. How much? Sorry, no can do.'

'I need some size in County Bev. No. Get back to you.'

They hung up the telephones and watched the screens. It had to happen. Morgans were first to knock up their price by one lousy penny. Lehmans followed with their token penny. UBS duly obliged with a full two pence. They smiled. A minute later Mitchells and Goldman upped their prices by three pence. The rest followed the US market leaders.

The word was out amongst that incestuous group of pseudo-professionals, the market makers. Blakes had bought lines of County Bev stock from all of them by stealth and was keen to buy more. So let's ramp the price up and make them pay. Only this special situations dealing desk wasn't buying anymore. Instead the team made for the coffee machine, their day's work completed by ten to nine.

Greg was already working on stage three. He ambled over to the research department on the same floor and made straight for Barbara Ashby, their highly rated star analyst, and not too bad at equity research either. He sat deliberately on the edge of her desk, here to stay until he got the answer he wanted.

'Are you going to any AGMs today?'

Barbara swivelled round on her chair and brushed back

tresses of auburn hair from her eyes. She looked great today. Even better than she had at six a.m.

'Nope.'

Greg was so distracted, this close to her. He kept his mind on work only with difficulty.

'Can you do me a favour? Go to County Bev's AGM in the West End today? Otherwise I'll have to send Hooray and he'll fuck it up totally. I need to know what transpires there, as it happens real time. It's a real hot stock today. There's a big buyer of size in the market and the price is drifting up already. Expectation is rising. It might come to a messy climax this afternoon in a room in the Dorchester Hotel.'

She refrained from passing comment at his loaded innuendo.

'Let me know when you are going by lunchtime. I'll give you a call on your mobile when you're there.' He didn't take no for an answer. Never.

Barbara checked her screens. The County price was indeed rising. She talked to her research colleagues. Yes, there was some morning action in the stock, some buyers of size according to the trade volume data on Datastream. Believe the hype. They were now expecting an announcement at the AGM that afternoon, maybe even a positive trading statement from Sir Gordon Harvey, the Chairman. She would have to go to the Dorchester and pen a research piece for tomorrow morning's meeting.

She enjoyed the leisurely view of Greg as he walked away, flexing those shoulders again and giving her a backward smile and a lazy wink of a clear blue eye. They would both know soon about County Beverages. The waiting was the worst part.

CHAPTER TWO

OLD BROAD STREET, LONDON EC2

Today's date was circled in red in Mark Robinson's desk diary. He had waited six months and was well prepared for the rapidly approaching meeting at ten o'clock. Still, he couldn't resist a brief mental reminder of the facts. He unlocked the bottom drawer of his awful 1970s MFI veneer desk, ignored the pile of miserly pay slips and took out a thin manila file marked Personal. No one was nearby. No sign yet of his tardy colleague. Ever since his engagement to Claire last month, Peter was regularly late for work. Too much sex in the kitchen over breakfast perhaps. Norris had told him off. Mark opened the file he knew so well and dared to flick through the accumulated evidence for the prosecution.

First that single faded piece of pink paper, torn from the *Financial Times* nearly three years ago, still jagged along the edges, some salient words underlined by him in black ink. The job advertisement he had naively believed at the time. 'The London Stock Exchange plays a vital role in maintaining London's position as one of the world's leading financial centres.' They had a vacancy and Mark had obliged them by filling it. Not the smartest career move in hindsight.

It went on, 'You will need a number of personal and

professional qualities including diplomacy, patience, initiative, an eye for detail and an ability to remain calm under pressure.' Mark possessed these qualities although unfortunately he rarely got the chance to demonstrate them to the world at large. 'A competitive salary and an excellent working environment.' Definitely not true. 'The chance to develop your career.' Not true either. 'Please send your CV to Clive Norris.' He had.

'Are you ready, Mark?'

Almost caught in the act. Norris had appeared from nowhere and now stood before him, Director of the Enforcement Department and Mark's boss. The man who had sold him the party line three years ago and still didn't feel the need to apologise for that sham of a job interview. Mark followed him into the biggest office on the floor and took the chair by the desk. Immediately he felt at a disadvantage, sitting at least six inches lower than his adversary. What an office it was. They sat surrounded by grey filing cabinets loaded with bundles of papers and files collecting centuries of dust; half-drawn window blinds with knotted drawstrings locked into position for decades; stained beige carpet curling at the edges along the walls; last year's calendar hanging awkwardly from six-inch masonry nails. Every item of furniture clashing with the other antiques that would never appear on any BBC roadshow.

Up close Norris looked drained. Massive bags under his eyes, thin grey hair in need of a decent trim, over-washed white shirt from C&A with yellowing shiny stripes. If Norris was the result of thirty years spent in the dedicated service of the London Stock Exchange, then Mark needed to get out soon before he faded to the colour of that shirt. Norris's present primary interest seemed to be in the pension scheme of the LSE. Three years to go to the compulsory retirement age of fifty-eight and then the eagerly awaited end of a lifetime's early morning commuting on Network South East and the Drain to Bank.

Norris also had a file: Mark's personnel file. The job advert was stapled to the inside cover. So was an old version of his CV. Norris didn't know that there was a much more recent version available. Just in case. The file also held Mark's previous appraisals over the past three years. They had been positive enough.

'So, Mark, appraisal time. How do you think the past six months went?'

What an uninspiring opening question. Wasn't it obvious? Didn't Norris know that Mark was becoming more and more disillusioned working in this sleepy department? He needed a challenge.

'Do you want an honest answer, Clive?'

'Of course.'

Might as well go for it then. Nothing to lose but his job. 'I'm bored here.'

Norris sat back in his chair, shrugging his shoulders in apparent surprise.

'Really? What's wrong?'

'I've been here for almost three years. The first year was all photocopying, boxing archives, filing and making coffee for everyone. I expected that and thought it would get better afterwards but not much has improved. I need some more interesting work. I would like to be considered for promotion.'

Norris grimaced behind his inter-linked hands. 'We can't promote you yet. You must show that you've earned it.'

'That's the issue. I'm still working on irrelevant investigations, widows' complaints, penny shares, the wording of company announcements and routine market surveillance. I need to be assigned to a decent investigation. How can I prove anything to you if I never get a chance? It's Catch 22.'

Norris was visibly uneasy at the confrontational tone that was developing. Amicable appraisals weren't meant to be this way. Management training courses hadn't prepared him for this. He hedged.

'I think you're doing well, Mark. I will try to allocate some

15

of the more interesting investigations to you when they arise in the future.'

'Do you mean that or are you saying it because it's my appraisal?'

'I mean it.'

'Good. Otherwise . . .'

'Otherwise what?'

It had to be said. It had been on Mark's mind for months. Get it out in the open.

'Otherwise I'll leave.'

Norris was clearly unhappy; visibly distressed at the thought of losing an experienced minion, but also angry at the disloyalty. People didn't leave the LSE.

'But we need you here. And where would you go anyhow?'

Didn't Norris ever read the FT on a Thursday? Or did he stick to the *Economist*?

'I've seen the job adverts in the newspapers. Most City investment banks are queuing up to hire experienced Compliance staff. I think I would have better career opportunities in the banks. They pay well too.' He would be a gamekeeper turned poacher.

At least the hint about pay worked. Norris leant forward and passed over a sealed LSE envelope. Mark knew that it would be rude to open it right now. Clever ploy.

'I am pleased to advise that your salary has been increased.'

'How much?' asked Mark bluntly.

Norris didn't care for such dangerous informality.

'It's in the envelope. You can open it afterwards.'

Mark smiled thinly. 'Thank you very much.'

They waffled on for an age in a pointless discussion, Mark growing more frustrated, Norris more defensive. He gave Mark an Above Average rating on the last page of the appraisal form. They signed it as if it held some major contractual significance. Waste of time. Norris could give him a Truly Stellar or better rating, he still wouldn't be impressed. They parted company after thirty minutes.

Peter arrived belatedly and took off his trademark Walkman. Mark sat at his desk and opened the envelope. His colleague grinned. It still unnerved Mark to look at Peter. He could never understand how Norris had come to hire a veritable Mark Robinson clone. He was terrified in case Norris somehow saw something of himself in his two juniors. Perish the thought. But they were so alike, everyone said so. Shocks of dark brown hair, although Mark's was combed; Peter would no doubt buy a comb soon. In the meantime Mother Nature sufficed. Same strong build, round face and square shoulders. Same easy smile and alert eyes. To top it all, Peter's optician had made him buy reading glasses too. They'd both go for a different pair to Norris's.

Peter was watching, looking for his immediate reaction to the number on the single page. Mark had to smile to make the right impression. The number was twenty-seven thousand pounds per annum. He faked the smile. Peter knew him well enough, knew disappointment when he saw it.

'Still not enough then?'

'Not really.'

Mark had commitments. The biggest was to the Halifax for the monthly mortgage on his Battersea apartment which he might have the chance to actually own in twenty-three years time. He was also well acquainted with the minimum monthly repayments and exorbitant APR rates of Barclaycard. And the ten-year-old VW Golf with the loud exhaust was continually breaking down and needed an upgrade. The RAC knew Mark personally by now.

Peter was more intuitive than Norris. 'Still thinking of moving on to pastures new?'

Peter had six months service and was still learning. But Mark had experience and market knowledge and still earned only a lousy 27k. He started to fantasise. Compliance staff in the US investment banks a few hundred yards down the road earned double that in a year, and got a mortgage subsidy, a company Gti and an annual bonus. Not fair.

'Who'd have me, Pete?'

Mark folded the appraisal form, thought about the bin then put it into his drawer. He took one last look at his personal file again. His CV still needed some work but not right now. Later. The early parts wouldn't change. School in East London. University. The Business degree: a 2.2 Honours, although he had worked damn hard and had hoped for a 2.1. Pity. A year wasted behind the counter of a high street bank handing out crisp ten-pound notes to old dears and cashing hot cheques for dubious customers.

Ambition forced him to leave prematurely, rather than waiting until his late fifties. Then some temping in a few City offices, some insurance broking and fund management. Decent names on his CV but never the chance of a permanent job due to 'headcount freezes', 'downsizing' and 'involuntary parting'. Careful phrases courtesy of the politically correct HR departments. When the LSE job came along Mark jumped at the chance of a permanent job. Jumped too early.

He was walking. Definitely. Time to call a recruitment consultant ... unless Norris gave him the next substantial investigation that came the way of the London Stock Exchange Enforcement Department.

Sir Gordon Harvey rose to his feet and faced the assembled audience in the Hunter function room of Park Lane's Dorchester Hotel. As Chairman of County Beverages, he enjoyed these annual occasions to speak to his loyal shareholders, with the attendant media presence and the City of London observers. He straightened the Old Etonian tie, loosened the top button on the chalk pinstripe suit, smoothed his perfect parting and knew he would look good in the newspapers tomorrow.

The turnout this year was most satisfactory. A public

company never knew how many shareholders would turn up on the day. They could hire a tent in some dingy side street in London for thousands of eager punters, or take the Royal Albert Hall for ten sad bastards with nothing else to do on a sweltering Wednesday afternoon. This year's venue had been judged to perfection by his under-utilised Corporate Affairs staff.

He delayed his opening remarks. He had to. Mobile telephones annoyed him intensely. Some of the flash City types never knew when to switch off.

When yet another mobile rang, every attendant research guru went for his or her own corporate telephone. No need. Barbara immediately knew it was hers. It was Greg.

'Hi, Barbara. Any news? It's after three o'clock.'

'Not yet. They're running late, the Chairman's about to speak.'

Barbara had taken an aisle seat near one of the side speakers so that the pronouncements from the podium would be fully audible back in Blakes' dealing room. She had passed the last ten minutes eyeing up the competition from the other investment banks. She immediately recognised many of her peers. Everyone who mattered in this business now had a representative here. They couldn't afford to be the last to know about this afternoon's possible announcement in the Dorchester. Word was out. The Chairman was enjoying making them wait. He knew every trick in the book thanks to the media training essential for every head of a plc walking into the lion's den.

Barbara remembered something she had noticed on her way into the hotel.

'Greg. Guess who I saw in the lobby?'

'I've no idea. Is this important now or just a wind-up? Who was it? The Queen?'

Americans were obsessed with the Royal Family.

'I saw half the board of Provident Bank coming out of a private dining room and heading upstairs to a meeting.

Surrounded by lawyers and advisers and other parasites in good suits. It looked serious. Something big might be going down at Provident. I saw the Chief Executive, Webster, and that guy Soames, the Finance Director. What do you think?'

A momentary pause on the line. The background sound of mumbled dealing chatter in Blakes.

'Interesting.'

Then the hum of a live PA system in the hotel function room. Barbara was near enough for some excellent reception. Greg sat with his team around the squawk box on the special situations dealing desk, worshippers at the altar of enlightenment. This was the moment they would learn what was going to become of their ten-million pound bet on a previously unfancied stock. Harvey finally began to pontificate.

'Thank you for coming today. The other Directors and myself are delighted at the turnout this year. It is a tangible sign of your continued interest in our company.'

The usual corporate bullshit from the Chairman. Shareholder attendance had picked up in the recent past merely because free samples of products were dispensed to those present at the AGM. This might not be well received at a waste disposal or metal bashing company but it was a real attraction for any food and beverage manufacturer. A six pack of beer and a big box of candy would help to sweeten any bitter pill.

'Before we go through the list of motions for the meeting and the approval of last year's accounts, I would like to comment on our recent trading performance since the last year end.'

This was it. They waited for his first utterance, positive or negative.

'I am pleased to advise . . .'

They didn't need to hear anymore. He had used the one magic word. They were home free.

'. . . that we have experienced most favourable trading conditions in the past six months. Sales of all our main products have risen sharply, particularly in the beer, soft drinks and ice cream markets. I believe it must be the great weather we are having.'

They could hear polite laughter in the function room. They were laughing at the dealing desk too. Greg turned down the volume on the squawk box. The others didn't mind. Their attention had shifted from Harvey's mellifluous tones to the SEAQ screens in front of each of them.

It took less than a minute. Deutsche flashed up a higher price for County Beverages. 506 pence – 512 pence. They would buy at 506. Greg was already sitting on a paper profit in theory, albeit minuscule. Then SBC flashed up with a 507–513. Excellent. Mitchells killed them dead with a 509–515 quotation. Beautiful. As the price goes up, the spread widens by an extra penny so the market maker shares in the gains. Greg did some quick mental calculations. Two million shares. Bought at 504.5. Now at 509 pence. Almost one hundred thousand pounds profit. Nice. Chas had more pressing thoughts on his mind.

'The price is on the up, let's shift some of this paper. I'll never be able to sleep tonight knowing we're sitting on two million County Bev shares. The Chairman's speech could be the usual verbal diarrhoea. Let's sell into the rising market.'

If it was difficult to buy shares sometimes, it was equally difficult to sell without hammering the price. There was always a price for selling shares, and another price for selling shares quickly. Greg was never a forced seller. The price was rising because he had taken two million shares out of circulation this morning and he was not going to release them back in the market yet. The market makers were caught short and were covering their positions. There might be more money to be made here, which meant waiting until tomorrow. Chas would have to endure a sleepless night. Greg made the decisions on the desk.

'No. We sit on our position overnight.'

And that was all there was to it. The others rose to knock off for the day at three-thirty.

'We're finished here. Let's celebrate at the Bull & Bear. Coming, Greg?'

'I'll follow you. I want to check the Bible. Give me a hour or so.'

Simon Fry charged his blue-chip clients the very respectable sum of two hundred and twenty pounds an hour for his professional advice, so it hurt all the more to take time away from his oak partners' desk at the leading City law firm of Speake Windsor. The view from his Bishopsgate high rise office out over the east of the City confirmed that he had arrived, at least geographically. He was one of the youngest partners at the firm, with an impressive blue-chip client portfolio, a fast tracker on the road to an even more lucrative career. However, certain matters at Speakes were still outside his immediate control.

He had inherited his new office and his secretary courtesy of a retiring senior partner. Simon had trashed the plastic plants, the net curtains and the appalling art, but unfortunately she was still here. The perm with the purple tint, the over-sized NHS-issue glasses and those shapeless pastel cardigans drove him mad. He would hire a svelte PA who would oblige with civility and informality, it was only a matter of time, but until then this late twentieth-century dragon was impervious to his undisguised hostility.

'Have you left me a contact telephone number, Simon?'

'I'd love to but I can't. It's one of those confidential corporate meetings. A big deal,' he lied.

She did not give up that easily.

'Are you taking your mobile telephone?'

'Yes, I am,' as he reluctantly placed the telephone in his inner suit pocket.

'And are you sure it's switched on this time?'

Nag. Nag. Nag. Simon flashed her the telephone with the LCD display lit up, obviously powered on. When the lift doors closed he took out the phone, switched off the power, and replaced it in his suit pocket. He did not want any interruptions in the next couple of hours. He strode across Bishopsgate and used a cash machine outside the local bank branch to extract a wad of new notes. He caught a black cab at the endless rank outside Liverpool Street tube station, giving the cabbie a vague destination towards the East End.

'Isle of Dogs. Near Crossharbour DLR station. I'll let you know exactly where when we get there.'

They drew alongside the station at exactly seven minutes before two o'clock. Too early. Simon instructed the driver to pass his destination and drop him at an adjacent corner. He paid the fare with a ten-pound note and did not ask for change. It was too much to pay for the short trip but he didn't care, not with his salary and his equity interest in the firm.

He loped back down the street at a well-measured pace and entered Thames View, a cul de sac which contained a secluded group of red-brick two-storey townhouses. He prised open the stiff metal gate and brushed by the gleaming BMW 3 series in the tiny cobbled drive. Then up the five tiled steps to the door of number thirty-two. He pushed the doorbell as the minute hand on his gold Rolex edged towards two o'clock. Perfect timing. Eventually. Simon was pleasantly surprised as ever when the door opened.

They sat together in the modern lounge and nonchalantly discussed work, holidays and the July heatwave. He gazed out at the river flowing beyond the window and the balcony as he anxiously sipped a chilled mineral water in a solid crystal glass that grew heavier by the minute. His heart was racing and the glass became loose in his sweaty grip. No going back now. There never was.

After the requisite ten minutes of social pleasantries he was asked to make himself ready for what he was about to receive gratefully. Without a word of acknowledgement he descended the narrow wrought-iron stairs into the garage of the luxury townhouse that had not been graced with the presence of the

BMW for months, even years perhaps. There was simply no available room.

Simon took off his regulation City pinstripe, then the custom-made poplin shirt, the striped silk tie, the polished black shoes and penultimately the M&S socks. Last to be removed were the white boxer shorts, the last bastion of male respectability. His heartbeat was racing faster, perhaps even dangerously so. He placed the unnecessary clothes in a tidy pile in the wire basket in the corner as usual, knelt facing the bottom of the steps, lowered his eyes to the concrete floor and waited. He clasped his hands behind his back, so tightly that he felt a twinge of pain in his shoulder blades. It felt good.

The wait always seemed to be an eternity. He heard footsteps descend the stairs. His eyes first caught sight of the heels. Then the full-length boots, a one-piece leather basque restrained by pairs of solid steel buckles, a choker around a perfect elongated neck and a peaked cap pulled low over steely-blue eyes. As she turned he saw the blonde ponytail that ran halfway down the small of her arched back. Her face was exaggerated by shocking red lipstick that merely served to heighten the perfection that confronted Simon.

She circled him, the sound of the heels ringing out on the resonant concrete, waited more minutes for the tension to build, then spoke with her trademark cut-glass accent.

'Over here.'

She led him to the darkest corner of the garage. He complied as she secured him, then dropped the wooden crossbeam. His ankles sat in another cross-section. He stood yet leant forward simultaneously, knowing that without the support of the stocks he would fall forward onto the unforgiving concrete upon which his bare soles rested.

She began her work. In his prone position Simon had no opportunity to see the small microphone recessed in the ceiling, nor the wire that ran upstairs to the tape deck recording in the lounge above them both.

Forty minutes later he sat fully dressed in the lounge, finished the glass of Evian, took one last look at the river, placed ten crisp twenty-pound notes on the coffee table and took his leave, smarting yet wholly satisfied. He caught a cab near the DLR station and wasted another tenner on the fare.

Simon was sitting at his desk at Speakes, albeit somewhat uncomfortably, in time for his four o'clock meeting with the Managing Director of Sportsworld plc, a major client about to do a chunky corporate deal. The terms had been agreed. The Memorandum of Understanding had been drafted, the multi-million-pound consideration finalised. The legal fees for Speakes would be enormous. Excellent.

His annoying secretary immediately noticed his reappearance.

'There were some telephone calls, Simon. I tried to get you on your mobile but it didn't work.'

'I know. I was detained.'

CHAPTER THREE

BISHOPSGATE, LONDON EC2

Greg sat and worried. He worried about what Chas and the others might deduce, about what Barbara knew, about other dealers in Blakes, about Old Nick in the plush corner office, the aged Directors upstairs, the market surveillance by the LSE, the hated competitors in banks around the City. Most of all he worried about being caught. There was so much to worry about.

He worried about Blakes' Risk Management Department, who independently monitored his dealing positions and screamed if he exceeded his gross book limit of thirty million pounds. They also monitored his stock limit of ten million pounds, the maximum he could invest in any one single company stock. Right now he was up to that limit without a buck to spare. Thanks to County Beverages.

He worried about Internal Audit, who came around once a year to ask inane questions about what he did and then produced a one-sided audit report that he had to rebut ever so impolitely. He worried about James Ingrams in the Compliance Department, who independently supervised his trading activity and made sure he didn't buy shares on their restricted list and didn't trade on any inside knowledge.

He worried about the Credit Department, who checked

on the credit rating of the stocks that he dealt in. He worried about the gophers in Operations, who screwed up the booking of his deal tickets and made next day corrections and more unnecessary paperwork. He worried about the Treasury Department, who charged him an extortionate funding cost of several hundred basis points over the LIBOR rate on the cash funding for his dealing positions.

He worried about Cashiers, who checked his exorbitant travel and entertainment claims and bounced them back to him when he accidentally – or not – over-claimed or forgot to attach some lousy mislaid receipt. He worried about Systems and Technology, who delivered every dealing system change months late and even then it was what they wanted, not what he wanted.

He worried about the Finance Department, who produced a daily printout with the valuation of his positions and the resultant profit and loss statement, and who watched every cent whenever a dealing loss was incurred. Rare enough, fortunately. They called the one page The Bible at the desk. It came from Finance so it must be the gospel truth.

Greg had dealt in County to ease the omnipresent pressure to perform that emanated from Old Nick's executive suite. The pressure to earn millions like last year was intense. Nick got The Bible also and so he knew the figures that mattered. Nick, or Nicholas as he preferred to be known – no, he insisted – was out, probably enjoying the Season, off at some cricket or tennis or golf or polo event. Such were the privileges of a Director.

Now was the time for Greg to regroup without distraction. The Bible showed the value of the stocks that he held in his one and only dealing account, number 99007. The number was their own choice, a private joke at their desk. Gorgeous girl, smoking gun, monkey suit, moody Gladys Knight soundtrack, the name is Schneider, Greg Schneider. Roll the dice.

Today's Bible showed that the value of the shares had risen yesterday in line with the overall bullish tone. There were only two stocks in their dealing account and Greg knew them intimately. He had to. There would be three tomorrow. County Beverages would be on the report and in the money big time. He hoped that his decision to hold the shares overnight proved to be correct. It would all depend on what the collective wisdom of the City, research analysts and the press decided.

Ten million pounds were invested in the shares of Provident Bank plc, that former Bristol-based building society recently listed on the London Stock Exchange as a fully licensed bank. Greg hoped that Provident was ripe for a takeover by a larger financial group, hostile or otherwise, and he wanted to make some serious money on this stock. It might take a while for a deal to come to fruition but so far it looked good. The price was up twenty pence plus since his acquisition a month ago, and Barbara's observations today in the Dorchester looked promising. The rumours could be true. No smoke without fire.

Another ten million pounds were invested in shares of Sportsworld plc, a high street sports goods retailer based predominately in the southeast and run by an energetic Indian entrepreneur named Swarup Amir. Greg was hoping for better annual results and more. Retail spending was strong, leisure time was growing, sportswear was fashionable and people paid money for designer brands. Knock up the goods in Bangkok or Jakarta and stick on the swoosh or the three stripes. Michael Jordan earned more than their entire Far East work force. Easy money. The annual results of Sportsworld were due out in less than two weeks and who knew what might happen then? He could already feel another coup in the making, another few hundred k. How did he do it?

Barbara had worked a twelve-hour day at Blakes and it wasn't over yet. She had arrived at her cluttered desk at 7.10 a.m. Then ten minutes on the PA at the 7.30 a.m. research briefing with her buy and sell recommendations for the sales force. A research team meeting at nine to decide which incremental stocks should be included in next month's coverage. An eleven o'clock conference call with their six Continental offices to discuss pan-European strategy, the Euro and other similar waffle. Then that tedious lunch with Nicholas Crosswaithe and his fund manager cronies from the big pension funds. Two hours of expensive wine from Blakes' own cellar, raw red bloody meat, VSOP and stinking cigars, exterior smiling, interior grimacing, communal laughing, running her long fingers along the lapel of her feint check pink blouse to tease the clients. Or corporate flirting as others knew it. Nick had invited her for a reason and it wasn't only for her knowledge of the UK equity sector. Nick had then taken his pals off to the Blakes' box at Sandown for the 3.30 while Barbara returned to a life on the first floor.

The afternoon trip to the County Beverages AGM at the behest of the star dealer had actually been a welcome break and a chance to come up for air. Then back for a five o'clock interview with a hopeful yet dizzy candidate who turned out to be mere cannon fodder and who mentioned that her daddy was a partner at Goldmans at least five times. If Daddy wouldn't hire then why should Barbara? At six she raided the complimentary vending machine for a coffee and some calorie-ridden instant chocolate energy. At five to seven her temp PA put her head around the office door. She was on overtime and was glad to wait around at time and a half. Barbara wasn't so keen.

'They're here again, Barbara. Three of them as usual.' In that Aussie drawl the guys liked so much.

It must be Wednesday then; Barbara's turn on the magic media conveyor belt of leading research analysts. She stepped out of the safety of her office and recognised the friendly make-up lady from recent visits. She in turn appeared to spot the signs of fatigue and immediately began her professional work on the star of the moment. A dab of foundation, a magic eyeliner, a stroke of blusher, sparkly eye drops, a smear of lip-gloss and a run through those shining locks with a comb. Then a brush along the collar of the pink chemise and an adjustment to the solid gold chain around her elongated neck. The make-up woman was happy. Barbara could be on a catwalk if she so desired.

She was reborn, at least on the exterior. She was the research guru, and a guru had to be right. She had consistently called this market correctly and the City knew it. Last January when all was gloom and doom she had predicted this bull run of Pamplona proportions. Six thousand on the FTSE by end of June she had said. Six by six as they called it on the glossy research. She'd missed the target by a mere week but the Blakes' clients sitting on huge paper profits didn't mind that. She was known as a forecaster with almost meteorological skill. She could share the limelight with the weather guys after the news.

Historically Barbara also knew that a raging bull was listened to. No one wanted a sullen bear hanging around the markets, depressing them all with sombre realism and carefully tempered comments. She also knew her limitations, although no one at Sky TV seemed to share them. She could influence the FTSE for an hour or so but the market was a bigger animal and would always follow the fundamentals. Sometimes she wondered what would happen if she came on live and said that the bottom would fall out of the market and everyone should dump their shares. Would the market plummet? Would they listen? Maybe.

The arc lights were directed towards her. She inhaled. Go for it. She would use her analyst skills for the last time today: her ability to speak clearly and express technical concepts with readily comprehensible examples; particularly her use of aggressive metaphors, like pulling the trigger when it was time to sell. One of the Sky guys in a grubby black t-shirt and matching jeans grinned at her.

'Try it for sound, darlin'?'

Darlin'? Don't even think about it, mate. She noticed his greasy hair pulled back into a ponytail. But she obliged in the usual fashion.

'Testing. Testing. Testing.'

The ponytail nodded back in agreement. Sound and lights OK. Ready to pre-record for the slot in one hour's time. Almost.

'Move over a bit to the right, darlin'.'

Barbara shifted a foot to her right and knew why. The Blake Brothers logo was directly above her on the pillar behind. It had to be in full view. Old Nick wanted it that way. Free advertising. The crew knew the procedure by now.

'Back a bit to the left.'

She shifted again. A glance behind revealed the row of dealing screens. Even more authentic. It gave the viewers a background shot of the dealing floor, impressive even without those rugged dealers and oozing sales staff.

'Right. I'm ready.' The cameraman held up an open palm to her, ready to do a mock countdown.

Barbara stared down at the small monitor on the floor with a picture beamed over from some desolate industrial park on the outskirts of West London. The presenter with the blow-dried hair was sitting behind his studio desk as usual in his uniform of bold chalk pinstripe and crimson polka dot tie. Richard somebody or other. Dick for short and rightly so. She had met him at the launch of the business programme ages ago and he was all over her then. She'd had to fend him off and dodge his double entendres on the few subsequent occasions they met. He was a Letch.

She watched him record an allegedly incisive interview about global recession with a boring wispy economist from Bank of America. What an utter joke. Barbara knew that a mildly educated research assistant prompted the questions down his hidden earpiece. The City knowledge of the Letch could be written on one side of the prompt board that he so often referred to in times of crisis when spontaneity was required. He didn't know the FTSE from that thing on the end of his leg. Ponytail man spoke again.

'We are next.'

The Letch waffled on solo about things he knew nothing about: meetings at the ECB, next week's Monetary Policy Committee at the Bank of England with the guv'nor, gloomy trading statements from plcs, even a mention of County Beverages today. Then her cue, a market round up with red down arrows and green up arrows for the simple minded, closing prices on the DAX and CAC, current prices on the Dow and NASDAQ still trading away merrily across the pond, cross currency fx rates, Japan's GDP, inflationary pressures. All Greek to him.

'Three, two, one. We're running.'

The light above the camera lens went green. Barbara smiled as required.

'And now we go over to Barbara Ashby of Blake Brothers.'

She saw her face appear on the monitor. Not too bad for a twenty-eight year old on the go since leaving college. Except for the shadows under the eyes. She must remind the make-up girl next week. She knew the next line. It was the only one the Letch ever delivered without the use of an autocue.

'Good evening, Barbara, how have things been today?'

Predictable as ever. And he wasn't interested in the City traffic or the lunches or PMT or thirteen-hour working days or leering clients or the wealthy talent all around her. In truth the market was toppy as they called it. The FTSE had run up too fast this week and was in line for a correction. The big players were sitting today out, waiting for a definite trend to emerge. But Barbara knew the party line.

'We had a good day in the City. The FTSE rose to an all-time high.'

'And why was that, Barbara?' He switched on his interested expression.

Careful here. This wasn't an economic forum for the informed sophisticated ABC1 viewers. This was for the masses who tuned into Sky TV's evening business programme. She had her brief. Be positive. Be optimistic. That's why they loved her at Sky. If in doubt then default to humour.

'I guess it must be the good weather we're having, Richard. It's the feel-good factor.' Hah bloody hah.

They'd loved her simple one liners. Like the time she compared shares to coats. If they are cheap then everyone buys them and no one cares about the quality. But when they're dear, *caveat emptor*, check the goods carefully, count those buttons, look for those loose threads. Or when she described an increase in base rates as being like a flu jab. Short-term pain but good for all in the long term. Barbara beamed back at the four point two million viewers, simultaneously boosting the TAM ratings for Sky.

'Several leading stocks made good gains. There's a lot of cash out there amongst institutional investors and banking shares are still strong amidst rumours of some possible industry consolidation. Provident Bank was in strong demand today and was up ten pence.'

'And of course County Beverages had a good day?' That was her cue.

'As you say, County Beverages made a positive trading statement at their AGM today. I was there and Chairman Sir Gordon Harvey was positively ebullient. It's a good stock.'

Perfect. That would suit the worried widow in Surbiton with her meagre investments. It would suit the blue-collar worker with his two hundred BA and three hundred BT shares which he had held on to for ten years. Or the retired couple who had given their life savings to the man from the Pru to play with at his leisure.

'Thank you, Barbara. See you next week.' And the Letch signed off.

The arc lights dimmed. The camera stopped rolling. The make-up lady relaxed. Ponytail spoke.

'That's a wrap.'

Barbara turned off the light switch in her office, closed the door and thought that there must be more to life than this. Her

Breitling showed 7.52 pm. Thirteen hours plus. Five days a week. Sixty hours plus per week. Time for some play. St Johns Wood, here I come. Via the Bull & Bear.

And later at 8.30 p.m. in a one-bedroomed flat in deepest Battersea Mark flicked over to Sky from the dodgy blue film on Channel 5. He always watched the Sky business programme, it was a hazard of his job. He made especially sure never to miss a Wednesday evening broadcast. It was worth it to see that girl from Blakes in action.

The special situations desk staff sat in their regular window seat in the Bull & Bear. Got to be seen. It was usual to celebrate when they had made so much money in a single day, for Blakes and ultimately for themselves. Greg arrived. Better late than never. He was buying with the corporate AMEX card. He recorded it as staff development on the travel and entertainment expense claim and Old Nick approved it if the daily Bible was healthy. It certainly would be tomorrow morning.

Greg's attention was distracted by others from Blakes who were in the bar. There was a group of research girls, the much-prized City species whom all dealers hunted for sport and pleasure. Tall, thin-stemmed English roses with high IQs and even higher sex drives. Barbara arrived. Greg made eye contact with her, enough to tell her he was watching her. She mingled with her own team. Greg's team were getting settled when Jules's mobile rang.

'Todd? Sure, when? Tonight? OK. 'Bye.'

Jules was gone in an instant. It was the best offer she'd got all day from Goldmans. Hooray scanned the *Evening Standard* business supplement, glowing at the positive comment about County Beverages in the late edition. Anyone would think it had been his own idea to buy in size. Chas had more important matters on his mind. He needed the boss to buy more drink.

'Greg, where the hell have you been?

'Working.'

'You sad bastard. Let's drink!'

'OK.'

Chas killed time as they queued near the bar, looking for eye contact with the elusive staff.

'So tell me, what actually made you buy County today? We all wanna know.'

Greg took him over to the sheer glass windows. Sunlight bore down upon them and upon the assorted dusty pictures and empty beer bottles. Chas stepped back. Too bright even for this late hour of the day. Memories of last night's rake of pints and a searing Thai green curry flooded back. Greg spoke.

'Think about the basics. What do County Beverages make? They are into beer, soft drinks, snacks and candy. When do they score? Answer. When the weather is good and folks drink more liquids and gorge themselves on ice cream. County Beverages make that premium lager beer; they also make that luxury Belgian chocolate ice cream with cheesecake and meringue that I love.'

He pointed outside. The heat in London in recent weeks had been intense.

'So Chas, what's the summer been like? Oppressive if the truth be told. Had County Beverages done well? Who knows? But I thought they might have. All we needed was the Chairman to get up and say a few positive words today and we were in the money big time.'

Chas nodded. He may in fact have understood his boss. But his attention span was short.

'OK. But right now we're well on here. Another round is needed and you're buying.'

Greg went for his wallet. 'Champagne all right for you limeys? Bolly or Dom?'

Chas objected vociferously.

'Jesus, Greg, no. There's only one drink we can have today. You Americans are so bloody slow on the uptake sometimes.'

Greg was lost. Chas obliged.

'Get some beers in. Whatever brand County Beverage

supplies. We gotta support them. Get three of each, Greg. It'll boost their turnover in the next half year.'

He was still lost. 'Which brands do they supply?'

'From everything you said today I thought you knew about County? You're supposed to know about their brands. What sort of research did you actually do anyway? You're the one who bet ten million quid on them.'

Greg didn't know any of the brand names of County Beverage. He should have. It was a dead giveaway.

CHAPTER FOUR

ST JOHN'S WOOD, LONDON NW8

Greg admired Barbara's form as she lay in the bed beside him. She stirred, yawned and stretched, causing the cotton sheet to drop below her bare shoulders to reveal perfect nakedness. Six a.m. He rolled nearer and kissed those full lips. She was awake. She could research him any day.

'Do you know what's pink and hard first thing in the morning?'

She smiled back and responded in an instant.

'Easy. The *Financial Times* crossword. I too heard that one on the dealing floor yesterday.'

Damn. One step ahead of him. As usual. He gazed at her in admiration.

'So what are you thinking about, Barb?'

'I was wondering whether you are a short-term speculative punt or a long-term accumulate.'

'Go with the long-term view. I am.'

This was going well and they knew it. Barbara was tired of the other types in the City, the fly-by-nights who considered a meaningful conversation on the pillows next morning to be scary evidence of the start of a serious relationship. Her biological clock was ticking. Greg was under pressure.

He was out of bed and running on autopilot as he stood under a steamy power shower and downed a rushed breakfast. Barbara skipped breakfast, slipped on a sleek Jaeger number and left before him. After all, they couldn't be seen arriving hand in hand at Blakes. Old Nick would go mad. Greg gave her five minutes' head start and made for St John's Wood tube station in the breaking July sunshine.

He stopped momentarily by the steel blue coupe and recalled last night's late trip to Oddbins to pick up a bottle of wine. Why did girls always prefer white? Something in the genes perhaps? He had returned to the residents' parking bays but all he could find was a free disabled space. To hell with it. He used it. Now a fellow resident's aged Vauxhall Astra with the orange disabled badge was double-parked up the road. Best not to take any chances with parking attendants and tow trucks. He moved the Merc to a safer space. No harm done.

He recognised his peers in the half-empty seven o'clock Central Line tube carriage, not personally, merely by their collective behaviour and appearance. They voraciously digested today's *FT*, eyes grazing the headlines, compulsively looking at the time on their Tag Heuers. They had good haircuts and better shaves. Simply by being on this tube at this early hour, they confirmed to all that they were the dealers and the salesmen, the revenue producers who needed an early start in the City. The other lesser mortals who worked in bank operations and support areas struggled to arrive by nine o'clock in over-crowded tube carriages. They did not have the same sterling incentive to arrive any earlier.

Greg's own FT made satisfying reading. The front page of the Companies and Finance section included details of yesterday's action in the major London stocks. Great headlines. County Beverages Rises On Positive Trading Statement At AGM. Perfect. Greg was optimistic about the morning, although much work was required before he could cash in his chips and realise the paper profits. The FT showed a closing County Bev price of 520 pence, the mid price between the best bid and offer prices.

His enormous dealing position was no secret. The FT noted that Blakes were a big buyer of County stock and were rumoured to hold two or three million shares, perhaps even more. Not a difficult fact to discover in the incestuous City, where market makers love fielding telephone calls from inquisitive financial journalists at the end of the day, merely to sow the rumours required for the next day's successful trading. Buy on rumour and sell on fact. They all knew that. Time to sell? Greg was long, the market makers were short, and they were seriously pissed off about it.

Blakes' dealing coup was news for all to see. Others far more influential than he in the City would notice it too, particularly those who managed much larger dealing desks in the bulge-bracket investment banks. County Beverages would significantly enhance Greg's reputation. Might be a useful career move.

He alighted with those that mattered at Liverpool Street station. The few others stayed on the tube towards Leytonstone, Stratford and the East End, to jobs in shops, factories and warehouses. He walked through the arcade of designer clothes shops, picked up a strong coffee and sugared doughnut at the corner delicatessen, strode across Bishopsgate whilst dodging those who cut across his path, entered the ground floor lobby of Blakes and took the escalator to the first floor to sit at his dealing desk.

Working in the City as a dealer was all about getting your daily fix of adrenaline. Everyone else had the magic stimulant. If Greg rolled the dice today without his he would get a damn good kicking, which would cost him a sizable chunk of his dealing profits, his annual bonus, ultimately maybe even his job. Today his adrenal gland was already working overtime. Let the games begin.

* * *

Chas asked the most obvious question of Jules.

'How did it go last night?'

'Wouldn't you like to know?'

'So Goldmans shafted us twice in one day. Way to go, Todd.'

Jules needed revenge. Fast. She knew how to get the better of these male dealers.

'Hey, Greg. Did you hear about Chas and the girl from Operations yesterday evening?'

Chas immediately looked uneasy. Greg looked for news of the latest scandal. So long as he wasn't involved in any himself. Perish the thought. Jules obliged the team.

'This little teenage thing came down to us yesterday before we left. She complained about Chas and his tickets for the County Beverages buy, said he got some execution prices wrong. He had a real go at her. He said she should piss off upstairs, and that without his dealing, she and her like wouldn't even work here. He said she had him to thank for her job at Blakes. She left us in a flood of tears.'

'So Chas won the day? Good old Chas. It's what we expect of the man mountain.'

Chas still looked uneasy. Jules delivered the final coup de grace on behalf of the female of the species.

'Until this morning, that is. Chas found this giant envelope at his desk. It must have been two feet tall. It was a Thank You card from the entire Operations department, signed by about a hundred people who were here yesterday. Inside it's personally addressed to Chas. The words say thank you for our jobs. It's a real beaut. Chas is livid. The rest of us loved it though. One nil to the Ops department, I'd say. Eh, Chas?'

Chas looked as if he was racking his sick mind to recount the most sordid event in Jules's illustrious career. Greg needed harmony today. He was about to cut into the conversation to avoid hostilities developing when the PA system boomed out the first words of the seven-thirty a.m. research briefing for the dealers and sales staff. It took at least ten minutes of waffle about inflationary pressures, US producer prices, clampdowns on monopolistic utility profits and the Nikkei and Hang Seng closing prices, before his very own Barbara said the few words that really mattered to Greg's dealing team.

'Finally, we will be raising our profit estimates today for County Beverages following yesterday's positive noises at the AGM. Full year profits are now estimated at ninety million pounds, up from seventy-five million pounds. We will upgrade the stock from neutral to buy. Music to the ears of any dealer sitting on a line of two million shares which was heading distinctly north.

Greg eyed today's still warm laser-printed copy of his 99007 account. It was a glorious sight to behold on this particular morning. The closing position valued at 518 pence each, the official best bid price at four-thirty p.m. yesterday. Then the magical figure of two hundred and seventy thousand pounds profit. Greg could sit looking at this printout for hours, or at least until Chas interrupted him.

'The first prices are going up now.'

The major market makers displayed firm dealing prices by eight-thirty each morning but some put their prices up on the SEAQ screens before eight so they could capture the early trade activity from the other investment banks. The best price for County Beverages was shown at 518 pence – 523 pence. Every penny on the price meant twenty grand more profit for the desk. Greg decided it was time to realise some cash. He eyeballed the others.

'Let's sell some of the stock.'

Chas immediately disagreed. Maybe he'd slept better than he had expected last night.

'Why not hang on for a few days? The price is ticking up. Barb in research likes them a lot. We can make some more loot.'

But Greg had already made up his mind.

'We bought them for a short-term punt. We had a good day yesterday, let's not push our luck. We'll sell some County Bev on the quiet. Take one house each and offer them a hundred thousand at best. Take whatever price they give you. Do it quickly. Don't haggle. Sell.'

'Shouldn't we check with Old Nick first?'

Greg stamped on Chas. Hard.

'I decide what we buy and sell here.'

The telephone calls were as short as yesterday's.

'Hundred thou County Bev, yours.'

'Best offer on County Bev?'

'Hundred County Bev all to go. What's your best?'

'Do you want what I have to offer, Todd?'

They were done in minutes. Four hundred thousand sold at an average price of 518 pence. Over fifty grand profit realised. No one could take that away from them. It felt good. A fifth of their holding had been shifted. They nervously watched the County Bev price on the screens. It didn't move. The market had absorbed the stock effortlessly. Greg took another instant decision.

'We can get away with some more. Sell another two hundred each. Try different houses.'

This was the big gamble. This was size, and size always mattered. The calls took longer. The price came back by a few pence. They did eight hundred thousand shares at an average of 516 pence. Another hundred thousand quid or so in the bag. This was going to plan. The screen price stabilised around 514 and Chas tried to intervene. Talk about changing your mind.

'Let's do the rest now. The price is falling. We're going to lose some of this profit.'

Greg disagreed. The day was still young. They would wait to see if the price recovered in the next few hours. Eight hundred thousand shares left.

'No. We can sit on the rest for a while longer.'

*   *   *

Mark knew he was late even before the noisy neighbours above woke him up with their screaming kids. The road outside was too busy. It was after eight. Shit. Eight-twenty-six on the cheap alarm clock that seemed to have off days when it too failed to react on time. The water pressure was still low and a shower was too much like hard work, running around trying to connect sweaty flesh with the evasive droplets of water escaping from the showerhead.

The fridge was devoid of edible items, the contents being predominantly past their 'best by' day. Someone had thrown up a pungent curry last night right outside his communal hall door. Further evasive action taken. The queue at the first bus stop was too lengthy, the cabs passing by were all taken. No choice but to walk, no, scurry, to the nearest tube station on the north side of the river. Bad start.

It was nineteen minutes past nine when Mark exited Bank station with the lazy types. Norris would not be impressed. A five-minute canter along the narrow side streets of the City, teeming with office folk, messengers, Royal Mail and DHL staff, guys in flash suits, girls in flashier suits. The heat of the City even now becoming oppressive, no sunlight amongst the canyons of offices, yet somewhere up there above the City, the sun glared down on a single square mile that annually generated billions in invisible earnings.

The figures were amazing. Last year the value of shares traded on the London Stock Exchange totalled a thousand billion pounds. Seriously. It was the first time it had topped the thousand mark, up a staggering thirty per cent from the previous year. Long may this market roll on. Bears, get lost. The number of share dealings in the year rose to thirteen million trades. Seventeen million new individual shareholders were created among the UK public as former building societies like Provident Bank plc made the mad dash for de-mutualisation and easy cash for their members. Hundreds of new companies had joined the market in the past twelve months, many from overseas. The LSE should be a great place to work.

Mark didn't agree with this widely held sentiment as he crossed the threshold in Old Broad Street for another day of not so stimulating work. He stood in the lobby waiting for one of the ancient shuddering lifts and eyed the names of the LSE departments on the wall. Alternative Investment Market. Capital Markets. Company Listings. Company Announcements. Press Office. Publications. Regional Offices. SETS and RNS, whatever the hell they were. And of course Enforcement. His own dismal choice.

The Exchange could trace its roots back to the London coffee-houses of the seventeenth century, where those who wished to punt bought shares in dodgy joint stock companies. As the numbers of brokers and stock-jobbers expanded, they opened their own subscription room on Threadneedle Street, and in 1773 officially became the Stock Exchange. Later the Exchange was transformed by Britain's industrial revolution into today's financial powerhouse, with thousands of staff and three hundred elite member firms in the City, amongst them the world's leading investment banks. The LSE existed to provide a well-regulated market for companies to raise finance in a cost-effective manner, to facilitate trading in their shares, to operate the markets on a daily basis, to provide investor protection and to ensure the widest access possible to market information. God. It sounded like that damn job advert.

Regulation was all the rage now, primarily due to the recent scandals in the City and overseas. The LSE assessed the suitability of companies to join the official list and had the devastating power to approve, suspend or cancel share listings. They monitored market makers' quotations on dealing screens all around the City using the lesser-known IMAS system, ensuring share trades were reported to those who needed to know. Most important of all they regulated the flow of information to everyone at the dealing desks by validating and publishing the crucial price-sensitive information on the Regulatory News Service. If it wasn't on RNS between the hours of 7.30 a.m. and 6 p.m. then it probably wasn't worth knowing about.

Mark had learnt much in three years; all about listed equities dealt on SEAQ, overseas equities dealt on SEAQ International, UK gilts, corporate bonds, listed options, covered warrants. He knew how companies came to the market by offers for sale, by placings, by intermediaries' offers or by introductions. He knew about rights issues, takeovers, mergers and corporate actions. He knew the difference between the Official List and AIM; between the primary market and the secondary market. But when was he going to get an opportunity from Norris to utilise his knowledge?

Mark slumped opposite Peter and thought about discussing the latest draft of his CV with his eager colleague. Nope. Best to keep it to himself until something positive developed. Peter peered at him through his designer specs from Boots Opticians near Embankment, almost identical to the pair that Mark had bought in the same end of season sale. The need to look out for the sales when considering any purchase was a hazard of existing in London on a modest LSE salary. They both needed the specs to read the tiny digits on the bulky computer printouts and to stare at rows of numbers on the PC screens all day.

He definitely needed a change of scenery before he went blind or bankrupt. Or both.

The morning lull in any dealing room was always a bad time, but particularly so for Greg in the venerable yet sleepy investment bank of Blake Brothers & Co. His thoughts turned away from the dazzling screens around him to other more personal matters. Yesterday had shown that he was one of the few people who individually moved share prices of billion pound companies like County Beverages. When he bought and sold, others followed. Yet he wasn't a true player in the City. They worked elsewhere.

Greg blamed his past. His education in a relaxed school in Sayville was, well, relaxed. There weren't many jobs in the sleepy coastal town on Long Island so he did what everyone else did and took the Long Island Railroad west to Manhattan in search of a life with pace. In hindsight it must have been the frenetic activity that attracted him to the bustle of downtown Wall Street. He drifted around for days looking for a job in any bank or broker dealer that would have him. He had heard that they paid top dollar, even for mailroom staff and clerks. He eventually got a job through an agency on the dealing floor of Mitchell Leonberg Inc., the biggest domestic broker on the street. His friends back in Sayville were madly impressed. They thought he was a dealer, a punter, a Master of the Universe. If only.

Greg's initial responsibilities on the equity dealing desk were running to the deli for food for the ravenous big hitters, hours of photocopying their dealing records, correcting badly written tickets, keeping hostile operations staff at bay and taking telephone messages from wives, girlfriends and mistresses, or all three. It was a demeaning job but in a great location and he learnt up close and personal from the professionals.

The better dealing staff moved on to other jobs within Mitchells but Greg stayed at that same securities desk. In time he took calls from other brokers and called counterparties and began to put a few good trades together and to make some money. He passed the Series 7 exam. There was never any one particular day when he graduated to becoming a dealer. It just happened. Then, after years of loyalty, Mitchells made him an offer he couldn't refuse.

Mitchells were beefing up their presence in London and needed some experienced securities traders to man the desks. They needed people they could trust. Ironic. Greg had no choice. His boss handed him the plane ticket personally. He had been chosen and you don't say no, otherwise you are history in Mitchells. He was one of the first to swap Wall Street and Battery Park for an equity desk in Moorgate and a two-bedroom company let in Chelsea. They were the good times. Until the day that word spread from New York and Mitchells asked him to leave their employment. The official reason was that he wished to resign. A good ruse. Less damaging too for the firm.

Then weeks of job hunting, this time in London, not being able to return to New York. Interviews with various banks. No desire to work for the Japanese. Nor the Germans. He couldn't even contemplate working again for a US house. Then an offer from Blakes to run their Special Situations equity desk. They were small, parochial, under-capitalised, but it was a living and he knew that he wouldn't be there forever.

The Special Situations desk was perfect for Greg. It didn't involve detailed analysis and research, mathematical computations or rocket scientist wizardry. It was trading on instinct. The desks brief was to buy special stocks, those where there was a possibility of major corporate action. Maybe good company news or a takeover in the pipeline. The desk held the shares while praying for a press release or a takeover bid from a competitor company and the chance of immediate big percentage profits.

Greg made millions for Old Nick every year, yet it was an unfortunate and inescapable fact that Greg did not personally receive a sizeable share of the profits that he garnered so assiduously. In his not so humble opinion he merely received the leftovers. The bulk was spent on basic staff salaries, the luxury City dealing facilities and the overheads of the back office operations areas. His colleagues at the dealing desk got a deserved share. Chas got the most as his unofficial desk deputy and local equity market expert. Then Jules, since she possessed one of the best pairs of pegs in the entire City. Hooray Henry got a share too despite being more interested in his landed gentry lifestyle and the Season.

Greg resented most that portion of their dealing revenue which went towards the Blakes' Directors' salaries and bonuses, that group of prematurely ageing City gents who allegedly knew more about the markets than a young Turk like himself. Especially Nick, the Director of Dealing, with no imagination, no personality and even less appetite for market risk. He was more interested in the social whirl than reviewing Greg's trading. Who was he to tell Greg what his dealing strategy should be, to query what he bought and sold, to ask why? Nick had seniority and experience light years ahead of Greg's, but no one knew these special situation shares like Greg did. No one anywhere in the City. Guaranteed.

Blakes was a mistake and he knew it. Working for them was like unilaterally taking on the whole financial world on a daily basis. His permitted dealing positions were tiny compared to the multi-billion dollar positions that US investment banks a few hundred yards down the road held right now.

Greg would do literally anything for a job with a real industry player, that symbol of ultimate peer recognition. The US banks weren't worth the risk. He needed a Deutsche Bank, who currently utilised the bottomless pockets of their awesome Frankfurt parent to buy the scarce talent they needed to compete. Even the tea ladies and mailmen in Deutsche were the best paid in the City. Or another European giant like ABN or ING or CSFB or UBS or anyone else with a few initials in their name. He would even take a Japanese bank now, as long as it was solvent, which reduced the likelihood considerably.

He needed a magic telephone call from a Mr H. Hunter. He needed to be poached from Blakes to sit at another desk down the road and do the same job with double the position limits, double the staff, double the salary and bonus. Meanwhile he was here and had to wait. The biggest mistake would be to call a headhunter first. That would make Greg look eager to leave, desperate, anxious, even cheap. Perish the thought. He needed that call. Otherwise he was stuck at Blakes for the rest of his working life. Definitely time for a change of scenery. Time at least for lunch with a hot date.

CHAPTER FIVE

OLD BROAD STREET, LONDON EC2

Peter made the executive decision for both of them at half past twelve.

'There's no way I'm going for stodge pudding in the canteen today. It's too damn fantastic outside. Let's get a quick sandwich and eat *al Fresco*.'

Mark agreed and left his suit jacket on the back of his chair. Too hot for that today.

'I know your game, Pete. And you almost a married man too.'

'Well, why not? All the talent will be out there today. Just because I'm on a diet doesn't mean I can't look at the menu. Claire won't mind. Nothing wrong with a spot of ornithology. Anyway, *you're* still young, free and single.'

'Don't remind me.'

They purchased some low-cal sandwiches from Boots and walked to the plaza at Broadgate. Everyone was walking in the same direction. Mark knew that the best seats would be long gone. Harder to get a front row position here than it was for a Lloyd Webber opening night in Shaftesbury Avenue. The tiered marble steps were the only alternative. They loved this place. Even the signage spoke volumes. Lehman Brothers Inc. Warburg

Dillon Read. Corney & Barrow at Broadgate, the very best wine bar. Espresso à la Carte, and the ludicrous assertion that *espresso makes you smarter than you really are*. Compaq Systems Inc., so good they power the world's money trading. The Nat West Jazz Band playing for you today in the City. They enjoyed the sax appeal. Peter put on a pair of shades and roamed his eyes around the scene before them. He had lost none of his lifelong bird-spotting skills since his engagement to his childhood sweetheart.

'Urgent. Three o'clock. Bearing directly towards us. Two ICIs. Check it out.'

Mark waited a polite moment and averted his gaze to the right. Bullseye. Two girls in blouses and dark skirts stood looking for somewhere to sit with some degree of modest respectability. Their form-fitting pencil skirts were almost too dangerous for such a manoeuvre. Their shoulder pads, jewellery and tans gave them away. Mark guessed they were from a European sales desk in some investment bank, probably selling Italian equities to fund managers who were queuing up to listen to their sultry accents. They were so utterly unattainable that it wasn't even worth continuing to gaze at them. A waste of time. Peter persevered.

'Now bearing ten o'clock. Single target on top step. Eating French stick in distinctly erotic manner.'

Mark would have to warn Claire about the bizarre sexual fantasies of her future husband.

'C'mon, take a look at least. I'm doing all the work here.'

He obliged. Peter was indeed on form today. She looked great from afar, whoever she was. Sunlight glinting off long, auburn hair. The French stick descended from those lips and Mark looked again. He knew her.

'Pete, that's her.'

'Who?'

'The girl from the telly. Barbara from Blakes.'

'Never heard of her.'

'She's on the Sky evening business programme.'

'I never watch it. It's crap.'

'I know it is. But she makes the Wednesday evening show worthwhile. She was on last night.'

Mark stared across at her. It was rude but he had to. She was perfect. He had never seen so much of her before. All he ever saw on his Sony was a shot from her waist up. Reality dawned.

'She's got legs.'

Peter peered over at target number two. He couldn't see through the dark shades. He took out his work glasses and stared through the throng.

'You're right. She definitely has. Not bad either. You're eventually getting the hang of this, Mark.'

This was his opportunity. He could go over and sit next to her, throw her some social aside and see if he could engage her in conversation. Would she be interested? Nothing to lose. Mark turned.

'I'm impressed. C'mon, Pete. We're moving to the other side.'

'No way. This is a great spot. Other reconnaissance experts would die for a perch like this.'

Mark stood. This was a solo job. But shyness overcame his enthusiasm. He watched as a tall, swarthy guy with dark wiry hair and a strong chin walked up to his Barbara on the steps and sat down beside her. Damn. His space had been taken. She smiled at the guy. He leant forward and kissed her on the lips. It was a long kiss, much more than just good friends. She held the moment. Mark sat down.

'Shit.'

Beaten to it again. Mark watched as the guy with the rolled up shirtsleeves and the loosely-knotted tie put his left arm around Barbara. She leant towards him and he placed a hand on her perfect knee. Peter was on form.

'Wow. He's all over her. They might go for it here and now in Broadgate Plaza. Unprecedented.'

Mark couldn't watch anymore. He couldn't compete with some hot shot like that, some star dealer in the City who could treat Barbara to a life of luxury. All the talent was at large in those investment banks. Monetary and sexual. He needed a job there just to get on the first rung of life.

Greg returned from his excessively long lunch with his endorphins at an all-time high. Barbara was hot today. But his elation turned to horror when he saw the price of County Beverages on SEAQ. The best bid price from the mercenary market makers was Morgans at 505 pence. It was back down to the price before yesterday's action. And he still had eight hundred thousand shares to unload into the market.

'What the hell's happened here, Chas?'

'I dunno know exactly. I was out at lunchtime.'

'We have an agreement. If I go out, you stay here. Where were you?'

'I went out to get a haircut.'

'Jesus, Chas, don't get a haircut on company time.'

'Well, it grew on company time, didn't it?'

'It didn't all grow on company time.'

'I didn't get it all cut.'

'Chas. Forget it. What do you know about the County price?'

Chas cast an unfair glance at Jules.

'Goldmans screwed us again. We couldn't do anything. Half an hour ago Scottish & Colonial dumped ten million shares of County Bev. They've had a major stake in the company for years and they used yesterday's rise in the price to unload most of it. The stock was placed with institutional investors through Goldmans at 504 pence. Goldmans probably made more on the placement than we will make on our two million shares. When they announced the placement, the price nose-dived on the screens. I didn't know whether to sell or wait for a recovery. What do we do?'

Disaster. Goldmans had cleaned up. They had used the rise in the share price to tempt a client to sell a large line of stock. Even with his edge in the market, Greg and Blakes had been well and truly nailed by a far superior competitor. Scottish & Colonial was a big fund manager working out of Edinburgh like so many of their peers. If they were selling out now then it was the start of an unstoppable force that Greg could not control. S&C owned more shares and could dump them at any moment. The overhang would depress the County price for the foreseeable future. Greg shouted the instructions.

'Sell all County shares now. Get whatever price you can.'

You can always sell shares; it's the price that is the difficulty. Jules and Hooray even unloaded some of them at below yesterday's acquisition price. They incurred a loss and this hurt deeply. Greg winced as he worked out the final numbers.

'We almost broke even on the last sale. We made our money this morning, so let's forget about this afternoon. We weren't to know what Goldmans or S&C were going to do.'

It was a downer after a twenty-four-hour trading period that had been profitable, albeit not hugely so. One hundred and fifty thousand pounds profit was a welcome contribution to the bottom line. Greg was always reminded that in order to meet his annual target of seven million he had somehow to make one hundred and thirty-four grand per week. Only just winged it this week.

In the late afternoon he rummaged around in his wallet, found what he needed, scribbled some figures and approached Nicholas Crosswaithe's corner office. He held the outrageously large expense claim in his hand. Last night in the Bull & Bear had come back to haunt him. Two hundred and fifty quid on drink for four of them plus a few too many rounds for the guzzling research girls and assorted hangers on. He needed to get a Director's signature. Old Nick had more pressing interests.

'Greg, what happened on the County Beverage shares? The price is weak. I hope you sold out in time?'

Weak was an understatement. The price was fucked but this fifty-year-old Director never swore, preferring to use an archaic version of the English language. Old Nick had seen the County

Beverages position on his daily reports, and the price on his SEAQ screen on his desk. Greg nodded to reassure him.

'Yeah, we're all done. All square. Some profit.'

Nick sat there in his suit of wide white pinstripes, half-glasses and handmade shirt. Overly long silver hair combed back and curling at the ends. Ruddy complexion from too much port at lunchtime and hunting for defenceless game on his country estate. Greg resented Crosswaithe's frequent absences, his large Air Miles collection from self-indulgent business trips, client meetings and conference boon-doggles. Old Nick was a world apart from the American observing him, twenty years younger and twice as ambitious.

Who was Nick to ask him about his trading? Just because he was one of the old partners of Blakes before the float and thus a personal holder of several million Blake shares. He should have retired long ago, got out of the City and left Greg and the team in peace to play the market. But in reality Greg was grateful for the lack of close supervision of his dealing. Old Nick got to the end game eventually.

'How much did we make on County Beverages?'

Crosswaithe wasn't the sort to abbreviate company names to convenient slang. Strictly Queen's English, old chap.

'About a hundred and fifty, Nicholas.'

They didn't dare call him Nick to his face. A young guy had made that mistake on his first day in Blakes. They never saw him again on the dealing floor. Rumour had it that he worked in the Operations Department now.

'Most satisfactory.'

'Yeah, the team did well.' Make it look like a group effort. Cover his tracks. 'Can you sign this?'

The bill was a small price to pay for a profit in the bank's dealing account. Nick scribbled an illegible initial on the expense claim that only the cashiers upstairs would recognise before they reimbursed Greg.

'Risk Management was on to me this morning. Those County Beverage shares put you over your thirty million pound dealing limit. I was going to tell you to cut some positions but now that we've sold off County for cash today, there is no need for any other action on your part.'

Those damn bean counters in Risk Management on the third floor spent all day looking at The Bible and totting up columns of figures with pocket calculators in their interminable search for dealing position excesses. Running around with glee when they found a dealer who had overstepped the mark and over-bought. Never having the balls themselves either to come downstairs and talk to dealers face to face, but preferring to send proforma memoranda in the internal mail or to telephone the Directors to tell tales about their star performers on the first floor. Which basically meant that Crosswaithe hadn't had the guts to walk out on the dealing floor first thing today either and tell Greg to sell. Typical.

'Sorry, Nicholas. We were OK when we bought them. I guess the rise in the stock price pushed us over the limit. It's impossible, isn't it? The more money you make the more hassle you get sometimes.'

Crosswaithe did not want to criticise those in Risk Management. It wasn't to be expected of a Director.

'These other positions we hold? Provident Bank. Sportsworld. Any sign of selling these soon? I see Provident is up twenty pence again today. Should we sell?'

Should *we* buy? Should *we* sell? Buying Provident was solely Greg's idea. His decision to buy and thus to sell. No way, Nick. Provident Bank was, well, a banker.

'No. I am holding the positions in the hope of further price increases in those stocks.'

Crosswaithe gave up. Almost.

'Tell me, Greg, how do you do it?'

'Do what?'

'How come you deal in nothing for days and then suddenly you get into County Beverages on the day they make a positive trading statement? I'm amazed at how you follow the market so closely.'

'I have a secret weapon. I call it common sense. You can see all around you that drinks and confectionery and ice cream are selling well in this heatwave. County Bev was a sure thing.'

'Seriously though, Greg.'

'It's a trade secret, Nicholas. It's all I have. If I tell you, I'll be out of a job, won't I?'

The trite answer seemed to suit Old Nick. Less thought required. Less worrying for him.

'Please don't rest on your laurels. Go out there and do your best to make me some more money.' Even when Greg made 150K in twenty-four hours, Crosswaithe wanted more. 'Whatever you're doing out there, keep on doing it.'

Old Nick had made a valid point. Greg's instant profits were too obvious. He should have bought the County Beverage shares last week. If only he had known about the positive trading statement earlier.

Alexander Soames's thirty-one years of unbroken loyal service with Provident Bank plc had crystallised into this four-hour meeting with his fellow directors and a bunch of blood-sucking City advisers in a Dorchester Hotel conference room. As Finance Director his views should matter, but this week Alexander had somehow lost his authority. And the plot. The others around the mahogany table were not receptive to his views. He was losing not only the battle but also the war. His Chief Executive, golf partner and long-time friend, David Webster, got to the crux of the matter. Time for them all to vote.

'Gentlemen, I suggest we put this motion to the Board. All those in favour please raise your hands.'

Nothing in his working life had prepared Alexander for a vote like this. Since joining Provident at the age of eighteen, he had risen from mere office junior to the main Board via a series of self-financed night courses, accountancy qualifications, hard work, enthusiasm and effective corporate networking. Provident had come a long way from its humble beginnings as a regional building society, had survived the carnivorous UK property crash of the prior decade and by subsequent organic growth become one of the largest building societies in Britain. Alexander Soames had played a significant part in the society's success as prudent and conservative management paid real dividends to both depositors and borrowers. For his contribution to date he had been handsomely rewarded. Provident was his entire life, and now nothing would ever be the same again.

'Alexander, we're waiting for you.'

A look from Webster at the head of the table. How had it come to this? Soames blamed the selfish moneymen in the City who saw mutual building societies simply as an incremental stream of lucrative fee income to be tapped. Provident had succumbed to the wave of industry peer pressure and paranoia that swept their market sector and de-mutualised as customers and recently arrived carpetbaggers chose easy cash above tradition. After the unprecedented workload of the listing on the London Stock Exchange, he'd looked forward to a period of stability. Then came the move to the new corporate headquarters in London and a new home for Helen and the family.

Then the pressures of being a public company, meeting the demands of a bunch of City research leeches feeding off your every move, every AGM, every forecast, every set of interim results, every sharp intake of breath. Soames had to deliver the results that Webster demanded. Anything less and Provident would be a public embarrassment to them all. That was when he'd first started cooking the books. So far, so good.

'Alexander?'

There was one other significant downside. Provident was now a public company and as such was vulnerable to the advances of any wealthy predator. One such predator had arrived sooner than the Board expected. There seemed to be no going back to the good old days in Bristol.

'Your turn to vote, please.'

One by one the Directors had voted on the motion. Webster faced down Soames, who in turn looked around the table at his fellow Directors and colleagues whom he had worked with and trusted over all those years. They all had one hand raised decisively in favour of the motion. His Chief Executive applied the final tourniquet of peer pressure.

'Alexander, it would be nice to have a unanimous vote approving this deal.'

This bloody deal. Last month Webster had received a telephone call at home on a Sunday evening from the Chairman of British Commercial Bank. It came just after the end of *The Money Programme* on BBC2. They all watched it religiously. The call signalled the arrival of an unsolicited bid approach from their competitor. British Commercial were a major corporate bank desperately in search of a retail customer base to whom they could flog pensions and life assurance and insurance products, and Provident's customer base fitted their marketing requirements perfectly.

They would pay to acquire Provident in an agreed takeover that would avoid the acrimony and mud slinging of a publicly contested hostile bidding war. British Commercial wished to deter others from bidding for Provident with a knock-out multi-billion bid. It would be the end of Provident, its identity, and its unique role in helping the communities of the West. Everything that Alexander had worked for would disappear in one corporate mega-deal.

'We need a decision, Alexander. One way or the other, please.'

The deal was all about the six billion on offer; the eyes of his fellow Directors were glazed over at the prospect of the largesse on offer. To hell with the loyal Provident investors and borrowers. The Directors knew that in the event of a takeover of their company, they would be handsomely rewarded when the acquirer broke their five-year fixed service contracts. Their City lawyers had been through the contracts with a fine-toothed comb; British Commercial would have to stump up the cash.

Alexander's vote made no difference. There was an overwhelming majority in favour already. It was only token resistance but he was adamant. He sat on his hands lest he involuntarily signal his approval of the deal.

'I'm against the motion, David.'

Damn. Webster winced in displeasure. He'd wanted unanimity. He'd never imagined that Soames would be this difficult. He had misjudged the pride of the man who had made that impassioned speech yesterday to those around the table. That had scared the City advisers who had thought the deal might be off. Now the lawyers and accountants knew they were close to the end of a successful week of negotiations, and were already salivating over the fees they were about to earn. It was good to work in the City of London, no matter what occupation or profession you had chosen.

A few people rose from their seats and walked over to the tables of drinks and canapés, a physical expression of the mutual relief felt in the room. Others stretched back in their chairs. One or two left the Waterloo function room. Webster approached the single dissenter.

'I'm sorry that you couldn't see our viewpoint. I know this is difficult for you but this deal means a lot to us. Thanks for your input this week.'

It had been an awful week, trapped in the Dorchester on Park Lane. By day they sat in a secretly booked conference room populated by professional piranhas as the terms were thrashed out. The hours dragged as they discussed the merits of a cash versus paper offer from British Commercial, prospective dividend policy, shareholder rights, minority interests, consolidated profit and loss statements, deferred taxation accounts and the crucial aspects of deal confidentiality. At midnight the Directors returned upstairs to their hotel rooms to catch a few hours' sleep in rooms booked by in-house public relations people under the wholly unimaginative names of Mr Smith, Mr Jones, Mr Brown and others.

It would have been easier for Soames to return to his West London home but the deal required intensive work in a short period of time. The media advisers were paranoid about news of the deal leaking out to the City. Once market makers got wind of a mega-merger like this they would pile into Provident stock big time. The board had watched the share price each day and so far there had been no massive reaction to the stupendous news that was about to break. Just a few pence increase each day in line with general bullish market sentiment. Then twenty pence yesterday. No one in the City could possibly know about the deal.

It was almost half past six, the earliest conclusion to a day's work since Soames had checked in at this hotel. Webster still persevered at building some bridges.

'Let's all have a drink to mark the occasion.'

He didn't feel much like a celebratory drink. This was more like a wake. He thought guiltily of Helen and their two children, Emma and Louise, whom he had not seen for four entire days.

'No, thanks. I need a break outside. What happens next, David?'

'We'll have a final board meeting at nine o'clock tomorrow morning to sign the papers and agree some of the media timings and announcements. Take the evening off if you want, Alex. The rest of us are staying here. Go and see Helen and the kids. Recharge your batteries.'

Good idea, and almost the one he had been harbouring for the past few hours as his attention changed from a lost battle to a personal diversionary manoeuvre. He made his excuses and went downstairs to use his company mobile in a corner of the spacious yet crowded public area. Today was a perfect opportunity that only rarely presented itself, and with the future demise of his job with Provident there would be less such opportunities in the future. No work, no play. Another night's absence from family life wouldn't matter at this stage. His call was answered immediately.

'Helen, hi. I'm sorry but this meeting isn't over yet. I can't tell you about it now but all will become clear soon. I will definitely be home tomorrow some time. Give my love to the twins.'

She would think that he was still staying in the Dorchester and would never be any the wiser.

There was no choice. The cupboard was bare. Mark pulled the hall door behind him and walked across the road to his VW Golf. Or rather his sister's Golf. Ever since she had headed off for that working summer in Oz three years ago she had allowed him to borrow her car, or at least rack up ten thousand miles a year in it. There was no alarm on the car. Who the hell would nick a piece of junk like this, even in Battersea? Mark prayed, crossed his index fingers, waited with baited breath, then tickled the key. The engine sprang into life at the third time of asking and he set off amidst a plume of grey exhaust smoke. It wasn't the ultimate mode of transport but it was preferable to standing for twenty minutes on the packed 44 bus back from Lord Sainsbury's finest shopping emporium.

Forget about nightclubs, bars, pubs, restaurants and the workplace. This was where the action was in South London on a Thursday night. There wasn't a married couple or a child in sight. Only twenty-something singles wandering around with a squeaky trolley that they knew was too big for their dismally small weekly shopping. Mark ambled from the fruit and veg to the fresh smell of the bakery and back up to the wine, while simultaneously eyeing up the opposite sex. They did the same. There was the occasional eye contact, a smile, a frown, a stare, with always the hope of something more to follow.

Mark played the one and only known supermarket game. Imagine a date with anyone you like here tonight. The girl in a loose Adidas t-shirt and khaki shorts was a strong candidate until he spied the engagement ring as she manhandled the loose tomatoes. The girl with the jet-black hair near the dairy products was promising until she turned around with a clutch of bio-yoghurts and a smoking fag. The awesome sight swaying up ahead in the faded Levi's with a dangling leather belt, pushing the reluctant trolley, was his definite final choice. Then her towering boyfriend appeared from the next aisle, placed his left hand inside the back pocket of her jeans and gave her all the assistance she needed.

As always, Mark's hopes were dashed and he stood alone by the sweets on display. The queues at the checkouts were horrendous. He listened to two sales assistants chattering at the next unused checkout. They were too loud, as if they wanted to be overheard. One said that she loved working here. Why? Obvious, she replied to her colleague. The talent was great in the evening with all the gorgeous guys. Really, asked the colleague? Yes and she knew who the single guys were by what they had in their basket or trolley. Mark looked over. She looked back. She knew. He knew. It was all about sex.

He was reminded of Peter's favourite joke of the moment. One that had been sent by email from a former colleague in another anonymous City office. Guy goes up to a checkout and places the contents of his basket on the conveyor belt. One apple, one orange, one banana, one tomato, one potato, one pint of milk, one tin of beans. The assistant says to him, 'I bet you live on your own, don't you?' The guy says, 'Yeah, I do. Did you guess that because I'm buying one of everything?' 'No,' she says, 'because you're an ugly bastard.' Peter thought he might use it in his forthcoming groom's speech. Sometimes Mark didn't find the joke so amusing.

The contents that he progressively emptied out betrayed his own lifestyle. Health conscious yet with a sweet tooth. A trainee gourmet chef with a simultaneous fondness for microwaved ready meals. A desire to consume the finest while minimising the damage that his Switch card would inflict on his Barclays current account that regularly dropped into the red at the end of the month before pay day at the LSE.

Low-fat milk, fresh OJ, heat 'em up quick croissants, ripe bananas for the potassium, yoghurts for speedy desserts, prepared salads, some token Kenyan vegetables for one stir-fry, cans and cans of lager, gotta have some doughnuts and a large Banoffi pie to sate today's sugar craving. Finally Mark emptied that essential staple item of the single diner: the corn-fed chicken breast fillet. Someday Mark would be in the market for substantially more. Legs, thighs and two breasts. The entire bird. Chicken, that is.

CHAPTER SIX

BISHOPSGATE, LONDON EC2

Greg was alone on the dealing floor. Twenty minutes to six. He couldn't wait any longer. He needed to know what was going on uptown. Yesterday Barbara had inadvertently given him the lead that might make all the difference. There were millions at stake. He needed to make another clandestine trip.

Some preparatory work was required first. Gotta be ready for every contingency, have an excuse in case some busybody asked him some leading questions. He took today's tattered *Mirror* from the bin at the desk, placed it into a Blakes' white A4 envelope, wrote the words 'Provident Bank – Confidential' on the front in big letters and sealed the envelope. Perfect. It looked like the real thing.

He hailed a cab near London Wall and slumped in the back seat, mentally rehearsing his plan. What could go wrong? The side windows were down and the passing lead oxide was a poor alternative for some decent air con. Jesus. Every cab in Manhattan had air con. Why the hell didn't the cabs here?

'Are you over here on holidays from the States?'

He still hadn't managed to lose that accent. To them he would always be a tourist.

'No, I live here.' Regrettably.

The driver mouthed on about the heatwave, pulling the peak of a blue Chelsea FC baseball cap over his five-pound pair of sunglasses to shade his eyes from the oncoming glare. They made good time until they hit a typical tailback near Park Lane, just minutes from the Dorchester. It was in sight.

'Pull in here. This will do me.' Best not to arrive too publicly at the front door by cab.

'Are you sure, Guv? You've got to cross over to the other side.'

'It's OK. I'll walk over.'

'It's your life, mate. Mind the five lanes of traffic, though.'

Greg unbuttoned his Brooks Brothers work shirt, undid the silk tie and peeled it all off to reveal the white under-shirt. It looked like any old t-shirt. The cabbie was not impressed.

'What are you doing back there?'

'A quick change. Can you wait here? There's a fifty in it. And can I borrow your cap?'

'Are you windin' me up, Guv? You a Chelsea fan too?'

'Yeah. Great team.' Greg had never been to a soccer game in his life. Give him baseball any time.

Greg loosened the under-shirt, grabbed the cap before any protests were forthcoming, and legged it over Park Lane and the deadly stream of combative traffic. Into the Dorchester, envelope in hand and over to the lobby noticeboard listing the usage of the in-house function rooms. A quick eyeball revealed no mention of Provident Bank plc. Just as he expected. Top secret. Next bluff required. He eyed the nearby reception desk, picked out the youngest, most hassled girl and approached her.

'I've got a message for the Provident Bank people who are meeting here. It's urgent. Which room are they in?'

She wasn't hassled enough to roll over and die.

'There's no meeting here in that name. Sorry.'

He spied her silver name badge. Go for the personal touch. Dear Rita.

'Look Rita, I know it's all confidential but they asked me to deliver this.' He held up the envelope.

She saw the words written boldly on the front and cast a glance over to her manager who was even more stressed out with an invasion of the world's biggest Japanese tour party; bags, video cams, wives and all.

'Is it OK to send this guy up to the Provident room? They want it to be private, don't they?'

He gave her a frustrated nod in reply. Excellent. He didn't give a damn either.

'They're in the Waterloo room. Fifth floor. Last door at the back. Knock first.'

Greg was in the lift before Rita could speak to the next guest. The fifth floor was deserted. He walked past several sets of closed doors to a covert reconnaissance position behind a row of plastic palm trees near the door to the room. Six fifteen. Decent enough timing. He could wait maybe a maximum of an hour before the cabbie would drive off or else come looking for his favourite baseball cap with a vengeance. Greg waited. Snack time? A leak in the john? There must be some action soon.

He waited. And waited. A few inquisitive people passed by. Greg held onto his envelope as a visible excuse for his solitary presence amongst the palm fronds. Then a sudden creak and the old wooden doors of the Waterloo room opened to the world. He leant back into the foliage. There were a few suits standing around aimlessly. Some handshaking. Good sign or bad? Jesus. This was risky. Someone might recognise him. But it had to be done. He had ten million quid of Provident paper sitting in account 99007 and if this deal didn't happen then the position would be going south.

He recognised Alexander Soames, the finance guy he had seen twice at City functions. Soames looked confused. Hard to tell. The deal may have hit trouble. Maybe it was off? More suits emerged in huddled twos and threes. Soames went off on his own, walking slowly down the corridor, eyes lowered to the deep pile carpet. A solo dissenting voice? Hopefully. Then that CEO, David Webster, appeared all smiles and chatted to other suits. Encouraging. Some laughter. Excellent. This was going to plan. But more evidence was required.

Then the cast iron assurance. A bunch of far more affluent suits emerged. Greg recognised another ex-pat banker from Morgans, a corporate financier from Barclays and a director from Deutsche. They were the investment bankers co-advising both companies on the deal. They were mutually ebullient as they slapped each other on the back. Wow. Great vibes here. This takeover deal was sure happening. They knew that this was big bucks and they were soon to be in the money. Roll on those lucrative advisory fees.

Greg left the celebratory party, ditched his envelope into the palm fronds by the lifts and pushed his way past the ever-increasing swarm in the lobby. There wasn't room to swing a cat, let alone a Japanese tourist. He dodged the melee and brushed up against some guests making calls on the public telephones downstairs. One suit turned to him in annoyance. That face again. Soames from upstairs. Damn. Was there a momentary mutual recognition? A pause. Soames went back to his furtive phone call in hushed tones. Strange. All of these City guys had their own mobile phones. Why bother making a call on a public telephone?

Barbara couldn't see Greg anywhere on the dealing floor. He'd said to meet on the way out at six but he wasn't at his desk nor in the lobby at the foot of the escalator. This secret relationship had been going on for too long. She needed him to make the next move soon. She would wait half an hour.

Her reputation was on the line once again. The City would judge her by her actions tomorrow morning. She sat in her office behind closed doors, her fingers poised above the keyboard as she looked for inspiration from the blank PC screen. It was time to write the research piece on one of the most closely followed stocks of late. The sales team had heard her bullish comments this morning. Now their institutional clients wanted something A4 size in black and white on Provident Bank.

The job of the City research analyst had changed so much. Years ago it was a mole-like civil-servant activity, where economic and literary academics put quill pen to parchment and wrote lengthy discourses on long-term profitability, gross profit margins, market share, product development, R&D and consumer feedback. These bone-dry documents were posted out in their thousands to the cautious institutional clients. They in turn pondered the salient facts for days, held tedious internal meetings, drew price charts and ultimately decided to buy or sell a few shares, or sit on the fence and do nothing.

Now speed was of the essence. As soon as tomorrow morning's meeting ended the salesmen would whack out her words in e-mails to their client mailing list and ten seconds later they'd be on the phones to get the client to buy or sell. Just to do something, anything, that generated incremental sales commission. They didn't care. The research was the excuse to call a client. Guess what? Our girl took the stock down a peg. You might wanna consider lightening up? She upped the stock. Get in there quick before the herd. It was all about short-termism. No client wanted to know where the Provident share price was going next year. They wanted to know what would happen next week, tomorrow, today, this morning, now.

The job was no longer about fundamental research. It was about showmanship, entertainment, glitz, flair and personality. Barbara scored a ten. Her opinion mattered and the market knew it. They saw her on Sky too. Last year she was rated number four in the Institutional Investors' Poll of Polls of City equity analysts. Some star players from the US giants always got the top spots, but fourth was good for a girl from Blakes.

Good for a twenty-eight year old with only five years' experience in the City, two in a dead-end credit department at a nearby French bank and three in Blakes' UK equity research.

She had single-handedly risen to her media-friendly position, irrespective of a privileged upbringing in a country estate and the munificence proffered by her retired self-made father and former stewardess mother. Ambition, intelligence and a Colgate smile combined to make a potent force in the high-flying world of the City analyst.

There were real conflicts in her job. She had to please all the parties. The sales force wanted big buy decisions. The clients wanted the truth, most of the time. The companies they rated wanted the best possible opinion and called her up when they weren't happy. The corporate brokers at Blakes wanted buy recommendations, otherwise they couldn't do client deals when their own in-house expert was negative on the stock. Blakes' own dealers always wanted buy research for the stocks they were sitting on. She tried to put one particular American equity dealer out of her mind and concentrate. It wasn't easy.

There was too much noise out there. She had to avoid the corporate spin put out by the PR and Investor Relations Departments of the big plcs, run by the sort of oily public school types who had mastered the art of talking to you for ten minutes while saying nothing. They were that good at their obsequious jobs. She knew that a sell recommendation from a leading light like herself would knock the stuffing out of Provident's share price for weeks. A buy would push the price even higher. She tried to avoid going neutral on a stock. What's the point of saying nothing?

Provident had in truth been a dull stock for months. But the Datastream price chart on her other screen showed a rise of five per cent in the past month. The stock was almost hot; the big clients were piling in, no one was selling. Last month Barbara reluctantly rated Provident a neutral. Now she wasn't so sure. That sight of the board in the Dorchester intrigued her. Something was afoot.

Her words would move millions into Provident, or out, just as quickly. Such a responsibility. Decisions. She went with her gut feeling and typed the first few words of the one-page research report in bold. Provident Bank – Buy. The office door opened. He didn't even bother to knock.

'How ya doin'?' inquired Greg, leaning into the room.

'Fine. But where have you been?'

Did she know about his Dorchester trip? Hardly.

'Whad'ya mean, Barb?'

'You know very well. We were due to meet here at six.'

Greg had forgotten. Provident Bank had filled his thoughts.

'I had to go out for a while. It was short notice,' he lied.

'So where were you then?'

Jesus. This was some inquisition. Why didn't she back off?

'I was seeing some people.'

'What people? Anyone I know?'

Back off, doll. Now.

'No one you know.'

'Are you sure? Tell me who it was.'

'Look, for Christ's sake …' He paused, recovered his composure.

'Greg, you and I aren't supposed to have any secrets,' she persevered.

'I'm sorry. It was about work. Dealing. You know that I can't talk to you about that. So then, what are you working on?'

'You know that I can't talk about that,' she replied as she instinctively turned her screen away.

'Ah. So we can have secrets then?

'This is different. You shouldn't be in here, Greg. Old Nick will be livid if he catches you hanging around in Research again.'

'To hell with him. I just wanted to see you.' He caught a glimpse of the screen. 'Provident? What's the story?'

'I can't tell you what I'm working on. We've got to follow these Chinese Wall procedures here. I'll be in trouble.'

'Go on. You can tell me. I am long of Provident shares.'

Barbara was insistent. 'I don't want to know your positions.'

'Barb, you know all my positions.'

She didn't appreciate the innuendo. 'Go away. See you in twenty minutes in the lobby.'

He eased back through the half-open door.

'All right. Anything to please you. You're too much of a professional.'

'Greg, don't be like that.'

'Too late for regrets. See ya.'

Old Nick caught him leaving the Research Department and stopped him by a row of desks.

'Dealers are not supposed to be in Research. You know that. I've told you before.'

'Nicholas, make an exception for me.'

Old Nick was always making exceptions for Greg. That was the problem with having a star on the first floor who made them millions every year. The dealer had him over a barrel.

Alexander Soames knew that the hotel lobby was full of guests, but there was no choice. His secretary reviewed his mobile telephone bill each month before passing it to the Accounts Department. The less she knew about his private life the better. Public telephone boxes might be noisy, germ-laden and prone to breakdown, but their call records were wonderfully anonymous compared to an itemised mobile account from BT Cellnet. His enquiry was immediately answered and the conversation was succinct.

'Alex here. How about an eight o'clock overnight appointment?'

A pause. The moment of truth. Where would he spend the night? Then an affirmative response.

'Yes, that's possible. See you then. Bye.'

He returned to room 812, his luxury padded cell for the past few days. He hated it. Immediately he telephoned down to reception to block any telephone calls to the room. He was too tired, he said. That was fine, Mr Smith, they replied. There would be no disturbances. Room service, sir? No thanks. Not again. He knew the menu off by heart and if he stayed there one more night he would turn into a club sandwich himself, cocktail sticks and all. He could get some proper food on the way to his destination.

He thought about changing out of his City suit into some casual clothes but decided against the extra effort required. Eight o'clock was fast approaching. Tomorrow morning he would change in his room into a freshly laundered shirt and tie before receiving his breakfast at the usual time. No one would ever know.

The hotel lift took him directly past the lobby floors and into the underground car park. He drove his Volvo towards the narrow exit ramp at excessive speed. He slowed momentarily by the barrier manned by a spotty youth in an over-sized uniform, not wishing to draw undue attention to himself. He turned left and drove south down Park Lane, through Victoria and then eastwards along the Embankment towards the City. Some might think he was going to some clandestine City meeting at corporate HQ. Not too far from the truth.

Soames had not stepped outside the hotel since he had arrived last Sunday evening, although the waiter who delivered his room service breakfast of coffee, OJ and croissants at precisely seven o'clock reliably informed him that the July heatwave was still blazing outside. It was the sort of heatwave that only London can have, miles from a beach or a breath of fresh air, stuck in airless tube carriages, sitting at office desks looking out enviously at the rays, wondering why all your holidays have already been taken, carrying suit jackets over your shoulder as sweat dripped down the inside of your shirt, tourists on the TV news sitting with their feet dangling into the water at Trafalgar Square under the watchful eye of none-too-impressed policemen.

He was on time. Capital FM played on the Sony quadraphonic

stereo system, and the sunroof was open to let in a much-needed breeze. Side windows down too. The car reading indicated an outside temperature of twenty-six degrees, even in the evening. London looked well as locals dressed to suit the summer season. Lots of talent about. Distracting.

His thoughts wandered to the amount of money that he was about to spend. It was a lot for most people but insignificant for him. He had his two hundred thousand pound salary, his annual bonus, his share option package, lucrative pension scheme, his mortgage subsidy on the family home in W9 and his metallic company S40 2.0 10v se auto estate complete with SIPS and ABS. According to the advisers in the Dorchester, he would receive over one million pounds in cash when his Director's contract was prematurely terminated. He would be unemployed but he wouldn't need to worry about money. He might look for another job in the longer term, but he was also looking forward to some well-deserved holiday.

He stopped at two different cash machines along the Strand and by Tower Hill to draw out five hundred pounds in cash from the personal current account that his beloved wife Helen knew nothing about. There had been many similar withdrawals over the past few months, even years. A few hundred once or twice a month. Now and again he whacked in a few grand of company expenses cheques to top up the account. The statements on the bank account were marked private and confidential and went directly to his office address, never to his home. It wasn't worth the risk of discovery.

The analogue clock on the dashboard showed it was seven-fifteen so there was indeed time for a detour to his favourite McDonalds beside The Tower of London, much frequented by overseas tourists returning from viewing the Crown Jewels and engaging in a bit of portly Beefeater baiting. No risk of bumping into anyone that he knew here. Perish the thought.

'Big Mac, large fries, onion rings, large coke no ice, apple pie, chocolate doughnut. To eat in.'

He slumped into a plastic corner seat, ate a lukewarm gherkin-infested hamburger and emaciated fries, read an *Evening Standard* and nursed a cold cup of coffee to kill time. He felt guilty, not particularly over what he was about to do, more about his passion for clandestine junk food.

It definitely contributed to his overweight frame. He certainly couldn't blame Helen's dedicated efforts to convert him to low-fat milk, yoghurt, salad leaves and gallons of Evian. She'd made him sign up for membership of that West London gym but he was never around to actually visit it. Gloomily he lit a well-deserved cigarette, something else the company doctor warned him about at his last check-up.

He had a high-stress job and that was why he was overweight, out of breath, unfit and continuously tired. Today was worse. That omnipresent heat was having a debilitating effect on his energy levels as the evidence of damp patches emerged under his arms and beads trickled down his brow. Hot. Too damn hot.

He arrived at the southern tip of the Isle of Dogs as planned. He did not park the car inside the narrow confines of Thames View because discretion was of the utmost importance. He had his instructions and knew how to obey. He left the car in an adjoining street with the engine immobiliser switched on. He took the coded security cover from the multi-play compact disc stereo and placed it in his suit jacket. Too much crime about in London these days. He walked the short remaining distance to number thirty-two.

After a typically civil conversation he took a hot shower and finally felt refreshed. He managed to erase the clinging McDonalds' odour and replace it with that of England's finest Imperial Leather. He used the facilities of the bathroom, his last chance to do so for some time. He did not replace his suit and tie. Instead he wore what had been left hanging for him on the rear of the bathroom door. It was generously splashed inside with talcum powder so that it was easier to wear.

The black rubber body suit clung to his still moist skin. He placed the hood over his head so that the open face was positioned for maximum comfort. He rolled up the arm-length gloves and then the socks so that he was wholly encased in his favourite material. The best was yet to come.

He descended the wrought-iron stairs to the garage. She minutely examined the suit and ensured that it completely covered his flabby body. It was not a pretty sight but they both knew that the tactile sensation and heavenly smell were more important than mere visual appearance.

'Over here, Alex.'

She directed him to the long wooden bench at the back of the garage that he knew so well. He lay horizontally on it, head nearest to the red-brick wall. He shifted slightly to the left and then again to the right. He had to be comfortable, to endure what was to come. Ten hours to go and counting.

She expertly secured his body with leather straps positioned along the edge of the bench. Another larger strap went around his waist and was buckled. The last strap went loosely around his neck, purely to provide the illusion of total restraint rather than to serve to impede the essential respiratory process. She stood back to examine her professional work, wholly satisfied with the end result.

'Goodnight, Alex.'

The sound of her heels grew distant as she ascended the stairs to her home. The adjoining door to the converted garage closed behind her. He heard the key turn in the lock, unnecessarily so, as if he was somehow going to break free from this self-imposed predicament. The fluorescent spotlights flickered and went out and he was left in total darkness. He could neither move nor stretch nor turn in any direction.

He would have to remain here until the mutually agreed time of six o'clock tomorrow morning. Bliss. This millionaire-to-be was going to get a good night's sleep. Eventually. But it was so hot.

Barbara knew Greg's routine verbatim but she still couldn't get enough. A girl likes to be truly spoiled and, as everyone knows, everything is bigger and better in the States. Everything.

First came extended foreplay. He ran his tongue along the inside of her lips for an apparent eternity. Back and forth, worshipping every molar. So much more pleasurable than any half-hour spent in front of the bathroom mirror with strands of floss. She'd cancel her next dental appointment for sure.

Then the tips of his fingers took her erect nipples, one by one, teasing them until he felt the wetness between her legs. Repeatedly stopping and starting again. He took them between his lips in turn and savoured the taste of pure carnal arousal. He blew onto them from close range and heard her inhale, felt her shudder.

His hands moved down and caressed her other lips. She was so wet already. She closed her eyes and enjoyed the journey. He rose up in the bed so that she could take him in her hands. Her index finger ran circles around his tip. She was so close to the edge of ecstasy. She was ready. He knew.

Suddenly he was on top, inside, all around, in and out. She couldn't resist. His body weight was too much. The palms of his sweaty hands were pressed against her extended palms, held down firmly on the cotton sheets. He was almost too much; it nearly hurt her. She cried out. He thought it was pleasure.

Afterwards Greg lay there and marvelled at how wonderful the sex was and how he didn't have to pay for it anymore. Barbara lay there and wondered if she would ever see an engagement ring and whether her mother was right about Greg.

CHAPTER SEVEN

THAMES VIEW, ISLE OF DOGS, LONDON E14

Sarah Hart awoke at 5:59 a.m. courtesy of the screaming clock radio that was essential for such time-sensitive occasions. Without even showering or downing the life-bringing caffeine drug, she put on a sensible cotton robe and descended from the living room of her townhouse via the wrought-iron steps to her guest in the garage.

A flick of the wall switch flooded the room in fluorescent light. Much too harsh at this time of the morning but it was essential. There were no windows in the garage. The door was two inches of solid aluminium. God, it was hot in this basement, too hot and with no air conditioning either. Like a pressure cooker. Dangerous. She must do something about it for the next overnight guest.

Her garage was unrecognisable as a place in which to park motor cars. Rather it was whatever her clients wished it to be. The basement was uniquely equipped at considerable expense, but Sarah viewed the assorted equipment as an investment upon which she made a daily return. Massive handmade items of customised furniture dominated the room. She sat in the chair raised on its base to a foot off the floor. The high back had an initial S set in metal studs.

'Morning.'

Alexander Soames lay on the bench. He hadn't moved. How could he? A FTSE plc Director who paid five hundred pounds to sleep bound in a rubber suit. Bizarre. She didn't want to disturb him. His eyes were closed serenely. He was in a world of his own in every sense. But she had her instructions. Alexander had a business meeting this morning in a West End hotel. He had explicitly said so ten hours ago.

'Alex, it's time to get up,' she encouraged him.

The garage was exactly as she had left it. Small wonder. He couldn't do much in his present condition. The walls were a deep burgundy red, the ceiling an oppressive black. The floor was simple grey concrete, effective for stiletto boots but not for bare male soles. The spotlights were recessed into the ceiling, each one operated independently by dimmer switches. The black velvet curtains could be pulled across various parts of the room to make each individual experience even more intense and intimate.

Sarah undid the straps around his wrists, then arms, and stood back expecting some reaction.

'Come on, Alex, it's six o'clock. Rise and shine.'

She held his rubber-clad hand in her own. He was cold to the touch. She held his skin-tight glove. Real cold. Still no reaction. She looked closely at his head framed by the open-faced rubber hood. He was perfectly still. Too still. She placed one hand nervously on the side of his face and immediately withdrew it. His cheek was hard and cold. She began to think the unthinkable.

'Alex. Please ... please.'

It was a one-way conversation. She took both his hands in a vain search for warmth. She shook his arms vigorously. They were so stiff, so reluctant to be moved. She rocked his portly frame from side to side on the bench with great difficulty, hoping the act would somehow re-awaken him. She leant over his head and listened intently. There should be a sound, some murmur, anything. There was nothing. She placed a finger by his wrist in search of a pulse. Nothing.

'Jesus, Alex. Come on, come on. Wake up, damn you.'

The dreadful reality dawned. Alexander Soames was no more. She collapsed into her throne chair in the awful knowledge that she now had a corpse on her hands instead of a living, breathing Finance Director.

How could he possibly have died? Had she tied some of the straps too tightly and affected his circulation? Had the hood around his face been too much for him? Had he become too aroused? Had he experienced breathing difficulties? Or succumbed to the claustrophobic atmosphere in the airless garage in the July heat? Did he have a health problem he had never spoken about? And if so, why the hell did it have to catch up with him here in her home?

The natural course of action was to do what anyone else would. Dial 999, give her address and wait. The police would come around and take charge of the situation, bring a doctor or a coroner, remove the deceased and the matter would be neatly resolved. Not so easy for Sarah.

The police would investigate how Alexander had died. This was not a natural death. They would question her circumstances and her lifestyle. Her untaxed immoral earnings and hidden offshore assets in Jersey would be exposed. Her City clients would become common knowledge. Sarah could see the *Sun* headlines already. Her much-valued privacy would end with tabloid interest in the sordid events at her Wapping den of vice. She could face a manslaughter charge or even one of murder. What was the going rate for murder these days? Twenty years? She wasn't going to risk it.

Sarah Hart had run a successful solo business from her home in Wapping for four years. She was wholly self-employed and no burden upon the State. In so many ways she was perfectly normal except that her livelihood consisted of beating the living daylights out of punters in the convenience and privacy of her Docklands residence. Life could have been a lot worse.

She'd moved south immediately after escaping from a Newcastle comprehensive school with passable results. She'd worked hard to lose the memories of a tough childhood and even harder to lose that northern accent in favour of something more cultured and overtly southern. The only problem with London was finding the money to live on. No one wanted an unqualified beauty. No one except the men she met. She always blamed it on friends of friends. They knew girls who used to work in the modelling business. They in turn had friends who wanted other friends to spend time with them at a price. Let's all be friends. Revolting at first. Easy money later. Ultimately a lifestyle.

Certain clients wanted more bizarre services. They were loaded. The money was better, the control was all hers and sexual relations were neither requested nor offered. Her dominant personality, born out of survival under her father's iron fist, came to the fore. It combined well with her physical attributes. Each client liked something special about her. Her height at five foot nine. Her lean body, fit as any thirty four year old could be. Her muscled arms from morning sessions at the Wapping Highway health club. Her broad shoulders when she arched back wielding an implement of correction. Her legs that looked even better encased in sheer stockings and thigh boots with metal tips. Clients truly worshipped her.

Sarah had a focussed business strategy like so many of her affluent corporate clients. She targeted a market segment of wealthy influential gentlemen, many with harsh public school backgrounds which they fortunately wished to re-visit behind her closed doors. Clients liked to think that they had chosen Sarah, but in reality she had chosen them. The two-line advertisement in *The Times* always worked: 'Strict lady seeks City gentleman for just rewards in convenient discreet facilities'. Of late she had placed some Box number advertisements in specialist magazines. They worked too.

She knew how to keep good clients, and more importantly how to lose bad ones. She treasured those polite middle-aged well-connected gentlemen from the City flush with ready cash. She gave them her all, bringing them to the edge of ecstasy, meeting their every whim and twisted fantasy, prolonging the agony past her usual one-hour time threshold, conversing freely before and after, and asking for enough notes, but not too many. It was different if some opinionated hormonally-charged pseudo-athlete visited. She ensured he never returned by providing an unfriendly half-hour, serious rattan marks and a quick exit stage left.

Her choice of a Docklands home was no accident. It was near to her target market, where clients could take an hour or two off from work for some spurious reason. They caught black cabs or parked their company saloons in nearby roads where most net curtains went unmoved when pinstriped strangers arrived. Wapping was almost devoid of locals during the day. Residents worked in the City and were gone from first light to late evening. The only exception was the old widow across the road who sometimes watched the arrivals.

Sarah received two clients at lunchtime and two in the early evening. They often voluntarily paid more because they were so satisfied. What's a few hundred for an hour of personal service unlike any other in London when you earn a six-figure salary plus bonus? She offered extended stays of several hours and overnights for trusted clients like the late Alexander Soames where the tribute was higher. The several thousand tax-free pounds that she earned per week was paid into her sterling account or invested in unit trusts in an offshore bank in Jersey. The welfare state did not provide a pension plan for Sarah's chosen profession.

Then two years ago fate had thrown her a curved ball. He had called about her advert in *The Times*. She should have recognised that awful American drawl. She should have remembered him from that Knightsbridge hotel room many years ago. He'd invaded her Wapping home and tried to renew old acquaintances, simultaneously rekindling violent memories. She wasn't interested. He had roamed the basement garage. Even he could work out how she made her money.

The City banker whom he saw on his way out, parking his Granada Ghia in the adjacent cul de sac, set his sick mind in motion. A scam. It had been his idea. He needed inside information and would pay her well for it. She needed more money to get out of this work as soon as possible. Why not? He scared her. Do it for a while. Two years so far and no way out. The American had made sure of that.

Sarah sat upstairs in the lounge for hours, afraid to venture down below to the scene of death. She lost track of time but eventually there was no choice. She had to do something. She took the first tentative steps downstairs. She approached the body and then reluctantly stepped back. Fear overcame her. She couldn't stand so close to her client, couldn't look at the lifeless hands hanging over the edge, couldn't view the peaceful face.

She compromised and picked up the wire basket from the floor beside the bench. It contained his clothes from the night before. That was the practice for overnights. Undress upstairs. Stow it away downstairs. She examined the sad contents, the guilt growing deeper by the minute. Nothing as sordid as rummaging through a dead person's possessions. Sorry, Alex.

Two items tumbled from the pile of clothes. First was a leather wallet crammed full of fresh notes. Sarah thumbed through them. Her five hundred pounds was here, and more. She thought about the morality of taking money from a dead man, but five hundred pounds in anyone's wallet was odd. The less suspicion the better for all concerned. She took the cash and stuffed it into the side pocket of her robe. She didn't know at what time during the night Alex had breathed his last. Perhaps she had earned it.

Then a metal object on the concrete, a key ring with a silver Volvo crest and an attached sonic car alarm button. Sarah thought about the implications. Alex had driven here from his City office. He had said so many times, about how the traffic was awful but that it was easy to park down here, one of the other reasons why she'd chosen Docklands. Had he driven down this time and was his car parked outside her discreet townhouse? She ran to the front of the house and looked up and down the road. No Volvos, but it was too important to leave to chance. Someone might be looking for it already. Such as the police.

She ran upstairs and changed into the most anonymous outfit she could find. Faded jeans, black t-shirt, baseball cap, flat shoes, no make-up, sunglasses. She left home and walked down the side streets but no sign, until suddenly she spotted a blue Volvo estate parked in a nearby cul de sac. It was an unusual place to park. Could this be it? One easy way to find out. She pointed the key ring alarm at the car, pressed firmly, watched the indicators blink twice and heard the central locking de-activate.

This evidence was too near to home. Better move it fast. There was no one else in the road. Might as well go for it now. She took out a pair of black leather gloves. She had five pairs that she used for her work. Safety first. No fingerprints in this car at all costs. She pulled her hair under the baseball cap. No need to leave tell-tale blonde hairs either. She got inside and moved the driver's seat well forward to a more comfortable driving position. She turned off the security immobiliser with the key ring.

The car started first time. Typical bloody Volvo. She pulled off in the direction of Wapping Highway, driving aimlessly until she saw the gridlocked traffic heading westwards towards Tower Hill, the City and ultimately the West End. She hung a right to follow the juggernauts towards the A12 and the East End, thinking all the time about the best place to leave this luxury car. Anyone want a freebie Volvo?

A set of amber traffic lights near Mile End forced her to a sudden halt. She could crash the lights but not today. A marked police car with two uniformed officers stopped directly beside her in the outside lane. She sat nervously with hands poised on the steering wheel deliberately avoiding eye contact with the occupants of the adjacent panda car. She wondered if anyone was looking for this S-registration Volvo yet. Hopefully not. She had to get rid of it before the next police car pulled her over and asked her what she was doing driving the car of a missing City Director.

She hated this part of the East End around Stratford. Youths hung around traffic lights looking menacingly at vulnerable lady drivers, derelict office buildings were boarded up with For Sale signs, and lone shops with metal shutters sold take-away convenience food and beer to the local unemployed population. In dives such as this a luxury car might not be safe for long. Perfect.

She approached the grim 1970s Stratford shopping centre. She could not leave the car inside the centre's own car park; too many closed circuit cameras pointing at customers. She had no wish to be recorded for posterity today, and perhaps ultimately for subsequent Crown prosecution. She searched for some anonymous side street near the back of the centre and went around the block twice to make sure.

She chose Burdett Avenue, lined with red-brick terraced houses, small front gardens and aggressive coloured youths in baseball caps and shiny Nike tracksuits strutting off to loiter in the shopping centre. She parked up on a kerb without yellow lines. No desire to get a parking ticket today; the less official records the better. A shiny estate could easily be stolen here if the correct security procedures were not followed. She checked the interior. Nothing of hers was left inside but more temptation was needed.

Sarah was puzzled. The base unit of an expensive stereo was in the dashboard, but the coded security panel was missing. She ran her hands under the seat and around the glove box but there was no sign of it. Pity. Still worth a try though. She put a few compact discs on the front passenger seat as an added temptation, stepped out of the car, left all the doors unlocked and threw Alex's key ring onto the front driver's seat. Gloves off. Sunglasses on. Walk fast, head down.

If that Volvo wasn't nicked in the next few hours then Sarah Hart wasn't the best dominatrix in London. And anyone caught in that car would have a difficult time explaining to the police that they had no knowledge of the late Alexander Soames. Honest Guv, the car was parked on the road with the keys left on the seat.

Tube stations and buses had CCTV cameras that ruled them out as modes of transport on this extraordinary day. Sarah hailed a black cab back to the Isle of Dogs and safety.

The feelings of relief evaporated as she opened the hall door. She was back at the scene, feet away from the body still downstairs. She had to find a solution. She made a strong coffee in the kitchen and almost downed it in one gulp. She stood watching the passing traffic outside in the Thames and thought about the effect Alex's death would have on his wife Helen and his twin daughters back in Little Venice. He talked about his family so much that she felt she knew them.

But she was a hardened businesswoman with no other means of support, and as the hours passed the corpse became no more than a problem looking for an easy solution. She was so alone. No one to help her. No one she wanted to call. She couldn't call *him*. And she didn't dare call Lenny. The Mandarin couldn't help. All the City lawyers she knew couldn't help. Yet her satisfactory lifestyle must not be jeopardised by one unfortunate event. There was too much to lose. Alexander Soames was her first fatality and he would be her last. She needed a plan, one to minimise the considerable downside.

She could drag Alex upstairs with some difficulty and lay him out in her lounge fully clothed in his suit and tie. Then tell the police that he died in her living room, that she was his lover and that he had been literally dying for sexual intercourse. But it wouldn't work. Too much could go wrong. The mere thought of inviting the police into her home left her as cold as Alex's present condition.

Sarah stood in front of her sunlit window, looking out at the barges and tourist traffic plying the grey Thames, stirring her second warm cup of coffee methodically. She was even more convinced that a clandestine disposal of the corpse was the optimal solution. Her first thought was to bury the body nearby but her townhouse was sadly lacking a grassy rear garden, the communal areas around the complex being tastefully cobbled in old red brick set in neat geometric patterns. There was not a blade of grass nor flowerbed in sight and she didn't even possess a shovel. In any case she could not live next to a corpse.

A slow barge laden with London's accumulated urban rubbish passed by. She realised that the best solution to her murderous dilemma lay before her eyes. Alexander Soames was going down the river.

CHAPTER EIGHT

DORCHESTER HOTEL, PARK LANE,
LONDON W1

David Webster was puzzled. The Provident Board sat in their usual function room. The assembled suits were about to sign the takeover agreement and agree the text of the press announcement to be issued that evening to the news media. But there was one empty chair where their expert Finance Director always sat. Alexander Soames was usually reliable. It was unheard of for him ever to miss a Board meeting, particularly one as singularly momentous as this. Webster spoke to the suits.

'Does anyone know where Alexander Soames is?'

Silence around the table. Blank faces. Webster's days as Chief Executive of Provident Bank were numbered and he couldn't afford to wait for anyone. Every passing day increased the risk of the news leaking out. Many dealers would kill to hear about the takeover by British Commercial Bank before their peers in the City. The media announcement had to come after the London market had closed so that no one traded and ultimately profited by using such price-sensitive information. Webster probed further.

'Anyone seen him since our meeting yesterday?'

Further silence. He delayed the meeting while an assistant

telephoned up to Alexander's hotel room. The call went unanswered. Webster instructed one of the hired-hand accountants to go upstairs. Perhaps Soames had over-slept or was unwell? The bean counter knocked noisily yet unsuccessfully on the door of room 812. He reported back that a tray of coffee, orange juice and croissants lay untouched in the corridor outside the room. Obviously room service had had no success raising him earlier.

An assistant manageress called Rita on the reception desk provided a master key to the room. They found the covers still intact on the double bed as testament that the room was unused during the night. Soames's personal possessions were there, his shaving kit was in the bathroom, his clothes hung in the wardrobe, and the co-ordinated luggage stood in the corner of the room. He must after all have left the hotel to see Helen and the twins. Four days of intensive business discussions was a long time away from loved ones.

Webster made the next call. Helen Soames answered from their Little Venice home.

'Helen, David here. Is Alex there?'

She too was puzzled.

'No, he's not. He's at some secret meeting in a hotel somewhere. With you, I thought? Isn't he?'

'No, he's not here at the moment. Have you heard from him recently?'

'He called me yesterday evening. He said the meetings were almost over and then he would be home.'

Webster did his best to disguise his concern.

'Never mind. I'm sure he'll be with us soon.'

Helen recognised a bluff when she heard it.

'Is everything all right, David?'

No need for undue alarm at this early stage.

'Perfectly all right,' he lied. 'Bye.'

He started the Board meeting and focussed everyone's attention on the key terms of this mega-deal, still wondering where his trusted Finance Director was. Today of all days. The senior PA taking the Board minutes spoke to him.

'What shall I record in the minutes regarding Alexander's absence?'

Webster gave him the benefit of the doubt.

'Show him as being absent with apologies.'

By mid afternoon he took matters into his own hands. He needed his Finance Director for this evening's high-profile press conference. He telephoned their head office in the City. No one there had seen Soames in the past twenty-four hours. He checked with their in-house travel department. No one had booked Soames on a flight to foreign parts or given him a Eurostar train ticket. He organised some calls to Central London hospitals. No one of that name had been admitted overnight.

Then a breakthrough of sorts. Rita at the front desk had used her initiative and pursued some investigations of her own. Soames's Volvo had pulled out of the hotel car park at half past six last night according to the staff who manned the exit. It was on the CCTV still. That's all they could see.

Webster was still puzzled. Where had his Director been going? Had he had enough of Provident? Had the takeover deal and the Board's decision been too much for him to stomach? Had he driven off into the sunset for good? No, Webster thought, this was unlikely. Alex had a Director's contract and a termination deal worth a million in cash. He was a professional. Webster knew him well. But obviously not well enough.

Sarah was suddenly stirred from her nightmare day by the telephone. It rang and rang. No way was she answering. No way was she meeting another client today. Still it rang. The answering machine kicked in and she smiled. No other clients ever left her a potentially incriminating message on the tape. They were too worried about the thought of their cultured

ABCI accents being recorded forever. If they only knew what happened down in the basement.

Her smooth voice played. She had practised hard to get that message right. It was the first impression that potential clients got and it always hooked them. Then an instantly recognisable voice spoke.

'Hello, it's me. I've got some good news. I'll be down at about four o'clock. See you then.'

His voice. He was visiting today. She made a lunge for the phone.

'Hello? Hello?'

She got the dialling tone. He had hung up. She had no direct telephone number for him. Many clients knew her home number but they never reciprocated. Perish the thought of a wife or girlfriend answering her call in reply. She knew the name of the bank where he worked in the City and could call the main switchboard, get put through to his desk and tell him to stay away. She held the phone and thought about dialling directory enquiries. Then second thoughts. No. That would be exceptional. It would worry him. Best to make everything seem as normal as possible. Even if it wasn't.

She went downstairs, held back the nausea, avoided eye contact with the body, took a black latex sheet and draped it over him. Then she pulled one of the heaviest velvet curtains all around the bench in the corner. Out of sight and out of mind. She would make sure no other visitor went down into the basement until her previous client had made his final exit.

Greg needed to get out of Blakes and a late lunch followed by a visit to his local gym was the perfect excuse for the other staff at the special situations dealing desk.

'Chas, I'm off early today. Keep an eye on our stocks this time. Don't screw up. No haircuts.'

He left Blakes and went to the over-priced Italian delicatessen in Broadgate for some wafer-thin Parma ham and mozzarella on herbed ciabatta bread. He sat in Devonshire Square for ten minutes while he wolfed it down with a Diet Coke and a packet of Walkers salt and vinegar. He strolled back towards Bishopsgate, into his local bank branch and was immediately frustrated by the length of the queue.

He needed cash and the electronic hole in the wall outside wouldn't deliver a sufficient quantity. After a closely examined personal cheque with banker's card and a conversation with an overly inquisitive junior teller, Greg folded three thousand pounds in sequentially numbered notes into the inside of his Boss suit pocket and took a black cab from the rank at Liverpool Street tube station.

The familiar journey to the riverside townhouse was mercifully free of both traffic and banal conversation with the sullen cabbie. He rang the doorbell and heard the heels approaching the door. She did not seem particularly pleased to see him. Bad day perhaps?

They didn't need to shake hands or kiss. Latent hostility was like that. He reached inside his pocket and placed the wad of cash onto the stripped pine coffee table. He pointed at it proudly from where he lounged on the over-sized couch.

'That's for you. I had some more good news this week.'

Sarah didn't know what good news was anymore. She looked disdainfully at the bundle of notes, not wishing to be tainted by picking it up with her manicured fingers. She had more important matters on her mind. She had to act normally.

'So where did this come from?' As she was usually required to ask.

'I made a killing this week.'

He wasn't the only one.

'You remember Sir Gordon Harvey's visit here and what he said about County Beverages? County made a real bullish trading statement at this week's AGM and the shares took off on the day. I bought and sold a few, got out in time and realised some damn good profits. I kicked the ass of most of the market makers out there on the street. That's your share.'

His explanation somehow justified the presence of the money for her. She pretended to be enthusiastic, ran her hands briefly through the notes, inhaled the inky odour and placed the money inside the drawer of her corner bookcase unit. Her own little temporary bank account here at home. There was no need to count it. She didn't know how long he wished to stay as he sat back comfortably on the couch, but she hoped he would leave soon. She feared he might be here for some time. Then fate smiled on her.

'I can't stay. I must get to the gym this evening. Got any more news?'

News. That dreaded word. She knew what he meant. She had almost forgotten about the information gleaned from her recent visitors given the recent turmoil. In the drawer, she immediately found what she was looking for. Make everything seem normal to him. She had feigned ignorance of the City and the listed shares that moved so magically. It seemed to have worked so far. He had no idea what she was doing.

'There's only one tape. Some company called Sportsworld. It's all here as usual.'

She gave him a single audiotape with the company name written on the front, a C90 with plenty of time to spare for the private and painful conversations that mattered. Greg put it inside his suit jacket, already looking forward to playing it later. And suddenly he was gone without ever asking to look around downstairs.

It was an easy three thousand pounds but Sarah would have gladly foregone the cash just to be able to talk to Alexander Soames again.

There was fifteen minutes to go before the start of the press conference in the domed Dorchester function room and the financial news media were assembled. BBC, ITN, Sky, *The Times*, Reuters,

Bloomberg, the *FT*, the *Standard*. Rumours circulated amongst the magnificent chandeliers and mock Louis XIV furniture about trading statements, acquisitions, takeovers, mergers and mega-deals.

There was still no definite news of Soames. Webster wasn't pleased. There were times when a Chief Executive needed his Finance Director and this was one of them.

'Where the fucking hell is Alex?'

His aides had no answers. Wild thoughts ran through the CEO's mind about industrial espionage, spying, kidnapping and counter-surveillance. There was no logical explanation for Alexander's absence but this deal could not be delayed merely because of one of the players. He had to start the press conference. He would call Helen and tell her to contact the police. Sometime soon. Once he was sure.

The Corporate Affairs staff called for silence as Webster straightened his collar and checked the knot in his tie. He read the press statement to a stunned audience. The aides handed out photocopies. The heading was bold: British Commercial Bank Acquires Provident Bank. Webster handled the questions from the floor, wishing that he had the assistance of his Finance Director to field the more technical probes.

'Are you expecting any other parties to bid for Provident?'

'Don't you think that the purchase price of six billion pounds is too cheap?'

'Why do you think Provident is a good fit with British Commercial Bank?'

'What do the directors get out of this deal personally? What about your contract and share options?'

'Aren't the board a group of fat cats getting as much from this deal as possible?'

He answered the questions deftly and concisely until the last question came from a scruffy guy from the *Evening Standard* standing at the back of the room. It threw him.

'Hey Mr Webster, where's your Finance Director today?'

*   *   *

Mark was almost wracked with guilt as he sat in the plush reception area of the Covent Garden office. This was treachery, treason, subterfuge of the worst kind. In all of his three years in the employment of the London Stock Exchange he had never stooped so low. The groomed receptionist with the pancake make-up and sharp charcoal suit stood authoritatively behind the marble-topped counter.

'Mr Robinson, if you'd like to come through now.'

He sat in the meeting room of City Selections with the recruitment consultant. He knew this was a good firm because the best job advertisements in the *FT* were always in their name. The consultant talked about Mark's CV, his education, university, his work experience, his salary package, his aspirations, his interests, his career in the LSE, or lack of it. Mark found it easy. Recruitment consultants have that gift of making you feel comfortable and important. And everyone loves to talk about themselves.

Then the more interesting conversation. The consultant dazzled Mark with possible job opportunities in Compliance departments in the City. Goldmans, UBS, HSBC, ING, Deutsche, Morgans, the works. He would make some calls first thing tomorrow morning. Mark would find a job no problem. He dropped a few indicative salary numbers. Big numbers. Mentioned the bonuses, the Beamers, the cheap mortgages, the subsidised staff loans. After twenty minutes of the hard sell Mark was almost salivating over the polished veneer.

He left feeling informed, optimistic and with feet that were positively itching to move on. The sooner the better.

Greg spent a few hours at his West London gym and then had a snack and a beer in the adjoining clubhouse. By the time he returned home he had been out of circulation for too long. Fatal sometimes in his business. He was only half listening to the BBC1 news headlines as he sat in his kitchen reading the business section of the Standard. As soon as he heard the name he ran down the hallway of his apartment and slumped in front of the television screen that showed the Provident corporate logo in the background. He listened to the newsreader as she expanded on the attention-grabbing headline.

'Provident Bank has announced that it will be taken over by British Commercial Bank. A statement issued at six o'clock today by the Board confirmed that British Commercial would pay eleven pounds for every Provident share. The deal values Provident at over six billion pounds and is by far the biggest of recent deals in a rapidly consolidating UK banking sector. The price of Provident shares is expected to rise sharply tomorrow, having closed at ten pounds thirty pence earlier today.'

Greg did his usual instant calculation. He had a million Provident shares. They had cost ten million pounds. Minimum eleven pounds each tomorrow. Eleven million pounds. He fell a sleep thinking about the million pound profit that would surely hit his Bible profit and loss printout in the next day or so. He would make a sizeable chunk of the rest of the year's target in one ecstatic day. God was good.

His only regret was that this announcement had come so soon after his quick and well-publicised inter-day profit on County Beverage shares. It was unfortunate timing. Old Nick would give him a hard time again.

While the Thames snaked through Central London for miles, it was an unfortunate fact that there were few suitable places where one could clandestinely place a body into its murky waters without the risk of discovery. The river ran directly past the townhouse, but it was overlooked by her nearby neighbours. Sarah needed a secluded spot where she could get close enough to the river. She knew of one such location less than ten minutes' drive away.

She did the necessary maritime research in *The Times*. The tide would begin to fall at 10.12 p.m. and she was sure that the departing waters would take Alexander well away from her environs. The lunar timing suited her. Late evening was the only time to do the deed. Not too many local Wapping residents about. It was always quiet in Thames View after midnight.

She had left the BMW 3-series coupe in the driveway with the rear up close against the garage door. She didn't know if the boot was large enough to accommodate a corpse, not being the sort of thing that the perfectionist test engineers consider in deepest Bavaria. She spent the early evening moving heavy furniture and equipment to the rear of the garage, then draping any other items with white sheets so that no one could view them from the road while the garage door was temporarily open.

She tried to focus on the task in hand but it wasn't easy. The bulging latex sheet in the corner was a nauseating reminder of the grim work yet to be done. As she moved one smaller bench out of the way she knocked against the body. A hand swayed momentarily by her side. So life-like. If only. She put off the worst part until near midnight; once she'd had a malt whiskey upstairs and steadied herself.

There was a lot to do, many angles to be covered. Appearances mattered. Firstly Alexander had to be clothed in a suit, work that is, not rubber. Sarah took a pair of heavy leather gauntlets from a rail on the wall. No fingerprints please. She tried to remove the rubber suit but it stuck to him like a second skin. She took a pair of scissors from her basement, ran the sharp blade down from his neck to his feet and gladly tore the rubber away. Two hundred pounds' worth of mail order rubber gear down the drain. The exposed skin looked off-colour, with a bluish pallor. The spare tyre around his waist lay on the bench like a beached whale on the seashore.

She took his clothes from the wire basket and dressed him awkwardly. His boxers, work shirt, suit, shoes and socks, everything he had been wearing when he had arrived. That was the way he must be found, if he ever was. She hoped not. It took several futile attempts for her to knot the silk tie adequately, not having as much experience of men's ties as she did of collars, chains, padlocks and six-foot ropes. It took even more effort to close his shirt buttons and fasten the belt buckle at the well-worn notch. She placed the almost empty wallet into his trouser pocket.

The strain was almost too much. The feeling of her warm hands on his cold body was the worst part. Alex had never been just a client. He had been a friend, their relationship garnered over years of familiarity and intimate discussion. She went back upstairs and downed a second malt. Any more and she wouldn't dare take the car. Any less and she couldn't complete the job.

The aluminium garage door hadn't been opened for months due to the hardware that lay beyond the sliding door. It was impossible to budge. She pushed against it, wishing that she had the strength of a man to help her. She finally prised open the stiff door and rolled it upwards. Shit. It creaked so noisily, in need of some oil, but no one nearby seemed to notice. She reversed the BMW into the garage and closed the doors.

After an unseemly ten-minute struggle she rolled the body off the bench and into the boot. Alexander lay lifeless in his suit and tie, hopefully looking the part of any normal Finance Director who had accidentally fallen into the Thames. She closed the boot on her former client and drove the car out of the garage. She locked the door and left her home, glad that she didn't transport bodies too often as the car performed sluggishly with the extra weight in the boot.

Down Westferry Road on the Isle of Dogs and towards its southernmost tip directly opposite Greenwich. The roads were deserted. She stopped at the Isle of Dogs Rowing Club and parked near the entrance to the slipway. She killed her headlights. A quick reconnaissance tour revealed nothing of concern at this crucial moment. No inquisitive onlookers or courting couples or wandering kids. She unhooked the heavy metal chain that ran across the slipway and reversed the car down the concrete slope until the rear alloy wheels were but a few inches from the lapping edge of the river.

One last look around. Silence except for dogs baying in the distance and a barge engine further down the river. She stood in a few inches of the cold water and felt it enter her shoes. She opened the boot. Gotta keep thinking that it's not Alexander. It's only a body. It's only a problem. She dragged him from the boot. He was so heavy. She rolled him over and into the water with difficulty but he still lay beached on the pitted concrete, as if somehow reluctant to leave her side.

She rolled him over one more time, further into the water, and suddenly began to fear that he would not float, rather he would lie half-submerged on this spot for all to see as the tide fell. She would never get him back into the car boot again. This was all going wrong. Then relief as the body seemed to take on a life of its own again. It ebbed in and out alongside the shore, then rose and fell with the flowing tide. She stuck out a pointed shoe and gave the body a decisive push.

The body moved further out and picked up a modest speed, heading downwards past Greenwich and perhaps even further on towards the working docks of Tilbury and then into the English Channel. Hopefully Alexander Soames would cover much distance before tomorrow morning dawned.

CHAPTER NINE

HARROW ROAD POLICE STATION,
LONDON W9

Detective Inspector Ted Hammond was enjoying an uneventful day at the CID desk in the station until one of the uniformed officers from the dingy communications room disturbed him.

'We took a telephone call from a Mrs Helen Soames in Little Venice. She says her husband's missing.'

Missing person cases were the responsibility of CID. There were no other available officers in the briefing room. Ted knew that the majority of missing persons turned up safe and sound soon afterwards. Easy case?

'I'll take it.'

'I said you'd be around in fifteen minutes. She lives at 22 Regents Drive, W9.'

No problem. Ted would pay Helen Soames a visit to ease her troubled mind. A service to the community and all that. He estimated the walk would take eleven minutes, give or take a milli-second. One minute for contingency purposes. Three minutes left in the CID room. He downed the remnants of his coffee and saved the Twix bar for later. No need for a coat in July, even the suit jacket was too much.

He checked himself in the glass on the way out. He had

to look his best for the general public. Well-ironed white shirt. Dark suit. Plain, sombre navy tie. He hadn't worn any other colour since that pile up on the A12 near Dagenham when those joyriders in the Escort Cosworth ruined his family life forever. Somehow it didn't seem right to wear a garish tie. It would sully the memory of his late wife.

He ran a cheap plastic comb through his receding hair. It was getting worse every day, literally falling out. Must be the stress. He was like that guy who went to the barber with only three strands of hair left. Guy tells the barber to comb it back. The barber combs it all back but loses one single strand. The guy is livid but says to part it down the middle. The barber is a bundle of nerves by now and loses another single strand. The guy resigns himself to the inevitable. Fuck it, he says. Leave it tossed. Ted knew how he felt.

Out into the big bad world, another chance for a DI in his mid-forties to get his fix of modest daily exercise and stay lean and healthy. His ambulatory visit would also be more discreet than if he borrowed a marked police car for all the wealthy neighbours to stare at and wonder why. Knowing the local residents as he did, the missing husband would surely turn up, perhaps even before Ted arrived in Little Venice.

Harrow Road was alive. Shoppers plied their way up and down the pitted pavements, stopping off in Halal butchers, fruit and veg shops, Seven-Elevens, Iceland, Boots, leaving each with a bigger collection of bulging plastic carrier bags. There must be people who live in London with nothing to do but shop all day? The more organised types sought out the bookies, the laundromat and the dry cleaners. Aggressive traffic bustled between the A40 and the north of London, much of it double parking and unloading under the watchful eye of mercenary traffic wardens from Westminster Council. Twenty minutes' maximum loading time here, mate. No more.

Ted liked this West London neighbourhood. A better class of crime. There were more missing cats and dogs, erroneous burglar alarms, parked cars without residents permits, nicked car stereos and petty thefts. Far less muggings, knifings, wife battery, rapes and assaults as in the bad old days in Walthamstow, Dagenham, Stratford, Leytonstone and Romford. Did he miss those wonderful East End boroughs? Nope.

He was a modest individual but even he knew that the move to Harrow Road and his elevation to DI after twelve years on the beat were well deserved. Give him this tree-lined drive by the dappled canal with wandering American tourists and pampered poodles any day. Far better than a shopping centre in Stratford populated by unemployed youths apparently sponsored by Nike and Adidas.

Number twenty-two on Regents Drive was impressive even from the pavement. White walls topped by immaculately painted black and gold railings, then a swing gate that creaked open onto five substantial polished stone steps. He stood between two pillars framing the black door. There was even a great view of Regents Canal, with branches of trees bending into the still water. Brass numbers on the door, matching letterbox and heavy doorknocker. Ted used the latter as he checked his watch. Yep. Eleven minutes precisely.

A middle-aged woman greeted him, looking distressed. Must be Mrs Soames. He showed her his warrant card and was ushered in. Her eyes were reddened and watery. She was dressed in the height of casual chic: beige chinos, white t-shirt under an open blue canvas shirt with rolled up sleeves and cream open-toed sandals. Looked like Mrs Soames was a big Gap customer. The interior of her home proved that her good taste was not merely confined to fashion. Stripped wooden floors were half covered by enormous patterned Persian rugs and surrounded by cavernous sofas with matching throws and co-ordinated off-white cushions.

Ted sat in the spacious drawing room by the full-length window and resisted the temptation to watch the barges in the narrow canal outside as they ferried sightseers and bohemian types between Paddington Basin and Camden Lock. He knew that letting her talk would be best.

'My husband has been missing for more than a day. What's happened to Alex? Where can he be?'

He used his years of experience to calm her obvious anxiety.

'The vast majority of missing people turn up safely. There's always a good explanation for where they've been, although few of us think of it at the time. I'll take some details from you and we'll investigate where your husband might be.'

Standard lines of comfort for the distressed. Out of the Met manual, page 75. True in any event.

'Tell me more about your husband.'

'His name's Alexander. He's 49. He works in the City. He's a banker'.

'When did you last see him?'

'Last Sunday evening at about eight.'

That was days ago. What's with this one day? She was only calling in the police now?

'Why did you wait so long to call us? You just said he has been missing for a day.'

'It's not like that. He calls every evening Alex has been in a series of secret company meetings all week. Eight a.m. to eleven p.m. stuff, so he stayed in some West End hotel. He wouldn't even tell me the name of it. I only found out today that it was the Dorchester. There's a big takeover. It's in the papers today.'

What's with these secret meetings? Sounded a bit unusual even to a DI with little knowledge of the weird and wonderful workings of the City of London.

'So he could still be working there? In secret?'

'No, he's not at the hotel. His boss, David Webster, called me again an hour ago. No one at the company has seen Alex since yesterday. He's definitely missing.'

'Has he ever done this before? Gone off at short notice somewhere?'

'No. It's so unlike him.'

'Do you have any idea where he might be? With friends, relations, at a club?'

'I've telephoned around everyone I know. No one's seen him for days.'

'What was he wearing when you last saw him?'

'Dark suit and silk tie, as usual.'

Her lucid conversation suddenly gave way to tears and she held her head in her hands. Tresses of mousey brown hair tumbled out of the velvet hairband. Her hands left thin red lines on her cheeks. Her nails were too long. Ted stood up and walked over to the window, partly in search of inspiration and partly to break the conversation that was becoming more desperate by the minute. And minutes mattered.

'Rest assured, Mrs Soames. We will find your husband.'

Through the front window Ted saw a black cab slowing down. It stopped directly outside the gates. A middle-aged man stepped out and thrust a bank note at the driver. A well-dressed man, City suit, combed-back hair and good tan. Stripey shirt. Ted had one immediate thought. Helen's husband? Ted had only been on this case for nineteen and a half minutes and had already solved it. Surely a record for the Met? He was about to advise Helen of the possibility of imminent good news when the doorknocker sounded again in the hallway. Bad sign. No key.

'More policemen?'

'No. I'm not expecting anyone else. It's a gentleman in a suit.'

Ted could see the hope on her face but he dared not say any more. She jumped off the sofa and ran into the hallway. He heard the door open and greetings were exchanged, then he saw the two embrace in the hall. It wasn't a lovers' embrace, nor that of a desperate wife and her lost husband, but one of mutual sympathy and comfort. They returned, hand in hand.

'Inspector, this is David Webster, Alex's boss at Provident.'

The suited gent shook hands with Ted. David was used to taking charge.

'I had to come round to see if we can help at all. What's the next step, Inspector?'

Ted's thoughts returned to the unfinished business.

'We'll put out a description of your husband to all our stations. Do you have a photograph?'

Helen needed no second bidding. She went to the mantelpiece, took a colour picture taken at a black tie corporate presentation of some sort out of silver frame, tore off a part of it and handed it to Ted. She had destroyed a memento of value in her rush for photographic evidence. And she knew it.

'Don't worry about that. There are lots of copies about. But there's only one Alex.'

As Ted folded the photo into his notebook, David offered one other piece of information.

'We know now that Alex left the Dorchester car park in his company car when our board meeting ended at 6.30 pm. It's a blue Volvo estate. Registration S 50 ALX. Easy to remember, I guess, a personalised plate. If you can find that car it might help in finding Alex. Is there anything else we can do?'

Ted had all the information he needed. Time to get back to base and set the wheels in motion.

'I'll make some enquiries but if he's still missing tomorrow may I call in to your offices in the City?'

'That's fine by me. Any time.'

This case was going to be more difficult than he first anticipated.

Helen persevered. 'When will we hear some news?'

'I'll call you with anything, or you can call me at Harrow Road station.'

Two pretty little girls in Gap Kids outfits ran into the drawing room. Identical girls in fact. Twins with matching brownish hair like their mother. School summer holiday time

and they were at home. Helen introduced them as Emma
and Louise. They looked about nine or ten years old; much
the same age as Ted's youngest son. These twins may have
temporarily lost a father but they didn't know what it was like
to lose a mother forever. They were the fortunate ones. Ted
wondered if they knew what was happening today. He avoided
the painful issues, changed the subject and glanced instinctively
at his watch again.

'I must be going.'

He shook hands with Helen and David. One of the twins
gambolled up closer to them and hid behind her mother in
shyness as they stood by the open hall door. Her impish freckled
face appeared at waist height beside her mother's chinos and she
looked up at Ted. She did know.

'When's Daddy coming home?'

The old lady on Burdett Avenue was worried. It was rare enough
for a car to be parked directly outside her two-bedroomed
terraced council house, but the estate car was still there in
the morning. And it was such a nice shiny blue car. Brand
new with an S-registration plate. It should be gone by now but
not so. Had the owner forgotten about it overnight? Unlikely
with such a valuable car.

Curiosity got the better of her by mid-morning. She ambled
out to the newsagent and on her return had to look inside the
luxurious interior. She saw the leather trim, the arrayed compact
discs, but worst of all she saw the keys on the front seat. This
was an invitation for a thief to steal the car. She opened the
door, took the keys and locked all the doors. The car would
be safe until the police arrived.

The local PC turned up on foot an hour later. Hardly a
national emergency. He was puzzled by his immediate inspection
of the car. He couldn't find the removable security cover for
the flashy car stereo. He had a look in the usual places: under
the driver's seat, in the glove box, in the side pocket of the

door, under the dash, but no sign of it anywhere. The base unit was still lodged securely in the dashboard, utterly useless without the front cover and its million-to-one-chance matching security code.

The PC drew a reasonable inference from the facts as presented. The owner had purposefully taken the security cover when he or she parked the car. The driver was coming back. This was obviously a false alarm. It was only a matter of time. Nevertheless he noted down the registration details, the minimum work required to demonstrate to the neighbourly do-gooder that a genuine effort to trace the absent driver was underway. He used his handset to communicate with his colleagues back in Stratford Police station. The old lady was much impressed by the modern technology.

The PNC check confirmed that the car was owned by Sentinel Fleet Leasing in Sheffield. The station telephoned Sentinel. They had eight thousand cars plus on their books. An utterly disinterested girl on the other end of the line said that she would check the name of the current driver of the car on their computer system. She miraculously returned their call in a mere ten minutes. The car was leased to Provident Bank in the City of London. The named driver was an Alexander Soames. The station staff looked up Provident's City head office in the telephone directory and placed a call to their Personnel Department. They too would ring back. Sometime.

It was that time of the month for Sarah. No, not that time, the other one. The doorbell rang at eleven o'clock. Punctual as ever. He always called early on the first Monday of each month. That way he never met any of the clients and didn't scare away their valued business with his ominous presence.

Sarah checked outside through the window first. His maroon Jaguar XJS was parked by the kerb. Not a brand new Jag, but a grubby, anonymous one with an E-reg plate, a few scratches on the door and a botched paint job. Recent enough to have all the creature comforts but old enough never to draw conspicuous attention to himself from the boys in blue. The moronic minder sat in the driver's seat. He brought a minder everywhere, to the private back room in Stringfellows, to Soho cappuccino bars, to the dogs at Walthamstow, to the casinos in Victoria, to the pubs in Bermondsey and Rotherhithe, to the shops on Regent Street and to the dens of vice in Streatham and Paddington. But he hardly needed a minder, thought Sarah.

She opened the mortice locks. He walked into the lounge and somehow enveloped the sofa in one single motion. A neat and tidy man, five ten or so, black oiled hair with an immaculate side parting, permanent tan from regular golfing trips to the Costas and a deceptively reassuring cherubic face. He looked normal enough. Pleasant almost. But that's what they said about the Kray twins too on their better days. Sarah knew the truth.

He wore his trademark gear, a shiny grey double-breasted suit and black polo t-shirt with all the top buttons closed. Miami Vice, eat your heart out. He thought that it was fashionable and Sarah didn't dare to enlighten him further. The other noticeable feature was the ugly scar on his right hand suffered when he pushed one of Sarah's more difficult former clients through a full-length glass mirror in a suite in Brown's Hotel off Piccadilly many years ago. The razor sharp shards of glass went everywhere.

She had known Lenny ever since she had started seeing men. It was dangerous work, meeting strangers in smoky bars and nightclubs, going off with them in limos with blackened windows. Lenny was a friend of a friend of a friend from up north. She had needed him then for protection. Lenny had helped get her a start of sorts in life. Now it was pay back time. Literally.

'Is everything OK today, Sarah?'

If only it was. If she were going to tell anyone about the recent death in the basement it would be Lenny. He would understand, probably shrug his shoulders and say that these things happen, that the stiff should have been more careful and such is life. Or death. But no one must know. Not even Lenny. And in any event the body was gone for good and there was no connection to her.

'Yes, same as usual,' she lied.

She knew the form. Lenny wasn't here for a social chat and he definitely wasn't a client. She went over to her favourite desk drawer and presented the white envelope that she had carefully prepared earlier.

'There you are. It's all there.'

For some reason, Lenny always counted it. Force of habit in his line of business where cash was king. He thumbed through the bundles of twenty-pound notes, the slow speed of the manual exercise giving away his lack of a decent numerate education. She had as usual extracted the right notes from all the cash that she'd received in the past few days from loyal clients. Crisp notes, not brand new or sequentially numbered direct from ATMs, yet neither old nor torn. Lenny liked his twenties that way. Like his women. He didn't like fifties at all and he hated hundreds with a passion. It was best to keep Lenny happy. She knew that from the bad old days. Fifteen hundred pounds in cash. He closed the envelope.

'Is the house OK, too?'

Lenny surveyed the interior of the townhouse. His townhouse. The one he bought five years ago for a hundred grand in cash in a suitcase. Always cheaper when you pay cash on the nail. Delivered in person by Lenny and a different minder in another Jag to the bent builder in a half-finished St Albans housing estate. The Isle of Dogs townhouse was now worth two hundred grand plus with the Nineties property boom. A tax-free eighteen grand a year in rental income from a hundred grand investment. An annual eighteen per cent yield that many a property fund manager in the City would be proud of. Another great investment for Lenny in his London property portfolio. Put it into bricks and mortar. The filth can never touch that.

'It's fine Lenny. No problems at all.'

And even if there were a leaking tap, a bust electricity socket or an odorous gas leak, she would say nothing. Best not to complicate the visit. Lenny seemed content. He had the loot. Business as usual. Same time next month then. Sarah opened the hall door as he placed the envelope in his inside pocket. The minder got out of the Jag to open the passenger door for his boss. He knew how to keep Lenny happy too. Lenny paused by the Beamer with a simultaneous furtive glance around the deserted cul de sac.

'Car looking good, too?'

Her Beamer but courtesy of Lenny also. Sarah had paid five grand for the two-litre injection coupe, cash of course. That was a busy few weeks' work for her. She never asked why a great car like this was so cheap. Lenny had mumbled something about it being a sign of his appreciation for her being such a good tenant. He also mumbled something about taking without the owner's consent, car ringing rackets and vehicle identification number plates soldered onto the inside panels of front engines. It was definitely a good buy. She would have been lost without it, particularly on the way to that murky slipway last night.

His Jag pulled out of Thames View. Relief. It had all gone smoothly. Lenny had noticed nothing different about his number thirty-two. Safe. Lenny gave her the creeps. As the years went by she thought he got more psychotic and unpredictable. But Lenny was an insurance policy. Sarah didn't need him right now but she might someday in the future. Sooner than she realised, in fact.

Mark knew about it. Even Clive Norris in the corner office knew about it. Everyone in the office did. Everyone in the entire City in fact. It was all over the papers that morning. The headlines in *The Times* and the *FT* said as much. Mega Banking Merger Creates Financial Powerhouse. Six Billion Acquisition of Provident by

British Commercial. Some even dared to call it the Deal of the Year. Again.

Norris had the newspaper open on his desk as he was prone to do between the hours of nine a.m. and half past while he digested his currant scone courtesy of the canteen lady with the trolley. Scones were exclusively for the executives within the LSE. It was a sort of civil service tradition. The lesser mortals made do with the coffee. Mark had years to go to earn a scone of his own. He wondered about the morning fare in those City investment banks. Surely not scones, more likely cream cheese bagels, buttered croissants and sugary doughnuts. Then he got the royal summons.

'Mark, have you got a minute? In my office?'

Norris sat across the desk from him. Was this a follow-up to their appraisal confrontation or something better? Did it really matter at this stage? The recruitment consultant had said that finding a job would take only weeks. Or was this related to the main story in the open newspaper? Provident Bank and all that? Was Norris finally going to deliver on his recent promise?

'Do you want to take a look at this for me?'

Norris *was* delivering. He handed Mark a thin file with a company name stencilled on the outside. Provident Bank. Something decent at last to work on, but was it too little too late?

'You see, I do keep my word. This is front page stuff and it's your case.'

Mark expressed his thanks. This investigation wouldn't be any different to the others he had conducted, except that this was the biggest company by market capitalisation that he had been entrusted with to date. Norris's instructions were clear.

'Provident is an enormous takeover, Mark, so we have got to cover all the angles. This file is all we have so far, press comments, details of Provident and British Commercial Bank, contact names, the company registrars and the rest. You need to check the recent activity in Provident shares to make sure no one has traded when they shouldn't have. Do the usual. Get the details of changes in the registered owners. Look at who owns the shares now. Look for any big purchases made recently. Look for any involvement by offshore shell companies in the Channel Islands, BVI, Luxembourg, Lichtenstein, Panama and the like. Look at the Directors' personal dealings in both banks. Look at the dealing activity of all the leading market makers and investment houses in the City. Give me an interim report in a week.'

Mark left with the file under his arm but with mixed emotions. This case was a great chance to impress the boss, finally show him his worth, but it was too late. Would it be his last assignment before he exited the LSE? What would happen when he walked into Norris's office next week to deliver the mother of all investigative reports and his letter of resignation at the same time?

Mark was a professional at heart. He would do the job well. If anything untoward had happened in Provident shares in the recent past, he was determined to uncover it.

CHAPTER TEN

BISHOPSGATE, LONDON EC2

Today was one of those days when being a dealer was the best goddamn occupation in the entire world. Greg sat at his desk with the others and watched the glorious Provident share price. Simply by doing nothing at all he was earning hundreds of thousands of pounds as the price ticked up a few pence at a time. It had opened at 1085 pence, just under the agreed announced takeover price. The small difference was attributed to the funding cost. If investors knew that they were guaranteed to get eleven pounds in a few months' time then they were prepared to pay only ten-eighty-five today, the difference representing the interest they could earn on their money in the intervening period.

Everyone on the floor knew that Greg and his team were sitting on one million Provident shares and passed by with congratulatory comments or jealous jibes. After the initial euphoria subsided, Crosswaithe called Greg into his office. The Provident price was now 1090 pence, dangerously close to the offer price. If it went over the eleven quid mark, then the real action started. If.

Not a word of congratulation from Old Nick at the good fortune that Blakes had encountered. Only a worried and indecisive Director of Dealing.

'So what do we do with these Provident shares? Sell or hold?'

Greg felt like telling him to answer the question himself. Surely the Director should have all the answers rather than Greg, a mere desk head? But he was shrewd enough to answer politically when so required.

'I wanna hold the stock, see how the end-game develops. The market is strong this morning. The banking sector is up all round as other folks realise that there could be more takeovers on the way.'

His boss had other ideas.

'I think that's a risky strategy. We should sell some and take our profit. Prudence before greed.'

Greg lost it.

'I disagree. Greed is the reason I came over from the States. It's the reason we're all here. Why not earn another few hundred bucks on this position?'

Old Nick shook his head. In any case, it wasn't bucks over here. It wasn't even the Euro. It was good old pounds sterling.

'In my capacity as Director of Dealing, I am advising you to sell some of the position.'

'Then I'll sell one lousy share and hold onto the rest.'

Old Nick leant forward and stared at him hard.

'Don't take that attitude. I'm in charge here. Sell a decent line of the stock.'

The conversation was coming to a head when Chas knocked and simultaneously barged into the office. Old Nick was visibly annoyed but could not get a word in before Chas.

'Greg, the price has gone through eleven quid. Provident's in play. It's 1110 pence now.'

Excellent news for Greg. A share price at a premium over the eleven pounds offer price meant that the market now thought someone else might be prepared to pay more than British Commercial. The fact that both banks' Boards of Directors had agreed the mutually beneficial takeover meant nothing.

The ultimate decision lay with the shareholders of Provident, a fickle mixture of institutional and private individuals who valued money and profit way above tradition and loyalty. Greg hardly needed to state the obvious but he did anyway. He enjoyed his moment of triumph.

'Every cent is ten grand. In the past five minutes while you and I have been sitting here arguing, the price is up twenty pence and my holding has increased in value by two hundred thousand. Let's agree to hang on in there for a day or so. Show the world that Blakes really has got balls of steel.'

Old Nick couldn't find a dignified response. Greg left his boss to his own thoughts. One nil to Greg, who was beginning to think that his profit on Provident was going to be the final piece of his plan to gain wider recognition in the market and nail that lucrative job offer. He needed to be with a major player, someone with oceans of capital, top talent, bigger bonuses, international clout. Anywhere but Blakes.

Ted Hammond sat at his desk at the station and logged the key details of Alexander Soames's life into the mother of all police computer systems. Big Brother was alive and well and living in Central London. Name, date of birth, address, occupation, marital status. Prior police record? None according to the computer. Then the missing persons screen. Last seen where? When? Wearing what? Known friends, relations, family. Business interests. Car.

The surprise came when he logged in the personalised registration plate. The computer flashed back at Ted immediately. The interrogation routines in this damn machine actually worked. 'Possible abandoned car found in Stratford this morning. S 50 ALX.' This was quicker than he hoped. He called Stratford nick to tell them to keep an eye on Burdett Avenue and this time he borrowed an Astra from the car park. Thirty-five minutes' drive to the East End at this time of the day?

The local police had cordoned off part of the road with obligatory striped tape but a uniformed officer raised it for his superior officer upon sight of Ted's warrant card. Another uniform greeted him as he stopped by the Volvo. Both passenger doors were now wide open. The PC was evidently aware of the importance of his find and was keen for the whole world to know about it.

'PC Braithwaithe, sir. I was first to the car this morning.'

'How did you find it?'

'A lady inside this house called us.'

'Did she see anything?'

'No, no one. Says the car was here overnight. It was unlocked. She locked it this morning.'

'Did she sit inside?'

The officer knew the implication behind the question. Fingerprints and forensic evidence. If the need arose.

'No. She touched the door handle, that's all.'

'Very good. Has anyone been inside it?'

'Only me.'

'Did you have gloves on at the time?'

A somewhat optimistic question given the July rays bearing down. The PC looked crestfallen.

'No, I never thought of it. I'll remember next time, sir.'

Ted gave the car the once over.

'Get a tow truck and take this back to Stratford station. Keep it secure there. We may need to dust it. And where's the car stereo? Was it nicked?'

'Dunno. I wondered about that, too. The base unit's still here but the cover is gone. Do you think the owner's coming back?'

Ted hoped so. It was the only glimmer of hope that he could pass on to Helen Soames.

Greg looked at the collection of newspapers on his dealing desk. There was no doubting the story of the day. The *FT* had devoted two entire pages to it. The broadsheets featured it on their front pages. Even the tabloids wrote it up as prominently as they could between the page three pictures and the showbiz gossip. The Provident story had particular relevance since so many of the shareholders were ordinary Joe Public punters who had received free windfall shares a year previously when Provident de-mutualised. They were all looking forward to eleven pounds a share for no work whatsoever. Just like Greg.

The story was done to death, so when the early edition of the *Evening Standard* came in, Greg didn't think there could be much breaking news in it. He was wrong. Chas interrupted his thoughts.

'Seen today's *Evening Standard*, Greg? Bit of new information on the Provident story.'

Greg didn't believe him. All the news he needed to see must be on the screens before his eyes.

Chas held up a page from the business section. The last paragraph was circled in pen. Chas read aloud.

'An unusual twist in the Provident takeover story ... missing from the recent press conference was Alexander Soames, Finance Director. Company sources today still did not know the whereabouts of their Director.'

Chas enjoyed stating the bleeding obvious.

'Bit strange for the Finance Director to go AWOL at a time like this, isn't it?'

Greg slowly realised the implications of what Chas had read but was careful to show no outward reaction. He took the single page for a closer examination. This news did not look good at all. Soames's absence was a worry and Greg didn't need any more worries at the moment. Provident was worry enough.

'Don't sweat it, Chas. Maybe this guy Soames has turned up since. This rag is hours old.'

Greg walked over to a corner of the dealing floor to a spare bank of phones. No need to make this call from his own extension. Best to do it anonymously. He dialled the head office number of Provident and asked to speak to Alexander Soames. He was connected to a mature sounding lady who announced she was Mr Soames's secretary. Greg faked the familiar touch in the hope of getting through and tried his best English accent. Like the one he'd used successfully on Rita at the Dorchester.

'Hello, is Alexander there please?'

He noted she paused for too long before replying. Soames's close friends probably called him Alex, instead of Alexander. Obvious mistake.

'No. I'm sorry. Mr Soames isn't available.'

'Do you know where he is?'

'I'm sorry, I don't.'

Then she paused to retract that statement.

'I mean, I know where he is, but I can't divulge that.'

'Can I get an important message to him?'

She sensed another example of press interest in the affair of her missing boss.

'Can I say who is calling?'

Greg hung up. She was being careful but she had said enough. Soames was definitely still missing. She was worried. Time to get the latest news from the screens. Greg hit Bloomberg with a vengeance. Hit the equity code PROV LN Equity and got the screen with news. The latest was go at the top. There it was. This got worse.

'Police sources confirmed that the car of missing Provident Director Alexander Soames was found in East London by a local resident. There was no sign of the owner. DI Ted Hammond said at the scene that the search for Mr Soames had been stepped up and that he remained optimistic about the outcome.'

Greg hoped that this cop's sentiments were founded on fact, not wishful thinking. There was too much to lose here. Time to find out more from his sources.

'Chas, I'm out of here. I'll be at the gym. See you guys tomorrow.'

*　　*　　*

Sarah had the *Evening Standard* open on the stripped pine coffee table. She had cancelled all her appointments today in the light of the week's events, citing an adverse reaction to the record high pollen count as the reason. The submissive men who regularly telephoned didn't dare question her any further. They were like that.

She read the story about Provident. She had shares in the company herself and knew that she would make money on them. But it was the last paragraph that she had almost memorised word for word by now. Alexander Soames was officially missing. True enough. No one knew where he was, not even her. She felt guilty about being the last person to see him alive and tried not to think about how his wife and children felt right now. Was it worse for them to know or not to know?

The doorbell rang. Strange. She had no appointment with any clients tonight. She eyed the security peephole. A familiar face. He hadn't called in advance as per their agreement, but she had to open the door. No choice. Greg barged past her and stood by the bay window, looking first at the passing Thames traffic, then turning to face her.

'Sarah. What the hell's going on here? Where is Alexander Soames?'

She had to act. Convincingly. It was easy. After all, she spent hours every day acting downstairs; schoolmistress, nanny, boss, diva. Whatever was required. Time to act the innocent now.

'What do you mean?'

'You know what I goddamn mean. Do I have to spell it out for you?'

He did.

'Soames is missing. You see him regularly. Do you know anything at all? When was he last here?'

'Days ago, maybe even a week.'

'And he left here in good shape? No worries at all?'

Time to inject some reality into this conversation.

'No, Greg, he left here feeling pretty sore. A few marks but that's all. What are you saying?'

Greg wasn't convinced. He looked at the *Standard* on the table.

'You've got that open at the page on Soames. You're worried too?'

She had to placate him. He was growing angry and that was something she wanted to avoid.

'Of course I'm worried. I know him and like him. Professionally. I'm wondering what the hell is going on too. He's a good payer and I don't want to lose him as a client.'

Greg sat down. Perhaps he had jumped to conclusions too quickly.

'The pressure is getting to me. This is serious shit. I'm into Provident for eleven million. On today's prices I'm up a million or more in dealing profits. Nothing must go wrong here. I can't believe Soames has gone missing just as this deal happens. I can't afford to have anyone fuck up on me. We know from those tapes that he was dead against this whole deal from the outset. I need to know what the hell he's up to now.'

Sarah knew that at this precise moment. Alexander Soames wasn't up to much at all. Swimming with the fishes perhaps? Greg stormed out shortly after his unwanted intrusion. He'd come too damn close to the truth.

Greg had to be alone. No one else could hear what he was about to hear or the game would be up. He placed the C90 audiotape into the state of the art Bang and Olufson hi-fi, sat back on the elongated futon, took out a pen and notepad and hit the play button on the remote control.

There were a few seconds of nothingness and then the sound of background noise. A car and a dog barking. Far enough away not to interfere with the all-important sound quality. Then the sound of heels descending the iron staircase. The cue for the action to begin. Silence for a minute or so. Tension rising. Even

Greg felt it and he wasn't in the townhouse basement, naked and bound.

'Arise.'

Sarah's first words were spoken in that acquired cultured accent. The sound of wood on wood. Must be the stocks this time. Sound of heels again. Walking over to the wall to select an implement? Sound of air in motion. Testing. Building the atmosphere. Then the first questions of the inquisition.

'So, Simon, what are you working on at the moment?'

Simon Fry of Speake Windsor & Co paused and then answered defiantly.

'I can't tell you that. It's confidential.'

The well-worn routine had begun. No way out for him now.

'Simon, you know that you can tell me. And you must. You have no choice.'

Stubbornness from their youngest legal partner.

'No, I can't. I can't. Please don't make me.'

Her cue. An invitation she was glad to accept.

'You know you have to tell me. There's an easy way and a hard way to do this. Which is it to be?'

Sound of air in motion and then contact with skin. Pain. Pleasure. What's the difference to Simon? More strokes in quick succession. Too much surely?

'Start talking, Simon. Tell me, who are you meeting today?'

Then a marked change in attitude. Her voice hardened at precisely the right time.

'Don't mess me about. You will talk.'

Then a succession of blows. Greg winced. Jesus. At last some talking.

'Amir ... Swarup Amir. That's who I'm meeting today.'

Anything to stop the pain. He couldn't move. No way to avoid the blows raining down.

'And what's the meeting about?'

'I can't say.'

He knew the immediate consequences. More blows. Too many. The pain threshold had been reached. Then a crackle and a hiss. What was this? Silence for a few seconds, then the sound returned. Greg wondered if there was something wrong with the hidden microphone. Better check it out next time.

'Amir's still going to buy out his biggest private competitor next week. It's a really cheap price. Sportsworld will clean up the competition in the high street.'

'Not enough. More. More.'

'No one will touch him in the market. It's a licence to print money for the future.'

Still Sarah wasn't satisfied.

'Tell me more.'

'No. I don't know any more. Please . . .'

In vain. More pain. Then a pause for a rest. Greg knew the procedure. There would be no more information from that City lawyer today. He stopped the tape and looked at the key words scribbled on his notepad. Sportsworld. Buyout. Cheap. Competitors. Clean up in the high street. Future profits.

Everything he had suspected since Simon's visit last month to the Isle of Dogs was on course. This deal was going to happen. Those Sportsworld plc shares in his dealing account had been a good buy. Thanks again to Sarah's hard work. He could trust her. Soames would turn up. Everything would be fine. Must fix that microphone next time. He left the tape in the deck.

Greg could not agree with Doctor Johnson's famous sentiments of more than a century ago. He had a love–hate relationship with the world's most exciting city and had done for years. What started off as a lucrative overseas posting had become a life sentence without a crime. Yes, he was tired of London.

There had been good times, like his first summer there. Those evenings after work in rolled up shirtsleeves on open-air sun-drenched boats along the Thames by Tower Bridge with his colleagues from Mitchells and a cold bottle of Bud in hand.

Those weekend jaunts in his first decent Merc to discover Oxford, Cambridge, Canterbury, Brighton, Dover, Stratford upon Avon, as the boy from the mean streets encountered new culture and did his best to assimilate as much as possible. Those corporate trips to the Centre Court box at Wimbledon, to the marquee at Henley, to the reserved seating at Lords in St John's Wood, to the barbies on the country estates of the heads of the other dealing desks, each one outdoing the other for culinary and sartorial supremacy. Those days had been short and sweet.

Then the dark times when winter set in and London lost any perceived glamour. The early rising in the pitch-dark mornings to get to his desk at some ungodly hour. The pissing rain and biting wind. The delayed tubes and the greasy streets. The mad rush at Christmas time, the sad drunken office parties and long-distance loneliness of an American trapped in London over Thanksgiving while the other ex-pats took a week off to be with family and friends. And that night of despair when he found his saviour.

It all seemed like eons ago but was only a few years in truth. The first October was the worst. The star American investment banker was utterly sick of his Knightsbridge hotel. Twelve weeks since he first touched down from JFK, when Mitchells had promised him a luxury serviced flat in Chelsea. He was still waiting for some other ex-pat from a global oil multi-national to move out.

The team at the equity dealing desk had left early for the stag night of a former colleague somewhere down the West Country. Greg wasn't invited. Never met the guy. The Brits at work were sociable enough but they hadn't yet taken this loud New Yorker to their hearts. They would in time, he was sure of that. He needed several killings on the market to impress the hell out of them.

Alone in a new job in a new city. Alone in a hotel room that looked like a million others around the world. Alone with an untouched complimentary fruit basket, the Hot Tickets listings magazine courtesy of the sympathetic concierge in the lobby, and his own dark solitary thoughts. Alone in the most vibrant city in the world with an evening to kill.

He paged through the freebie magazine. The last pages were the small type of the classified personal advertisements. Single white female. Attractive middle-aged guy. Divorced Jewish forty-something. Separated mother of four. Part-time model. Free spirits. Successful self-made millionaire. Dream on buddy. Take a reality check.

He missed Katherine. He should have taken her with him but she didn't want to leave Wall Street to join him in London. He knew why. That time when his drunken alter ego beat her black and blue outside a bar in midtown Murray Hill. And worse later. He hadn't had sex in twelve weeks and was suffering. She would enjoy that. If she even thought about him anymore.

Then the classified professional advertisements. He grazed them until he came to the only advert that was suitably worded. 'Attractive cultured blonde seeks upmarket gents for evening rendezvous. Hotel visits a speciality.' He needed company badly. He was in a hotel room. He had a telephone within reach.

Forty minutes later he heard the lift doors open in the corridor. He eyed her through the spy hole in the door and was suitably impressed. A shadowy figure beside her had melted into the darkness before she knocked twice. Lenny, she said his name was later. Her chauffeur, she said. Minder more like.

The sex was great, in no way cheap and nasty. Not cheap anyway at two hundred for an hour. Sarah was her name. He liked her. She had determination, ambition and independence. A bit like him in a way. They could do business. He would see her again.

Once she had left, Greg leant over the crushed pillows to the array of tempting fruit by the bedside, took the biggest, ripest orange, deliberately peeled back the messy layers, downed it in one gulp, enjoyed the bitter after-taste, let the sticky citrus juice run all over the tossed sheets and threw the roll of peel vaguely in the general direction of the bin in the corner. He missed. Fuck it. He could do what he damned well liked.

CHAPTER ELEVEN

CITY OF LONDON, EC2

Mark was looking forward to visiting the leading investment banks in the City, and not solely for the vital information he would glean for his Provident investigation. Rather, it was his chance to see the previously hidden workings of these great banks from the inside, meet the people, go with the flow and find out which of them might want to hire a former disgruntled employee of the LSE. Game on.

He left the office with a briefcase containing the barest essentials. The file from Norris, an A4 pad, a calculator, and his co-ordinated pen collection. He would gather the initial evidence from the Compliance Departments of each bank, review their trading history in Provident shares and talk to dealers or salesmen as required. It was an ambitious itinerary to be packed into one week. That was all the time he had before Norris wanted his interim report.

First up were the big US investment banks, the best according to legend within the Square Mile. Mark agreed with the City's sentiment. They were impressive animals. Enormous dealing floors, dazzling screens and telephone equipment, no expense spared. So unlike the LSE. A great audible buzz permeated the workplace, like before the start of an epic rock concert at Wembley Stadium or the Three Tenors at the Royal Albert Hall. Rows of colourful international flags hung on pennants at the foreign exchange dealing desks, global clocks on the wall, and the mixture of British, Americans, Asians and Europeans gave it a truly cosmopolitan atmosphere.

The dealers talked to Mark about their positions, the size of which amazed him. Millions of pounds invested in stocks he had never even heard of, millions invested in international bond holdings, billions of daily trading volume, all supported by the even greater billions of liquid capital of their NYSE-listed parent corporate back home in downtown Manhattan. The ex-pat dealers talked about their strategy, their best buys, their disasters, their hunches and lunches, their sources, the news in the *FT*, the results of the 3.40 at Lingfield and the personal attributes of today's page three in the *Sun*.

The people in these market leaders impressed Mark the most. Young, energetic employees, educated and ambitious. Well-bred American males in white shirts with button-down collars and subtly patterned ties. No rolled up shirtsleeves or brown shoes here. Groomed girls in pencil skirts and silk blouses with Sloaney or Harvard accents, confident, alluring, flashing their eyelids at all around. People who knew how to have fun at work and still get the job done. American footballs thrown around the dealing floors amongst players of a different sort. Half-finished snipes of champagne left upon chaotic desks. Research staff speaking confidently on the PA to the thundering herd. Maximum bullish. Yes, these banks personified sex on legs. And sex worked for Mark.

They simply oozed money, as if it was seeping out of their pores. They threw fivers in tips at the guy from the Italian deli who delivered the avocado and bacon or prawn and crabmeat on wholewheat granary at midday. More loot was offered to the shoeshine boys who kept Church's finest black leather highly polished. They used their platinum Amex cards to book flights, holidays, flowers and gifts. They returned from the West End at lunchtime with bags from Blazer, Pinks and Austin Reed.

If even a small portion of this omnipresent affluence rubbed off on a recently employed Mark in their Compliance Department then he would indeed be a happy man. Much happier than at present and far more solvent in the longer term. Enough to trade up house wise and car wise. And repay those people at Barclaycard.

It was different elsewhere in the City. The buzz was missing at the few remaining British investment banks. The staff knew that their parent companies, those prudent high street clearing banks, were pulling out of investment banking. Fear of the unknown. The Americans killed them dead too often. The elderly retail bank management didn't understand the dealing risks, panicked at even plain vanilla derivatives and didn't understand why successful staff in their mid-twenties had to earn six figure amounts to prevent them from leaving. It was all so different in their day. And now and again some accountant or auditor uncovered a hidden multi-million-pound loss on an exotic option trading book or at a bond arbitrage desk and it confirmed their worst fears. The atmosphere was one of retrenchment and the dour staff reflected it. No thanks, thought Mark.

The Japanese banks were even worse. Those who were still partially solvent and without a rogue trader in the past few years soldiered on against the odds, relying solely on their domestic Yen business to keep afloat. Mark didn't like what he saw. Rows of timid cloned Japanese dealers in a factory assembly line, continuously watched by middle-aged bulging bosses sitting in goldfish bowl glass offices along the dull dealing floors. No laughter, jibes or banter. It was too serious and unexciting for someone like Mark.

He was still unsure about the Continentals, those few remaining German and French investment banks. The German houses were soulless places while the French staff looked like they were counting the days to getting back on the safer side of the English Channel, away from their sworn historical enemies.

Case closed. A bulge-bracket American investment bank was the place to be. A Mitchell Leonberg, a Goldman or a Morgan would suit him perfectly. Mark would need to extend his modest shirt collection, his assorted cuff links and his patterned ties. With a decent haircut, a new suit and an *FT* under his arm, he would blend in perfectly. They would never know that he was an escapee from a civil service mindset, a one-bedroomed Battersea resident, an antique Golf driver. Mark advised his eager recruitment consultant accordingly.

Simon Fry's secretary intruded on his quiet afternoon as he perused some legal files at Speake Windsor. He could still see no obvious way of replacing her, short of breaking every bloody rule in the EEC's employment legislation. Bloody bureaucrats. She was here for the duration.

'Simon. Mr Amir and his party from Sportsworld are here to see you.'

He was puzzled. The three o'clock meeting had been arranged with Swarup Amir alone. Amir was a successful entrepreneur who had started his sports empire from a rented market stall in Petticoat Lane twenty-two years ago. He was now the Chief Executive of the largest quoted sporting goods retailer on the London Stock Exchange. Sportsworld had booming outlets all over the West End, the southeast and the Midlands, with new flagship stores in Lakeside Thurrock and Brent Cross. His annual turnover was close to five hundred million pounds and retained profits approached forty million per annum. Not bad going for an immigrant who had arrived on a spice boat from Bombay in the sixties with little education or English. Asian Businessman of the Year award winner for two of the past three years, he was the recent proud owner of a struggling first division soccer club in the Midlands with some upside commercial potential.

This was to be a routine chat to confirm the legal details of the forthcoming acquisition by Sportsworld. Simon had drafted the Memorandum of Understanding two weeks ago and had the contracts ready for Amir. He now planned to dot the Is and cross the Ts and charge Amir two hundred and twenty quid an hour for the pleasure of doing so. But Amir led three other suits into his office.

'Good afternoon, Simon. I'd like you to meet my professional advisers from the City. Geoff and Mike are with CSFB. John is my accountant. I thought they should join us for this meeting.'

Fine by Simon. With three more attendees there was a good chance the meeting would drag on for an extra hour or more. These City types never knew when to stop talking. Simon's billing clock was already ticking in his mind as Amir set the scene for them all, newcomers included. Amir dabbed his forehead with a white handkerchief, suffering in the London heat ... Hotter than Bombay?

'We need to talk about this proposed acquisition of our biggest high street competitor, Classic Sports. I have seen the draft contracts you sent to their legal people but something's come up.'

It was a done deal. What could have possibly happened since? Amir obliged.

'I was keen to make this acquisition because I knew the purchase price of sixty million was great value for us. Unfortunately I have been proved right in hindsight. The Parker family who have owned Classic Sports for generations went into the City with their local accountant and hired some expert assistance from a big City investment bank. Those rocket scientists have valued Classic Sports at a hundred million pounds. So now old man Parker wants to tear up the Memorandum of Understanding that we signed and increase the purchase price to a hundred million. Can he do that at this late stage?'

Smart move by Classic Sports. The invited advisers awaited Simon's definitive legal opinion.

'Yes, Parker can do that. All we signed two weeks ago was a memorandum. It's not a contract and it's not binding on either party. It's bad form to break it but there's nothing we can do about it. It's their right. We could do the same if you wanted to walk away from the deal right now. It cuts both ways.'

Amir shook his head in annoyance. The advisers weren't happy either. Simon could see his enormous fee income on this deal disappearing before his eyes.

'So does that mean that this acquisition is off?' he dared to ask.

Amir hadn't got to where he was today by rolling over and dying, however.

'No. It's definitely still on.'

'Are you sure? A hundred million is a lot of money to pay for a family business of this size.'

'I know, but I have to acquire Classic. Otherwise someone else will and I must eliminate the competition. I have come this far and I am not going to fall now.'

Simon knew enough about Sportsworld to foresee another immediate problem. Loot. Or specifically the lack of it.

'But where will you get a hundred million in cash? Sportsworld only has fifteen to twenty million stashed away. You'll never borrow enough from the banks to cover the balance. Sixty in total was hard enough, a hundred will be impossible.'

Amir nodded and turned to Geoff. The banker made his initial contribution to the meeting.

'Correct. Sportsworld will undertake a rights issue and raise the necessary funds in the market.'

Simon wasn't an expert in this area but he didn't like the sound of it. Firstly, Sportsworld were going to shell out a load of money for a possibly over-valued business. Secondly, rights issues sometimes gave the wrong message to shareholders and to the market, as a company issues new shares to existing shareholders at a discount to the current market price. Because there are lots of new cheaper shares in the market, the share price always falls on the announcement. Sometimes by a little. Sometimes by a lot.

'Swarup, the stock market is not expecting a rights issue from Sportsworld. What sort of price are you thinking of issuing the rights at?'

The banker made another contribution, pulling out a spreadsheet with rows of different what-if scenarios, as bankers were prone to do when considering a range of financing options.

'We are looking at a rights price of seventy-five to eighty pence based on prevailing bullish market conditions.'

Simon followed the fortunes of his corporate clients. He knew the current share price of Sportsworld: 105 pence as of yesterday. The rights would be at a big discount to the market. But he resigned himself to the wisdom of the City experts who sat before him. He wanted his fees.

'OK, gentlemen. You're the financial advisers. I'm here to do the legal paperwork. It's your call. Fine by me.'

The meeting broke up after two hours. Another four hundred and forty quid in billing time and the deal was still on, only bigger. Everything had changed in the space of a week or so, from a lucrative deal where Sportsworld bought out a competitor for next to nothing from their own cash and bank resources, to an overly expensive acquisition that the shareholders would pay for out of their own pockets.

Simon wasn't bothered personally by this. He didn't own any shares in Sportsworld. He had done his utmost to keep the terms confidential. In fact, thinking back over the past week, he had only told one person about this deal. He'd had no choice. She'd made him talk. And it had been enjoyable.

Sir Gordon Harvey wanted to celebrate. Last week had been a great week. First there had been the County Beverages AGM in the Dorchester. Everyone who mattered in the City had given it favourable comment in the press the next day. The share price had risen nicely as soon as he started his speech. His fifty thousand share options in County were now worth so much more. His photograph in the Companies & Finance section of the *FT* had been flattering, taken from his good side too.

Secondly, the company was making great profits through this summer heatwave. Sir Gordon knew the exact numbers that mattered. He got the confidential management accounts every week. The year end executive pay reviews would be generous if profits continued for the second half of the year.

The only downside was that one lousy investor, Scottish & Colonial, had sold out big time and had adversely affected market sentiment. Sir Gordon didn't like their apparent loss of faith in his management abilities. He blamed the US investment bank who'd advised them to place their shares in the market. All they wanted was their commission on the deal. Parasites.

His celebratory mood could take many forms. A night out at the opera, a day's racing at Glorious Goodwood, a test game at Lords, polo at Windsor, the company box at Wimbledon, a West End first night, a Cotswold break or a weekend trip to a European capital. All, of course, in the company of his perfectly preserved wife of twenty-seven years' loyal and mutual devotion.

Sir Gordon knew one other sure-fire way to celebrate. Time to regress into the past. His company chauffeur was always on call from the underground car park below. Jack had been his driver for eight years and Sir Gordon could trust his utterly discreet approach. Sir Gordon summoned him to the front door of the Pall Mall office and gave him the usual directions, having telephoned ahead. The high pollen count had fortunately receded.

The three-litre company Rolls purred eastwards past Tower Hill and Canary Wharf onto the Isle of Dogs. Jack knew not to park within residential Thames View. He chose instead the cul de sac two roads further on to the left. Sir Gordon made the short walk alone back to the steps to the door of number thirty-two. He noticed a net curtain twitch in a window across the road. That happened sometimes.

His favourite scenario was the schoolroom. Sarah would be the stern head mistress, this captain of industry her errant pupil. It reminded him so much of those first harsh days in his public school where his landed parents abandoned him for nine months of the year. He had hated it then. Now he looked forward to it.

Barbara would have preferred an anonymous restaurant nearer home in Kensington. Less risk of bumping into anyone from Blakes. Instead they sat together across an allegedly quiet table in one of Conran's newest mega-Brasseries in Soho. Greg had wanted somewhere brash and busy, reminiscent of NYC. Sometimes she wondered how much they had in common. Different backgrounds, different interests, different aspirations. But the same basic carnal instincts. And there was the dilemma of her biological clock. Tick. Tock. Thirty.

Her girlfriends told her there were several essentials that every girl needed before she reached thirty. An old boyfriend you could imagine going back to, and one who reminds you how far you have come. Thanks, Greg. Enough money to live on your own if you so wished. Thanks, Blakes. Something perfect to wear if your boss or lover needs to see you in an hour's time. A set of screwdrivers, a cordless power drill and a black lace bra and briefs. Eight matching plates and wineglasses with long stems for that special dinner party. A skin care regime and an exercise routine. A past juicy enough to enjoy re-telling in the future.

But there was also so much more to learn. How to fall in love without losing yourself. How to feel about having kids. How to quit a job if you found it taking over your entire life. How to walk away. How to kiss a man so that he knew what you wanted to happen next. How to still please your parents. How to keep a secret from your colleagues. How to survive late night bouts of great sex during the punishing working week.

Barbara regretted the subterfuge of trying to date the best looking, most eligible and loaded guy on the dealing floor and not getting caught by Old Nick. She hated the thought of all the wasted time they had spent apart already. Hated the uncertainty of not knowing where this relationship was going, the thought that at any time he might hop on BA and go back Stateside, despite his promises to stay on in the UK. The stock markets hated uncertainty. She did too. Life was moving on.

Every encounter, every glance, every smile in the office from Greg was like his dealing strategy. It was a risk worth taking. It was more than a year since that Blakes' offsite in Hertfordshire when they had found themselves side by side at the same dinner table and the Bolly flowed to drown their transatlantic inhibitions. Greg never did get to use his two-hundred-pound country club suite that night. She could have saved Blakes some money.

This relationship was getting serious and sooner or later Old Nick or some other Director at Blakes would twig the romance. She knew the angle that Nick would take. It wasn't the clandestine nature of their relationship. It was the fact that his star special situations dealer was sleeping with his star research analyst. The fact that the guy who made apparently inspired trading decisions was exchanging pillow talk with the girl who spoke to company Chief Executives and anticipated interim results and mega corporate deals. He would put two and two together and get a million or so.

Greg seemed worried too, distracted about something. Perhaps it was his dealing, his profits and losses. She knew the rules in the City. They never talked shop together, it wasn't worth the risk. He played around with a fork and a plate of pasta, growing colder by the minute, the pomodoro sauce slowly congealing.

'Are you not hungry at all tonight, Greg?'

'It's a big helping,' he explained over the din of the restaurant. Next time here, if there was a next time here, he would get a better table. The maitre'd had stiffed him by giving him a crap table near the doors to the kitchen and the toilets. He'd get them back. Fuck the tip tonight.

They never saw the party out for a hen-night meal before they took on the crew-cut bouncers at assorted West End nightclubs. They wouldn't have recognised any of the eight girls sitting at table twenty-nine anyway. The temp in question had only been at Blakes for a week or so, filling in for Old Nick's regular sweetness and light secretary who was away on her well-earned annual break in the Canaries.

The temp knew Greg from her seat near the dealing floor and from his frequent visits to Old Nick's office. And what a wonderful view it was. She also knew Miss Perfect media star who had accentuated her looks so effortlessly last Wednesday evening. She knew both of the diners. And she'd seen the lingering kiss at the start of the meal. She'd seen the close body and eye contact. She'd seen his left hand disappear below the tablecloth to rest upon her leg. This was certainly no City meeting between a dealer and a research analyst. This was foreplay with the promise of much more to follow. Something juicy to talk about innocently in the office tomorrow when Miss Perfect wasn't around.

CHAPTER TWELVE

HARROW ROAD POLICE STATION,
LONDON W9

Ted had a full day planned. Three different locations to visit. So little time. He checked his watch, waited at the door and took a car and a uniformed driver with him on the short trip to his first destination.

Helen Soames was at home, probably still waiting by the telephone for news of her husband from friends, relations, anyone. Ted knew that there had been no telephone calls from the police. He wanted to deliver the news personally. They sat on opposite sofas and he accepted the offer of tea. Up close Helen looked older than on his first visit. He must have formed an overly flattering initial impression of her or else the uncertainty was getting to her. He empathised. He remembered the night a DI had called round to tell him his wife wouldn't be coming home, never again. There was a right way and a wrong way to do this. Tact was important.

'We have made some progress in the search for your husband.'

'Yes?' Her eyes lit up.

'We found his car in the East End near Stratford.'

'Was there any sign of him?'

'Unfortunately not.'

Ted didn't mention the fact that the keys had been left in the ignition and the doors unlocked. Rather uncharacteristic behaviour for a prudent Finance Director of a plc. Still, he had to sound optimistic.

'It's a good start.'

'Do you know where he might be?'

Slow down, Helen. These things take time.

'I was hoping you might. Does your husband know anyone in that part of London?'

'No, not that I know of. He wouldn't be seen dead there.'

Unfortunate turn of phrase. They both knew it. Ted left her on a hopeful note.

'Remember this is definite progress. The car was parked carefully at the side of the road and the stereo security cover was removed. It looks as if your husband intended to return later.'

She didn't seem to share his optimism but acknowledged his efforts.

'Thanks for coming around here. It helps.'

He left her alone in a house he knew would be too big for a widow and two children.

The SEAQ screen showed the bid offer on Provident was 1105 to 1120 pence. Theoretically speaking, Greg could sell all his million shares right now at the best bid of 1105 pence each. In reality he knew the price would drop with that sort of volume in the market. He debated the relative merits of taking the money and running. At times like this he needed the advice of an experienced player in the markets. Pity there was no else like that working on the dealing floor of Blakes.

'Chas, what do you think?'

'About what?'

'Jesus, what else? The weather? Last night's TV? The talent at lunchtime? Provident, of course.'

Chas looked uncomfortable. Decision-making was not his forte. Greg gave him a not-so-subtle hint.

'Do we hold or do we sell?'

Chas went for the easy compromise.

'Do what I do when you are away on holiday. If in doubt, hedge our bets. Let's sell half our holding. That way we can crystallise some of the profit but still leave ourselves open to benefit from future gains.'

Not a bad idea, but would there be any future gains? The share price had been stuck in a tight trading range for days. Always in the low eleven pounds or thereabouts. Greg had a better idea. Time to turn the tables and make Old Nick do some work for a change. Get his pseudo-expert opinion.

He passed the temp outside the corner office without a word of acknowledgement. Crosswaithe was sitting at his desk signing some intra-office memoranda with his trademark Mont Blanc. He looked uneasy at Greg's intrusion on his domain.

'I need your advice, Nicholas.'

Old Nick didn't know whether Greg was serious or had been put up to this by his twisted colleagues. He glanced out at the special situations desk. The staff weren't staring back in at him. It must be serious.

'About what?'

'Provident. Do we sell or hold?'

For once he actually took an immediate decision. Amazing.

'The shares are doing well now. Let's hold them.'

'I was thinking about dumping half of them today. Cover ourselves.'

'That's not the way I dealt when I was out there on the floor. You either like a stock or you don't. You either hold or sell. Let's not fudge the issue.'

'Times have changed in the big bad world of dealing.'

'Not at Blakes they haven't.'

Greg was about to get stuck into a good row with him when Chas came in unannounced. Did he have to keep doing that?

'Greg, great news. It's on Reuters. It's the closest thing to an official company announcement.'

'What is?'

'There's a rumour that another bidder for Provident has emerged. Kapital Bank AG has called a press conference at short notice for tomorrow morning in Frankfurt. Our research team, including Barbara, all think that Provident would be a great fit for Kapital Bank. They're dying to get into the UK banking market, and they're a risk adverse bank so the residential mortgage portfolio in the southeast would be a big attraction for them. Provident shares are up forty pence on the story on the wire. 1145 now.'

It was the end of their conversation. Greg and Old Nick both knew it. Another bidder in the market was music to their ears. British Commercial and Kapital were both loaded with cash. They could push up the Provident share price to astronomical levels. They would be scraping the share price off the ceiling in a few weeks' time. Blakes were definitely holding onto the position.

Greg left his boss in the knowledge that forty pence on a million shares was another shedful of profit. This dealing position could be his best gamble ever. Everyone in the City would know that he had made a bundle for Blakes and that he was the best damned special situations dealer at any desk with the best of sources for the inside track. And then surely the headhunters would come knocking at his door with their promises of sky high bonuses, job security, prestige and power.

Next stop for Ted and his PC was the blatant opulence of the Dorchester. They left the car illegally parked outside on Park Lane, snarling up one of the five lanes. They could do that. Smart guests in the hotel stared at the uniformed officer as they walked through the lobby to the duty manager's office. This was obviously a rarity in the Dorchester and was giving off worrying signals to American Suits here on business, while simultaneously providing photo opportunities to Nikon-waving Korean tourists recently back from Buck House and the Changing of the Guard.

The duty manager asked a girl called Rita to show them up to room 812. Ted grilled her on the way.

'Who has been in this room since Soames went missing?'

'No one but myself and his Chairman, David Webster. We kept the room locked when we heard that our guest was missing.'

'So for all you know Mr Soames could be in there now, having a deep sleep on the king size?'

Rita didn't share this optimistic assertion.

'Unlikely.'

Ted noticed the stapled sign on the bedroom door. 'Room Out of Use – Contact Duty Manager.' An efficient touch from an efficient hotel.

The bedroom was deserted. Ted went thorough the expensive possessions: hanging garments in the wardrobe, empty luggage on the floor, toiletries in the bathroom. No packed luggage in sight. It was giving out the same signals as the parked Volvo. Alexander Soames had expected to return.

He found a leather carrying case with some papers inside and thumbed through them. Looked like minutes of Board meetings held days ago in the hotel about a takeover by another bank. Must be the takeover by British Commercial, that story that had been all over the news this week. It made interesting reading even for someone not acquainted with the ways of the City. All the comments attributed to Soames in the meetings about the deal were decisively negative. Ted wasn't a City expert but he knew a disagreement when he saw one in black and white. He could get more background at the next stop on his journey through Central London. By the lift, he spoke to Rita.

'Did anything unusual happen while Soames was here? Were any visitors asking for him? Any phone calls at all?'

She thought back over the past few days on life at the dull reception desk, drew a mental blank and then lit up.

'Soames and Provident were here in secret for many days. No one knew they were locked away upstairs in a function room. No one until the day before the press conference, that is.'

'The day before the press conference?'

'Yes. Strange. Some courier guy called with a package for them.'

'What did you do?'

'I sent him up to the function room they were meeting in. It's on the fifth floor'

'Show me.'

Ted examined the interior of the Waterloo function room. It was immaculately clean. Rita explained.

'These rooms stink of food and alcohol and cigarette smoke, so we clean them well afterwards. You won't find anything in here. Sorry.'

As they stood by the lifts waiting for one to descend from a higher floor, Ted pointed to a large brass urn containing an almost extinct palm tree.

'What's that?'

Rita turned around and extracted a large white envelope in surprise. 'Provident Bank – Confidential' was written on the outside.

'Wow. That's the package that the courier delivered. How on earth did it get there?'

Ted opened it and withdrew a copy of the *Daily Mirror*. He looked into the envelope, shook it a few times and was disappointed at the sole contents.

'Why would anyone send a *Mirror* over here? Don't you sell newspapers in the lobby?'

Rita nodded. He paged through the paper but nothing fell out of the middle pages. Ted folded the front page over and then saw the scribbled writing on top of the loud masthead. Special Situations.

'What does that mean?'

'No idea.'

'What firm did this courier work for? FedEx, DHL, UPS? Did he wear a uniform?'

'No. I remember he wore a Chelsea baseball cap and a white t-shirt. Good-looking. Dark. American or Canadian.'

Greg was worried. Not about the unearned fortune he was sitting on in Blakes, but rather about that last visit to Sarah. All those questions he had posed, those accusations, the latent hostility. He had over-reacted and that was unwise. He needed her. She wouldn't dare to stop the flow of taped information or else she would be front page of the *News of the World*. He had told her as much. But he had to keep her sweet and knew one certain way to do that. Money always talked.

A trip to the bank, a bundle of notes, a black cab, a short walk, a knock at the door and he was with her again. The dull thud as five thousand pounds in cash hit the coffee table.

'This is an advance payment for the Provident Bank information. I haven't sold a share yet but the price keeps ticking up every day. There's even talk of a counter-bid today. This position is going to make my name in the City. And it's you I have to thank.'

She didn't react favourably at all. He was surprised. Sort of like the last time with the County Beverage cash. What was wrong with her these days?

'You want the cash, don't you?'

'Of course I do. Thanks.'

She left the bundle of cash on the table. The conversation died. He was about to leave and then he remembered the other reason for his sudden visit.

'I listened to the tape of that City lawyer Fry from last week. It looks like the Sportsworld tip will turn out all right too. They've got a great takeover deal with Classic Sports in the pipeline. It's fucking dirt-cheap.'

He watched her glazed eyes and laughed on the inside. She had no idea what was going on here. She was so stupid. These basement tapes were dynamite. They were a sure thing, a one-way bet. Yet she never talked about the contents, about the companies mentioned or the upside on the share prices. She had never sussed out the importance of inside knowledge in the City. She was a dumb broad from up north. Always was and always would be. He remembered the problem.

'There was a glitch on the tape. The damn sound went in the middle for a minute, sort of came and went. I'm gonna check the mike downstairs.'

She couldn't stop him. Yes, go ahead. Visit the scene. There's no evidence left.

Greg descended into the basement reluctantly. This place gave him the creeps. Who were these people who came to play here? What's wrong with plain vanilla sex like he and Sarah had enjoyed in the old days? Or he and Barbara now in his St John's Wood pad.

He stood on the studded bench along the wall to reach the microphone hidden behind one of the spotlights. It moved to his touch. That was the problem. Loose connection. He pulled out the microphone and fixed one of the red wires at the back.

Standing on the bench gave him a new perspective on the basement. His eyes came to rest upon a small black object lying in the darkened corner, near the wire basket used for visitors' clothes. It gave off a faint reflection as the naked bulbs shone into the darkest recesses of the room. He would never have seen it from the floor, only from up here. It looked like someone's mobile telephone.

No. Up close, the green luminous display gave it away. It was the front panel from a car stereo. An expensive one too. The owner must be pissed to lose this. Time for Greg to do his only good deed of the day. Of the week in fact. He brought it back upstairs to Sarah.

'Look what I found down below.'

Jesus. He knew it all. Did he? Could he? No. Impossible. He had found the one piece of evidence Sarah had been unable to locate in the Volvo but he didn't appreciate the significance of it. There was nothing about this particular item yet in the media.

'Someone must have left it behind. What shall I do with it?' he asked.

Sarah didn't want to taint herself with the last of Alexander Soames's possessions.

'Leave it on the table. I think I might know whose it is.'

'No problem.' He placed it on top of the wad of cash. 'The mike works now. There was a loose wire. It should be fine for the next poor bastard. Back to business as usual.'

And then he was gone. Back to his dealing desk, no doubt to watch the Provident share price tick upwards again. She sat numbed by the evidence on the table. The two items told their own story. Was Alexander Soames's life worth five thousand pounds? The horror came flooding back to her.

What was she to do with this stereo, this damning piece of evidence? Chuck it in the bin? No, too risky. Drop it, too, into the depths of the Thames at the end of her cul de sac? No, too public. Take a hammer and smash it to pieces? No, too messy. This was important. Think about it in time. There was no hurry.

She took the bundle of cash in two hands, the stereo cover still resting on top, and walked over to the open drawer. Carefully she placed the items inside. She didn't realise it but as yet she had not touched the evidence. Fortunately.

Ted arrived at Provident's City office later than planned. Last stop but still ten minutes late. David Webster was expecting him and he was ushered immediately into a plush Chief Executive's office with oil paintings on veneer walls and a commanding view of the Thames from the desk which dominated the room. David greeted him anxiously.

'Helen called me to say that Alex's car's been found. Any other news, Inspector?'

'No. I'm sorry to report that there are no other leads. We have some of our people going over the car and local uniform are calling on all the residents in Burdett Avenue. We may yet turn up something.'

They sat in adjacent leather chesterfields, edges tastefully worn by decades of corporate use.

'What can I do for you then?' Webster asked cordially.

'I'd like to ask you about when you last saw Soames at the Dorchester.'

'Sure. The meeting finished around six. Alex went off but didn't turn up to our meeting the following day.'

'How did he seem?'

'Well, frankly he was unhappy about the deal.'

'How unhappy?'

'What do you mean? How do you measure unhappiness?'

'I mean, was he suicidally unhappy? Could he have done something stupid afterwards?'

'Absolutely not. Alex wasn't like that. He was a chartered accountant. That's how rash he was.'

Ted opened the file of papers recently retrieved from the hotel room.

'These minutes of your meetings were left in his room.'

'Damn. I thought that I had taken all the papers out of the hotel room. At the time those papers were highly confidential. Now of course everyone knows about the takeover.'

'Yes. Even me. I've had a look at these. Mr Soames was vehemently against the deal going ahead. He seems to have been alone in that?'

'Correct. I thought Alex would come round in time but he didn't. He was adamant.'

Ted placed the file on the low table between them.

'Do you think this takeover has anything to do with Soames's disappearance?'

'In what way?'

'You know, big deal going down. Lots of money to be made on both sides. Everyone keen to push ahead at full steam except one lone objector who miraculously disappears from the scene.'

Webster did not like the inference that was being drawn by his visitor.

'I can't see any such scenario. That's pure supposition. Totally unfounded.'

'Do you think anyone might want to see Mr Soames removed from the deal? A person with a big enough stake to make it worthwhile?'

'Absolutely not. Unthinkable. This is the City not the Old Kent Road.'

Ted stood up, then paused by the door and went into his Columbo mode. He watched too much solo TV these days.

'One last thing. Did a courier try to deliver a package at any time to you at the hotel?'

'No.'

'Are you sure?'

'Of course I'm sure. No one knew that we were there. No one at all.'

Ted returned to the car outside and headed back to Harrow Road, one eye on the dashboard clock and one on the traffic ahead. Then he stared out at the ebbing Thames that ran along the Embankment to his left-hand side. He hoped that Soames would turn up soon, yet he was beginning to fear the worst. He thought of Helen Soames and the children and the long wait that might never end. He'd been there, he knew the feelings and he wouldn't wish the uncertainty on anyone.

Sir Gordon Harvey was back. His second visit in a week to Thames View. Sarah didn't know why he needed to return so often, but it was two hundred pounds every time. She gave him his instructions in the hallway.

'Go downstairs, Gordon, and prepare yourself for class. I'll be with you shortly.'

Over to the wardrobe in her bedroom. She selected the uniform he needed. Flowing black gown, mortarboard and sheer black stockings with visible garters. Sarah was ready to teach. She descended the stairs and saw that Gordon too was ready. He stood by the bench in a pair of underpants. Disgusting off-white Jockeys in fact. Sarah wondered why this captain of industry insisted on such childish regression.

'I see you have misbehaved again.'

Her errant middle-aged pupil kept his eyes lowered to the concrete floor.

'Yes, teacher.'

He loved this. She knew it. What an act. What an actress. Her forte.

'Come over here, Gordon.'

He lay over the bench as instructed. She selected a rattan cane from the assorted items on the wall. She let the implement sing through the warm air for the effect. He shuddered in anticipation. She expertly lowered the Jockeys to his knees with the crook of the cane. The row of neat welts from the prior visit was still visible. She'd be more careful this time. Gordon didn't want many marks. Otherwise his wife might pass comment as he ambled from the bathroom with the his and her washbasins to the walk-in wardrobe that housed the sartorial evidence of his accumulated wealth back home in Hampstead Hill.

'You're getting six of the best, Gordon. You deserve it.'

It was so damn hot down here today. She prayed he wouldn't keel over and die on her. Again. She'd take it easy on him this time. Sarah started her correction but immediately he spoke out of turn.

'What about the questions, teacher?'

'Questions?'

'Yes, teacher, like normal. Questions about my work.'

Jesus. She had forgotten her routine. She was losing it.

Gordon always told all before he took the full force of the cane. What was she thinking of? She was addled today. Badly. That death. That visit.

'So, Gordon. What are you working on? Tell me.'

'No, I can't.' Jesus. Wish he'd make up his mind. This acting lark was almost of Oscar proportions. She started. He cried out and then warbled on about new brewing deals, pub acquisitions, leveraged buyouts and premium lager sales. Sarah was drifting away. This was all so irrelevant. She had forgotten to set the tape upstairs to record this for posterity. She was really losing it. She was a million miles away.

'Ahhhh ... no more, teacher, please.'

The signal. Gordon collapsed onto the concrete, hands out of sight, moaning uncontrollably like those lonely nights between the cold sheets back in the Upper Sixth dormitory years ago.

And Sarah stood over this drained man, cane still in hand. She wondered how this twisted human being could ever run a major plc, wondered how she'd ever begun this sordid lifestyle, wondered if she'd lose her sanity, if she'd saved enough sterling by now, if there was a better life elsewhere. Most of all she wondered if Alexander Soames's death would come back to haunt her.

CHAPTER THIRTEEN

BISHOPSGATE, LONDON EC2

Mark waited in the marble-floored lobby of Blake Brothers. He had a ten o'clock appointment with James Ingrams, the Head of Compliance. The secretary on the other end of the telephone line had said that her boss didn't do nine o'clock appointments. Even for the LSE. It was his ninth visit to a City investment bank and Mark didn't expect this to be any different from the others. So far, Goldmans off Fleet Street had impressed him the most. He would work there if they wanted him.

Blakes surely couldn't be as impressive as the big boys, except of course for one important factor. Barbara Ashby was on his mind and she worked here. His impressive sighting in Broadgate had whetted his appetite. If he kept his eyes open today he might even see her around in the flesh. He was eventually ushered upstairs by reception staff. It was well past ten already.

First impressions of Ingrams made even Clive Norris look good. A visibly tired middle-aged man with jaded eyes and a jaundiced pallor, Ingrams warbled on about ancient LSE investigations over his many years in the City. His three-piece grey suit bore the hallmarks of twenty years dedicated service to its owner, food stains and all.

Mark asked for the standard information and Ingrams

tottered about while he sat and waited patiently. The poky office was devoid of other people, with two empty desks piled high with reports and boxes of A4 listings. Mark made some effort at polite conversation as the Blakes' Compliance guru sifted through the morass of paper. So much for the paperless office of the future.

'So how big is your Compliance Department here?'

'This is it.' Ingrams saw his surprise. 'There are three of us. My deputy is away at the moment.'

'Is he on holiday?'

'She, young man. Maternity leave, in fact.'

'For long?'

'Five months so far. Due back soon.' Ingrams hesitated. 'I think. I must ask Personnel in fact.'

'Five months is a long time. Do you have a replacement while she's away?'

Ingrams could see what Mark was driving at.

'In her absence I keep an eye on everything. I'm make sure all your rules are followed.'

Mark wasn't convinced. Blakes' Compliance Department didn't look that pro-active. Or even reactive.

'And the other member of the department?'

'My secretary, Lisa. She's a temp but we might make her permanent in time.'

The one Mark had spoken to on the telephone last week. As if on cue a mousey girl walked in, steaming coffee in hand.

'Lisa, do you know where that Provident Bank printout is?'

'The wha'?'

She was of no use whatsoever. Ingrams finally found a listing.

'Never mind. Here it is. I had this run off last week.' Ingrams opened it out onto a spare desk. 'It's from our systems people and shows all our activity in Provident shares for the past two months as you requested. It contains all our proprietary accounts and client accounts. It's yours.'

Mark sat down and quickly paged through it, circling the larger positions. Ingrams watched him work, apparently amazed at his speed. It didn't take Mark long to find the biggest position.

'Looks like you've got a million Provident shares in a house account. Number 99007.'

Ingrams was temporarily lost.

'Have we? I see. Yes, indeed, you're right.'

Obviously Ingrams hadn't been through the listing before Mark. Every other bank's Compliance Department had bothered to do this, so that they had the easy answers ready for the man from the LSE.

'Who uses this dealing account in Blakes?'

'One of the dealers downstairs. I don't know who exactly. Does it matter?'

It was the only dealing account worth looking at in this second-tier bank. This would be a short visit.

'Yes, it does matter. The shares were bought three weeks ago. I need to talk to the dealer.'

Ingrams hit the speaker telephone, peered at a scribbled internal telephone list for a minute, dialled an extension and got through immediately. The hum of the dealing floor was audible in the background.

'Nicholas Crosswaithe.'

'Ingrams here. I have a visitor who wants to talk to one of your dealers.'

'Who is it?'

'Someone from the Enforcement Department of the Stock Exchange.'

'Would you mind taking me off the speaker then?'

Ingrams picked up the handset as requested.

'Yes, sorry. Yes. I see. Sorry. I'll send him down to you. His name's Robinson.'

He doth apologise too much. Easy to see who ran this bank. The dealers did, not the back office. The inmates were running the asylum. They parted company, Mark holding onto the printout, Ingrams holding onto his job. Mark didn't see himself ever working in Compliance at Blakes.

A conservative-looking middle-aged gentleman met him at the lifts on the dealing floor.

'Morning. What's all this about?' asked Crosswaithe.

These guys were too anxious. Time to put them at their ease.

'It's purely routine. I'm looking at recent dealing in Provident shares.'

They sat in his corner office. Mark guarded the printout closely. Crosswaithe stole furtive glances at it.

'I need to speak to the dealer who trades proprietary account 99007.'

Mark observed Crosswaithe's reaction. He wasn't keen but he knew Mark had the right to ask. He pointed out of the glass window at a tall guy with a short haircut, white shirt with button-down collar and animated facial expressions.

'The dealer is Greg Schneider. He's an American. The gentleman standing over there with the phone.'

Mark stood up to leave. He could see Crosswaithe debating his next move.

'Will I introduce you to Greg?'

It was always best to talk to dealers one on one without their boss eavesdropping on the conversation.

'That won't be necessary. I'm sure you are a busy man. Thanks for your help.'

Mark was getting that gut feeling already. Blakes were disorganised. The Compliance Department was a non-event. Ingrams was technically incompetent. Crosswaithe was edgy. Schneider looked to be a difficult character even from this distance. Mark always used moments like this to spring the element of surprise. Schneider wouldn't know who he was.

'Greg Schneider?'

The dealer spun around, telephone still in hand, other hand in his right pocket scratching his balls.

'Yeah? Who wants to know?'

Mark thought he recognised this guy from somewhere. But that was impossible. He had never been on Blakes' dealing floor before. He must have seen him somewhere else, with someone perhaps? Or else it was just that this guy looked like any dealer in the City. Loaded. Pushy. Hassled. Agitated. Objectionable. Volatile.

'Mark Robinson from the Enforcement Department of the LSE.'

Mark flashed his identity card, complete with dire photograph and offered a handshake. Schneider had to hang up and oblige. The chatter on the desk stopped. A girl with great crossed legs stared back at Mark from her seat. Hostility personified or else she fancied the pants off him. Had to be the latter he told himself in vain. A fat guy in a bulging shirt leant forward on the other side of the desk. An Oxbridge type with a foppish haircut appeared from behind a copy of *The Times*. They had all heard the words. Enforcement Department. All eyes were on Mark. Schneider did his best to smile but patently it required an effort on his part.

'Sure, Mark. Pull up a chair. What can I do for you?'

Mark put the printout down on an already cluttered dealing desk piled high with research reports, plastic bottles of Highland Spring water junk mail, *Mirrors* and *Suns*, and stinking McDonalds' styrofoam boxes.

'I want to talk to you about your large position in Provident shares in light of the takeover.'

They all got his drift. What he meant was the possibility of insider trading. Only he couldn't say that.

'Large? It's all relative, I guess. How many shares do I have now?' pondered Schneider.

What a crass question. Name one dealer in the City sitting

on a pile of paper like this heading north who didn't know the exact number of shares that he owns. None. Mark was obliged to open Ingrams's printout on the page with account 99007, as if proof was required before this doubting Thomas.

'You have a million shares according to the bank's records. Bought twenty days ago at a weighted average price of ten pounds. Currently trading per that screen in front of you at a best offer price of eleven fifty two pence. I make that an unrealised profit of one and half million pounds.'

Shit. They knew they were up against a pro here. Someone who could read an SEAQ screen and knew the jargon. Greg had also been caught with the Provident price displayed on his screen. Not a crime in itself but still circumstantially incriminating all the same. The dealer decided it was best to say as little as possible.

'Can you tell me why you decided to take a position in these shares so recently?'

Another loaded question. The dealer debated the answer then went with the party line.

'I thought they represented good value at the time.'

'Did you think that there might be a takeover in the offing?' pushed Mark.

'I always hope that there will be a takeover in every stock I own. It's called optimism, isn't it?'

Mark wasn't there to answer rhetorical questions. This dealer was playing hard to get, watching his every word as if a Crown lawyer was sitting beside him. Mark didn't like it. He recalled the characters he had met at comparable desks in Goldmans, Deutsche, UBS and the others. All ebullient characters wanting to tell him how good they were. Those guys chatted about the market, the hot stocks, the gossip, and the afternoon's nags. This guy was different. Careful with his words. Too careful?

Mark wondered how far to take this conversation. A mobile phone rang. Everyone at the desk made for the inside of creased suit jackets hanging over the backs of chairs. The mobile still rang. Mark then realised it was his, and interrupted one stalled conversation for another.

'Mark?'

It was Norris back in his office. The nerve. Mark had told Peter that he had got a freebie Nokia courtesy of his car insurance. It was all he could afford. Then Norris had insisted he provide his mobile number.

'Yes?'

'Mark, I haven't seen you in the office for a few days. How are you getting on with the Provident investigation? The powers that be were asking me about progress this morning.'

Mark couldn't discuss this case on the floor of Blakes, not with Schneider and the others so near. He walked over to a quiet corner behind a partition and spoke.

'Everything's fine. I've visited nine banks. Three or four more to go. No news to report.'

Mark shifted impatiently and used the moment to look around for his quarry. Not the dealer, but the ever wonderful Barbara. No sign of her. Pity. He looked back at Schneider just as the dealer leant forward and placed a hand on the printout. Shit. Mark had left it on the desk. No dealer should see all of the bank's positions, particularly those held by the bank's clients. Mark tried to quickly end the conversation with Norris but to no avail.

Schneider looked furtive, flicking back through the pages of the printout. Once, twice, three times and then more pages. Nosy bastard. He stopped suddenly and peered at the text, scribbling on a dealing blotter in front of him. He had found something all right. Mark frantically tried to recall how many times Schneider had turned back the pages. No way to tell.

Norris finally let him go. When Mark arrived back at the dealing desk, Schneider had turned the pages of the printout back to his own dealing account. Mark's curiosity was aroused. The dealing blotter was in front of them. Schneider had a red pen in his left hand. Look for red ink on the blotter. A light flashed on the dealing board. It was another bank looking to do some business. Schneider couldn't refrain from taking a lingering look at the phone board as he swore at the leggy girl to pick up the call.

There it was, written in the corner of the blotter. A number in red. Mark committed it to memory. 2024 something. He gave Schneider a reassuring farewell that neither of them believed and reluctantly left Blakes, wondering why he had not even caught a glimpse of his favourite Sky TV star.

Ten minutes later Mark sat in the Prêt à Manger deli near Broadgate. Chrome ruled here. He digested an exotic seeded baguette that came with assorted salad dressings, herbs and condiments, yet nevertheless was essentially a sandwich. It was complemented by one of the world's most expensive cappuccinos and a packet of matured English cheddar and corn potato snacks, or crisps as others call them.

Four pounds seventy-five pence for a snatched lunch in the City. Mark could have had meat, potatoes, two veg and sticky toffee pudding back in the LSE staff canteen for far less. Only these City types could afford to eat regularly in the City. Not civil servants.

He opened the printout again on a counter in the corner of the deli while ensuring no one else could snatch a look at it. First to account 99007. Then he trawled backwards page by page looking for 2024 something. And there it was. Account 20245.

It was a private client by the name of Ms Sarah Hart. No address given, just care of Blakes' office in Jersey. Her account manager was a Penelope Swales in Jersey. The account held ten thousand Provident shares. They were bought twenty-one days ago. Same time as Schneider's purchases. Recent enough.

Mark wondered why Greg Schneider could possibly be interested in this one offshore account.

Sarah was anxious. Too much grief and confusion in recent

days. And a death. Time to take stock. Literally. See where she was in her life. Check her liquidity. There were no other client appointments that day so she would not be disturbed. She powered up the Dell mini-tower PC in the spare room, chose the Excel option, and clicked on her favourite file on the drop-down menu. Liquidity.xls. She needed a password to access the file. Hartless always worked for her. A bad choice in hindsight. Unnecessary too. Who else would ever get to see this single spreadsheet that she guarded so carefully?

She started on her investments. Exactly 100k in UK gilts. Last priced a few weeks ago courtesy of the Saturday *FT* at par of almost a pound each. The price never changed that much anyway, only when UK interest rates moved. That was why she bought gilts in the first place, it was her pension fund, completely safe until the UK government defaulted on its entire public debt of billions. Never in a million years.

Her biggest shareholding was first. Ten thousand shares of Provident Bank. Originally priced at 985 pence, the price she bought them at three weeks ago. Definitely time to update their value. She flipped over the screens and pulled up the Internet icon, logged in with another password, and was instantly connected to the World Wide Web courtesy of BT. The pages were slow today. It wasn't called the World Wide Wait for nothing.

Then into the Yahoo! Finance page and on to their stock quotes screen. She picked the London Stock Exchange from the list, keyed in the acronym PROV. Today's closing mid-price was 1155 pence. The spreadsheet did the work for her with a new valuation for the shares and an unrealised profit of seventeen thousand pounds.

The Provident listed options were the real sweetener. She had learnt about the benefits of options after having read three books on the topic as recommended by the Open University Business Studies Degree tutors. Never too late for an education in life. All that wonderful option leverage with so much profit potential for so little up front capital. Much more risk too but not when you had the inside track on certain shares. Sarah also owned thirty thousand Provident options bought at a pound each.

They gave her the right, but not the obligation, to buy Provident shares at any time in the next three months at 1050 pence. At today's price these options were a pound in the money, as the pros tend to say in the City. She knew the jargon all right. She never mentioned it when the dealer invaded her home and basement. She had doubled her money in three weeks; a performance that many a City fund manager would die for. Pity about that particular analogy.

Next were the Sportsworld shares, bought on the day before Alexander Soames's death. Before his evening visit she had made a telephone call to her ever-receptive account manager. Fifty grand invested and Sarah was counting the days to the mega-deal and more instant loot. It was a no-lose situation. She checked the Sportsworld share price on the Web. Still 105 pence.

Then her other educated gamble. Ten thousand County Beverage shares still shown at the purchase price of 480 pence. She had given her usual instructions to her account manager to sell before close of business on the day of the AGM. She had received 520 pence per share and an instant realised profit of four grand. She deleted the shares with the edit key and moved the four grand into the cash account below. All this was adding up quite nicely.

There were a few other incidental investments on the screen. Far East mutual funds. Sentimental stuff like the first shares she had ever bought and some privatisation stocks which she meant to stag at the time, sell for a quick buck, but she held onto them. She kept her eye off the bottom right-hand side of the screen where the cumulative total was updating real time. Save the best till last.

She always had ample cash, enough to dive into any fancied stock at short notice when the information came to hand. Her spreadsheet showed eighty-six thousand sterling in the high interest money market deposit account. That was her estimate and she would confirm with Penelope in due course that she was correct.

Sarah had explicitly instructed that all statements and trade confirmations were to be held at the bank's office. She hadn't seen a hard copy bank statement on the account for a few months, not since her last visit in person to her account manager. It was too risky to have them arrive in the Royal Mail, getting lost or left around the townhouse to be seen by her many daily visitors.

Her less liquid possessions were not listed. Like the cheap BMW with the ample boot essential for that covert nocturnal manoeuvre, and the customised furniture down in the basement. They weren't worth including in liquidity.xls. Not liquid enough. She owned no property. That would only tie her down to a particular location. Perish the thought. She would be off soon if all went well.

The temptation was too much. She looked at the bottom line, as so many of her accountant clients enjoyed doing from nine to five at their desks. Five hundred and thirty-two thousand sterling. A good improvement on the prior spreadsheet of a few weeks ago, thanks primarily to Provident.

Could she live on that sort of money? She could get a yield now of five per cent that would give her an annual income of twenty-five thousand per annum for the rest of her life. She knew she couldn't live on that in London, not with her lifestyle. Maybe somewhere overseas? Somewhere safe where Alexander's death and the law and the awful memories could never catch up with her.

It was time to visit her account manager, to confirm these big numbers, and drop off some cash that she had recently accumulated in her drawer. A day trip would suffice. It was only an hour's hop on the turbo prop. Funny how she had immediately thought of one suitable offshore bank two years ago when she opened this account. Somewhere secure, traditional, secretive, discreet and genuinely British. Somewhere that American kept talking about when he visited.

Blake Brothers & Co in St Helier Jersey, private bankers to the rich, suited Sarah's needs perfectly.

Greg was hoping to leave the dealing floor quietly but Old Nick cornered him on the way out.

'My office Greg. Five minutes. Now.'

He had no choice. Crosswaithe pulled the door closed. This looked serious. Worse than usual.

'So what was that all about today?'

'What?'

'Don't come the innocent with me. That investigator from the LSE. They never visit us.'

Why hadn't he asked the same question of the visitor instead of grilling Greg?

'He wanted to ask me about my Provident dealing position. Why I had bought the shares.'

'And?'

'I told him I liked the stock. That's all there was to it.'

His boss looked unconvinced.

'Don't short change me.'

'I'm not. He said he's visiting lots of banks in the City. As far as I'm concerned that's the end of the case. He won't be back here.'

'Is that all there is to it? You and I have spoken about this before. You're either a good dealer who makes us millions every year or you know more than you're letting on about the market. Which is it?'

Shit. Nick was getting warm. Too warm.

'The former. I'm on a roll at the moment. Don't knock it. I could have a bad second half of the year. I might lose millions of bucks before the year-end. Would you be happier with that?'

'Don't give me that attitude. If I ever hear of anything untoward going on at the Special Situations desk, I'll fire all of you. Blakes is a reputable bank and I will never allow one rogue trader in our midst to ruin our reputation. Remember that.'

Old Nick wouldn't recognise a rogue trader if Greg had it printed on his business card. The inquisition was over but Greg had one last thought as he made for the door.

'By the way, I'm taking a day's holiday on Monday.'

'Are you? What are you doing?'

Greg's time outside Blakes was his own. Crosswaithe had no right to ask. Lie.

'Nothing. Relaxing.'

Days like today made Greg want to leave Blakes sooner rather than later. Where was a decent headhunter with a six-figure job offer at a big name bank when you needed them?

He wasn't resting at home on Monday. He had a full day planned and had to be up at seven o'clock. Two telephone calls earlier today had been enough. He couldn't make those calls from the dealing desk where all the lines were recorded in case of a dealer error or counterparty dispute. He had made them on his mobile phone outside the office during his lunch hour.

One call was to Jersey European Airways reservations office in Hounslow to book a club class seat on a 9.30 a.m. Heathrow departure. The ticket was to be collected at the airport. The other call was to a colleague, Penelope Swales, private client account manager at Blake Brothers & Co. in St Helier.

CHAPTER FOURTEEN

ST HELIER, JERSEY, CHANNEL ISLANDS

Today was the sort of lazy summer day that made living in Jersey worthwhile. Penelope Swales always maintained that she didn't actually reside there on a full-time basis. Sure, she worked there from Monday to Friday but in reality she saw the island as the perfect intermediary base between the UK and the Continent. Weekends could be spent back with Mummy and Daddy in the family home. Or she could catch a flight to her aspiring model friends in Paris. Visit family friends in their Tuscan vineyard and sample the local produce. Vino, men and all. Ski in the Alps with her college chums. Veg out on the beach near Marbella with an ex-colleague who lusted after her company. So many locations, so little time.

After a long shower, she blow-dried her long hair and swept it back into a neat hairband. She elected to wear a cream one-piece sleeveless summer dress and navy blazer with gold motified buttons. Perfect for the seventy-five degrees of heat that was forecast by midday today but nevertheless giving the right impression to clients. Smart and fashionable yet prudent and conservative. Last to go on were the sunglasses, a quick spray of Sure and the not-so-modest collection of jewellery. Time to go to work. If that's what they called it.

Her complimentary company let was perched on the hill overlooking the bustling harbour of St Helier. It was near enough to the impressive bank edifices lined along the waterfront. Penelope always left home on foot each morning, her token gesture at maintaining a healthy lifestyle. If she closed the hall door behind her at quarter to nine then she was always at her desk in Blakes before nine.

Penelope was not a morning person. She couldn't see the point of rising at the unsociable hours that were primarily the preserve of unfortunate postal workers, office cleaners, corner shopkeepers, milkmen and tube drivers. No thanks. Although London's equity markets were alive and kicking well before seven-thirty a.m., most of her private clients were still curled up under the duvet in their four posters in the Home Counties, waiting for their staff to deliver the morning toast and a well-ironed *Times* paper.

Penelope started three years ago in Blakes' Jersey office as a sales assistant for one of the biggest producers, old man Stevenson. Her initial tasks were menial, writing out his sales tickets, typing up his letters and faxes and e-mails, making coffee for his discreet visitors, maintaining his client files and taking phone messages. But she eased her way into Stevenson's life. She took orders from clients, passed them to their London equity and bond dealers, read up on Blakes' research and rehashed it back to clients and filled out cheque requisitions for withdrawals from client accounts. When Stevenson retired at forty-six years of age to live in the sun-kissed Marbella pad that she knew well, he left his clients in the capable hands of Penelope.

And what a varied bunch of clients they were. Retired country gents with estates of both the hunting and BMW variety. Widows with so much more than a meagre war pension living in Bath, Bournemouth and Eastbourne. Criminal lawyers and leading QCs in London. Investment banking and dealing types in the City with massive salaries and annual bonuses to invest. International accountants flying the world to work for US multi-national corporations and escape from the overly zealous taxman. Oil engineers risking their life in Libya, Iran and other Middle East hotspots. Doctors and surgeons living in Saudi and Bahrain security compounds. Property owners with dodgy rental income to invest. Ex-Formula One drivers. Geologists in Colombia and Zimbabwe. Sportstars, musicians, comedians, writers, producers and TV celebrities looking to avoid the attentions of the Inland Revenue.

Penelope was less well disposed to some of her other clients. Those who turned up with cash to lodge to their accounts. Those who never talked much about their personal life or business activities back in the UK. Those who never wanted a telephone call from her to their home or to their office. They would initiate the contact. Those who never wanted a trade confirmation or a bank statement in the Royal Mail. Penelope didn't know enough about some of her clients but surely that was a compliance issue.

Others in the office had noticed the effect she had on Stevenson. Penelope couldn't help it. She had the dress sense to impress the affluent, she could put on the plummy accent when so required, she knew how to converse effortlessly over a dining table in Jersey's best Michelin starred restaurants, she took a weekly manicure and pedicure, she had the tan from time spent on the south-facing balcony of her subsidised pad. Stevenson had insisted she accompany him on his trips to Cannes, Verbiers, Nice and the like. Penelope just thought the others were jealous of her success.

Blakes paid her a basic salary that allowed a very satisfactory lifestyle, but they also operated a sales commission structure, which they had copied from the US retail securities houses. Account executives like Penelope took a third of all commissions they earned on their accounts. Penelope had inherited a range of profitable accounts and was clearing six figures gross per annum.

Not bad for a twenty-seven-year-old only child who'd performed with mediocrity at public school and who had never quite lived up to her father's grand expectations. He thought his Penny would be married with two kids by now and settled in rural England with other landed gentry types but not so. She'd spent a few years after Oxford with a backpack and a friend from Uni finding most of herself in the deepest jungles of South America. Then her father had somehow miraculously procured this Jersey posting for her. His personal friendship with a Director of Blakes, one Nicholas Crosswaithe, was pure coincidence, of course.

She hadn't looked back since. The share purchases and sales continued, the clients kept coming back for more, and the commission income kept flowing into her own personal account at the Jersey branch. She was mixing in the right circles, the client entertainment was great, the travel was all on Blakes and she had recently graduated to having her own sales assistant Gabrielle, to do all the mundane work for her. Full circle.

Penelope looked up some opening prices on the Reuters screen at her desk. The FTSE was still hovering around the 6,500 mark. Some blue chips were up; some of the stocks with Far East exposure were down since the Hang Seng had fallen one per cent overnight on fears of economic recession and a property slump. The Nikkei closed down on rumours of another Japanese banking collapse.

She passed a few buy orders to the London dealers that she had received overnight on her answering machine, then took a long coffee break with the *FT*. She checked her on-screen PC diary that was maintained by Gabrielle outside in the general office area where the mere mortals sat.

Her first appointment of the day was an eleven o'clock with a colleague from London.

It was one of those mornings you can only have in London. A nightmare. With hindsight Greg should have taken a Jubilee line train and then changed at Green Park for the Piccadilly line. Or he should have gone to Paddington to catch the express train

service. Famous for fifteen minutes. Instead he was stuck in a
black cab on the hump of the Hayes bypass off the M4 looking
down on the three lanes of solid morning traffic. The rows of
red rear brakelights ahead were a bad sign. The meter in the
cab was rapidly approaching twenty-five pounds and Greg was
going nowhere fast.

In the distance planes swooped down on Heathrow from
the direction of Central London at regular one-minute intervals.
Tantalising. So near yet so far away. He eyed his watch nervously
hoping that he would still make the 9.30 departure. He had an
appointment to keep.

His absence on business always seemed to be public knowledge in Blakes but this trip was different from the others. Greg
had said he was on the mobile today. They could try him
at home. No one must know about this clandestine journey.
Especially Old Nick who always signed his expense claims. This
time he had paid his own fare. No claim could be proffered. He
checked his mobile for the second time. Yes. It was powered
off. He was uncontactable today. Perfect.

Greg's other trips were approved by Nick on the pretext
of an allegedly essential stock market briefing in Amsterdam
or Milan. Some trips out to the Far East were justified by a
visit to a Blakes office in Honkers or Singers. Some trips were
company offsite meetings when the powers that be decided that
a private château in Normandy was the best place to discuss
complex arbitrage strategy or equity underwriting, rather than
using a Trust House Forte on the M25 orbital.

Greg had not crossed the threshold of the Blakes office in
downtown Manhattan in all his years of service. Ironic for an
American living in London since he missed the best freebie
opportunity Virgin Atlantic to see his relations, friends and
former broking colleagues back home. He had missed the trip
to New York last year due to an alleged almost fatal dose of
gastro-enteritis in a West End seafood restaurant. A conference
in New York the year before last had clashed with a wedding

where he was the best man. At least that's what he had told the others. He was rapidly running out of annual excuses to avoid going home.

He arrived in a packed Terminal I departure lounge and waited impatiently as the old dames boarded ahead of him. Jersey attracted them in droves. It must be the sunnier climes, the exciting annual Flower Festival, the ankle-deep paddling in the sea, the fact that the locals also spoke the English lingo or that the food was as bad as back home.

Retired couples hand in hand in matching M&S pastel jackets with too much carry-on baggage from the Sixties shuffled off nervously down the air bridge, looking for non-existent railings to hang on to for support. Then they stood in the aisle ahead of Greg, peered at their boarding cards and wondered where was row 25 and which was seat C or D? Give me strength.

When you regularly travelled in Boeing 747's double-deckers and magnificent Airbus beasts, the interior of a British Aerospace turbo-prop was not an enticing prospect. Greg was too tall for the cabin roof and crawled to his seat in row I. He felt cramped in the tiny fake leather seat. The unpleasant Suit in the adjacent window seat had got there first and claimed their dividing armrest as his sole property. Greg eyed up the hostesses but found little to get excited about. None came close to Barbara.

The in-flight service on Jersey European Airways was miserable. The food consisted of boiled pink sweets before takeoff and after landing, interspersed with a luke-warm breakfast. He had never heard of the brand of French champagne on offer. There was no complimentary *FT* available. No comment. Just the *Express* and the *Mail*. If this was business class, what was it like back in coach? The turbulence was bad too. Give him BA or Virgin any day.

He knew nothing about Jersey and more to the point he had no interest. Some middle of nowhere place stuck on a rock in the ocean. Nothing to compare with the buzz of the world's great financial capitals. They flew in low over dark waves with white-peaked crests and then down to the runway set in the middle of what was essentially a field.

The airport terminal was a relatively modern edifice at the end of the field. Greg had no luggage. He left the old dears worrying about their assorted cases by the conveyor belts and was the first London passenger to get into a taxi outside.

'Blake Brothers Bank. In St Helier.'

Greg was impressed when he walked into the sumptuous private office. Not particularity by the fine walnut desk, the set of Regency chairs, the oil paintings of hunting scenes on the wall nor by the harbour view framed between the drapes held back with gold tassels. He was more impressed by the stunning private client executive in the cream dress who rose to greet him with a wide smile. Greg placed his briefcase deliberately on the floor beside his chair.

Penelope was in her automatic sales mode, sensing that another affluent client was about to join her select stable. Roll on the commission.

'So how are things back in head office, Mr Schneider? Any excitement there?'

Apart from million pound plus profits in Provident shares, between the sheets action with a lithe research colleague, arguments with his ageing boss, vain hopes of a call from a headhunter and a missing plc Finance Director, there was absolutely nothing of note going on.

'No excitement. After all this is Blakes, last bastion of Britishness in the City.'

They both smiled. Penelope knew the corporate image that the Directors did their best to project.

'That's what I tell all my clients. Don't knock it, it works for me. They like the sense of security.'

They talked about Blakes as she poured coffee into two fine porcelain cups, both of them knowing that some informality was necessary before they got down to the serious business. Penelope knew when the time was right. That was another skill she had acquired from Stevenson. Great timing. He always said so in an ecstatic gasp, in and out of the king size in his split-level Marbella pad.

'I take it that you're interested in opening an account with us, Greg. If I may call you that?'

She could be as informal as she liked.

'Sure thing, Penelope. I wanna open an account.'

'Call me Penny. When we open an account for staff, we need to know more about them. What is your position in our London office? Who do you work for there?'

'I run the Special Situations dealing desk. We're hot. We deal mostly in UK equities.'

'Who is your boss?'

'Nicholas Crosswaithe is the Director in charge of dealing there.'

Penelope acknowledged the name but omitted to mention the family connection. Small world.

'So what can I do for you?'

A lot, babe. A lot. But not right here and now. Barbara may have some competition.

'I wanna open an offshore deposit account for some spare cash that I have.'

She saw the prospect of her lucrative equity commission income rapidly disappearing.

'How much were you thinking of investing with us?'

'How about five grand for starters?'

She tried to hide her disappointment. Five grand was the minimum amount required to open a new account. She knew that. So did he. A City dealer like him had far more cash at his disposal. Five k was an insult to her. It was pocket money. This was a waste of time yet she remained in sales mode.

'Sterling or dollars?'

'Hey, bucks of course. I prefer hard currency.'

'Excellent. I'll open an account for you immediately.'

She handed him a proforma new account form. He paused before putting pen to paper to ask a loaded question.

'I don't want any mail. Can I have my account statements held at the office here? How does that work?'

'Certainly. We'll title the account in your name but show the address as being care of the office here. We'll keep any correspondence and statements in my files over there and you can pick them up whenever you're in Jersey.'

Penelope pointed at a single four-drawer metal filing cabinet in the corner of the room. It looked grotesquely out of place amongst the fine furniture and fittings but it was obviously a corporate necessity. The top drawer was slightly ajar by a few inches. Greg could see that the cabinet was unlocked.

'That's fine by me,' and he signed the account opening form with a flourish and handed over a personal cheque for 5k. Done deal. Next step. His briefcase lay flat on the floor beside him. He covertly pushed it away with his shoe so that it lay partly hidden under her desk. Perfect for later. She would never know. The meeting was over. She thought about her usual modus operandi. It was nearly twelve o'clock. Hunger pangs beckoned.

'I usually ask my new clients out for lunch on Blakes. Are you interested?'

It killed Greg to turn down such an invitation from the most fanciable private client executive that he knew, but this situation demanded a negative response. Maybe next time.

'I'd love to, but I've got a flight back to Heathrow real soon. Gotta run,' he lied.

They parted company at the main reception. Greg made sure the girl on the reception desk noticed him as he pointedly asked for the nearest taxi rank. She gave him an address a few streets away.

Greg wasn't going for a taxi yet. He had come too far to leave empty-handed now. Instead he sat alone inside a darkened bar across the road from the entrance to Blakes and waited. And waited. One o'clock approached; he was on his third bottle of Miller and there was still no sign of her.

Then, as if on cue, Penelope emerged, accompanied by a young guy who looked like a Blakes' colleague. She had found someone else to dine with. Greg was sure there was never a shortage of interested parties when it came to invitations from Penelope. The two took a sharp left down a side street to a bistro. He gave her five more minutes to make sure it was safe, paid the tab in the bar, and ran across the road back into Blakes. Up to the girl at the reception desk. She recognised him. He flashed his Blakes' head office business card at her in an open palm. She recognised that too.

'Hi. Me again. From London head office. I need to see Penelope.'

He wasn't disappointed by her reaction but he did his best to make it look that way.

'She just stepped outside for lunch. Would you like to wait for her?'

'I can't wait. I've got a flight real soon. And I left my briefcase in her office. I'll get it.'

She half rose to stop him, then the telephone rang on the reception desk and her attention drifted. He strode past her and down the corridor towards the private offices. Then he was out of sight. Greg entered Penelope's office in the next twenty seconds and pushed the door firmly closed.

The top drawer of the filing cabinet was still open, key sitting in the lock. She was careless when she left the office. He half thought about closing his new account. The files were in alphabetical order. He made straight for the H surnames. Time to see if the Sarah Hart on the dealing printout that the LSE guy had brought with him was the same as his Sarah Hart in London. It couldn't be, she was surely dumb, wouldn't know what to buy or sell. She never even listened to those tapes. Did she?

He found the file immediately. It was thin. Must be a relatively new account. He read the account opening form, like the one he had completed so recently. There it was. A hold mail account. No post to be sent to 32 Thames View, Isle of Dogs, London E14. It was definitely her, fuck her.

He heard sounds outside in the corridor. He would be caught in the act. He made for his briefcase on the floor but the sounds passed. One last look. He opened the file at her last account statement. Jesus. Look at those goddamn shares. Provident Bank. Sportsworld too. She had sold County Beverages for a big profit. Same as him. All that loot. She was dealing in the shares.

He passed the receptionist with his briefcase prominently displayed. Later, he sat in the taxi, stunned by the knowledge that Sarah was playing his game too.

The return flight was no better. There was hardly enough elbow room to open the *Evening Standard*, delivered on the last incoming flight. Greg made straight for the pink middle pages of the inside *Business Day* supplement. Force of habit by now. Two headline stories immediately caught his eye.

Kapital Bank Confirm Counter Bid for Provident Bank. It had happened. The Germans had entered the bidding war. Chairman David Webster was quoted as saying that British Commercial would review the terms of their original offer. Excellent. A bidding auction was developing. Greg looked at the Provident share price at the opening in London. Up forty pence to almost twelve pounds. Another 400k made in a morning and he hadn't even been at his desk today. What a wonderful business this was when all went well. Maybe it was getting close to the time to sell up and cash in his chips?

Missing Bank Director. Shit. Still no sign of the guy yet. Alexander Soames's car had been found in the East End of London. Greg read the small print below. It was found in

Stratford. Greg thought back over his modicum of A–Z street knowledge. As an American abroad he didn't yet know all of central London but he knew that Stratford was near enough to Thames View on the Isle of Dogs.

CHAPTER FIFTEEN

BISHOPSGATE, LONDON EC2

Old Nick made straight for Greg as soon as he arrived at Blakes. Greg had been at his desk for an hour already, celebrating the rise in Provident's price with Chas and the others, watching the flashing quotes on the FTSE 100 screen. Blue meant rising prices. Red meant falling prices. Orange meant going nowhere. Provident was flashing blue today. They were in the money big time and everyone on the desk knew it. Roll on bonus time and the year end.

Old Nick was livid. Greg saw the blood rising to his face as he slammed his office door behind them both. Inquisitive pairs of eyes out on the dealing floor glanced back at the two of them inside the glass office. Crosswaithe saw their interest and almost closed the full-length blinds to get some privacy. Rare enough. They knew this was serious. Greg was about to get a bollocking but they had no clues as to why.

'Greg. I told you before that if I ever found out that your dealing was suspect in any way, I would come down hard on you. Do you remember that?'

Greg nodded, Old Nick had new information. What had he inadvertently given away?

'So tell me, are you seeing Barbara in the research department?'

Greg's immediate reaction was a dead give-away.

'You are, aren't you? It's damn well true.'

Nick obliged with a clue to his source.

'When you want to keep an office relationship secret in future, may I suggest you don't go out together for a meal in the West End. London can be a small place at times. You have been seen.'

'By who?'

'That's none of your business.'

He moved onto the next stage of this interrogation.

'So what do you and Barbara talk about together? Takeovers? AGMs? Annual results?'

Greg had to defend himself. His very livelihood was at stake.

'Of course not. I'm not dumb. We never talk shop in or out of work hours.'

His boss persevered.

'Do you get your ideas for buying and selling shares from Barbara?'

'No goddamn way. I know the rules about observing Chinese Walls between the dealing desks and the Research Department. I am telling you straight up I would never breach those rules. I'm damn good at my job. I read the market well. I do my own research. I look for good value in shares. I buy and sell at the right time. My relationship with Barbara has nothing to do with the millions of bucks in profits I bring in every year for you. I made money for you long before I dated Barbara. End of story.'

It was an intemperate outburst but the words had been carefully chosen. They seemed to do the trick. The mention of millions of profit always worked. Crosswaithe was too scared to lose his most valued income stream. He'd love to fire Greg right here and now but what would the other Directors say in the Boardroom at the loss of their star dealer? He sat back, resigned to the lack of real proof. Gut feeling wasn't enough on which to base a P45.

'I hear what you're saying but I don't want to see the two of you together at work ever. Remember I am watching both of you. Don't bring your love life to Blakes. Leave it at home.'

Greg understood their discussion was over. He made for the door. Too soon.

'Hold on, Greg. There's something else.'

Old Nick held up a single faxed page. The heading on the top was clear. Blake Brothers & Co Jersey.

'This was faxed over to me yesterday from Penelope Swales in our Jersey office. Did you know that when a Blakes' employee opens a deposit account there, our Jersey office asks for a reference from their current boss? To ensure that they are a genuine employee of the company and not a gangland drug lord engaged in international money laundering and the like. And of course to ensure they are entitled to favourable rates and staff discounts on the standard commission levels.'

The bitch. Swales had told Old Nick on day one. These fucking compliance procedures were a pain in the ass. He bluffed.

'That's fine by me. Give her a reference. There's no law against opening up an account out there.'

'You're right. But why all the cloak and dagger stuff two days ago when we spoke? This fax says you were over in the Jersey office yesterday.'

Greg did his best to field a decent answer in the light of incontrovertible evidence.

'Yeah, I was. It was personal biz.'

'And you didn't bother to tell me about it?'

'Like I said. It's personal.'

Nick wasn't impressed.

'It's a long way to go to open a deposit account. They have them in the Nat West down the road, you know. Or most people can open a deposit account by post. It's so much more convenient that way. It's the way I manage my own account with the Jersey office. Penelope is my account executive too. But you felt the need to be physically present?'

Greg had one hand on the door handle, dying to leave.

'I needed a break for a day and I'd never been to Jersey before.'

'It must be a big deposit then?'

This was no business of Nicks and they both knew it. He was pushing his luck.

'That's personal too. I'm going back to my desk.'

'Sure, but be careful out there. I'm watching your every move.'

Greg left for the safety of his dealing desk. At least he could get some peace there. If only.

'What was that all about?' asked Chas.

'What?'

'In Old Nick's office. We could see enough from here. He was fuming. What's his problem?'

'Nothing at all. Let's get back to work and speculate on something else.'

'OK, Greg. Hey. There's a good piece in the *Sun* today. A survey from the States. Do you want a laugh about back home?'

'Sure. I could do with a laugh.'

'Some academics in a Florida university researched American workers and the sports they play. They found that the blue-collar workers play basketball. The office clerks go bowling. The managers play American football. The Senior Vice Presidents play tennis. The really top guys, the CEO's and the CFO's, all play golf.'

Chas paused for effect. Greg fell for it.

'So Chas, what does that prove?'

'Easy. The more senior you are in the organisation, the smaller your balls are.'

Greg smiled and looked over at the corner office.

'I guess that explains a lot about Old Nick's dealing appetite. He ain't got balls at all.'

Jules returned with a coffee. She'd seen it all too. She was more perceptive than her colleagues. Or so she thought.

'Old Nick wants to know how you do it, doesn't he? How you buy such great shares?'

It was the easy way out. Far easier than laying his secret love life out in public for all to pick over.

'Yeah. You got it in one, Jules.'

Chas wasn't giving up.

'So how do you do it? Like Provident? How do you pick 'em?'

'Call it experience, skill, intuition, savvy, common sense, even luck. It's my secret.'

'I know how you do it, Greg. I've seen you at work,' interjected Jules.

Now he was worried.

'Yeah?'

'Sure. You're always going to visit the Research Department in the evenings. We're not supposed even to go near there. Who do you go over to see? Are you reading up on what they're working on after hours?'

That was it. Jules was well out of line. He snapped.

'Jules. Shut the fuck up and check those screens. One more word and you'll be working on your CV.'

His tone gave it away. She had gone too far. Touched a raw nerve. They sat in silence at the Special Situations desk, knowing there might be more to their glorious leader than met the eye.

Mark had given Norris a twenty-page interim report on his investigation into the recent share dealings in Provident. It wasn't much but then there wasn't much to report. Only one item still troubled him.

'Mark, this all looks to be above board. There's no unusual dealing at all?' queried his boss.

'Correct.'

'No personal share dealing by the Directors of Provident or British Commercial in the past three months?'

'Correct.'

'No unusual dealing by the big investment banks?'

'Correct.'

'No large purchases by unknown shell companies in offshore tax jurisdictions?'

'Correct.'

'So we can close the file on this mega-takeover?'

Mark was about to give another similar utterance but he hesitated. Norris noticed.

'Is there anything I should know about?'

Mark recalled his visits to the City investment banks.

'It's not in the report, but I have a sort of hunch about one of the smaller banks.'

Norris closed the file and leant forward with interest, elbows on his desk.

'Which one?'

'Blake Brothers.'

'Really? They're small fry, aren't they?'

'That's just it. They are second-tier, yet one of the dealers there is sitting on a massive profit on a million Provident shares that he bought only weeks ago.'

'There's nothing wrong in that per se. I presume he told you why he had bought them?'

'No. All the other dealers talked to me about how wonderful they were. Yet this guy Schneider said nothing. He was edgy, reluctant to talk. And his boss, Crosswaithe, was edgy too. As if he wasn't keen for me to talk to the dealer. As if he suspected something untoward himself.'

Norris gave Mark the benefit of his years of experience.

'That's good work, but it's still only a hunch. Did Schneider do or say anything unusual at all?'

Norris had struck a chord.

'Yeah, he did. I left a printout with him and he was surprised by one of the Blakes' accounts on it. He wrote it down on a dealing blotter at his desk. I got the account number later.'

'What's the account?'

'It's a private client account in Blakes' Jersey office in the name of Sarah Hart. She owns ten thousand shares in Provident too. It's a lot for a private client. And she bought them one day before Schneider bought his million for the Blakes' Special Situations dealing account.'

'Jersey? That's more interesting. I think it's worth pursuing.'

'How do I do that?'

'Give Blakes' Jersey office a call. Say you are from the LSE. Tell them you want more information on this Sarah Hart person and her account. See if there is any connection to Blakes or to this guy Schneider.'

Mark knew sound advice when he heard it. Norris was getting better to work for of late. He took the file with him back to his desk. This case wasn't closed yet. Peter eyed him enviously across the desk in the knowledge that Mark was on the biggest case of late and that he was spending a lot of time one on one with Norris, while Peter was left to plan the wedding guest list with his fiancée over the phone.

Mark dialled Blakes' London office and asked for the number of their Jersey office. In two minutes he was through to the Jersey switchboard. He knew who to ask for, that account executive whose name appeared on the printout.

'Penelope Swales speaking.'

'Mark Robinson from the Enforcement Department of the Stock Exchange here.'

He always paused for effect after the introduction. It fazed some people. She went quiet too.

'I'd like to ask you about a private client account you have there.'

'I can't discuss our accounts with a total stranger.'

Hardball. Two can play at that.

'Then ring me back immediately at the LSE in London. Then you'll know you are talking to a regulatory official, not a total stranger.'

He hung up. Would she ring back? Most people did. He waited. She took her time. The phone finally rang.

'Hello, Mark. Penelope here. I had to make sure to whom I was talking. You appreciate that I can only answer limited questions. Client confidentiality is paramount here.'

'Do you had an account there for a Sarah Hart?'

She didn't need to trawl through her list. She knew her best clients well.

'Yes, I do.'

'Is her account operated in a satisfactory manner?'

'Yes, it is.'

Mark widened the scope of his investigation.

'What does Sarah Hart do for a living?'

'She has property interests in London.'

Too ruddy vague. Mark took a gamble.

'Has she ever mentioned a guy called Greg Schneider to you at all?'

'No, she hasn't.'

Dead end?

'Does Schneider have an account in Jersey too?'

Penelope was beginning to think that this LSE guy was well briefed on recent developments.

'Yes, he does. But it's a deposit account. He doesn't buy and sell any shares.'

'Are you sure? Maybe he has done so in the past?'

'I'm one hundred per cent sure.'

'How come?'

'He only opened the account with me here yesterday.'

'He was in Jersey yesterday?'

Penelope knew she had already said too much.

'Yes, yesterday. Listen, that's all I can say now. Goodbye.' She hung up rather abruptly.

There had to be more to this. Mark advised Norris immediately. He was of the same opinion.

'Get over to Jersey. Have a look at Sarah Hart's account. Talk to this account executive about what Schneider was doing there. Look at his account and let me know what happens.'

Ted Hammond arrived at Stratford police station and made straight for the back car park where he knew the Volvo estate was parked in an end lock-up garage. One of the forensic officers from the Met's specialist unit was finishing up, taking off white overalls and latex gloves. Ted was hoping for a lead.

'Any luck with the examination?'

The forensic guy was apathy personified.

'It's a perfectly normal vehicle. The inside is covered with fingerprints, as you'd imagine. Most are on the steering column and the dashboard but are too smudged to be of any use to us. There are better prints in the rear and by the lock to the boot. We have copies of Mr and Mrs Soames's prints and also those of their kids. There's no positive proof that anyone else was in the car recently. Maybe you're reading too much into the disappearance of this guy?'

Ted didn't have to take this sort of opinion from a junior officer.

'That may be your humble opinion but I can assure you that it's not shared by Mrs Soames. How about hair samples in the car?'

'Same result. A few greying gent's hairs that match the ones found on Soames's suit at home. A few hairs from Mrs Soames on the passenger seat. A few kids' hairs in the rear. Dead end otherwise.'

'Anything unusual left in the car?'

'No. We made a list of the contents and showed it to Mrs Soames. She recognised all the items.'

'So we're back to this missing front panel of the car stereo?'

'What?'

'It's not in the car. Didn't you notice that?'

He evidently hadn't. Some forensic specialist. But he agreed with Ted.

'That would be a real lead. Those security panels are unique. The codes in them are all one in a million shots. It would be easy to link the panel back to this car, and ultimately to Soames.'

The only problem was finding the item. Ted turned to leave in disgust and collided with a new DC from his station. The youngster was excited.

'Guv, we've been through Soames's personal records, bank accounts, mobile telephone and credit card bills. We got some new information from his bank about one of his current accounts. He used his cash card twice in an ATM an hour after he was last seen alive in the Dorchester.'

'Where and when?'

'Once on the Strand at 7.03 p.m. and then again at Tower Hill at 7.09 p.m.'

So Soames was indeed heading east towards Stratford. But twice in ten minutes?

'How much did he withdraw?'

'Two hundred and fifty quid at each machine.'

Ted was one step ahead of his less experienced colleague.

'See if there are any CCTV cameras on the ATMs. See how Soames behaved at the time. Was he alone?'

Why exactly does a guy take out five hundred quid in cash before going to the East End? Ted's first thoughts were of drugs. A deal to feed a secret habit? A lot of the players in the City were known to take a line now and then. They blamed the pressure and the stress. Nasty strung out types did drug dealing in the East End. Unpredictable at the best of times. Ted wasn't looking forward to his next visit to Helen Soames.

Greg's first instinct back in London was to go down to the Isle of Dogs and confront Sarah. She was buying and selling on inside information. He had been careful not to get discovered but he didn't know what a stupid bitch like her might have done. But real care was needed here. She brought in the clients, the recorded tapes, the knowledge, and the ideas for buying and selling shares. Those deals were his ticket out of Blakes. Someone would soon hire him elsewhere. He needed her so badly. He had to keep her sweet.

The telephone rang on the dealing desk. Chas shouted over to him.

'Greg, line three for you.'

He hit the flashing board and took the call immediately.

'Schneider speaking.'

'Good afternoon, Mr Schneider. Is this a good time to talk to you?'

This was it. Those magic words. They all knew them off by heart. A headhunter calling at last.

'No,' as he was required to say. They knew the secret code. Would the caller oblige with the next required line?

'Perhaps it would be better if we meet up this evening to talk?'

He did. He knew the code. Greg had to give short answers to stop others on the desk picking up on the nuances of this soon to be truncated conversation.

'Where?'

'Café Java. Liverpool Street station upper level. Five o'clock. I'll have a *Standard* open on the back sports pages.'

Greg hung up. Great choice. This guy must be good. Sometimes they chose stupid places to meet, like big noisy pubs and wine bars right in the midst of the Square Mile where the odds of bumping into someone else from Blakes was about five to one on. Yes. A trendy coffee bar with muted lighting was an inspired choice. This could be his chance to get out.

An hour later he left the office, crossed Bishopsgate, dodged the buses and other pedestrians and used the escalator to the upper level. The station was alive with rush hour commuters shuffling over the acres of gleaming white tiles on their way home to the safety of the suburbs. Café Java was situated towards the end of the upper concourse. It looked quiet. Perfect. Greg was five minutes late but that was to be expected. The headhunter would have been there since at least a quarter to five, staring at the same redundant sports page but taking nothing in, probably now on his third cappuccino. He had to arrive first. Otherwise it was considered seriously bad form.

A well-dressed man in his forties rose from a barstool and greeted Greg. He had the sort of firm handshake known only to real estate agents, former US marines and of course other headhunters. A stocky build, sharp suit and alert eyes. They moved over to a quiet table in the corner and ordered a cappuccino and a large espresso. No one within earshot. No faces they recognised. This was like a spy movie. The *Standard* was instantly discarded.

'The name's Nathaniel. You can call me Nat. I'm a freelance recruitment consultant in the City.'

Greg recognised another American accent. Sounded like a New Yorker too. They made small talk about living in London versus Manhattan until the oversized cups arrived courtesy of the Irish waitress. Nathaniel didn't look like he ever wasted time. Maybe he had three or four clandestine meetings lined up this evening. He would overdose on caffeine.

'Greg, word is out on the streets, you're a star dealer.'

Greg didn't like to discourage this opinion. He shrugged.

'Everyone knows about your big Provident position. Is it true you made five million pounds for Blakes in those shares in the past month?'

Hey. The guy was overdoing it but the less said the better. It was only two million so far. Only?

'Thereabouts, I guess. What's a few million between friends?'

'So what's a dealer like you doing working in a sleepy place like Blakes?'

Greg threw him the line Nathaniel really wanted to hear.

'Waiting for a better offer from someone like you, of course.'

They both laughed nervously. Nathaniel knew that merely by agreeing to meet, Greg had signalled he was mobile. Now he was giving out definite signals. Nathaniel could see his fee for this placement in his wallet already.

'I am retained by one of the most prestigious investment banks in the world.'

They always said that. Who was it? Greg needed to know. Fast.

'My client has an equities dealing desk, massive position limits, piles of capital to invest, great people but they need more expertise on the UK equity side. They like what they hear about you in the *FT* and the *Standard*. Money is no object to them. They are willing to pay you an extra hundred k over your Blakes' basic salary, whatever that is. And they will guarantee you a one hundred per cent bonus next year.'

Great offer. The guaranteed bonus was the sweetener. Even if Greg had a crap year and made no money at all, perish the thought, then he was certain to get his salary in a lump sum all over again at year-end. Ideal. But he still didn't know the identity of the mystery investment bank. Would it be a big German name or a Japanese house or a French place? Time to find out.

'Who's the bank?'

Nathaniel winced. The nerve of this guy, asking the big question so early on. All the dealers were pushy. This was the card that he held closest to his chest and this guy was asking him to play it early. Too early. Yet he had to hook Schneider. This was a big deal he couldn't afford to blow.

'The bank in question is Goldman Sachs.'

He'd expected a reaction from Greg but none came. He persevered.

'I don't have to tell you that they're the global players. The very best. What do you say?'

Greg tried to bluff it out.

'I don't really see myself as a Goldman's person. It's a strange culture there. I've heard some bad things about the place. I'm not that keen on moving there.'

Nathaniel couldn't believe it. That was all there was to it? This guy was going to turn down the offer of a lifetime in an instant. Or was he?

'Greg, is this an opening gambit? Are you bullshitting me? Because if so we can do an even better deal. Do you want a Carrera or a TVR, something flash like that?'

'No. I don't want this opportunity. Thanks all the same.'

He rose, shook hands and left. Nathaniel sat, empty cup in hand, wondering where he had gone wrong. No one ever turned down an invitation like this. He must be losing his touch. How would he break the news to the millionaire partner at Goldmans who was already clearing desk space for Schneider in anticipation of his imminent arrival?

Greg was gutted. It had sounded so promising initially. If only it had been a European bank, not one from the US. Then it would have been a job worth taking to get out of Blakes and away from Old Nick's probing. But a US investment bank was no good to him at all. He could never work with a US bank again. Not after what happened at the last one in New York. He needed a drink.

Barbara looked for Greg on the dealing floor but there was no sign of him. Chas sat alone at the end of the bank of screens, feet up on the edge, belly too, tired eyes glued to today's page three. He had drawn the late shift. She couldn't ask him about Greg. That would be too obvious, even to someone as intellectually stunted as Chas. She might as well take out a full-page advertisement in *The Times* and announce the relationship to the entire world. It would be news to all except Old Nick. Greg must be at home in NW8.

She walked the few hundred yards from the office to the mainline station. She must have trod this pavement a million times. Outside Liverpool Street she saw a familiar figure up ahead. He brushed past slower commuters and dodged oncomers. That great male frame. That confident walk. The drive. It was her man in person, still in the City. She ran with difficulty in her high heels to catch him before he descended the incessant escalators into the manic pit of Network South East at rush hour.

But instead he turned right and into Hamilton's, a pub never frequented by Blakes' stars. It was too much of a depressing spit-on-the-floor place to be seen dead in, being more suited to back-office and finance folk than the players in dealing and research. Barbara stood inside the open door, taking in the stench of warm bitter and watched him from afar. He leant against the bar, ordered what looked like a neat shot of Jack Daniel's, threw his head back and downed it in one gulp. He looked stressed. Anxious. Strange on the day that Provident came into play and soared. He ordered a second immediately. Down again. She was amazed at his consumption.

'Greg.'

He turned around, so safe in this wonderfully anonymous pub.

'Barbara.' He was lost for words. It doesn't often happen with a big swinging dealer.

'What are you doing here, Greg?'

'I'm . . . I'm meeting someone.'

'Who?'

'Some friends.'

'Which friends?'

'You don't know them.'

Very evasive. There must be more to this. He didn't seem to want to tell her more.

'Well, then?'

'Well, what?'

'Are you going to buy me a drink?'

He was relieved to redirect the conversation.

'Sure. Whad'ya want?'

'A bottle of Becks. With a glass.'

They sat on adjoining bar stools amidst the smoky haze. This was truly a disgusting place.

'What made you come here? What's wrong with the Bull & Bear?'

He shrugged his shoulders.

'Look at Provident go. Everyone knows. You should be in good form today.'

'So I should.'

She probed.

'I haven't seen you drinking Jack Daniel's like that before.'

'Like what?'

'So fast.'

'This is my first. There's nothing wrong with that. I'm not a goddamn alcoholic, you know.'

Lies. Change this conversation. Fast.

'So what sort of day did you have, Barb?'

'An awful day.'

'Why?'

'Old Nick had a go at me about you and I, about confidentiality and Chinese Walls at Blakes.'

Greg didn't seem interested.

'Yeah, he had a go at me this morning too. But I didn't take any crap from him.'

'Nick spoke to you this morning?'

'Yeah. So?'

'So, you could have warned me. It came as a real shock. Nick almost had me in tears.'

Greg deliberately avoided her accusing gaze. He looked back at the empty glass on the counter and wished he could order another shot.

All she needed to hear was some sort of an apology. One word would do. It never came.

CHAPTER SIXTEEN

TERMINAL 1, HEATHROW AIRPORT

This was a real treat for Mark, his first trip on business anywhere in his time at the London Stock Exchange. The morning tube ride out to Heathrow was cheap and definitely quicker than the expensive luxury of a black cab amongst the combative traffic of West London. Norris would appreciate the three-pound fifty tube fare over a thirty-pound cab fare.

The staff at the check-in handed him a boarding card with the words Executive Class printed boldly on the front. He only had an economy class ticket. That was the prudent cost-conscious LSE policy. The relaxed girl behind the counter said there were lots of free seats in business class this morning. Mark was in a good suit. He looked smart and pleasant. He was, as they say, suitable for upgrade, and it all came courtesy of Jersey European Airways. Enjoy.

He boarded the 9.30 a.m. flight in the company of groups of holidaying pensioners. They were excited at the prospect of a trip to the sun with no long haul travel involved. He carried some of their hand baggage down the airbridge and helped a fragile couple find their seats in the middle of the plane.

His last flight had been a year ago on a lad's trip to Ibiza. They had flown out on Go, BA's discount airline. One of his inebriated mates had asked a stewardess if the plane would be called Return on the way home. Sometimes on his holidays he wondered why the crew couldn't spice up the repetitive cabin announcements before takeoff or after landing. How about after takeoff, 'Anyone found smoking in the lavatory will be asked to leave the aircraft immediately.' Or, 'There are fifty ways to leave your lover but only four ways to leave this aircraft.' Or after landing, 'Please take care when opening the overhead compartments because sure as hell everything has shifted.' Or, 'Please gather your belongings as you leave since anything left behind will be distributed evenly among the crew.' Or at disembarkation 'Thanks for flying with us today and join us next time you feel the insane urge to go blasting through the skies in a pressurised metal tube.' But he had always wanted to ask the crew as he exited after a particularly bad landing, 'Did we land or were we shot down?'

Mark savoured the wonderful business class service. A complimentary copy of *The Times* allowed him to catch up on news in the City. Provident shares were up another ten pence. The seat next to him was empty and he enjoyed the space amongst the luxurious leather. He started with the sparkling bucks fizz proffered on a silver tray and had seconds when the crew spotted a half-empty glass. He downed the full English breakfast including the bubble and squeak on the side, polished off the croissants and pastries, took refills of coffee and freshened up with a hot towel afterwards.

He spent the last ten minutes of the flight looking through the ever-growing Provident file. He had the dealing printouts from Blakes, he had Sarah Hart's account number verbatim and he had a list of questions jotted down on a single page of his legal pad. Who was Sarah Hart? How did she operate her account? Did she make money? Did she know Greg Schneider? Why was Schneider in the Jersey office earlier this week? He hoped that Penelope Swales would have all the answers for him. She had sounded amenable over the telephone. Maybe that was the sales person in her?

They covered the hundred and seventy miles from Britain in under an hour. Jersey looked wonderful from the air. The northern coast was protected from the sea by huge granite cliffs. In contrast golden beaches dominated the southern coast between lush green countryside and clear blue sea water. The ebullient atmosphere on the plane was almost contagious as several of the veteran holidaymakers voluntarily clapped with joy as the wheels skidded onto the hot tarmac.

Mark had done his research, it being a hazard of his job. Jersey. Nine by five miles; 85,000 inhabitants living on an island world-renowned for its rich cream, Jersey Royal potatoes, flowers, fine restaurants and twenty miles of great beaches. Eighty banks housed eighty billion sterling deposited on the island in cash and investments. No VAT. Income tax was a mere twenty per cent. There were more millionaires per square mile here than anywhere else in Britain, even in the City, evident in the many J-reg Rolls Royces driven by tax exiles and celebrities. You needed a minimum of eighteen million quid in liquid assets to become a resident. No worries.

The airport was small and friendly and much easier to negotiate than the dark warrens and mile long hikes of Heathrow. He took a taxi which set off in accordance with the rather tame forty mile an hour speed limit on the island.

'Blake Brothers Bank please. In St Helier.'

Penelope was more accustomed to ingratiating herself with monied types with excess loot to deposit or to spend. She welcomed her regulatory visitor as best she could but it still required an initial effort. She had set aside the minimum time in her diary for this intrusion, since there was nothing in it for her. Or was there?

Robinson made a pleasant change from her regular visitors. Well, he was under forty for a start, probably about the same age as herself as they both approached that dangerous thirty-year milestone. He was good looking in an unconventional, almost roguish way. Warm friendly blue eyes. He sat confidently in his regency chair. Good build too, maybe five eleven in height. Perfect. Three inches taller than her. Well matched.

Her early reconnaissance revealed that her man from the LSE did not wear a wedding ring. Perhaps like herself he was still searching for that elusive life partner. She was distracted when they shook hands as she spent the first minute deciding whether or not it was worth flirting with him. Yes. It probably was. She subconsciously fingered the top pearl button of her collarless blouse.

Mark was sure that his host had loosened an additional top button on her blouse. He couldn't be absolutely sure but he didn't think that it had been open so low when he had first arrived. He would have noticed. She was idly playing with a single strand of curly hair that dangled by her matching pearl earrings. This was distracting. He had to appear more interested in work, rather than in the temptation personified before him. Norris would expect that at the very least.

'Thanks for agreeing to see me, Penelope.'

'No problem, Mark.' And it truly wasn't. 'Call me Penny. Do you have any identification so I know that you are who you say you are? For the record, of course.'

Her voice was even better in person than over the telephone yesterday.

'Sure,' as he made for the his LSE identity card. He always kept it in the inside pocket of his wallet. There was a photograph on the laminated card that always reassured doubters. It wasn't a great posed photo, more like that of a seasickness victim, but he hoped she wouldn't be put off by it. Damn. The card wasn't in his wallet. Where the hell was it? It must be back in London somewhere. He had last used it in one of the banks he had visited. Maybe it was just as well. Skip the photograph.

She wouldn't be impressed at his fumbling. Time for decisive action. He offered her his LSE business card. He liked the way she held it in her manicured hands and ran a finger over the embossed letters of his name, as if in some way validating his presence before her. This office was getting hot.

'Where do you want to start, Mark?'

All this first name stuff. Very informal and friendly. Was it a come on or was she using all the means at her disposal to unnerve him and his investigation today? Hard to tell. Mark could have given her a dozen loaded responses to her inquiry but he chose the work-related response.

'I'd like to see Sarah Hart's file and her account statements.'

She made for the corner and leant against the filing cabinet. Her navy skirt rose over her knees and revealed a perfect form. Great calves. This was hard work, thought Mark. Stay focussed. She found the file and opened it on the desk. She sat down again. Now all he could see was the waist up. Like Barbara on Sky TV. Pity.

Penelope was puzzled. The account opening form with the client name and address was at the front of the file. She'd never looked at that form after day one. Someone else had looked at this file recently. But there was no need to bother her visitor with this detail.

Mark was lost in more carnal matters. Concentrate. As the supermodel said to the carton of orange juice. They made direct eye contact across the narrow desk. Two feet away maximum. Her *parfum* was wonderful. They were on the same wavelength.

Mark made some notes as they turned the pages together. He jotted down the address of Sarah Hart in E14. It might be worth a visit some time to see what sort of a place she had given all that wealth.

The Provident shares he had seen on the Blakes' London printout were there, very much in the money today. She had some call options on Provident too. Mark deduced that she was a sophisticated investor since she knew about these more exotic instruments. They always joked back in the LSE about the legal definition of a sophisticated investor. Peter said that it was someone who existed solely on Bolly, smoked salmon and beluga caviar. Possibly.

There were a few other investments. Hart had bought and sold County Beverages shares very recently for a quick profit and had also bought some Sportsworld shares. She had 100k in UK gilts, 80k in cash, some UK privatisation issues and mutual funds. A tidy sum indeed. Time to ask some searching questions.

'I take it that you've met this Sarah Hart. What's she like?'

Mark had visions of a stooped widow in her sixties with calcium-deficient limbs. Not so.

'Mid-thirties, confident, pushy even at times, demanding about having her account instructions carried out to the letter, very keen on confidentiality, no mail, a flashy dresser, likes wearing black a lot, English, affected London accent, business like.'

'Does she visit here?'

'She comes over every few months.'

Mark looked at the file again.

'She signed the new account form with a London address. Is there anything else in writing from her? Any correspondence, faxes or e-mails at all?'

'No, she never puts pen to paper. She always calls late and leaves a voice mail message on the phone for me to act on next day.'

No clues there. Mark tried a different approach.

'You said yesterday she has property. Is that where her funds come from?'

'Yes. From rental income. That's what she said when she brought the cash here.'

'Cash?'

Penny wished she hadn't mentioned that. Cash lodgements always alarmed the more prudent types.

'Yes. She makes cash lodgements with us. It's all on the statements. They are under our twenty-five thousand reporting threshold.'

Mark went down the pages. He could see the statement credits. Ten k, fifteen, twenty.

'So does she make good profits in her account?'

Penelope deliberated while glancing through the recent history on file.

'Yes, she's an astute investor. I don't give her any specific investment ideas. She always gets them herself. She seems to buy and sell at the right time.'

That didn't come out the way she'd meant to say it. They both knew that no one wins all the time. Then the killer question.

'Are you happy with the conduct of her account?'

Followed by the killer answer.

'Yes, Mark, I am.'

'Fine, then give me a copy of the contents of her file to take back with me to London.'

She was uneasy but felt she had no choice with the man from the LSE. Gabrielle, the PA, returned on demand and headed off for the nearest photocopier, file in hand. Mark moved on to the next topic.

'Let's discuss Greg Schneider.'

Penelope feigned disinterest.

'There's not much to discuss. He came here two days ago, opened a cash account and left.'

'What do you make of him?'

This account executive was definitely feisty. Alluringly so. Mark was wondering how well she knew Schneider. If this was the way she teased regulators, imagine the reception she gave ex-pat dealers with a big wallet and a bigger sex drive. She leant forward.

'He's like any other City dealer. Loud, brash, demanding, opinionated.'

'You mean, he's a total bastard.'

'Precisely,' she smiled. They were definitely bonding.

'Has Hart ever mentioned Schneider at all to you?'

'You asked me that question on the phone. I've already answered it.'

True enough. She was sharp. Good memory too. An apparent dead-end.

'Did Schneider mention Hart when he was here?'

Penelope was thinking back to Hart's file. She wasn't happy. Someone had been through the file. It wasn't Gabrielle. She knew she would be fired for less. Penelope had been out for a long lunch the day Greg Schneider had shown up, and then sex for afters back at her place. But this wasn't the time to volunteer her suspicions to a total stranger. A desirable stranger all the same.

'No, he didn't mention her.'

A definite dead-end. Mark knew what to do next. Go back to London. Regroup. Get Schneider's dealing account for recent months. Compare it to Hart's account statements. See if there was a pattern, any connection at all. Maybe even also get out his battered mark-one VW Golf and take a drive down to Thames View for a curious look.

'You've been very helpful, Penelope.'

This was the moment of decision for her. Mark wasn't a Blakes' client and never would be. He didn't earn as much in his civil service type job as she did in her banking job. He might never return to Jersey in her lifetime. They might never get a chance to meet up again. She had the expense account and the corporate credit card to play with. An eligible American male visitor had turned her down once already this week. Surely she couldn't fail a second time?

'How about lunch before you leave?'

They sat on the upstairs stone terrace of a restaurant overlooking the bay. The view from the top of the sea wall was a million miles away from the City of London. The stone edifice of Elizabeth Castle shimmered in the distance against still water. Children with parents in tow ambled along the unspoilt sands below. Billowing yellow striped canopies protected the diners from the harsh midday rays that reflected off the pristine white tablecloths. The onshore breeze gently ruffled Penelope's hair.

The wineglasses were heavy, the cutlery silver-plated and the napkins real linen. This was a classy place. The staff on the door had been as snooty as possible when they had arrived, as required in Michelin-starred places. Mark didn't know what he had done to deserve this. The maitre'd evidently knew Penelope.

'Miss Swales, very good to see you again. And a very nice choice too, if I may say so.'

Nice choice? Did he mean this restaurant, this particular table, a Kir Royale as an apéritif or her choice of dining partner today? Mark hoped for the latter. The menu was extensive.

'What's good locally, Penelope?'

Apart from you that is.

'I like the fish here. Fresh this morning from the harbour. Easy on the palate too.'

They were spoilt for choice. Ravioli of lobster, fresh seared scallops, crab salad in the shell, sole on the bone and chargrilled seabass. Penelope saw his gastronomic indecision and she ordered for both of them, anticipating his every need. Almost. The sommelier hovered with the wine list, unsure as to which of the diners would accept it. Penelope did the prompting again.

'Your call, Mark.'

'Well, we need a white. How about a Chablis?'

Exactly what she would have chosen to complement the assorted *fruits de mer* for two. The latter arrived soon afterwards on a silver platter, overflowing with shells and claws. They worked industriously together on the fish. Mark had the last mussel. Penelope had the last oyster. God. The way she eased it out of the shell and then down between her lips was almost too much to watch. He'd love to be that mollusc.

They didn't discuss work. Neither of them dared to, nor were they interested. Instead they concentrated on the best things in life. Penelope spoke from experience, Mark more from aspiration. They had a pistachio parfait with Jersey ice cream for dessert, both sharing the wondrous guilt of a sweet tooth.

Two hours passed effortlessly until the waiter hovered again with another dilemma of his chosen trade, unsure to whom to give the bill. The lady or the gentleman? Penelope obliged with the corporate platinum. Mark could see from his seat that the bill was well over a hundred quid including the compulsory tip. A lot more money than a meal for two in the LSE canteen.

'Next time it's on me, Penelope.' He wondered if she'd even heard of Prêt á Manger.

'I'll hold you to that. Will it be London or Jersey?'

'Dunno. It depends where work takes me, I suppose.' All this business flying could be addictive. Well, one flight to date.

Time was running out. His return flight left in an hour. She saw his anxiety.

'Don't worry about your flight.' Was this an invitation to stay longer in Jersey? Perhaps even stay on in that hillside pad she had proudly pointed out on the way here from Blake's office? Nope.

'There is another one an hour later.'

She smiled in the knowledge that this had been one of the most entertaining lunches for a long time. Was it because she wasn't talking about the FTSE, gilt yields, offshore tax shelters, dividend income and dollar currency conversions? Or was it because the personable young man at the table had not once mentioned a steady girlfriend in the past two hours of easy conversation. She rounded off the meal with the only work-related anecdote of their brief encounter. His mention of flying had prompted it.

'The other day I met a wealthy Arab who flew here to discuss his US T-bond holdings and how to maximise his coupon income. I asked him when his flight left. He said it left whenever he told his pilot.'

Mark liked that. Yes, he would see her again. Somewhere.

CHAPTER SEVENTEEN

OLD BROAD STREET, LONDON EC2

Mark sat on the opposite side of the table in Norris's cramped office.

'So how did it go in Jersey? Was it worth the expense of a day trip?'

He assumed that his boss didn't want to hear about the business class upgrade or the long lazy lunch overlooking the harbour.

'This Sarah Hart character is a successful investor. She has about half a million quid in shares and her portfolio is growing all the time. She made some great money recently on FTSE shares and listed call options. Yesterday on my way back to Heathrow, I called Pete on the mobile and asked him to have a look at the timings of her purchases and sales. He told me this morning that she's an uncanny investor. Truly inspired, Pete says.'

'In what way?'

'She always buys shares before some good news is announced, like a big interim profits hike or a bullish trading statement from the board, or a great corporate deal or a mega-takeover, like in the case of Provident. Or else she sells shares before bad news breaks. She's wasted owning property on the Isle of Dogs. She should be on a City dealing desk.'

'Maybe she is something in the City?' inquired Norris.

'No. I checked with our Registration Department. They don't show her listed as a dealer or a salesperson at any bank in the City. Either now or in the past. She doesn't seem to have a day job at all, but has some London property interests which produce cash rental income.'

Norris saw his frustration.

'There's no law against being independently wealthy, Mark.'

Sometimes Mark wished there was. More to go around for the rest of them.

'I know but . . .'

'But you don't like what you see?'

'Correct. I talked with her account executive, Penelope Swales. There's no proof on Hart's files at Blakes of any property being owned. She lodges cash to her account. She turns up every month or so with ten or twenty grand in crisp notes. Blakes don't like cash much but they take her word as to the source. They have an internal cash limit imposed by their Compliance Department. They won't accept more than twenty-five grand in cash at any one time. Hart is always under that limit, so Swales doesn't need to tell her London Compliance department about it.'

Norris tried another line of attack.

'And do you still think that the dealer in Blakes knows Hart?'

'Yes. He definitely recognised something about her account when I was last at Blakes. He visited Jersey the day after I met with him to open an account. I'm wondering why out of all the private client account executives in the office there, some much more experienced, he picks the same Penny Swales to manage his account.'

Mark was calling her Penny. Very informal. They had indeed got on well.

'Why did Schneider open the account? Is he buying and selling shares in his personal account?'

'No. He lodged five k in a cheque drawn on Nat West in Bishopsgate.'

'Small change for him, I'd say. It's a long way to travel when the mail would do just as well.'

'That's what I'm thinking. It doesn't feel right.'

'So what are you going to do next?' asked Norris.

'I'm going to return to Blakes and have a look at Schneider's dealing over the past few months. See if he is dealing in the same shares as Hart and making the same excellent money. Maybe they are doing something together? I've already asked for a report of his dealing from Ingrams at Blakes.'

Norris gave Mark a reassuring look as if he felt his pupil was learning from the expert.

'That's exactly what I would do, Mark. Visit Blakes. Annoy Schneider. Give him a scare.'

Greg had a revolutionary idea for any dealer in the City. He needed to lose some money. Badly. Fast.

The recent confrontations with Old Nick, the great Provident profits soon to be realised upon completion of the takeover after the increasingly dirty battle, and the inter-day profit on County Beverages, all weighed heavily on his mind. He hadn't seen the light before but now it was obvious. He was too good at his job. Others were asking questions. A decent dealing loss on a big position would show that he was human, fallible and normal. Like the others at dealing desks in Blakes and around the City.

He knew a good way to lose money. Take a sure thing, a one-way bet. Easy. The Sportsworld plc results were due out today. He had the tape from that basement encounter with Simon Fry. Sportsworld were about to buy out a big competitor for a song, then they would dominate the sports retailing business. Swarup Amir was no dumb ass. Sportsworld shares were heading north and the announcement must come today with the interim profits statement. The SEAQ company announcements screen said the results were due out at 2.30 p.m. Enough time to lay some smoke first.

'Chas, what about a mega deal today?'

Chas did not look enthused at the prospect of any incremental work above doing absolutely nothing.

'Jesus, Greg, give it a rest. How can you think about anything today other than Provident?'

'Provident is a done deal. It's history. Toast. We gotta move on to the next killing. Be ahead of the game, Chas. That's the way to make serious bucks. Do you know who's announcing interims this afternoon?'

'Lots of companies. Anyone I should know about?'

'Sportsworld, Chas. We're sitting on ten million quid of the stock. What do we do? Sell or hold?'

Chas had no idea. He fudged the issue again.

'I guess if we are in doubt then we hold?'

'What if the results are really crap and the stock price tumbles? The prices of this designer sports gear are falling, your quaint football season is long over so people aren't buying those expensive club shirts any more and there's acres of bad press about the underage locals in Far East sweatshops paid fuck all for making branded gear for Western sports clothing multi-nationals. If Sportsworld's results are less than good, the stock price could take a hammering today.'

'Then let's sell them all damn quick, Greg.'

'On the other hand, Sportsworld are dominating the high street, their market share is rising, they've opened twenty plus new stores since last year and their head honcho, Swarup Amir, is publicly bullish about the company he's taken this far in such a short period of time.'

Chas was all over the place. Indecision personified.

'Jesus, don't do this to me, Greg. Then let's buy some more shares.'

There was no competition at the desk. Good news from Sportsworld was on the way and the only sure way to forego his profit was to sell all of the Sportsworld position as soon as possible.

'My gut feeling is to dump the lot of them. But I'll tell you what we'll do, Chas. Let's take a gamble. Here's a dime. Heads we shift Sportsworld. Tails we stay long. OK?'

The others at the desk stood up. Even Jules and Henry were surprised.

'You can't be serious, Greg?'

He was. Greg tossed the coin in the air and caught it in one fluid motion. He revealed the coin in his open palm. Jules and Henry saw it too. Heads it was.

'Right, we sell. But I've got an even better idea. Let's double up on the ante. Sell the stock we got and then sell the same amount over again that we haven't got. Let's take a short position of ten million. We'll buy back the stock cheaper this afternoon and take our profit.'

Greg put the double-sided coin back into his pocket for the next time. Chas objected.

'No, Greg. Going short is too risky.'

'That's why we are here. Battle stations, people. Let's sell twenty million quid of Sportsworld now.'

Chas, Jules and Henry did their best in the next ninety seconds and then they were all done.

'Do you feel like an early lunch, Chas, before the announcement later today? A swift half of bitter included, as you guys say.'

'Greg, I couldn't eat anything now, let alone down a pint. My stomach's churning over. I think I'm gonna throw up chunks over this SEAQ screen.'

Greg left on his own, safe in the knowledge that Sportsworld were going to announce a great corporate deal, the share price would rise, he would have to square his short position by buying back the shares at the higher price that afternoon, all leading to a big loss that would incense Old Nick yet leave a cold trail for the suspicious few in Blakes. And in the LSE. Perfect.

*   *   *

Mark entered the lobby of Blakes by late morning, but this time he knew where he was going. Ingrams rose from behind his cluttered desk in the Compliance Department, this time looking distinctly uneasy at the return of the man from the LSE whom he had hoped never to see again. Nothing personal of course.

'Mr Robinson, I didn't expect you back so soon.'

'Me neither.' No time for small talk. 'Do you have the listing I asked for?'

'Sure.'

This time Ingrams was better prepared. He instantly produced a twenty-page computer printout. It bore definite signs of having been perused in advance, crease marks, corners thumbed, the odd tear along the edges. Mark deduced that Ingrams had already reviewed the Special Situations desk dealing account that morning, but he evidently still didn't know exactly what Mark wanted.

'What are you looking for in this account? Is this still about Provident?'

Provident was now one piece of the jigsaw. There was more to this and the evidence proved Mark right as he turned the pages detailing the recent buys and sells in the dealing account. There were the stocks. Sportsworld. County Beverages. The same stocks that appeared in Hart's offshore account. The dates of the share purchases were almost identical in the two accounts. No need to alarm Ingrams yet.

'I'm looking to see if there are any dealing patterns here.'

Ingrams was getting smarter.

'I would imagine all dealing accounts have patterns. Otherwise the guys wouldn't be successful dealers?'

'Exactly. Can I see Greg Schneider again?'

'Is that necessary?'

'Yes.'

'When do you want to see him?'

'Now. It will save me making another visit later.'

Ingrams phoned Old Nick first. He needed his approval. No reply. A temp secretary picked up the call. Her boss was out for lunch. He tried Schneider directly but he was out of the office also. He couldn't put Mark off forever. Time to stall.

'Sure. We'll arrange for you to meet him. How about some lunch first?'

It would be impolite to refuse the invitation. The salubrious top floor executive restaurant at Blakes beckoned. This dining experience upped the count to two free lunches on Blakes in the week so far. Not bad going for an investigator more used to the grease and stodge of the LSE canteen.

They sat at the dealing desk counting the minutes to the Sportsworld interim profits announcement. Chas was visibly agitated. Jules chewed her nails. Hooray made paper airplanes from research notes. Greg slouched in the high-backed chair with his polished black leather uppers on the edge of the desk, safe in the knowledge of the events that were about to transpire at 2.30 p.m. Chinese Dentist Time as they always said.

Then disaster. Greg could see two men walking across the floor towards his desk. That useless Head of Compliance approached, the guy who gave them lectures every few months on some irrelevant legalistic subject and distributed inane Compliance memoranda that were also converted by disinterested dealers into streamlined inter-galactic fighter planes. Ingrams looked hassled. Having failed to track down Old Nick, he was about to bring an unwanted visitor onto the ever-sensitive dealing floor without the Director's prior agreement. It could be fatal for all concerned. He knew as much.

Greg saw the second man. A face he immediately recognised. That bastard from the LSE was back on his dealing floor and Ingrams was responsible for this visit.

'Greg, Mark Robinson is back and wants to talk to you again.'

He rose from his vertebrae-damaging position in his seat and faked a welcome of sorts.

'Sure thing. Grab a seat there, Mark.'

Mark gave Ingrams a long look, along the lines of, Thanks, I'm OK on my own, now please bugger off and leave us. Ingrams took the subtle hint and exited stage left.

'What do you want this time, Mark?'

This time. The loaded innuendo. The dealer was annoyed already. Perfect.

'I'd like to ask you about some other shares you have dealt in.'

'Such as? Gimme an example.'

'Shares like County Beverages, a few weeks ago. What made you buy then?'

This intruder was pissing Greg off. Time to be flippant.

'I like their beer and their ice cream.'

'And that's it?'

'Yep. If I like them, then most people like them. Then they sell lots and make more profit and the stock price goes up. Mark, let me lay it out clearly for you. There's no secret to this, no magic formula. We are well-paid gamblers and we're on a roll at the moment. The fact that the market is bullish and the Footsie is at an all-time high helps us a lot too. But we could lose money in the rest of the year.'

Mark was frustrated. He needed some hard evidence. Anything. He prepared to utter his next careful question but stocky Chas blatantly cut in, evidently keen to place their detested guest in his rightful secondary position and instead focus attention on the more important topic of their dealing profits.

'One minute to go, guys. Ready or not.'

Mark was puzzled.

'One minute to go to what?'

Reality dawned for Greg. He couldn't have scripted it better. This asshole from the LSE was investigating his dealing profits. Twice in two weeks too. Greg was making loads of bucks every few weeks. This odious LSE guy was suspicious. And now, in a mere sixty seconds time, Greg was about to lose a shedful of glorious loot and this guy sitting beside him was watching it all real time. Thank Christ for that.

'There's one minute to go until Sportsworld announce their interim profits.'

Mark thought he knew the desk's position from the dealing printout before him.

'Your desk is long ten million sterling of Sportsworld shares?'

'You are incorrect.' God, Greg enjoyed uttering those words. 'That was the case this morning. We have since taken a decidedly bearish view. We're not convinced about the medium-term prospects for Sportsworld so we went short in size this morning. We sold twenty and we are short a net ten mil. We need some bad interim results so we can buy back into Sportsworld immediately.'

That's the theory, folks, but it sure as hell ain't gonna happen in reality. Guaranteed.

'Here comes the announcement now on SEAQ,' obliged Chas.

They waited. No conversation. All eyes on the flashing screens as the digital clock ticked onto 2.30 p.m.

'Sportsworld announce interim profits up twenty-one per cent,' advised Chas, needlessly demonstrating his ability to read the announcement that they could all see on the foot of their screens.

No big surprise there. Great profit growth as predicted by Barbara and the research gurus. The market wouldn't react much. The price of 104 pence was unchanged. They were breaking even at current price levels. What else did Chas have to say? wondered Greg. As if he didn't know.

'Hold it. Sportsworld announces an acquisition.'

Tell us anyway, Chas.

'They are buying their arch-rival high street competitor, Classic Sports, in an agreed takeover deal.'

Yep. That basement sure was a great place to make quality tape recordings. But there were no smiles on the dealing desk. They knew that if the feared competitor was being swallowed up, it was good news for Sportsworld. The share price would surely rise. The desk team would be paying more this afternoon to get back to a square position. They would lose money. Loss. That awful word.

They turned to look at Greg who struggled to appear as if he shared their disappointment. He faked a resigned look, suppressing the elation inside. The guy from the LSE was two feet away and registered his disappointment. I'm only human. I lose too. Leave me alone. Then Chas broke the bad news.

'The acquisition will cost a hundred million and be financed by a rights issue at seventy-five pence a share.'

They paused, thinking over the implications. A hundred million was a lot of money for a small retail business and a rights issue truly sucked. Sportsworld had some cash and surely could have borrowed more, but they had gone for an easy rights issue instead. Make the shareholders stump up at a big discount to the market. They wondered whether their bearish views were shared on other dealing desks in the City?

The SEAQ quotes screen for Sportsworld flashed red. The mid-price was heading south. From 104 pence before the announcement it was fast approaching a pound even. Their peers had independently confirmed their views. This was a crap deal for Sportsworld. The price touched 99 pence. They had sold their shares at 104 pence this morning. They were up five pence a share on ten million quids worth. Five hundred k of dealing profit waiting to be bagged. Euphoria erupted. Chas was ebullient.

'Fucking hell. Look at that share price, Greg. Sportsworld are being buried. Way to go.'

Mark was still sitting two feet away from Greg and he saw

it. It was momentary but significant. No doubt in his mind at all. The others were elated, bullish, adrenaline pumping, standing up. Greg by contrast was confused, puzzled, uncertain and sat on in his seat. His optimism sounded hollow, almost forced.

'Great. Then let's buy back at ninety-nine pence and square up our position. You guys do it. Hit those phones now. There must be dozens of market makers out there who are dying to unload Sportsworld shares.'

Mark was still watching Greg. It was obvious. This dealer had been expecting different news. He had made a half a million quid profit but he acted like he didn't want the filthy lucre. He didn't even want to make any of the calls himself and grind the face of some pushy market maker into the dirt. Strange behaviour from a City dealer. There must be more to Greg Schneider than met the eye. This investigation was only beginning. Chas got in the last line, as ever. Pity.

'Greg, we simply don't know how you do it.'

Sarah Hart didn't feel as enthused about seeing clients of late but she didn't mind this visit at all. He arrived punctually at five o'clock after he had finished his day's work. He entered the living room without a word, looking the part. Middle-aged, combed back greying hair, immaculate shave, dark suit with waistcoat, white starched shirt and narrow, neatly knotted striped tie. He left his briefcase by the door, took off his suit jacket, put on the pair of green rubber gloves and started.

The hoovering lasted ten minutes, including all the ground floor rooms. He did the kitchen floor with a wet mop, the pine furniture with a yellow duster and the inside of the rear windows with a chamois leather. He tackled the congealed grime on the kitchen worktops and the greasy hob and oven, then the humid bathroom interior and matching wall mirrors. Within the hour the place was sparkling, back to its best since his prior visit three weeks ago. Sarah sat on the couch in a smart black business suit with crossed sheer legs and high heels watching his every move around her home. That worked for him.

She didn't know his first name. He never offered it; she never asked. So she knew him by her own private nickname, the Mandarin. Not because he was Chinese, but because he'd once said that he worked in some government department in Whitehall. He talked about the stress at work, but never about his wife and why she evidently did not let him carry out his dark desires in their own home. The Mandarin always left his wedding ring on the coffee table before he put on the rubber gloves. He said that it might snag the wafer-thin rubber of the Marigolds. Sarah believed that it lessened the guilt of his frequent visits.

'Are you finished, boy?', as she was required to ask at the end.

'Yes, ma'am. I am finished.'

She walked into the kitchen to give it a cursory examination. She ran a pointed fingernail along the shining surfaces and faked some obvious satisfaction at the lack of dust, while throwing a simultaneous glance at the wall clock as the smaller hand edged towards six. His hour was up. Time to end the charade.

'Very good, boy. You have indeed finished your work.'

And that was it. He removed the rubber gloves. A bundle of notes appeared from his trouser pocket. He placed the cash beside the wedding ring on the table, then put the ring back on the relevant finger. Easy money again. He should have left but he lingered. She was in no rush. She had been paging through the business supplement of the *Standard*. The page with the latest news about the counter bid for Provident by Kapital was open. Conversation of some sort was inevitable. All they needed was the topic. The Mandarin could see the headline as he put on his jacket and felt the urge to talk to someone. Anyone other than his wife, who didn't understand his inner needs.

'That Provident deal will never happen.'

Sarah looked up, startled by his sudden opinion, and then feigned apparent disinterest.

'Why won't it?'

'No one will be buying Provident.'

She didn't wish to declare her own sizeable interest in the proceedings. So she let him carry on. He said too much.

'I've heard the Minister say that he'll never allow a bid to go through. We don't want any more bank mergers in the UK. They just mean job cuts and less consumer choice. He'll block the Kapital bid on some obscure European cross-border ruling. He doesn't want the Germans buying any more of our banks. The Minister says that blocking the bid will be a good vote winner. He's from Bristol where a lot of constituents will keep their jobs.'

Sarah contemplated the worst case scenario and expressed fake naivety.

'And what will happen to Provident then?'

'Word will spread out of Whitehall to the City via the Old Boy network after a cosy lunch of Dover sole and Chardonnay in Bill Bentleys. The share price will plunge.'

He had said enough. He picked up his briefcase to go, closing the hall door behind him. It never ceased to amaze Sarah how small a place London was and how the right information was available if you knew the right people and engaged in the right bizarre pseudo-sexual practices. The Mandarin wasn't only a client; he was a friend who had now given her some excellent financial advice.

Sarah had too much to lose if this all went wrong. She dialled an overseas telephone number, albeit in the knowledge that her specific private client executive would have left the office by six o'clock. She was greeted by the answering machine. She left her all-important instruction for the next business day.

'Penelope. It's Sarah Hart here. Sell all my Provident shares and options at the best price at the open tomorrow morning.

Leave the cash proceeds in my account until further notice. Thanks.'

London was insufferable. Eighty-four degrees today according to the *ES* front page. Barbara's late evening tube ride from the City to St John's Wood was hell on wheels. Packed train carriages, unwarranted delays at stations, mysterious stoppages in humid tunnels, gasps for stale air out of open sliding doors, and stinking male hormonal BO all around. Not a civil gentleman in sight willing to offer a seat to a girl after a demanding thirteen-hour day. The only consolation was that Greg had left long before the Sky crew had arrived in order to get home before her.

She opened his front door with her own key and heard the water running in the over-sized bath made for two. They both enjoyed this well-practised and optimal solution to the remains of the day. She peeled off the grime and sweat of what used to be a smart suit and pushed open the door to the bathroom. He stood in only a pair of boxers and immediately gave her a long kiss.

'I'm nearly ready, Barb. Do you want the added extras tonight?'

She nodded and smiled in anticipation.

'Then you do the music and lights. I'll grab two snipes from the fridge. Then we're all set.'

He held her close as he brushed past to go to the well-stocked kitchen. Meanwhile, she lit the entire row of assorted scented candles and dimmed the recessed lights to create a subtler ambience.

'What sort of music do you want wafting through the apartment, Greg?'

'Whatever you like. Surprise me.'

She tried to negotiate the impossible mega hi-fi system in the living room. Damn. Boys like their toys. It was all dials, lights and switches. More knobs here than at a Royal Wedding. Cables and wires down the back like Spaghetti Junction. Who needed a graphic equaliser, auto-synchro editing and Dolby quadraphonic surround-sound anyway?

She tried a few of the buttons in the vain hope that a CD would kick in. Any CD. Nothing. Some more buttons. Capital FM boomed back. Doctor Fox at large. Hard rock. Too much for the erotic occasion at hand. She eyed the rows of CDs with some inner satisfaction. Half of them were her own. Always a good sign in a relationship. More buttons. One of the twin tape decks suddenly opened and a tape lay there. There was a scribbled word on the label. Sportsworld. That company. The one listed in London. Today's profit announcement and surprise nights issue? What did it mean?

'Greg?'

'Yeah?' he shouted back.

'What's this tape here?'

He appeared by the door. He had left the boxers behind. She was distracted.

'Which tape?'

'The one with Sportsworld written on it?'

He dived over for the remote control on the table, held her with one hand and with the other behind her back expertly reversed the tape back into the unit. Easy when you knew how.

'Forget the music, Barb. I can't wait. The water's getting cold. Do you want the tap end?'

She was still distracted. The tape didn't matter. She needed to relax. What an awful day. How long could she carry on like this? She needed a break from the City. And Greg was the man to provide it.

'OK. Give me a minute to slip out of these briefs. I'll join you but the tap end is yours.'

He was alone. She had come close. He took out the incriminating tape and hid it behind the rows of CDs. Must be more careful in future. Must trash this tape later like all the others before.

She enjoyed a luxurious soak until he stepped in. They faced each other. Eager hands rubbed aromatic gel into pores as they inhaled the hedonistic scent of the candles. He stood up and moved nearer her. They were enjoined after only minutes. They felt so clean. Physically at least.

'Next time, Barb, you definitely get the goddamn tap end.'
He was like that. It worried her sometimes.

CHAPTER EIGHTEEN

GREENWICH, LONDON SE1

The retired army lance corporal always took an identical route on his early morning constitutional in southeast London. He had no choice. If he altered his path by a mere few feet, Missie, his overweight Golden Labrador, soon let him know about it and put him back on the straight and narrow.

Out of his modest council flat, turn left towards Greenwich Village, into Greenwich Park, up the hill towards the Observatory but not all the way, it being a bit too steep for these two OAPs. Down to the pillars of the park gate and back along the Thames waterfront. Then into the newsagent by eight o'clock for his Daily Torygraph newspaper, a pint of milk for his cup of char and a fresh white loaf for toast. Twenty-three minutes was the existing record for his daily excursion before London awoke, kids hollered at him, cars ran him over and motorcycle couriers raised middle index fingers at the world.

It was like any other summer morning until they left the park and walked along the waterfront. Missie maybe noticed it first as she stopped abruptly ahead of him. This British Legion stalwart knew the local places and faces well. Anything out of the ordinary always caught his eye too. Twelve years in a gunnery battalion had decimated his eardrums but the squaddies on the sixty-millimetre guns always used to say he could see an Afrika Korps Panzer in a sandstorm before the others even spied a plume of diesel smoke.

The hunched outline was half submerged in the dank mud as tidal water repeatedly lapped up against it. His first thoughts were that someone had thrown some old clothes over the railings. It looked like the jacket of a good suit. But there was more. An extended left arm lay along the sand and circled inwards to a clenched fist. There seemed to be no legs on the torso. The half-visible head was dishevelled and matted with dirt and grime. The scene was of someone who had been fatally caught in quicksand, clambered desperately to get out, clutched at every available stinking grain of sand within reach, but nevertheless was pulled downwards below his waist by irresistible superior forces. The OAP knew it was a man's body.

It was the location of the awful discovery that affected him most. He had seen bodies in the mud of rat-infested trenches, stretched forms over taut barbed wire, charred remains trapped in burning Chieftains and severed limbs in unseen minefields, but he never expected to find one on his way to the newsagent. He leant over the rusted promenade railings, hoping they wouldn't give way under his frail frame and retched into the dull water twenty feet below. The thought of a breakfast of tea and white toast made him feel worse. He used a twenty pence piece at a pay phone on the high street to dial 999.

The first Greenwich station police officer at the scene clambered down the iron ladder affixed to the wall and found an expensive leather wallet on the body. It contained a collection of sodden business cards for a bank in the City. The surname immediately came up on the Met computer in the local nick. A missing West Londoner who disappeared two weeks ago. They knew that CID in Harrow Road were investigating.

Someone should have told Ted that the body was still half in the water. He wished he had brought his gardening wellington boots along as he gingerly tiptoed in his Marks and Spencer's finest black leather uppers amongst the odious slime and remnants of urban waste of the Thames waterfront. The stench down at sea level was almost overpowering. The heat of London bore down on him. The dead rotted. The flies and birds hovered.

He took in the scene for a few minutes, committing the view to memory. Behind him was the Greenwich Observatory and the Royal Maritime Museum, to the left the tall masts of the Cutty Sark in permanent dry dock and directly across the river was the Isle of Dogs and Canary Wharf off in the distance.

The body lay face down. One of the forensic police officers in a virginal white body suit and plastic gloves waded in the mud below. He was all right. He had his boots on. The officer gave Ted the nod. All the requisite photographs had been taken, both from up close and from the railings above. Ted had to do the ID before anything else at the scene was touched. He stood beside the kneeling officer who cradled the head in his two hands and laid the face sideways on the sand. It was so white, like chalk, badly bloated by the water, eyes closed, strands of weed and grains of sand entangled with the matted grey hair.

Ted took the photograph taken from Helen Soames's mantelpiece out of the inside pocket of his jacket. Same charcoal suit and silk tie, just as Helen had described. Same face moreover. Ted showed the picture to the other officer who looked and then nodded in reply. They were both of the same opinion.

Ted wasn't looking forward to breaking the news to Helen and the twins.

It was Chas who found it almost buried under the pile of newspapers, research documents and daily printouts at the Special Situations dealing desk. He stood up.

'Look what I found under all this crap.'

'What is it?' asked Greg.

'It's an ID card. Belongs to that fucker from the Stock Exchange. What an awful mug shot. He looks like someone on Death Row.'

Greg expressed nominal interest.

'Throw it over here.'

Chas obliged with a smooth delivery. Greg tried to concentrate on the ID card in his hand but it was difficult. The last few days had been hell on earth. Sarah Hart was insider dealing but he couldn't confront her. He needed her too badly for his own dealing. That asshole from the LSE had been round twice, talking to Ingrams in Compliance, to Old Nick in the corner office, looking at his dealing records, asking him where he got his trading ideas from. There was altogether too much hassle of late.

He could do without all this on a day when the Provident share price was down fifteen pence on some obscure rumour coming out of the City that the takeover deal wouldn't happen. Weird or what? Greg hadn't sold a single share yet and there was two million quid minimum of dealing profit up for grabs. No one could be allowed to step in his way. Especially some youngster with an attitude from the LSE.

Greg placed the ID card on the telephone board in front of him. He stared back at the face in the picture, his hatred growing deeper with every passing moment. He had to stop this do-gooder at any cost. There was too much to lose. In for a penny, in for two million quid.

Then the idea. Simple, once he thought about it. Nothing too serious. Just a delaying tactic. He dialled the LSE from a shared telephone on an anonymous empty sales desk and asked for Mark Robinson.

'Hello, Mark speaking.'

Greg hung up immediately. Robinson was at work today.

Perfect. Time for an early lunch break and a rushed sandwich in the back of a black cab on the way to the Isle of Dogs.

Sarah opened the door to her visitor from the City. This was an unpleasant surprise. He hadn't called. He wasn't expected. Was there more easy cash to be had today? Apparently not. Greg had other ideas.

'I have a problem.'

Oh yes, thought Sarah. Nothing as bad as finding a body in your basement.

'What sort of problem?'

'A problem at work.'

'Serious?'

'Potentially.'

Sarah didn't see how she could possibly help. She hardly dared to ask.

'Is it to do with those tape recordings that I make?'

He shrugged his shoulders indecisively.

'Not yet, but it might be in time. Do you still know that guy Lenny? The bastard who attacked me.'

Lenny? The same Lenny who called for his rent every month. Greg had a good memory. It was years since Lenny had punched Greg hard for going too rough on Sarah in a well-paid bout in a West End suite. She didn't like to think about the bad old days.

'Yes, I still know Lenny. You don't want to meet him again, do you?'

If this was her effort at a joke then he didn't find it amusing at all.

'Of course I don't. Can you contact him at short notice?'

'Yes.'

'I need something taken care of. Lenny might be the person to do it for me. I don't know anyone in that particular line of business and I'm not doing it myself. He knows me.'

'Who knows you?'

'The subject. So Lenny will have to do it, won't he? I'm sure if you ask him nicely, as you always did, that he would oblige. He has in the past anyhow.'

Lenny the Great Protector, of sorts.

'What do you want him to do?'

'I need someone from the London Stock Exchange roughed up a bit. Put out of action for a few weeks. Maybe a mugging or an accident of some sort. Nothing fatal of course. Scare him off.'

Sarah didn't like the sound of this.

'I don't want to be part of this. Why should I get involved at all?'

'Because you fucking well are involved. This guy thinks he's on to something and the stuff on those tapes leads directly back to you. You're up to your neck in this like I am. That's why.'

She was still looking for angles to avoid the assault and battery.

'Won't something like that alert this guy that something untoward is up, that he's on to something?'

'No. Not if it's done in the right manner. Make it look like it's random, with no connection to us.'

Sarah definitely didn't like the use of the word us. Were they in this together?

'Who is the guy you have in mind?'

'Mark Robinson. He works in the Enforcement Department of the LSE in Old Broad Street. I don't know where he lives but he's at work today. The rest is up to Lenny.'

'How's he supposed to recognise this Robinson?'

Greg went for his suit pocket. More cash? Nope. A work ID card instead.

'This is what Robinson looks like.' He offered the laminated ID card to Sarah.

She took the card in her hand, and as soon as she did, she realised that by doing so she had definitively accepted this contract, as they say in the trade in deepest South London. Nice looking guy she thought despite the glasses in the photograph. Pity that perhaps his face wouldn't look so attractive in the near future.

'When do you want this done?'

'It's gotta be today, like I said. He is definitely at work now. Make the call, OK?'

Sarah insisted that Greg left first, then she dialled Lenny's mobile number. His gruff voice answered hesitantly, then softened when he realised that she needed his help. That was what professional pimps did for a living anyhow. Whatever she wanted, he could arrange. Don't worry about it. Anything for his Sarah. Today? No problem.

Lenny and a sidekick were already in the area in his Jag and would immediately pick up the ID card for identification purposes. Old Broad Street? Yeah, they knew where that was. Consider it done, doll.

This was the worst part of the job. Standing on the steps of a family home in Little Venice, waiting for the door to be opened by a recent widow or a fatherless child. Helen Soames came to the door almost immediately. She looked at Ted and knew by his expression. Still she had to ask.

'Is there any news, Detective Inspector?'

'Can we talk inside?'

She definitely knew now. Bad news. How bad could it possibly be? Alexander was still missing? Injured? Or worse?

Ted searched for his opening line. There were no right words but he did his best, safe in the knowledge that the twins were out of earshot.

'I received a telephone call this morning about a body which was found in the Thames near Greenwich. I went down to identify the deceased. I am sorry to say that I believe it is your husband.'

At first she didn't seem to grasp the full implications.

'Are you sure? Couldn't there be some mistake?'

Ted was as sure as he could be from a good photograph and the set of Provident business cards found on the body.

'I'm sorry, but I am very sure.'

Then she understood. She shook visibly, her hands grasping one arm of the sofa, her face colouring as the tension of the past few days overcame her. She leant forward against Ted as she cried openly. Ted felt a tear running down the inside of his shirt collar, onto his ever sombre tie, as he gave her all the physical support that he could. He recalled how he himself had felt when he was told the news of the crash on the A12. All he could hear now was no, no, no. Why? Nothing changes. We all react the same.

Mark sat in front of the Head of Compliance of Morgans wishing that he were somewhere else. The recruitment consultant had given him no choice in the matter. The appointment was fixed for five o'clock in Morgans' flashy Embankment offices. Mark had faked an excuse with Norris about meeting some elderly relation at Stansted in order to leave earlier than usual. He hated white lies.

The sense of guilt was worse than ever. The past two weeks had been his best time to date in the LSE. An interesting high-profile assignment, visits to the leading investment banks, some promising leads yet to be followed up, a trail of possible intrigue that led to Jersey and an even better terrace lunch with a stunning executive. Without the LSE job and Norris's ideas, he would never have met the wonderful Penny.

The Compliance guy from the States droned on about how bloody wonderful Morgans were, how their Compliance Department was so well resourced and expertly staffed, how they were on top of all current compliance issues at the bank and how they synergised with the front-end business units. Such awful waffle. The more Mark heard the less he thought that Morgans needed someone like him.

After ten minutes he had switched off and his thoughts rambled to Provident, County Beverages, Greg Schneider, Sarah Hart and the half-undone row of pearl buttons on Penny's silk blouse. He hardly noticed when the Yank told him that the interview was over and that he would be in touch. Don't bother, thought Mark. I'm in no hurry to join this place.

He entered Embankment tube station, somewhat frustrated that he had agreed to the interview at all. He had lost a valuable hour or more at work. He had a meeting with Norris first thing next morning to discuss the next step in the Provident investigation.

He didn't know it yet but that pushy recruitment consultant had done him a big favour in retrospect.

Lenny and his sidekick were pissed off. They had been sitting in the sweltering Jag opposite the entrance to the LSE for the best part of two hours and there was still no sign of this guy Robinson. Lenny placed the ID card up on the front of the dashboard and they both threw glances from the card to each guy in his late twenties who emerged from the office as the end of the working day fast approached.

Pug scratched his shaven head, fondled his protruding ears, picked his nose and moved his massive bulk uncomfortably in the seat. He clenched two big tattooed fists together in a vain effort to relieve the tension. No use at all.

'Jesus, boss. Is this guy ever going to show?'

It was almost seven o'clock and Lenny was feeling the frustration too.

'Shut up. Just keep looking.'

This was not going to plan. Lenny wondered what could have happened. Was this guy going to work until eight or nine o'clock tonight, and if so how were they going to spot him in the fading light? Was there an unseen rear exit to the office? Had they already missed their target? Was this even the right fucking office building? Was there only one London Stock Exchange office in the City? Had dear Sarah screwed up on the information she had given him?

'There he is, boss.'

Pug put a sweaty hand on the handle of the Jag's passenger door. Lenny grabbed his arm.

'Hold on. Are you sure?'

They both looked at the photograph. It was a decent enough likeness.

'Yeah, I'm sure. Same looks. Dark hair. Glasses. OK, boss?'

Lenny reluctantly let him leave the car.

'Right, but make sure that he is the right guy.'

Pug was out of the Jag and down into Bank station before you could say street mugging. He followed his target to the platform and sat at the opposite end of the Central Line carriage. At every station he checked that his target was still in the carriage. The tube emerged from the tunnels and they travelled eastwards in the open countryside past Leytonstone and further out. Where the hell did this guy live? Was he ever going to get off the train? Pug was starting to get hungry. This was overtime.

They finally drew into leafy Hainault station and the target rose to leave. Pug followed him out of the station and down a series of criss-crossed residential streets. At any moment his quarry could turn into the gate of his semi-detached home and disappear behind the security of a bolted door. The job had to be done soon. The streets were quiet, practically deserted. No cars, no pedestrians, no onlookers. Only a stray dog or two. Pug was less than ten feet behind his target. Now or never.

'Excuse me, mate.'

The target in front stopped, then turned to face him. Pug looked hard. Was this the right guy? Better be sure.

'Do you work in the Enforcement Department of the Stock Exchange?'

'Yeah, I do.'

Wrong answer.

CHAPTER NINETEEN

OLD BROAD STREET, LONDON EC2

Mark sat side by side with Norris at the circular table in his office. He believed that this represented real progress, being far less confrontational than sitting on opposite sides of the awful wooden desk. His file on Provident Bank was open before them.

'So Mark, what do we have so far?'

'We have Schneider who has made excellent profits in Special Situations stocks, who won't talk to me about his dealing strategy, who hasn't had a dealing loss in months and who knows something about Hart's account in Jersey. And we have Hart who is buying and selling the same shares at the same time as Schneider. There's a lot of circumstantial evidence, but there is nothing that I can see to incriminate either.'

Norris paused to consider as he sat back.

'Mark, I've had cases like this in the past where my gut feeling was bad but I couldn't find what was wrong. Try a different tack. Forget about share dealing and all that City stuff. Consider instead the people involved. Find out all you can about this dealer, where he used to work, what he does, how he lives, where he goes. He's a American, so find out if he has a history in this business in the States. Then do the same for

Hart in the Isle of Dogs. Maybe even drop round to see her on some spurious pretext of protecting the interests of shareholders in some other company in which she has invested. Spin her a yarn to learn more about her. You know what to do.'

'OK.'

'Have you looked at Schneider's personnel file at Blakes?'

'I never thought of it.'

'Drop over and see what's in it. Look at any appraisals or annual reviews, any comments he might have received in his time there. See how much he gets paid and what incentives he has to make big profits. Go soon. Line it up with the Compliance guy in Blakes. Then visit this client in the Isle of Dogs. Let me know what happens.'

Mark liked the ideas. They were a good angle. Norris was delivering. He was about to get some further details when his secretary disturbed them.

'Claire called me. Pete won't be in this week. He's in a bad way. So is she, poor thing.'

Norris was surprised.

'Is he sick?'

'It's worse than that, he's in hospital. He was mugged outside his house last night.'

They both looked concerned.

'Is he all right?' asked Norris.

'I dunno.'

Norris turned to Mark.

'Do me a favour. Put this case on hold today. Get down to the hospital. Let me know how Pete is. Take as long as you want. There are more important things in life than Provident Bank.'

Norris was human. And he seemed to be surprisingly expert in nailing possible insider dealers.

Ted hated morgues. Bloody awful places. Especially the one in the basement of this East End hospital. The awful chlorine smell, the stagnant room, the clinical atmosphere, the cold air, the depressing sights and hollow sounds. But he had no choice. He needed to know how Alexander Soames had died.

'So what can you tell me about our man here?'

His question was directed at Dr Cameron Beath, the longest serving forensic pathologist in the Met and an old sparring partner of Ted's from his days in the East End. Trips to see Beath were fortunately far rarer now. Beath was two letters of the alphabet away from a far more appropriate surname, given his chosen vocation. Death and all that went with it. Last time they'd met socially was at a Met retirement party where Beath was paged urgently to examine a body during the bread and butter pudding. Despite thirty years working south of the border he would always be a Glaswegian and had the humour to match.

'Well, Ted, I'd say that he is definitely dead. No doubt about that whatsoever.'

Beath shrugged his shoulders and lowered his eyes behind the half spectacles sitting on the end of his ruddy nose. Ted gave him the obligatory sarcastic grin. The pathologist removed a pair of latex examination gloves drenched in human blood and threw them into the open waste unit with an ease practised over the years. They stood together surveying the rather considerable form of a middle-aged man on a metal trolley half shrouded by a green sheet that hung almost to the floor.

'Seriously, Cameron, what's the cause of death? Is it just a drowning?'

'No. The River Thames didn't help my examination but the facts are clear. His lungs are flooded with dirty water but there is no consistent pattern of seepage into the lining of the membranes. There was no gasping for breath as the water clogged the windpipe and the victim came up for air in vain.'

'Meaning?'

'This body went into the river after life was extinct.'

'How long was the body in the water?'

'For about two weeks based on the extent of the decomposition.'

As precise as that. About the time Soames left the Dorchester.

'So what's the cause of death?'

'There's no mystery at all. It's a good old-fashioned heart attack. Plaque built up over time on the inner wall of his right coronary artery, which supplies blood to his heart muscle. A blood clot formed and obstructed his artery. His heart muscle died from lack of blood. That led to electrical instability in his heart muscle tissue, in turn leading to severe ventricular fibrillation. When that happens, the heart simply quivers and can't pump oxygenated blood up to the brain. Permanent brain damage occurs after five minutes. Anything more than five minutes and you've got a body. Like this.'

'You said some sort of plaque built up? What's that?'

'Cholesterol plaque can build up in your artery. We all have it. It starts in your mid-twenties. A hard thick gunge that really screws up your system. Smoking and high blood pressure can accelerate plaque accumulation.'

'But heart attacks aren't always fatal? I've known people to recover.'

'Correct. The stats show that six in ten people who suffer a heart attack will survive. Heart attack deaths only occur when victims don't get prompt medical assistance. Ninety-five percent of victims who make it to an intensive care unit survive. You take them in, open up the blocked arteries and restore the blood flow to the heart muscle. I guess in this case no one knew that this guy had suffered an attack. Either that or else no one bothered to help him.'

'Anything else I should know?'

'One other thing, Ted. I could hazard a guess at the time of death.'

'You're joking?

'No. It's a well-known fact that heart attacks most frequently occur between 4 AM and 10 AM due to higher adrenaline amounts released from the adrenal glands during the early morning hours. Heart attacks do not occur when you exercise. Most happen in your sleep. So I'd say that he died early morning.'

Beath poked the body. Ted was still unsure. Perhaps this case was closed already?

'So, then, he died of a heart attack and fell into the Thames?'

Beath shrugged again.

'Not exactly. Rigor mortis set in many hours before he went into the water. The remains of the lungs prove that. They're over there in a metal tray if you want a look at them. Full of nicotine and black tar. Lovely stuff. But dead men don't walk. I'd say that this body was dumped in the river by someone.'

Ted thought he'd seen enough. But Beath had other ideas and made for the edge of the surgical sheet.

'Here, take a closer look at the body.'

Ted did not possess such voyeuristic interests. Beath saw his disdain.

'Don't worry. I'll leave the sheet on. But I want to show you something. You'll like it. Not a lot.'

They stepped closer to the trolley. Beath took the sheet in his hand and pulled the deceased's right arm out from underneath the folds of stained cotton.

'See that?'

Ted did indeed. A definite purple line around the wrist.

'What is it?'

'There are identical markings on the other arm and both ankles. This guy was carefully bound before he died.'

Ted wasn't sure.

'It doesn't exactly look like a rope mark to me.'

Beath stretched over the body to reveal the left arm. Then placed both arms crossed on the chest.

'Correct again. I'd say that he was bound with a strap or a belt. Same marks on his ankles. Look at the exact same width of the discoloration, an inch or more. And solid edges too with no other bruising nearby. It was a precise act. It's strange. I've never seen such a thing on a body before. Looks like the victim never even tried to get out of his restraints. As if he was happy to do it. Who'd do that?'

More questions than answers in the morgue today.

Mark hated hospitals. Fear of the unknown mainly, fortunately never having needed to visit one himself for any extended period of care. He shared the lift with a patient in a bed with wheels manned by two burly orderlies and disembarked on the fifth floor where he wandered around looking for the Waverley ward for ten minutes. Finally he saw Peter in an end bed in a ward shared with five others.

Peter didn't look good. One side of his face was badly bruised, partly covered with dressings. Mark could see a gash on the side of his head, where the hair had been shaved off only to be replaced by a row of eight neat stitches. And that was only the visible damage.

'Pete, how are you doing? What happened last night?'

Peter acknowledged his colleague and mumbled a few words through a cut upper lip.

'I was attacked on the way home. Some thug beat me up.'

'Do you know him?'

'Never saw him before in my life.'

Mark sat on the chair by the bed and deposited his modest gifts of a few car and men's magazines on the locker. Peter could see Mark's reaction to his injuries and went on to make a drama out of a crisis.

'Do you see this?' Peter opened a button or two on his NHS-issue pyjamas to reveal heavy strapping wrapped around his chest. 'He fractured a couple of ribs too. That's the worst damage. That's why I'm in here for a few days. Observation they call it. Imprisonment more like.'

Mark didn't understand.

'So some guy mugged you? What did he take? Money? Your watch? Your designer specs?'

Peter grimaced. Pain or else frustration at what had happened.

'That's the strange part. He took nothing at all.'

'Then why did he attack you?'

'That's what the police asked me earlier today.'

'And what did you tell them?'

'The guy spoke to me. Asked me if I worked at the LSE in enforcement.'

'How the hell did he know that?'

'Dunno. But once I said yes, he went for me. He knocked me to the ground, kicked me in the ribs, and ground my face into the concrete paving stones. He was a big bastard too. There was nothing I could do and no one around. Then he left me lying there ten yards from my front door.'

Mark didn't understand but he had spent enough time in the ward. He didn't feel comfortable in this hospital. He told Peter that he would call back again, strict visiting hours and Norris permitting. Peter asked him to bring *Loaded* and *Viz* mags next time. As he rode back down in the lift to the in-patients exit Mark couldn't help thinking that someone had got the wrong man.

He almost collided with Peter's fiancée, Claire, in the lobby area. He tried to talk to her but it was impossible. She was close to tears and kept fingering the engagement ring on her left hand.

Greg sat on Blakes' dealing floor wondering if it had happened yesterday evening. Had Sarah got Lenny to do the dirty work and got Mark off his case for at least a few weeks? He needed the breathing space. He hit the phone, picked an outside line, called the LSE and asked for the Enforcement Department. He did his best to disguise his fading American accent when he spoke with the departmental secretary.

'Mark Robinson please.'

'I am sorry but he's not here at the moment.'

'Do you know where he is?'

'I believe he's at the hospital.'

'Thanks.'

He hung up immediately. Excellent. It had worked. There would be no more visits to Blakes by the man from the LSE while the crucial Provident takeover battle was coming to a head.

Greg picked up the next incoming flashing red light on the dealer board. It was his personal line so it must be someone he knew, or at least someone who had his Blakes' business card with his direct number on it. He recognised the New York voice this time.

'It's Nathaniel speaking. I wanted to follow up on our recent chat. Can we meet up today?'

'Is there anything in this for me?'

'I hope so. Say same place, twelve-thirty?'

Within the hour Greg was back in Café Java, sitting opposite an enthusiastic headhunter who wouldn't leave him alone. Nathaniel knew that his target was still keen. Perhaps this was the job offer Greg was looking for, the one he couldn't turn down.

'Greg, I have another vacancy that would suit you.'

Greg needed to know where the vacancy was. Urgently. Otherwise this was a complete waste of time.

'Which bank is it?'

'Hold on a minute, let me tell you about the job first.'

'No, tell me the name of the bank first.' And don't let it be a US bank please.

'You dealers are in such a damn hurry all the time.'

Nathaniel shifted uneasily in his seat and took his left arm off his half-folded *Evening Standard*. Greg threw a glance at the newspaper, scanning the bold headlines purely out of habit.

'OK, I'll tell you then?'

Greg didn't understand the headline in the right-hand column at first. He read it again slowly. Just four words. City Banker Found Dead. And not any old City banker. The first paragraph mentioned Provident Bank. Greg was thinking about the missing Alexander Soames. Nathaniel wasn't.

'Greg, it's Deutsche Bank.'

He didn't hear the mention of one of the biggest non-US banks in the world. The investment bank division was currently recruiting the best talent in the City, and where serious money was no object. He was still reading the newsprint with his head tilted ever more sideways. Alexander Soames's body found near Greenwich. In the Thames for two weeks. Suspicious circumstances. Police investigating. Nathaniel repeated the magic words.

'I said, it's Deutsche.'

Greg heard the name and slowly focussed back on Nathaniel. Still wandering from mega-job offers to deceased clients of Sarah in the Isle of Dogs. Still unsure what was happening right here, right now.

'Don't you want to join Deutsche either? Am I wasting my time with you again?'

In an instant Greg knew that everything had changed. Something bad had happened and Sarah must be involved. She had last seen Soames two weeks ago. She lived by the river, opposite Greenwich. All change. Time to break the routine and do something else. Something more normal. There must be big money involved here with Deutsche.

'Yes, I heard you. I'll take it.'

'But I haven't even told you about the job yet. Let me at least give you the sales pitch on it. Earn my commission.'

'I said, I'll take it.'

Nathaniel felt the need to continue the hard sell.

'It's a job as Head of their UK Equity Market Making team. You'll be working with the guys that you currently deal with from the other side as a dealer. It's an excellent position with a great company.'

Market making. Perfect. No special stocks. No inside track. No need for Sarah. She was in deep. Like Soames.

'I said, I'll take it.'

'Deutsche are prepared to make you an excellent offer. They heard about the millions you've made on Provident, amongst others. They'll pay two hundred k basic and a guaranteed hundred per cent bonus for the first two years. Company car, whatever you damn well want. Massive mortgage subsidy. The works.'

Greg didn't know why Nathaniel was bothering. Deutsche was perfect. Time to go straight at last.

'I said, I'll take the fucking job.'

Finally Nathaniel understood. He had got his man. Greg was moving on. Bye bye Blakes at last. Time now for a hot date back home.

Barbara immediately knew what was expected of her as Saturday morning dawned. He wanted great sex again. Right here. Right now. Last night's climax just after midnight was only a distant memory for him. She wasn't so convinced, but she turned away from him and folded her knees up into an almost foetal position. This would after all require far less effort on her part.

Greg moved closer to her and explored her warm flesh. He ran his nails along her spine and she tingled involuntarily. He was ready. Maybe she wasn't. It didn't seem to matter to him. He enveloped her and moved inwards and upwards. She exhaled. Greg liked lazy Saturday mornings at home.

Ten minutes later they lay side by side and stared up at the cornice of the raised ceiling. Neither had spoken yet. They enjoyed the silence, each evaluating how the weekend was going so far. And it was still only nine-thirty. The silence in NW8 was broken by a definite thud outside on the maple floor of the hall.

'What's that?' she asked.

'The mail.'

Neither of them moved for another five minutes. She pushed Greg.

'So are you going to get the post?'

'There's no hurry. It ain't going anywhere.'

She rolled back the duvet cover and stepped naked into the hall. Greg admired the view from the pile of pillows. She threw a bundle of manila and white envelopes at him.

'Aren't you going to open them?'

'Nope.'

'Then I'll open them for you.'

'Suits me.'

She was surprised at the most impressive corporate envelope.

'Do you see this logo? A blue box with a slash in it. It's got to be Deutsche Bank.'

Greg sat up in the bed, as erect as he had been fifteen minutes ago. How the hell had the job offer arrived so soon? Their Human Resources department must have sent it last night in record time. German efficiency personified. He saw the express delivery sticker on the front. He had yet to resign from Blakes. Yet to confront Old Nick. No one must know until then. No one. Not even Barb. He didn't want her to discover his new job yet.

'Leave it. It's OK. I know what it is.'

'What is it?'

He bluffed. Quite a good bluff, he thought. Spur of the moment and all that.

'It's some stock research they send me.'

'Then I'll have a look at it. See what the competition's doing. See if they're as bullish as I am.'

Damn. Wrong bluff.

'No. Don't bother.'

'Why does this go to your home address? Why not to work?'

Another lie was required. This was getting more difficult.

'Deutsche won't send free research to me at Blakes so I get it mailed here. I told them I was an independent money manager and I would put some business their way. It was easy.'

'So you lied to them?'

The silence was too long until he made the admission of guilt.

'Yeah. It was a small lie. It's a hazard of this business. You know?'

CHAPTER TWENTY

BISHOPSGATE, LONDON EC2

Greg had waited years for this opportunity. He sat at his dealing desk, one eye on the SEAQ screens and one eye on Old Nick's corner office. His door was closed and the blinds partially drawn. Nick was leaning in towards the speakerphone, arms crossed in utter frustration. Some sort of Blakes' conference call with the overseas offices was concluding after an hour of serious corporate bullshit. Not a great time for an apparent star dealer to interrupt his boss with the news that he was leaving their hallowed environs for far greener pastures.

Everything was now in place. The interview with Deutsche on Friday evening had been great. His new boss was on the same wavelength, someone who thrived on risk and reward, not an old social dinosaur like Nick. Greg liked the market making team. Their offices were state of the art. Moorgate tube station was nearby. They had a well-equipped gym and a better restaurant. There was enough talent on show, even at six p.m. on a Friday evening. Always the best time to do a covert interview in the City, with few still there to ask questions about unknown visitors.

Deutsche, however, had indiscreetly sent that damn envelope to his home over the weekend. He had opened it alone. It contained company information, pension booklets, life assurance details, flash company car listings and mortgage subsidy deals. Most important of all it contained the offer letter on headed paper signed by the head of Human Resources and by the FVP in change of London equity dealing. The salary and guaranteed bonus numbers looked great. Lots of zeros. Time to act. No one knew.

Crosswaithe was still fruitlessly engaged, one hand hovering over the cut-off button on the telephone console. Greg chewed the end of a rotten Bic pen as he mentally rehearsed the words he was about to irrevocably utter. This was serious. Once he went in there, there was no going back. No one in the City wanted a departing employee sitting at a dealing desk. They were a liability. They could commit Blakes to a laughable stock market deal and be gone before the shit hit the fan in the month-end profit and loss Bible. Once Greg formally resigned from Blakes, Crosswaithe would ensure that he was promptly escorted from the premises, the meagre contents of his desk sent to him by another busy courier and his security pass extracted at the revolving door by uniformed security. Greg had ten minutes left at Blakes. Maximum.

There was one minor distraction. That SEAQ screen was bad news. Provident was already down thirty pence this morning. It was their biggest fall for many days. The wild rumours were still out there in the market. Barbara had said on the PA this morning that some thought that the takeover deal might not happen. There were horse whispers that the Treasury officials in Whitehall were not keen on further consolidation within the UK banking industry and might block the planned mega-deal.

The dealing volumes in Provident were up today too, with almost half a million shares traded in the first hour. A sign that some of the bigger players in the City were taking these rumours seriously. Widows and orphans weren't selling out today, more likely it was the pension funds and institutional investors. The screen flashed decisively. Red again. Down forty pence now.

Greg directed the obligatory question at Chas. More in hope than anything else.

'What do you think about Provident today, Chas?'

'There's nothing new, officially Greg. Only some rumours. Let's sell the lot now.'

Wishful thinking. How the hell could they ever dump a million shares in the market? The price would take a hammering and much of the profit would be lost in the bargain basement sale. They would have to sell on a piecemeal basis, a few hundred thousand shares a day, to keep the marketmakers guessing. Greg would soon be one of them.

'No way Jose.'

He knew he would miss Chas's company and the visual appeal of Jules alongside. It didn't matter. He couldn't make them both an offer to join him down the road at Deutche. They knew too much. Market making didn't require inside knowledge. For less stress. Easy money.

Fuck it. Provident was still ticking down but did it really matter now? The stock had made his name in the City. He had bought the shares in time. The *FT* had Blakes' name in the back page Lex column one day. The Deutsche equity guys saw it. They immediately knew they had a winner here. They made the outrageous offer. He had it at home on paper. Case closed.

Crosswaithe opened his door. Now or never. Greg ambled over, hands in pockets. Guilt?

'I need a minute, Nicholas?'

'Certainly.'

Greg pulled the door shut. His boss immediately looked worried. He knew the give-away signs of a closed office door.

'What's up, Greg?'

'I want to talk to you about my position here.'

Crosswaithe was thinking wild thoughts. Was Greg looking for promotion? More cash? A bigger bonus? Greg had prepared some words but still paused to get them out right. No point in being unduly rude. Deutsche would look for a reference letter from Old Nick in a week or so. Greg needed one. Pity about last time with his former employers when such a letter had not been an option. There was no need to burn any boats here. Might even get invited back to the Blakes' Christmas party in the Grosvenor?

'I've been at Blakes for nearly four years now. I have been thinking about my long-term career in the City.'

Chas knocked, and then opened the door in one swift movement. Did he still have to keep doing that? He saw the glare from Greg. Crosswaithe too.

'Sorry, guys, but we're in big trouble in Provident'.

'What sort of trouble?' asked Greg.

'The share price has gone into freefall. It looks like the deal is off.'

Nick and Greg didn't understand.

'You mean those rumours are true? Whitehall's going to block the deal on competition grounds?' Greg probed.

'Far worse than that. British Commercial have issued a press announcement that they are pulling out because their due diligence review revealed major holes in the loan book at Provident.'

'What sort of holes?'

'Many home mortgages that are in default. Bad debt provisions that are way below the industry norm. Bad commercial property loans hidden from the external auditors at the last financial year end.'

'How much are we talking about here? Millions?'

'Hundreds of millions. It looks really serious. It might be the end of Provident as we know it.'

How the mighty had fallen.

'Shit.'

Greg needed the facts fast.

'What's the stock price now?'

'Less than eleven quid when I left the desk two minutes ago.'

Crosswaithe swivelled around and looked at the screen on his desk.

'Ten seventy now. Jesus, the price is shot. Greg, get out there and dump the whole lot. Now.'

Old Nick never swore but this was different. He had told the Board so many times in the past month that his best dealer was sitting on an enormous unrealised profit and it was only a matter of time before they cashed in their chips. Pity. Greg left the office with Chas. He had entirely forgotten about the purpose of his visit. More pressing matters had overtaken the staff at the Special Situations desk. Greg pulled his chair up to the desk and watched the screens. Decision time.

The price was steady at ten pounds sixty pence. He thought back to only minutes ago when the price was so much higher. Still steady. When Chas had jokingly suggested selling the entire position. Flashing red. That was such a good idea in hindsight. Down ten more pence. He should have listened to Chas. Ten fifty pence. Steady again. Would the share price turn? Would it recover? He had bought at ten quid a month ago. His paper profit was fast disappearing before his eyes. Would he even make a profit?

'What do we do, Greg? Are we selling?' asked Chas.

No easy answers. Greg's every instinct told him to sell, but he still had a million shares. Every ten pence fall was 100k lost. His mind raced over all the alternatives. Flashing red again. Another ten pence fall.

'Greg, come on,' urged Jules, 'what are we doing?'

The seconds ticked by. Expensive seconds. While Greg waited, the world dealt. He felt cold. The past few weeks sped by. Press coverage. Job offers. Deutsche. How had it come to this? Was he losing it?

'Greg. Greg, for fuck's sake. Talk to us.'

Got to get out. Take whatever profit was there. Flashing red. Ten forty pence. Again. Ten twenty pence. Jesus. Then a twenty pence fall. This was the end. Breakeven had almost been reached. Unthinkable only minutes ago. Sell at all costs. He finally decided on the only way out.

'Right, let's sell the lot of them. Take whatever price you can get.'

They hit the phones to get through to their chosen banking sector market makers at dealing desks across the City but the lines were busy. The quotes on the SEAQ screen were changing by the minute. More red. Greg had lost over a million and a half quid since eight a.m. Chas saw it first.

'Christ, no luck, Greg. We're fucked. Look at that.'

The announcement flashed up on the news ticker service. 'London Stock Exchange suspend dealing in Provident Bank following the collapse of British Commercial Bank bid.'

That was it. They were long a million shares and the market was closed. They couldn't sell. It was the worst possible outcome. They were powerless as they waited for the LSE to pronounce on the fate of their dealing position. Greg was already thinking about the wider implications. Too depressing by far.

Ted sat with David Webster in the Provident City offices. He needed to know more about Alexander Soames. Perhaps his work was somehow connected to his premature death? An accidental drowning in the Thames or a man captured, bound, stressed out, suffocated and dumped? Hard to tell yet.

'Did you notice anything unusual about Soames in the days before he disappeared?'

Webster shrugged his shoulders, giving the distinct impression that he was preoccupied with other matters. Work, perhaps. The Deal of the Year?

'He was unhappy, distant. Alex was vehemently opposed to the takeover deal so we had drifted apart in the last days. But that was business. It wasn't personal. We were still friends at the time.'

'Did he have anything to lose in the takeover deal? Money for instance?'

Talk of money always made Webster sit up and think.

'Quite the opposite. Alex stood to receive a million pounds in compensation on the premature termination of his directorship and his executive employment contract.'

Ted thought back to the family home by the canal in West London. And Helen too. Alone.

'Did money matter that much to him? He didn't seem to be that badly off.'

Webster was evidently growing tired of the policeman's visit. The novelty was wearing thin.

'Doesn't it matter to all of us? You can live without it but have you ever tried?'

A screen on his desk distracted Webster's attention again. Ted could see a red share price. Webster was looking at the only share price that mattered to him at the top of the screen. Ted pushed his luck.

'You seem more interested in that screen.'

'I'm looking at our share price here. It's down fifty pence in the past few minutes. And it's still falling.'

Ted made a modest contribution to a conversation that was rapidly diverting to City matters.

'Do you know why it's falling?'

'No. That's the worst part. That's life in the City. These dealers and research analysts move share prices and there's damn all that we in the corporates can do about it. The analysts speak. The dealers sell.'

Webster was fixated. Then it happened. The screens flashed a news item.

'Jesus,' exclaimed Webster.

'What?'

'The takeover has been pulled.'

Ted was lost.

'Why?'

Webster read the small print aloud.

'The City accountants hired by British Commercial have

found a problem with the mortgage book. Many of the loans are in default and the loan book is under provided. They say we've cooked the books over the past few years and that our audited accounts are wrong.'

Ted needed to know more. The ways of the City were a mystery.

'Is that all true?'

Webster hedged his bets. Ted sensed he knew more than he was willing to disclose here and now.

'I don't really know.'

They sat and watched the screens. The time for questions was over. Webster was seeing his million pound severance payment go down the tubes before his very eyes. Reuters flashed more news. Provident Deal Collapses. It was now official. Rumours became fact. Ted had to leave. He dared to risk one more question of the corporate wreck before him. It was rhetorical. Sort of.

'Who would have known most about this problem?'

Webster reacted instantly.

'What do you mean by that? Are you accusing me of something?'

'No. Of course not. I was thinking of someone else.'

A black hole like this might be uncovered in a takeover deal. The Finance Director knew most about the books of Provident. Soames must have known the truth. Perhaps he couldn't face the inevitable discovery. Beath was wrong. Suicide perhaps? The depths of the Thames could have been a more bearable alternative to facing friends and Helen. Soames knew the million pound payoff would never happen.

'Do you think Soames knew this would come to light in the takeover bid and couldn't face the public humiliation. So he drowned himself in the Thames?'

Ted couldn't yet explain the marks on the deceased's wrists and ankles but this current theory was all he had to go on. Maybe he had help?

'You may be right,' Webster agreed, clutching at straws. Ted left in the comforting knowledge that he had made a breakthrough in this investigation.

Damn. Webster sat on alone following Ted's departure. This wasn't going to plan. The pressure to deliver stellar annual results to the City every year since the public flotation had been enormous. The takeover would make them all multi-millionaires but British Commercial were not supposed to find anything until well after the deal was done. If they did find the well-cooked books years down the line, would they ever stand up in public and say that they had been duped for millions of quid? Hardly.

He should have listened to the advice of his Finance Director. Alex had in retrospect been right to resist the bid. He knew the risk of discovery was high. Webster and the board had voted the wrong way.

It was all over the evening papers. The deal was off. Shares suspended mid-morning amidst record trading volumes and a plummeting share price. Mark's investigation wasn't even half finished. He had no idea where he was right now, except geographically. He sat with Norris, looking at the *Standard* headline.

'So boss, that's the end of our investigation into Schneider and Hart and Provident?'

Norris shook his head.

'Not necessarily so. Normally I'd say stop your work now and move on to another investigation, except for one overriding factor in Provident's case. The death of that Finance Director, Soames. I have never seen a takeover situation in twenty years where one of the main players disappears on the eve of the deal and dies. It's too suspicious. Could even be murder based on these press articles. There could be something big in this investigation.'

Mark was pleased. He too needed to see the end result. He left the office, still hoping that there was something to be uncovered after weeks of work. Norris's secretary accosted him on his way out and thrust a scribbled message at him.

'Some girl called Penelope Swales called for you. She's staying at Le Meridien Hotel in Piccadilly. That's her telephone and room number.'

She gave him a knowing look. She knew that he didn't get many exciting messages like this at work. Mark knew the reality. He never got messages like this at work. Promising.

A telephone call and a short trip later, he alighted from the cab courtesy of the red liveried doorman in the peaked cap who guarded the entrance to the interior magnificence of Le Meridien. Mark was excited. Had he made such a decent impression on the restaurant terrace in Jersey? He couldn't remember. What had they talked about? Did he have any conversation left? Was she even interested in conversation?

Penelope arrived in the lobby at seven o'clock precisely as arranged. Mark hardly recognised her. Casual navy chinos with a thin belt and a perfectly ironed crisp white shirt with sleeves rolled up. Shades sitting nonchalantly atop her carefully gathered hair. Flat deck shoes. She looked wicked. Absolutely wicked. She was on a date. Mark was honoured to step out of the hotel in her company.

They strolled east along Piccadilly's baking pavements, crossed the mass of fuming traffic at Tower Records, past the Statue of Eros and the masses of backpacking teenage tourists *en vacances*. They stepped into a hidden Italian in Soho, another restaurant that Penelope chose from her apparently extensive global experience. Mark eyed the lavish menu carefully and wondered if he could afford a meal for two in the unpretentious location. Perhaps if they stuck to the house red and stayed off the wine list.

It was a small table. They were only feet apart with a solitary candle dividing them. Penelope kept fingering the gleaming cutlery, running her fingers along the stem of her wineglass, accidentally or not touching Mark's hand when she emphasised a particular point in the conversation, connecting her foot with his foot underneath the draped cotton tablecloth. Serious eye contact on a continuous basis, lingering stares, long periods of mutual laughter, much smiling. The positive vibes were incredible.

They instinctively walked back together to the hotel afterwards. Could she seriously be interested in him? Was a high earning sales star from a leading City investment bank chasing a modest civil servant from the LSE? Hard to tell. He wondered if he would ever actually get to see the inside of a Meridien hotel room.

He could seize the moment and suggest going back to his more modest apartment. Panic. His unfinished laundry was everywhere. A week's collection of boxer shorts and socks lay on the various radiators, three days washing-up was piled up in the sink, unironed work shirts hung from doorknobs, the fridge was bare, the wine was cheap and the bath needed a good Jif scrubbing. He couldn't bring Penelope back home. The only option was a visit to her room in Le Meridien. She stopped by the entrance steps.

'Mark, do you know that this hotel has a lenient policy towards room guests?'

The king-size four-poster upstairs was so vast that they almost needed directions to find each other. Their tongues explored every mutually rewarding erogenous zone. They re-lived the Kama Sutra, page by page. Penelope gave him all the vocal encouragement he needed. The foreplay lasted an hour. The celebration of sex, when it came, was orgasmic. What else? As good as your very own tub of Haagen-Dazs strawberry cheesecake ice cream.

CHAPTER TWENTY-ONE

BISHOPSGATE, LONDON EC2

Greg hardly had the energy to get up and go into work. Somehow he made the super-human effort and slumped at the Special Situations desk. Not only had he thrown away millions of quid of profit yesterday, but Blakes' punting money was still tied up in shares that he couldn't sell, shares which would return to the market in the next few days at a far lower price. He was going to lose money on this sure-thing deal.

And worse still, everyone in the City knew it. The people at Deutsche would know. It was their own market makers that the team had tried to call at the last minute to shift the excess paper but to no avail. Were the people that he quaffed champagne with last Friday now laughing at him from behind the anonymous security of their dealing screens? Was his future boss in on their joke too? That was his worst fear. He wondered if they still wanted him at Deutsche? He would call Nathaniel later to discuss.

Old Nick strode out of his office. He was having a bad day too, taking the heat from the Directors upstairs. They hated losses as much as their dealers did. It didn't look like good news.

'Greg, I got a call. That investigator from the LSE, Robinson, is coming back here today.'

Greg was stunned.

'That's impossible. That guy is . . .' In hospital, isn't he? He had to be. Sarah had arranged it. Greg had called his office and he was laid up in hospital. He couldn't have made a recovery that quickly. Not if Lenny had done what he had promised. A good going over. Nick saw the indecision in his expression.

'What do you mean it's impossible? What do you know about Robinson?'

Greg had to attempt a cover-up.

'Nothing. Don't worry about it.' Change the subject quick. 'When is he seeing me?'

'He's not seeing you this time.'

Nick looked at the other colleagues seated at the desk. Greg was worried. Did Robinson want to talk to them now? Chas looked back, immediately worried at the attention he was getting. Jules smiled. She could sweet talk any guy from the LSE. A good corporate move on her part. Henry was oblivious to the impending visitor, oblivious to the world at large. Nick faced facts.

'Don't jump to conclusions. This time he only wants to meet with Personnel.'

Greg wondered what was on his file. That CV. This was getting worse and it wasn't even mid-morning.

Ted sat with the Super at the top table in the only large room in the police station and faced a wall of invited media types. He did not take kindly to undue publicity but his Super gave him no choice in the matter. Their investigation was at a dead end and had been for days. Maybe it was suicide. Maybe a murder. They had no clues from the hotel or from the parked Volvo in Stratford. Just a stiff with marks on his wrist and ankles. The forensic team had found zilch. They had come full circle back to the only lead and it now needed the maximum amount of media publicity in their search for a murderer.

There were only the two of them. The Super had wanted Helen Soames to be there too, had wanted to add some female drama to the top table, but Ted fought him. The Super claimed it always got them more exposure on Sky, more soundbites on BBC, more footage on ITN. It wasn't fair on her, countered Ted. The Super eventually backed down. Camera flashlights blazed back at them as the Super coughed into the microphone to gain the initial attention of the assembled journalists and TV crews.

'Good morning, ladies and gentlemen. We have asked you here today to seek the public's help in our investigation into the death of City banker Alexander Soames earlier this month. We believe his death to be suspicious and to date, despite the excellent help of the public, we have failed to make sufficient progress in the case.'

Ted winced at the untruth. The public hadn't helped him at all in the past month, but the Super was prone to uttering such excellent community-policing inspired one-liners. He loved the limelight but now he reluctantly handed over the floor to yours truly.

'My colleague, DI Hammond, seeks help to locate a unique item which is missing from Mr Soames's car.'

That was his cue. Ted rose. More flashlights. He picked up the identical item from the green baize draped over the tables and held it up at head height to his left. More photographs, although most of the snappers must have wondered what they were photographing. Cameras zoomed in on the latest car technology.

'This is the front security cover of a Sony CD 90X compact disc multi-play car stereo system. It's a relatively rare item of in-car entertainment since it retails at approximately four hundred pounds and is fitted as standard only in luxury cars like the deceased's company vehicle. Please note the prominent features on the front and the distinctive display and luminous dials.'

Not distinctive at all if the truth be told. It looked like every other bloody car stereo. This was a long shot. Ted felt a right prat as he stood there looking at the evidence in his hand. It was all he had.

'We believe that a stereo cover identical to this was removed from the car, either by Soames before his death or possibly by a murderer. We did not find the item on the deceased's person when he was recovered from the Thames.'

Ted knew the stereo cover wasn't in Helen's home nor was it on the banks of the Thames where they discovered the body. It was probably deep in the bloody water. Waste of time.

'We would like the public to let us know if they have seen an item identical to this. It may have been discarded after the death, possibly in the East End near Stratford or Greenwich. If so, they should contact their nearest police station or myself at Harrow Road.'

And that was it. The visitors departed. The Super seemed pleased at his moment of fame. Ted wondered whether the effort had been worthwhile.

Mark was looking forward to being back in Blakes' offices today. Not for the opportunity to meet James Ingrams of the Compliance Department again, or to observe Schneider at his dealing desk on the sly. More for the chance to see Barbara on the floor, even though she was surely out of his league. Penelope was in the office today. She had said so last night as she had peeled off her blouse and rolled back the duvet of the king-size bed in Le Meridien. That was the only time that they talked about work. The rest was play.

Mark was almost floating on air as he made his way down the corridors towards Compliance on the fifth floor. His mind wasn't really on dealing strategies, private clients, big profits and Provident Bank at all. More so on cotton sheets, Jersey sun tans, scented *parfum*, shared showers, morning coffee and warm chocolate croissants delivered by room service, his and her matching deep-pile bathrobes, simultaneous feelings of ecstasy and exhaustion. And then the second time. What a great close encounter. Beyond his wildest dreams before last night. Now a reality.

Ingrams greeted him with a dour expression.

'I'm surprised to see that you turned up here today as planned.'

'Why's that?'

'Haven't you heard about the collapse of the Provident deal?'

'Yes I have, but that doesn't change my work here.'

'Pity. The Dealing Director's not pleased with your recent investigations here. Schneider is at best breaking even on his investment. It doesn't look much like an inspired purchase now, does it?'

'Didn't he sell his position?'

'No. He couldn't get out in time in such size. He didn't sell a single share.'

They paused to consider the recent events. Ingrams pushed him further.

'What do you want to talk to Personnel about?'

'I want to see Schneider's personnel file.'

Ingrams winced. Mark hadn't mentioned Schneider's file during the telephone call, otherwise Ingrams would have had a look at it first. He wondered what was on it?

'So let's visit Personnel.'

Ingrams had no choice.

'This way.'

He took Mark down the corridor to a large room wholly populated by sparkling girls in their mid-twenties, mostly blonde, natural or otherwise, for some unknown reason, and all well dressed. A typical Personnel Department of any City investment bank. Full of Tanyas, Emmas, Louises and Samanthas. Every girl counting the days until she could hook a star dealer on the second floor and retire in her late twenties to a life of leisure in the country on his annual bonus. Unfortunately the Head of Personnel in her forties seemed to have missed the boat. No wedding ring on her left hand. Ingrams obliged with the introductions.

'This is Shirley Rhodes, Head of Personnel. This gentleman is from the LSE.'

Despite her tough exterior and horn-rimmed glasses, she made some effort for Mark.

'What can I do for you?'

'I wish to see the personnel file on Greg Schneider.'

She recognised the name immediately and turned to one of the Tanyas or Emmas.

'Schneider's file, please, for this gentleman.'

Mark sat alone at a spare desk in Personnel and opened the carefully ordered thin manila file. It was in reverse chronological order so he turned to the back pages and started there. First off was a word-processed letter from Schneider to Nicholas Crosswaithe dated four years ago, looking for a job. Strange. Most dealers were headhunted, not job hunters themselves. Schneider's CV was attached showing his prior dealing experience at Mitchell Leonberg in New York and in London. Five years in all at their Manhattan office and a mere six months at their London office. Short enough, thought Mark. He wondered why it hadn't worked out.

He looked for some references from former employers but he found only one. It was from Mitchells in London and was as good as you get from any investment bank. Short and sweet, nothing too enthusiastic, the wording was overly legalistic, showing the involvement of litigation-obsessed lawyers. No reason why you should not consider hiring Mr Greg Schneider. That was all. A one-pager with a covering letter signed by a Director of their London office. Someone called Brad Franklin.

Then more recent correspondence. Copy letters of annual

pay reviews. Schneider was earning a six figure basic per annum. Mark could only marvel at the numbers. Schneider's bonus last year was measured in percentage numbers of his basic salary. Same again please. Double your money. Blakes paid well thought Mark. Better than the LSE.

Mark took photocopies of the CV and references. He would check them out later, not while sitting at a desk in the midst of a gaggle of Personnel girls. One or two gave him the once over, evidently sizing up his bank balance. Mark would hate to tell them the truth. It would shatter their illusion that he was an important visitor. He accosted Ms Rhodes at her desk in a corner office.

'Anything else that I should know about Schneider?'

'Not that I am aware of.'

She killed his enquiry stone dead. Too late. Ingrams would have since briefed her. She was good. Mark left with the copies in his briefcase, took the lift alone down to the entrance, lurched when it stopped on the second floor and then his day was made. She entered and stood beside him.

'Hi.'

Penelope smiled back but she stood her ground. Mark moved closer to her. She pulled away.

'Not now, please. I'm at work.'

'What's wrong?'

'Nothing.'

'Don't you remember last night?'

'Of course I do. It was great. But it's one night. Don't read too much into it. I was alone. You were willing to come out with me. You wanted sex. So did I. What's there to discuss?'

The lift stopped and she stepped out. She didn't even say goodbye. The bitch. The rich bitch. He had been used for one night. A lonely international high-flyer in a luxury London hotel room picks a guy's business card from her extensive Rolodex and summons him over for the evening. Have him washed and scrubbed and brought to my tent immediately. Raises his hopes, his ego and a lot more beside. Then dashes them the next day.

There was a group of Suits at the revolving door in Blakes' lobby. Mark made to push through them but they ignorantly blocked his way. They were just dark Suits with tanned faces to him, waiting to go to lunch if someone else paid for it. Then a sullen face he recognised. Greg Schneider stood before him. They made eye contact. No smile. Some civility was required and Mark made the token effort.

'Hello, Greg.'

Schneider was looking hard at him. Looking closely at his face for some reason. Whatever he was hoping to find, the dealer was apparently disappointed.

'I can't talk now.' And Greg was gone.

Mark was back in the LSE office in ten minutes and knew something was wrong when he sat down at his desk. He badly missed Peter's company in the vacant seat opposite. Norris's secretary approached him.

'I don't suppose you've heard?'

'Heard what?'

'About Pete. He's taken a turn for the worse. They found internal damage. He slipped into a coma earlier this morning. The doctors say he has a blood clot on his brain. They moved him to intensive care. No visitors allowed except Claire.'

'How bad is it? I mean, could it be life-threatening?'

'The doctors say it's fifty fifty whether he pulls through'.

The call eventually came after lunch, this time tactfully made to Greg's mobile telephone, not to the general numbers in use at the dealing desk. When the shrill tone sounded, Greg immediately knew that it was the call he hoped he would not be getting today. Few people had his personal mobile number. Amongst them was Chas for work purposes and Barbara for social purposes. Both of them were in view. The other recent recipient was Nathaniel the headhunter.

'Greg, is this a good time?'

The regular code words spoken in that Manhattan drawl. Nathaniel all right. The moment of truth.

'Yes, now's OK.' Greg stood up and walked over to the coffee machines for some privacy. He tried to deduce Nathaniel's mood. He sounded hesitant. A bad sign. If this move to Deutsche weren't going to happen, then Nathaniel would be equally pissed off about it. No commission.

'I've got some news from Deutsche, Greg. I called you as soon as possible.'

This didn't sound great.

'I hope you haven't done anything rash at Blakes yet, job wise.'

Not great at all. Nathaniel had said enough. The hints were there. No job. Greg persevered.

'What do you mean exactly?'

'Like resigning? I hope you haven't resigned yet.'

Make Nathaniel suffer a bit. The leech had teed him up nicely and now he was about to dump him.

'And what if I had? Does it matter? Haven't I got the Deutsche job lined up for next week?'

Innocence personified. Nathaniel was not enjoying the hushed conversation.

'They have had second thoughts. The offer letter you received is null and void.'

'When did this happen?'

'Thirty minutes ago.'

The day after the Provident share price collapsed. No coincidence at all.

'So the job is gone? All because of Provident?'

Nathaniel lied.

'No, Greg, of course not. Deutsche need some time to reconsider.'

'Time? How much time?'

'A while. I'll be in touch if they wish to pursue this

opportunity further at a later date. Bye.'

In touch? At a later date? It wasn't a postponement. It was permanent. Greg was stuck at Blakes for the foreseeable future, his one possible escape route blocked at the last minute. He'd had enough of Blakes today. He left the office and made straight for a darkened pub nearby. One of the more disgusting pubs in deepest Spitalfields, solely frequented by builders, social welfare claimants, market traders of the fruit and veg variety and lounging council workers.

There were no other suits from the City to recognise him in his moment of despair. He ordered a pint of Budweiser but found the wait interminable. He ordered a double whisky chaser and downed it before the lager arrived. That felt much better. He would be all right once he'd had a few more and chilled out a bit.

Sarah sat at her PC and viewed her spreadsheet of hard cash and investments. There was only one recent share deal with Penelope to update, the sale of all her Provident shares and share options. The shares had been sold at eleven pounds seventy-five pence each, ten pence under the all-time high price achieved a day before. The options had been sold at an excellent profit too. She had done well thanks to the Mandarin's timely advice.

The spreadsheet totalled five hundred and ninety-two thousand pounds. Was she there yet? Perhaps. She looked up the sterling dollar exchange rate: 1.69 dead. She worked the numbers out. It came to a million bucks plus. She was there. She had reached her magic target figure. Time to consider her future. Did she really want to continue living life like this? A million bucks went a long way for a single girl.

The passage of time didn't make the death any easier. She had killed a husband and a father and she never wanted to relive the experience with any other client in that awful basement. On the last few occasions when she had descended the wrought-iron stairs to provide her unique service to an influential gent, she could feel the odious presence of death all around her. She couldn't work there. She needed a change. And now she had the change to spend.

It was a sordid life full of bizarre games. Lenny scared her. So did Greg. Four years' working like this in London had taken its toll, mentally and physically. She'd had enough. Work wise and financially. The loot was sitting offshore in Jersey in sufficient quantity. Game over. The doorbell rang.

As soon as she opened it, she smelt the stench of alcohol on his breath. Whisky for sure and lots of it. Greg lurched into the lounge and almost fell into one of the sofas. The odour of cigarette smoke followed him. He threw his creased jacket on the floor and put his feet up on the coffee table. He dragged his shoes sideways, marking the Mandarin's polished surface. His tie was loose and he slurred his speech.

'Sarah, this is a disaster. This is the worst fucking two days of my life.'

She was worried. He was seriously depressed. And drunk again. She didn't need to probe any further.

'I have lost millions for the bank in the past twenty-four hours. Fucking millions. Provident has been a fucking disaster. But worse than that, my new job at Deutsche is gone as a result. Four years of my life I've wasted with Old Nick and the others at Blakes and this new job disappeared this morning. All because of Provident too. If only I had known about it in time. Deutsche don't want a loser like me at their desk.'

She offered some token of hope.

'You're not a loser. You're a star dealer.'

'No, I'm not. You're the star. Without you, I have nothing. I need you so that I can deal.'

Now was not the time to advise Greg that she was about to end their business arrangement.

'And another thing. You screwed up on that job I asked you do. That thug Lenny was supposed to beat up that asshole from the LSE.'

Sarah countered.

'He did. He called me to say that his minder had done the job.'

'That's what he says. I saw Robinson this morning in Blakes. He's been around again asking Personnel questions about me and my dealing. There isn't a mark or a scratch on him. Lenny's lying.'

'Are you sure?'

'Of course I'm damn sure. Either you or Lenny fucked it up totally. That guy is getting too close to finding out what we did and if I go down, then I'll take you with me. You get back to Lenny and tell him to give this guy from the LSE a serious scare. Give him something fatal to think about.'

'I'll call him.'

'You'd fucking better.'

She didn't need this sort of language in her home. Greg wasn't quite finished.

'What a lousy day. Gimme a drink.'

'Don't you think you've had enough?'

'No, I don't. Get me a damn drink. Whisky. Now.'

She froze on the spot. This was going downhill fast. She hadn't seen him like this for a while. Not since the time in the hotel suite when Lenny had saved her from his anger. He moved first.

'I'll have to fucking get it myself then. Won't I?'

He stood by the array of liquor bottles on the side table and selected a bottle of scotch.

'Glass?'

'In the kitchen.'

He made for the door. It was hard work. He stumbled along, holding onto nearby chairs on the way. He almost collapsed onto one chair by her desk, then stopped. He was looking at the glare of the screen and that Excel spreadsheet which was still open. He was drunk, but not that drunk. He was seeing words and numbers. Sportsworld. County Beverages. Provident. Provident fucking bank with an enormous profit listed in the far right-hand side sell column. Lots of zeros. Sold at 1175 pence. Jesus. She had made a killing. The light dawned. He forgot about the glass and lurched back into the lounge.

'You bitch. You fucking bitch. You knew.'

'Knew what?'

'About Provident?'

She realised what he had seen. Her secret was no more.

'Yes. I bought and sold the same shares as you did. I'm sorry, but I realised there was easy money to be made and it did no one any harm.'

But she still hadn't understood what Greg had seen.

'Fuck that. I've known about you buying and selling the same shares for weeks. I've been to Jersey too. But you knew about the bad loans at Provident from Soames and you sold out just in time. Didn't you?'

Her expression said it all. She didn't deny it. No point. He had seen the evidence in black and white.

'And you never fucking told me about it.'

He was pissed. In every sense of the word. He stumbled nearer and clenched his fists in front of her, uttering a stream of verbal obscenities. She should have seen it coming but it was too late. He lashed out with his left hand and caught her on the side of her face. She toppled and fell upon the stripped wood floors. It wasn't enough for him. Millions of pounds lost in a day and she knew. He hit her again, easily brushing off her flailing arms as she tried to protect herself. The job at Deutsche snatched from his grasp. Another blow met the side of her head. That guy from the LSE was round today in Blakes. Another blow.

She screamed. This was all too familiar. It had been years ago but the memories flooded back. The pain and the hurt. The scars afterwards. At times like this in the past, in five star hotel rooms and corporate apartments in the West End, Lenny the chauffeur had been her saviour. Now she was alone in her own home and at Greg's mercy. It seemed like an eternity until he staggered out of her trashed home, a half-finished bottle of whisky in his hand, his shirttails hanging under his suit jacket.

Sarah lay listlessly on her sofa for hours. She debated going to see her GP or checking in at the local in-patients but they would ask questions. Maybe even call the police to report an attack. She didn't need that. She had to get even with that bastard from the City. Somehow.

She had to protect herself from discovery. She telephoned Lenny and told him that the job on the guy from the LSE had been botched. He swore over the phone and blamed his sidekick. Can't get the staff these days at all, he complained. He promised he'd sort it out this evening, Doll. Give the man a good scare.

She lay exhausted and played with the remote control until the ITN News at Six-Thirty came on. Not much of interest this evening until a short segment shot in a police station in West London. The mention of an executive of Provident Bank caught her attention. She wondered if the police were closing in on the suspect? Her.

A shot of a middle-aged detective holding something in his hand. It looked like a stereo cover from a car. She recognised it immediately. The detective warbled on about the evidence possibly being linked to the suspect in the investigation. Perfect. The clip finished and they cut to the sports news. Boring.

She used her remaining energy to shuffle over to the desk by the wall and open her favourite drawer. She fingered through a few bundles of cash that should have been lodged to her Jersey account by now. She might need to convert them to some foreign currency at her nearest Thomas Cook office. She saw the evidence. The stereo cover lay at the back of her drawer.

She pulled away for fear of placing an incriminating fingerprint on the evidence for the prosecution. The only fingerprints on it belonged to Alexander Soames, possibly also his wife and of course one Greg Schneider who had so kindly brought it up from the den of vice downstairs. She had an idea. Revenge would be sweet.

Barbara was worried about Greg. She hadn't seen him at Blakes all afternoon. No one knew where he was and he wasn't answering his mobile. She was due back on Blakes' dealing floor by seven so that she could do her star turn on Sky. Provident Bank was sure to be mentioned. But where was Greg? There was time to investigate. She left Blakes at five o'clock and took the Jubilee Line towards St John's Wood. A five-minute walk from the station brought her to the flat that she knew well from her many prior visits. She rang the bell out of politeness but there was no answer. She opened her handbag and used the key that Greg had given her months ago. She needed to check on him.

'Anyone at home?'

There was an indecipherable grunt from the main bedroom. He was here. Was he ill? She opened the bedroom door to be greeted by Greg lying on the duvet half dressed in a suit. The room smelt of alcohol. Drunk not ill. He was mumbling. She had never seen him this way before and was concerned. She knew about the events of the morning. The news was all over the first floor; many others were glad for once that they were not the alleged star of the nearby Special Situations desk.

'What's happened to you? Is this because of Provident?'

The mention of the word turned his stomach. That fucking bank. Two million quid lost. It all came flooding back. Why did she have to mention it? He rolled over to look at her. She stood a foot away in a muted pastel suit. She looked great. He stretched out a hand and grasped her leg. It felt good.

'No, Greg. Not now.'

He was sick of hearing the word no. No. No. All day today. Sick of it. He stretched out and encircled her legs with his arms. She protested and tried to move back towards the safety of the door. He had her.

'No, Greg. Leave me alone.'

He wasn't listening. His mind was on other more carnal matters.

'Come on, Barb. Let's do it. You know you like it.'

He was strong. Much stronger than her. He pulled her nearer and toppled her onto the bed. Then he rolled on top of her. He was heavy. His hands were all over her, grasping at the buttons on her blouse and exploring beyond. His fingers were sweaty and hot, his breath overpowering up close. She fought him, unsuccessfully. His trousers were off and he held her down on the pillows. It hurt. Real bad.

It was that time of the week. The time that Mark dreaded. Seven days had passed since the last trip and he had no option but to return. The cupboards were bare, the fridge was empty, the cheap French lager was gone and the cheese and fruit had turned mouldy. Thank God for late evening opening till 10 p.m. The Golf miraculously started first time as another plume of grey smoke emanated from the hanging exhaust. Kwikfit here we come. He headed off towards Sainsburys in Wandsworth for some pasta, poultry, noodles, booze, vino, and of course to watch the talent in the aisles. And to forget about Penelope.

He was later than usual but the traffic was still bad. He wanted to make it back in time for Barbara on Sky business. He overtook a crawling ten-year-old Escort with an L plate, dodged a lane-changing London bus but slowed when a hovering police car came up on the outside. A second glance in his rear-view mirror revealed a tailgater, a car right up his ass, just feet away. Annoying. Mark didn't like the look of the two guys in the car. One big ugly mug of a guy at the wheel and a dapper guy in the passenger seat. Mean characters. An ancient maroon Jaguar. A classic, unlike its occupants.

They were still on his tail. He slowed deliberately to annoy them, standing on the brakes. They didn't seem bothered. Their eyes stared back at him in the mirror. The traffic had cleared.

There was lots of room in the outside lane. If they were in a hurry, why didn't they overtake him and speed off into the sunset? They weren't in a hurry. They were following Mark.

He was about to see if the Golf could do fifty miles an hour and lose them when he hit the first set of amber traffic lights on his journey. He could have made it across the junction but common sense and the distant memories of the Highway Code prevailed over fear. He stopped precisely on the white line, like a Grand Prix driver on pole position ready for the off at Silverstone.

The Jag left his view momentarily but immediately appeared directly alongside. Mark could see the metallic paint and the shining chrome bodywork out of his side vision but he did not dare turn to look. He stared ahead, transfixed, waiting for the lights to turn green as soon as possible.

A partial sideways glance revealed that a side window in the Jag was being wound down. Mark had no choice but to turn to his right. The small man in the sharp suit stared back at him, his face partly disguised by a pair of heavy sunglasses. The man raised his hand slowly from his lap and pointed it in Mark's direction. It was the first time in his life but Mark knew a revolver when he saw one.

Fuck the traffic lights. Mark hammered the accelerator to the floor and the Golf lurched forward. He swung on the steering wheel and took a sharp left to avoid the oncoming cars that had screeched to a halt in the middle of the junction, horns screaming at the lunatic Golf driver who was jumping the lights. Mark wasn't listening to their protestations. He was attempting a world land speed record in a Mark I Golf as he put as much distance as possible between himself and the Jag.

Frequent glances in the mirror revealed no further sign of the Jag and after a manic ten minutes he pulled over into a deserted side road miles from Sainsburys. He slumped over the steering wheel, mixed feelings of fear and relief overcoming him. What the hell was going on?

Worse still, there was another minor disaster when Mark returned home. Barbara never made it on to Sky at eight-thirty. The anchor said that she wasn't available tonight at short notice. There would be no comment from the most alluring research analyst in the City. Mark wondered where Barbara was.

CHAPTER TWENTY-TWO

ST JOHN'S WOOD, LONDON NW8

Barbara awoke at seven a.m. She had overslept but it didn't matter today. She lay in the soiled bed. The sheets stank of alcohol, sweat and bodily fluids. Fear prevailed. The memories of the night were too much to recall. The pain remained. Physical and emotional. She could only remember crying herself to sleep in the early hours. She stretched with difficulty, extended her left leg from the bed onto the carpet and knew that he had hurt her.

She was alone at last. The bastard had already gone into work at his dealing desk. He had locked the bedroom door from the inside last night and forced her to stay. Now she could escape. What the hell had come over him last night? He had never been so drunk, so low, so strong, so sordid. He wasn't the man she thought she knew. Dreams of an engagement had become nightmares of abuse. Her mother had been right all along. Mind that American.

There were too many confusing choices. Her mind spun. Give her GP a call and go round immediately for a check-up? See if there was any internal damage done. Best to be sure. Or call the police. It was rape, but she and Greg worked together and had been a couple for months. She had called around to his flat and had stayed overnight. How would the police and a court jury see it? The indecision was too much to bear. She couldn't rationalise the choices. She had to leave and take the past with her. Got to get out of this flat that now held such terrible memories.

She skipped breakfast or a shower and instead gathered her torn clothes from the pile on the floor. Her work suit was unwearable, ripped along the side with threads hanging down. She went to the spare back bedroom where she had left odd items of clothing over the past few months for convenience. Mostly casual stuff, never good enough to wear on the second floor of Blakes. She found a pair of faded jeans and a Russell Athletic sweatshirt. They would do.

Into the kitchen where she took a black plastic bag from a cupboard. She packed the other few items from the spare room inside. A pair of sneakers, T-shirts badly in need of a wash, summer shorts, a skirt, sunglasses. Then into the bathroom to clear out her spare toiletries and make-up. She was desperate to take everything, not leave one reminder of how good the distant past had been.

She went into the lounge and looked for anything else. She grabbed a big bundle of CDs. Some were probably his. Fuck him. Then she noticed the single tape cassette lying behind the CDs. She read the label. Sportsworld. That tape again. Still here.

She couldn't think straight. Why had he got a tape like this? It must be from a press conference or some other corporate event. She placed the tape into the machine, examined the buttons this time, ran it back to the start, hit the play button and sat on the floor, her aching back supported by the sofa. She wished she could rewind the past twenty-four hours as easily.

'Arise.'

She heard some woman's voice with a false accent.

'So, Simon, what are you working on at the moment?'

'I can't tell you that. It's confidential.'

'Simon, you know that you can tell me. And you must tell me. You have no choice.'

'No. I can't. I can't. Please don't make me.'

'You know you have to tell me. There's an easy way and a hard way to do this. Which is it to be?'

A sudden crackle and a hiss on the tape. Silence for a few seconds. More air in motion. More cries. The tape ended abruptly. Barbara had no idea what this was about but her survival instinct told her to take it.

She threw the tape into her black plastic bag of bittersweet memories. She slammed the hall door behind her knowing that she would never return to NW8 again.

Sarah didn't dare to look in the bedroom mirror at first. She finally got up courage after a long soak in the bath. The evidence of last night's beating was clear to see. A discoloured bruising along the right-hand side of her face, so bad that it looked like a birthmark from hell. Her hand instinctively touched her tender cheek but she immediately withdrew it in pain.

The doorbell rang at his usual time. She had forgotten. Now she had to open the door. She took one last look in the hall mirror. He would see it and ask questions. The Mandarin was observant.

'My God, Sarah. What on earth happened to you?'

She backed up into the concealment of the half light of the hallway.

'Nothing happened.'

He put down his briefcase with the rubber gloves and cleaning utensils inside. He held out his arms to her. She stepped into them and gently he pulled her into a better light.

'You've been attacked. Who did this?'

She didn't want to implicate anyone. There had been enough violence of late. But he didn't give up.

'Was it a client? Tell me and I'll get something done about

it. I have contacts at the highest levels in the Home Office. I can pull a few strings. Arrange an arrest, whatever you want. Just name it.'

She'd had enough of deception and bizarre requests. She needed a career break. He was insistent. Perhaps he could help. The Home Office? That might be the answer.

'You can do me one favour.'

'Whatever you want, name it.'

'You say you have friends in the Home Office?'

'Sure. You want to get back at whoever did this to you?'

'No. I need a passport.'

He relaxed at this request. He was on home territory now.

'Haven't you got one already? You can get them easily enough, you know?'

'Not that sort of passport. I need the sort you use for sudden emergencies. A passport where you pick your own surname and it still looks like the real thing.'

He caught her drift. This could be a way of repaying her for all the understanding she had shown over the years.

'It's possible. I can get you one.'

'How much?'

'Don't worry about that. It's on Her Majesty's Government.'

'How soon can you get it?'

'A week. What name do you want on it?'

'You choose. Something anonymous.'

The Mandarin knew that this wasn't the time and the place for cleaning her home. He made to leave and almost fell over the recently arrived shopping from John Lewis in Oxford Street. Never knowingly undersold even when it came to fine co-ordinated luggage from the floor fifth. Two matching Samonsite hard cases still in their plastic wrapping stood by the wall.

'So you're going away somewhere?'

'Yes. I'm leaving London for good.'

He turned to her in surprise.

'Where?'

'You don't want to know where. It's best that way.'

'I'll be sorry to see you go. You've been a good friend. What about your home here?'

'It's rented.'

'What about the car?'

'It's stolen.'

'What about the hardware downstairs? You can hardly sell that sort of stuff.'

'I've got some friends in the business. I'll sell it to one of them. I'll give you an introduction if you like. One of them has a really old and dirty house. Her toilets are always in a bad way. The bathroom's a mess and even rats avoid the kitchen. You'll love it.'

The Mandarin smiled, a resigned look on his face. The end of an era.

'I'll work on my CV. It's been a great few years. Get me a photo and I'll get you the passport.'

He paused in the hallway, leant over to give her a polite peck on the cheek, then realised it was still tender to the touch. He pulled back. He cared about her that much.

Mark was distracted. How could he work when he was tormented by memories of that incident with the Jaguar? He had told no one yet. He didn't understand what had happened. Was it a case of mistaken identity? Was someone having a laugh at his expense? Was it for real? Was it a threat on his life? And why could he not remember the registration number of the Jag? One thing was certain. It was hard to focus on work. Maybe that was the plan?

He sat at his desk with a dog-eared copy of the A–Z open in front of him, wondering where the hell the lesser-known hamlet of Thames View was. Then success as the tattered index at the back revealed it was somewhere on the southern tip of the Isle of Dogs in EI4 land. His thumbnail came to rest on a small curved cul de sac near Mudchute Park. Might as well Just Do It. Nike would be proud.

There was no point getting a cab in the peak daytime traffic. Quicker by tube as they say. The nearest station was Crossharbour. Not a tube station though, rather a Docklands Light Railway station. He took a business card with him for identification purposes. He still hadn't found his missing LSE identity card. He stopped by Norris's door on his way out, so his boss didn't think that he was skiving off early.

'I'm off for an hour or so.'

'To where?'

'Sarah Hart's place like you said.'

Then Mark had second thoughts.

'Clive, what exactly should I do down there?'

'Use your eyes. Look around her place if you can. See if she seems like a normal private client.'

'What should I ask her?'

'Ask her if she knows Schneider at Blakes.'

'She'll never admit that to me, even if she does know him.'

'Of course she won't. But watch her face, her reaction when you ask her the question. You'll know.'

Mark left the office and entered Bank station. He waited for a few minutes on a busy platform before the space-age Docklands train drew in. He took a seat near the all-glass front and soon the blackness of the underground tunnels gave way to awe-inspiring views of Londons Docklands. The gleaming towers of Canary Wharf hove into view, intermingled with building sites, giant cranes and excavators.

Crossharbour was the penultimate station on the most southern branch line and a short walk brought him to the steps of number thirty-two Thames View. First impressions were uninspiring. A small townhouse, built say five years ago but well maintained. Mark used his non-existent property surveying skills and summarily valued it at a couple of hundred k. Not a particularly flashy place for someone with so much more stashed away in Jersey in cash, shares and government gilts. The BMW 3-series was gleaming. He was forming the immediate impression that this Sarah Hart was a tidy, organised individual.

There was no answer at the door. He tried again. She must be out. Typical. A wasted journey. He peered into the front window although the curtains made it difficult. He could see someone inside. She saw him too and knew that she had been seen. She had no choice. A voice called from behind the hall door.

'Yes?'

'I'm looking for Sarah Hart?'

A pause. She still had no choice.

'And you are?'

'Mark Robinson. I work with the Enforcement Department of the London Stock Exchange.'

Another pause. She recognised that name. It was the one that Greg had mentioned a few days ago. He was that poor guy who should have been beaten up by Lenny, but never was according to Greg.

'Do you have any identification?'

Mark pushed an official business card through the letterbox. The door opened slowly. He seized the moment and walked inside, without actually having been invited. She didn't stop him but looked at her guest properly for the first time. It was the guy in the photograph. He looked far better in real life. Alive, personable, relaxed. And he didn't have a mark on him. Just like Greg had said.

She noticed him staring back at her. Did he recognise her? What was he staring at? Of course. The bruising. She instinctively held up a hand to her face. He didn't know her at all but he was worried.

'Are you OK? Have you been injured recently?'

She used to know how to lie. A trick of the trade.

'Yes. I walked into a door.'

Old excuse. Bad lie. His suspicions were aroused. It was the sort of ugly injury you see on *The Bill* or on *ER*, when someone has been attacked by a drunken boyfriend or a jealous husband. It didn't look like she'd had any medical treatment for it. Raw, deep marks. Purple discolouring. Sore and tender, he guessed. She didn't like the scrutiny.

'What do you want?'

He had his story well prepared. He used the moment to glance around the interior of the townhouse. Normal enough. Nicely furnished. Wooden stairs leading to the second floor and a wrought-iron staircase leading down to a basement garage probably. He focussed.

'I am investigating recent trading in Provident Bank shares. I believe you own some?'

She had sold. She could tell the truth. Sarah went for the easy response but as soon as she uttered the words, she regretted her voluntary spontaneity.

'No, I don't own any.'

'The client records at Blakes' Jersey office show that you have ten thousand shares, and many more options?'

He knew about Blakes in Jersey. This was getting serious. How much did he know? Mark had extrapolated the implications of her answer in record time.

'Do you mean then that you have since sold your shares and options?'

No way out. She was cornered. He must have access to Blakes' private client records. Come clean.

'Yes.'

'When did you sell them?'

'A few days ago.'

Precise timing mattered in this instance and they both knew it. The black hole in Provident's loan book was all over the press.

'Did you sell before or after the British Commercial takeover collapsed?'

He probably knew the answer to that question too, or could at least find it somewhere in Blakes.

'Before.'

Mark was more suspicious. She had sold out in time and must have made some decent money. She could see his reaction. Still, there was no law against making a lucky profit on a share sale. He persevered.

'Can I ask you why you bought the Provident shares originally?'

'I thought they were a good speculative punt in the near term.'

He recognised the jargon. She knew her stuff. This was no amateur investor.

She wasn't saying anymore, wondering how far this conversation would go. Did this guy carry handcuffs? That bruise hurt.

'Is that it? Is there anything else you want to ask me?'

He had only one question left. He watched her closely, watched her eyes.

'Do you know a dealer called Greg Schneider who works at Blakes in the City?'

They definitely moved. Her pupils dilated. Only for a spilt second. A dead give-away. She lied.

'No. I can't say that I've ever heard of him.'

She was lying. She had been attacked by someone but would not talk about it. Something was wrong here. She motioned to the door. Mark noticed the stacked luggage and threw in a social pleasantry.

'Going somewhere?'

'Maybe.'

Mark stood in the cold corridor staring into the intensive care unit. It was scary to the uneducated. Tubes and monitors. Electronics and sensors. Charts and dials. Lighting as subdued as Mark felt right now. Worse still, the form on the bed lay motionless, mouth open and to one side, forced ajar by a ventilator tube, limp arm extended along the side of the bed and connected to a saline drip. Peter hadn't moved a muscle in the twenty minutes of Mark's lunchtime visit.

Mark recalled their conversation on his first, more optimistic, visit to the hospital. Someone had asked Peter where he worked. They knew about the LSE. And then those men in the Jag at the traffic lights yesterday. Was there any connection with Peter's current plight? Mark didn't feel much like returning to work but it would keep his mind off more depressing matters and he did have an appointment to keep.

Back at his lonely desk he avoided looking at the adjacent empty seat. It was almost time to go home but he still had one telephone call to make before he briefed Norris again. He looked up the LSE telephone directory of all the players who mattered in the City, found the number of Mitchell Leonbergs' office, and called the switchboard.

'Brad Franklin, please.'

An anonymous girl's voice answered in perfect Queen's English.

'I am sorry but Mr Franklin no longer works here.'

'Oh . . .'

She sensed the disappointment in Mark's voice. The trail had gone cold.

'Mr Franklin now works in our New York office. I can give you his direct number?'

Mark jotted down a 212 area code number, hung up and looked at his Swatch. Six p.m. in London. Lunchtime in Wall Street. Franklin might be out, but it was worth a try. He dialled and the phone rang.

'Franklin.'

The background noise of a busy dealing floor was audible. American accents shouted over the din.

'This is Mark Robinson from the London Stock Exchange speaking.'

The voice was hesitant on the other end, evidently worried about a call from the regulators.

'Are you sure you got the right number, Robinson? I'm in New York, out of your reach. We worry about the NASD, the SEC and the Fed over here, not the LSE. Whad'ya want with me?'

Mark posed the next question carefully.

'Do you remember a dealer who used to work at your London equity desk called Greg Schneider?'

'He wasn't on any equity desk. We call them securities. Sure he worked on that desk.'

'Was he any good as a dealer?'

Franklin laughed.

'He was no worse than the others. He made a lot of loot for us in UK securities.'

Someone in the distance shouted prices at Franklin. He was distracted but Mark continued anyway.

'Schneider only stayed six months at your London office before he left for Blakes. I saw your job reference for him yesterday morning. I wondered why his employment with you was so short.'

Franklin was puzzled.

'What reference did you see?'

Mark looked again at the photocopy on his desk. It was definitely signed by Franklin.

'The one you signed. It's in the personnel files at Blakes over here.'

'No fucking way. It can't be so. He's legged you over.'

'How can you be so sure?'

'Because I never signed a reference for Schneider. I was explicitly told not to do so.'

'So there was a reason for his early departure?'

'Sure. We fired him.'

More shouting in the background. The Dow Jones was moving stateside and Franklin was missing the ride.

'Why did you fire him?'

These questions were starting to annoy the American at his dealing desk.

'It wasn't my call to fire him.'

'Who decided?'

The tone was growing hostile. Exasperation was setting in. Mark didn't have much longer.

'A senior guy in our Compliance Department in New York told me to fire him. That's all.'

'You must know more?'

'Look, limey, I've said enough already. If you want any more information you'd better talk to Compliance here. That's all I can say. I gotta go to work.'

The line went dead. A short but useful call. Schneider's original job reference on file was a fake, albeit a good one on glossy headed notepaper and signed somehow by a Director who swore that he hadn't put pen to paper. Norris came out of his office, took Mark inside and asked for an update.

'Schneider has lost a pile on the Provident deal but it's a rare loss. He evaded me when I met him yesterday. He's must be getting edgy that we might be onto something. Sarah Hart buys the exact same shares and is living in an average townhouse despite her enormous liquid wealth. She has been in a fight recently. She definitely knows Schneider. I saw it in her eyes, like you said. And there's more.'

'Go on.'

'Schneider faked his job reference from Mitchells when he joined Blakes. He was fired from Mitchells but his former boss won't say why. He said I would have to talk to Mitchells' New York Compliance Department if we wanted to find out more. I could try but they won't tell me much over the telephone, will they?'

Norris was impressed.

'This sounds interesting and worth following up.'

Norris leant back, looked at a hand-written list of personal telephone numbers and dialled a Manhattan number on the speakerphone. An American accent boomed out at them.

'Good afternoon, NASD.'

Mark recognised the initials. The National Association of Securities Dealers, the organisation that registered and licensed all the dealers and salesmen who worked on Wall Street. Norris was about to call in an old favour.

'Herb Imperio in Registration, please.'

A New Yorker answered his telephone. Norris immediately recognised the friendly voice.

'Herb, Clive here in London. How's life in the Big Apple?'

'Rotten to the core and we love it that way. What can I do for you?'

'Are you busy?'

'Always. Shoot.'

'Do you have the registration details of all dealers who have worked on Wall Street?'

'I sure hope so because that's my job.'

'Have you got any records there on a former Mitchells' New York dealer called Greg Schneider?'

'Hold on.'

They heard a few keys being tapped as a surname was typed into a computer. Success.

'Yeah. He was on our registration system a few years ago.'

'Do you have anything unusual on him?'

'I can't tell. The data is too old. It's been archived on our system. But the paperwork is somewhere in the basement here.'

Then Norris went for it.

'Could you dig it out and send it over to us?'

'Gimme a break, Clive. These are our records. They gotta stay here.'

Norris re-evaluated the situation.

'If I sent someone over to you, could they have a look at the file?'

'Sure.'

Someone from the LSE was going to New York on business. Norris was getting carried away.

'And could you get that someone in to see Mitchells' Compliance Department? You must have lots of contacts built up during your many years.'

A wry smile from Norris. Mark swore that Herb could see the grin six thousand miles away.

'Yeah, Clive, I can do that. Let me know your timings and I'll line it up. Who are you sending over?'

'A guy by the name of Mark Robinson. He's one of our best. Keep an eye out for him next Monday morning.'

CHAPTER TWENTY-THREE

BATTERSEA, LONDON SW1

Mark stood by the window of his Battersea flat with one eye on the television. Sky TV was showing the review of the week's news, as they were prone to do on a Sunday morning. It beat spending scarce money on new programming. He was half hoping that they would cut over to that gorgeous research girl from Blakes but he knew that it was a vain hope at 10 a.m.

His other eye was on the world outside. The one-way street was lined with cars parked up on the kerbs. Wild kids glided amongst them on roller blades. Early morning shoppers walked back home with a pint of milk and *The Sunday Times* under their arms. Cats stretched to wake up on the tops of precariously narrow garden walls. The promised complimentary car service from United Airlines was late.

An engine stopped outside. Mark glanced out again. Surely some mistake? He didn't know the name of the enormous beast outside but it was the same make of car that the Queen used to drive down the Mall on state occasions, black with over-large windows and ridiculously elevated seats. All that was missing was the Royal standard fluttering up front and Philip in the back. The driver took off a peaked cap. Totally unnecessary too. He buzzed the doorbell below. It was Mark's lift to LHR. The embarrassment.

He was about to turn off the JVC and check the gas, electricity and water for the umpteenth time when he heard the Sky newscaster mention something about Provident Bank. City news. Perhaps Barbara would appear after all? He waited and saw an archive clip of a couple of plain-clothes policemen at a press conference. The caption in the top left of the screen said Wednesday. Four days ago. Mark must have missed it first time around. He wondered if it had any relevance to his dealing investigation.

A middle-aged man held the cover of a car stereo in his hand. The caption said DI Ted Hammond of the Met. It was a Sony stereo with a CD 90X something or other name. Hammond seemed hopeful at the prospect of finding the missing clue. Not likely, thought Mark. It was more likely to be sitting in the murky depths of the Thames. He killed the TV with the remote control and pulled the hall door closed. The driver took his one piece of luggage downstairs. Mark stared at the car.

'Don't you have anything less conspicuous than this?'

'Sorry Guv, it's all we had at the depot. The Mercs and Range Rovers were booked. Don't you like it?'

'It's a bit over the top.'

The chauffeur pushed through the melee of interested kids hanging around the car.

'Maybe, but the Arabs who fly on Emirates and Gulf Air love it. They say they feel like royalty in it.'

Mark had been excited when Norris had told him that LSE policy was to fly business class on all flights over six hours. His second trip on LSE business was to be a real experience. Now he wasn't so sure. Mark wasn't royalty and had no such aspirations. He slumped into the back seat.

They hit every set of red traffic lights. He noticed another drawback as they sat in the rows of fuming traffic. Other motorists alongside in their Vectras and Mondeos peered in.

Wives in front passenger seats and unruly children pinned into rear seats stared up at him, probably wondering who this guy was in the flash car and was he famous? Mark did not acknowledge their glances and wished that the windows were darkened. They headed through grimy West London, through Shepherds Bush Green and Chiswick, and onto the M4 and out of this damn car.

Heathrow Terminal 3 was manic inside, as if the last flight out of Saigon was about to depart. Mark avoided the queues at Economy, made straight for the Connaisseur check in and through Fasttrack passport control. Still manic. This wasn't an airport anymore. It was one big shopping mall that happened to have a few airplanes and a runway attached for passenger convenience. He stood on the gleaming marble floor near the odious x-ray machines and observed the shoppers who scurried around him like soldier ants, all aware that the clock was ticking remorselessly and they only had an hour or less before the departure gate to Tokyo or Johannesburg or Rio closed. So little time, so much choice, all suffering the social pressure of having to board the plane without a designer shopping bag. Mark thought about his current Barclaycard balance and made for the departure gate.

He boarded and eyed up the other passengers. Mr Big Shot Banker in his ochre Polo shirt made for the inside pages of the *Wall Street Journal*, then the glossy pulp of *Business Week*, lastly the utter boredom of *The Economist*. Mr P.C. Nerd in his cream socks opened up a Toshiba laptop and aimlessly toyed with Microsoft icons and drop-down menus. Miss Prim Academic put on over-sized glasses to peer at pages of dense mathematical formulae and graphs filed in weighty metal binders. Mrs Corporate Wifey sat beside her ten-year-old son who read the *Beano*, no doubt favoured by the ample home leave transport policy of some US multi-national, rather than being independently wealthy enough to afford the luxury of a club class seat. The fortunate child's feet couldn't even reach the floor.

Mark sat in silence beside an obnoxious investment banker in 5B. He knew his occupation because his briefing papers proclaimed the name of a second-tier US firm. Paine Webber Inc. And what a pain. The more he saw of these types the less he liked them. Could he ever work with them? This swarthy guy barked at the stewardess until she understood that he had wanted the *Wall Street Journal*, when he had mumbled the *Journal*. Then 5B immediately took over total ownership of the centre arm rest, wolfed the gourmet food down like a Big Mac, guzzled the vino like Coke, took the largest fistful of Belgian chocolates possible, farted repeatedly yet silently after he had eaten and stretched out in his holed socks to sleep. There wasn't a single word exchanged between them in seven hours and twenty minutes.

After the largest afternoon tea ever served, they touched down at JFK. Touchdown. Like Cape Canaveral. Mark's first time in the USA. Thanks to Clive Norris. He wasn't that bad as a boss. He had given Mark some useful pointers in the past few weeks; he knew the securities business well, and he had contacts in his peer group all over the world. Mark would stay on longer at the LSE, at least until this investigation came to a conclusion. He hadn't thought about moving jobs for weeks, not since Provident came up and that pointless job interview at Morgans.

The baggage was already waiting on the carousel when he cleared immigration. Bulky Afro-American NYPD police officers and customs officials stood about, some with pieces hanging from holsters. He stepped out of Terminal Six into eighty-five degrees of humid heat and took in a breath of fresh US air. Well, as fresh as you can get in Queens. He avoided the aggressive taxi touts at the exit and took a legitimate yellow cab.

They left the warren of JFK in the company of ridiculously elongated white Lincoln limos, Hertz and Avis transit buses, Carey airport transfer coaches and lost tourists in lost gleaming hire cars. Mug me please. The lunatic cab driver from Bombay hurtled down the pitted concrete of the Van Wyck expressway towards Manhattan. Periodically he found an opening in the traffic and Mark felt the surge of power in the battered Chrysler as the pedal hit the metal. They only slowed when they encountered the soul-destroying tailbacks of the tollbooths but by then Mark's mind was in overdrive.

There it was. A skyline. No, *the* skyline. Manhattan rose up before him. Awesome. Towering skyscrapers stretching from the left, the twin towers of the World Trade Centre near Wall Street, up past the Empire State, the PanAm building and the pink neon of the Chrysler Building and on further right to the Citibank Tower in uptown. In between a myriad of steel and reinforced concrete beckoning all-comers. Mark felt the adrenaline. Welcome to the USA, folks. Have a nice day.

Half an hour later he was in his hotel room on East 34th Street and Park, still awake although jet-lagged. He found nothing of interest in his anonymous hotel room. Beige carpets, beige wallpaper, beige duvet, beige everything. Cheap prints welded to the walls. Air conditioning filtering out reality. A mini-bar with the world's most expensive shorts. Hangers hooked to the rails to avoid petty theft. Free souvenir pens. Magnified shaving mirrors to shock. Toilet paper shaped into a neat point by some Latino housemaid. Too many mirrors to give the impression of space that simply wasn't there.

He flicked through the television stations with the remote. Forty channels of mere abbreviations. NBC, CBS, CNN, MTV, CSPAN, NYI, VH1, HSC, A&E, ESPN, TNT and the rest. Nothing worth watching. Too many adverts. Adverts for global burger chains, deep pan thick crust pizzas and oozing tacos interspersed with adverts for peptic acid, indigestion tablets, six-pack stomachs and better pecs, slimming and weight loss. Adverts for luxury sedans interspersed with adverts for treadmill running machines at 299.99 bucks plus p&p. Such irony. But he hadn't come all this way to watch TV.

He gazed out of his window from the twenty-ninth floor. He didn't think he had ever been so high, physically or mentally. The speckled lights stretched before him like the backdrop from *Frasier*. Cranes inter-mingled with roof gardens and steaming air-con units on rooftops. FDNY fire engine and NYPD car sirens wailed incessantly far below. Were there really that many fires or crimes in NYC or was it laid on especially for the expectant hordes of tourists? Cars moved lanes like beetles below on a mission to boldly go. The white roofs of MTA buses moved effortlessly like an aerial scene from *Speed*. Customers scurried in and out of corner Indian delis, still open at eleven o'clock. Capitalism reigns supreme.

What a city. Daunting yet challenging. And somewhere out there, amongst all the lights, the noise and activity, the eight million inhabitants, lay a story about Greg Schneider. Mark had to find out the truth in the next week or this trip would be a waste of time and money for the LSE.

Mark was lost. An Englishman in New York. He stood outside his midtown hotel on a sweltering August Monday morning wondering where exactly in Manhattan he was. Which way was uptown and which was downtown? How did the sequential avenue and street numbers run again? He needed a map. And a cab. The doorman did his best but it was rush hour and few passed by with their vacant light on.

'Where are you going, sir?'

'Wall Street direction.'

'Try the subway, sir.'

Was this guy serious? His first day in New York. Try the most dangerous train system in the world? How would he even know where to go? The doorman was a step ahead.

'It's over there. Thirty-third and Park Avenue South station. Walk down. Buy a Metro card. Get off at Fulton and Broadway. It's a few minutes' walk to Wall. You can't go wrong. Just don't stare at anyone.'

Mark took the chance, descended into the claustrophobic air of the station and pushed his way through the ticket barrier and onto the air-conditioned carriage. Packed but clean inside. People sat reading their *Journals.* Very civilised in fact. Six stops downtown later he alighted and exited onto Broadway with a modest sense of achievement. Not much of a feat for a local. More so for a Brit overseas.

The locals also emerged from subway exits with cups of double decaff latte and cream cheese bagels in hand. Men in regulation-issue white shirts with button-down collars, dark suits and highly polished shoes. Women with teased streaked hair, sombre suits, white Nike sneakers and dark tights, even in eighty degrees of sweaty discomfort. The shoes were soon to be exchanged for a pair of heels left under their desk last Friday evening. Welcome to Wall Street in rush hour.

The brass nameplate on the side street confirmed he was at the offices of the National Association of Securities Dealers. A quiet lobby gave way to bustling offices upstairs. He was escorted to a corner suite, totally chaotic with files and printouts scattered across every available inch of desk space. The sign on the door gave away the name of the deputy head of NASD Registration & Qualification.

'Herb Imperio. You must be Mark?'

An absolute bull of a man greeted Mark. The handshake hurt. Six foot three plus, broad and with a neck like a rugby front row prop forward. Imperio's top shirt button was open merely because no shirt had yet been designed by man to accommodate the extensive girth of his neck. Rolled up sleeves revealed equally thick muscled arms. A greying moustache was the only noticeable facial feature on an otherwise leathery face. The sheer physical presence belied the personality of a friendly fellow regulator.

'Clive told me more about the purpose of your trip. I hear you're on the trail of a real big scandal in London?'

'I hope so. Otherwise I've wasted a month or more at work.'

'Don't worry. Us regulators are like the Mounties. We always get our man. You know I did two tours in Vietnam? We hunted VCs, tracked them for days, crept up on their foxholes and wiped them out. It's like this business only the targets are harder to find and we ain't got any Napalm.'

Mark was wondering what it would be like to be in a platoon run by Imperio. Scary. They paused while the caffeine arrived on a tray. He surveyed the general office area outside. Imperio eyed him.

'Is this your first trip to good old New York?' asked the veteran.

'First time to the USA. First time to anywhere west in fact.'

'What do you know about what we do at the NASD?'

'Not much. Fill me in.'

Imperio eased back in his wobbly chair and delivered the party line.

'The NASD is the self-regulatory organisation for all securities firms and their employees in the US. That's a lot of work to do. There are five and half thousand member firms, sixty thousand branch offices scattered across every corner of this great country and half a million people who work as dealers, salesmen and the like. We police the industry, we ensure that the securities business operates in a fair and equitable manner. We got our rules, we review the members' firms, we protect investors and we operate the NASDAQ market. And we wipe out the wrongdoers when we catch them. Hey. Just like 'Nam.'

Mark had heard of the NASDAQ stock market. Unlike its more famous bigger brother a few blocks away, the NYSE, NASDAQ was screen based trading at its best, no dealing floors anywhere downtown, and it boasted some of the newest yet riskiest listed companies. Imperio saw his recognition.

'We're proud of NASDAQ. It didn't even goddamn exist twenty-five years ago. Now it's one of the biggest stock markets in the world with six thousand listed companies. Even ten years ago the companies listed on NASDAQ were dodgy technology outfits, pushy biotech researchers and FDA-busted drug companies. Now they are household names and everyone wants to buy them. Dell, Cisco, Compaq, AOL, Yahoo, Netscape, Amazon. They are worth billions. They're real hot. Do you know that one in six new jobs created in the US today is created by NASDAQ listed corporates.'

'I'm impressed.'

The intro was over. Time for business. Imperio knew it.

'So, I guess you want to know about what we have here on the dealers?'

'Definitely.'

Imperio was still doing the hard sell on the NASD. There was no need.

'We register and qualify every securities professional who works with a member firm, including the mighty Mitchell Leonberg. That includes every partner, officer, director, branch manager, supervisor, sales person and even the most junior grunt on the sales desk. We take great care with the dealers. When we register a dealer we get information about their prior employment, their disciplinary history, and even their police record if they have one. Every professional must pass an exam called the Series 7 before they can deal and that exam is pretty tough. We ask them hundreds of multiple choice questions about federal securities laws, NASD regulations, securities products, financial markets, economics, risk, order solicitation, new issues, accounting, portfolio analysis, sales practices, tax breaks and the like. They gotta get seventy per cent or more to pass.' Imperio pointed to a framed certificate hanging lopsided on the wall behind him. 'Those of us who work at the NASD even sit the exam ourselves, to show that it can be done. It took me two damn attempts to get it.' Imperio gave him a wry smile. 'Now for Schneider.'

Mark saw that at last some information was on the way.

'Herb, I know Schneider faked his CV and his reference

from Mitchells. His former boss Franklin told me so. He was fired from Mitchells' London office but I don't know why. What do you have on him?'

Imperio leant forward and spun a dirty desk computer screen around so that Mark could view it.

'This is our registration database. It's got the amazingly unimaginative title of the Central Registration System. It holds the name, address, employer, date of birth, experience, exam record, disciplinary record and much more on the employees in the industry. We got half a million names on here but only about half of them are actively employed in the biz. The rest got some sense, have gone straight and got a decent respectable job doing something more productive for the nation.'

Another grin. Mark enjoyed the dry sense of humour. Maybe a tour of duty in 'Nam wouldn't have been so bad.

'This is Schneider's record on screen. It says that his info is archived.'

'That's not much use to me.'

But Imperio had a file.

'This is Schneider's file from downstairs. It's four years old and a bit musty but don't mind that.'

Mark thumbed though the first few pages on the desk. Imperio guided him.

'That's his original application when he joined the Mitchells office here. Those are his Series 7 exam results. He scraped it with a seventy-three per cent. He was no rocket scientist apparently. That is his registration as a junior dealer on their domestic US Securities desk.'

All the forms amazed Mark. The NASD had a form for everything. Then he saw a page displaying what looked like two sets of fingerprints. Surely not? He was getting excited.

'What are these fingerprints for? Does Schneider have a criminal record?'

'Not that I am aware of. We fingerprint all the registered dealers. It's a unique identifier for every individual and therefore we never get our records confused. It also helps when we check if they have a criminal record. We don't want embezzlers and cheats selling stocks to little old ladies and orphans. Some here wants us to switch to DNA samples for ID purposes instead but I'll believe that when I see it.'

Mark marvelled at the row of ten perfectly inked finger-prints. The NASD was light years ahead of the LSE.

'You might find the last few pages a bit more interest-ing, Mark.'

There was a letter from Mitchells' Legal & Compliance Department confirming to the NASD that Schneider had moved to their London office and would no longer need registration in the US. Then another letter six months later confirming that he had resigned from the employment of Mitchell Leonberg and seeking explicit confirmation that the NASD records had been updated to reflect this. Imperio was reading the file at the same time.

'That's a bit unusual. Mitchells writing in explicitly to tell us that. It's as if they didn't want to be associated with Schneider ever again. It makes me think that he left for a definite reason.'

'Don't you ask firms why a dealer has resigned from the employment of a particular firm?'

'We can ask but it doesn't do us much good. This place is a legal nightmare. There are parasitical lawyers running around to see if you have defamed their client and they would love to take an action against a government department or a big wealthy investment bank. Bottomless pockets and all that. So the banks and brokers are real careful. They get all legalistic and say that the employee resigned. They don't want to hang out their dirty laundry in public. They say the matter is dealt with internally and that's that.'

Mark needed some more clues. Otherwise this trip to Wall Street would be a waste of time.

'Is there anything else to go on?'

'Mark, don't panic. This is a file note written by a clerk who used to work here. He telephoned Mitchell's and pushed a compliance guy for some more background. He sensed that Schneider had been fired for unethical conduct, but it was off the record and the compliance guy wouldn't confirm it publicly. There's nothing on the file officially. Only a scribbled note.'

'Can't we track down this clerk and ask him if he remembers anything else? Find out who he spoke to in Mitchells' compliance department? Ask them in turn?'

'We could try to find the clerk now but it's a long shot.'

'It's all I have to go on,' pleaded Mark.

'OK, we'll try. But you can also ask Mitchells about this yourself when you meet them.'

'When?'

'Today. Two o'clock.'

'Who am I meeting?'

'J. Edson Weaver, of course. Nothing but the best for you, Mark. He's the Head of Legal & Compliance at Mitchells. The top man. And he's a complete bastard too, so watch out. Do you want some lunch first on the NASD?'

Mark was expecting some loud underground Wall Street den with hazy smoke and bad light. Instead Imperio surprised him. They strolled down Church Street, across manic Liberty Square and down behind the immense buildings of the World Financial Centre, north and south towers. Suddenly there was utter tranquillity. Unheard of in New York in Mark's short experience.

Rows of trees lay between the red marble office buildings and the Hudson River. The residential apartments of Battery Park overlooked them, all reclaimed by the Reichmann brothers in recent years from the muddy shallows. An elongated low level waterfall ran beside the outdoor restaurants, each miraculously with one or two free waterside tables at the ready. A breeze emanated from the river. Millionaire cruisers moored at the wooden jetties, interspersed with more modest yachts from the Manhattan Yacht Club and NYMEX. River ferries despatched their passengers along the quayside.

The beautiful players from the markets carried unwanted jackets over their shoulders and sported the best in tinted sunglasses from Saks. Other obese types snacked on an extra lunch that would have nourished an entire family in Somalia for weeks. Puerto Rican messengers in pristine white overalls delivered bulging bags from nearby delis through revolving doors to those who couldn't afford to take an eye off their dealing screens. Yuppies in shorts and t-shirts did lunchtime Yoga class in the adjacent park under the watchful gaze of a lithe pony-tailed female instructor. Tourists with Nikons, Berlitz guides and open downtown maps stopped to gaze at the scene and wonder if they really were in Manhattan.

Mark and Imperio took an outside table at Cucina where the breeze flapped the tablecloth gently. Imperio, true to his apparent Italian ancestry, ordered the largest available pasta. Mark went for a Sicilian, pizza that is, and not the wait-ress who swayed between the tables in a dangerously short skirt.

'Do you like New York so far, Mark?'

He nodded. It made all the difference when you had a native New Yorker to show you around. Other less fortunate visitors took fewer chances and never strayed from the well-worn tourist trail.

'If Weaver doesn't tell you much, there's one other line of attack that we can take. The SEC.'

Mark almost choked on the pepperoni and cheese. The Securities and Exchange Commission. They were serious regu-lators, the enforcers. They made the FBI look like amateur theatrical students.

'Are you sure?'

'Yeah. The SEC might have investigated a dealer who's been in trouble with his firm. It's worth a try and I know some people there. I'll make a call this afternoon. Call in a few favours. Finished?'

Mark had failed to down the final quarter of the world largest double crust pizza. What was it with the meals in the US? Breakfast this morning had been a forty-minute endurance test and had almost wiped him out for the entire day. Imperio had long finished the pasta and didn't like to see good food wasted.

'Sure. Dive in.'

A mammoth right hand swooped on the pizza and it disappeared. In the midst of digesting, Imperio's cellular phone went off. Imperio mumbled through the short conversation on the phone but he did his best.

'That was my secretary. She tracked down that clerk. He still works with the NASD but in our uptown offices. He says he clearly remembers the file, and the person he spoke to in Mitchells all those years ago was J. Edson Weaver. That's some more ammunition for your conversation with him in fifteen minutes' time. Let's go then. This tab is on me. You can pay next time if you get a result from Mitchells.'

'Where are Mitchells' offices?'

Imperio swivelled on his seat and pointed towards the World Financial Centre. And so modestly titled too by its corporate creators. A door in front of them was guarded by two security men.

'There it is. The world headquarters of Mitchell Leonberg & Co Inc. America's finest. The most successful and profitable investment bank in the world. You're a bit early but wait in the lobby for a while. Take in the view and the people. They are the best. And be prepared for Weaver. He's a strong character and he doesn't volunteer much. Work him like you're interrogating a Charlie.'

Mark sat in the lobby and assimilated his new surroundings. This put places like Blakes' London office in the shade. He wondered how someone like Schneider could ever move from a domain like this to a poky office in London. He must have been mightily pissed off. Maybe he had no choice. Had to get out?

Weaver made him wait until three o'clock. Then he made him wait for another half an hour. Deliberate or not? Mark couldn't tell. Would Weaver even see him at all? A secretary appeared from the lifts.

'Mr Robinson, this way please.'

Mark entered a walnut panelled office but didn't acknowledge the man across the desk. He was distracted. The view from forty-five floors up was truly awesome, as they were prone to say locally. Manhattan stretched before him all the way up to Central Park and beyond. Mark wished that he had bought his camera to this meeting. He wanted a souvenir. His host was not so impressed.

'Mr Robinson. I don't usually see representatives of regulators from outside the US.' His diction was perfect, spoken in a measured manner, as if a bunch of lawyers were sitting around waiting for the first loose word to sue him. The accent was not authentic New York, nothing like Herb's. More educated and polished, maybe from further north along the coast. New England perhaps? Massachusetts? Probably Harvard educated and wanted the world to know it.

Weaver was a middle-aged guy, immaculately turned out in an expensive suit, with an even more expensive groomed haircut. His small weasel-like face was intense and alert, but mean. He was perfection personified, at least on the exterior. They shook hands briefly. Weaver's hand was cold yet clammy. His fingers were bony. His handshake was limp and affected. His watch was all-gold. His cufflinks protruded noisily.

'I agreed to this as a favour to Mr Imperio at the NASD. I have ten minutes free in my diary. Running Legal & Compliance in Mitchells is a full-time job.'

Mark grovelled as required.

'It's much appreciated.'

Weaver waited. The silence was awful. This was going to be difficult.

'I am investigating Greg Schneider.'

No recognition from Weaver at all. Not a flicker of an eyelid.

'Do you remember him when he worked here before moving to your London office?'

'Vaguely.'

'He left your London office six months later to join Blakes.'

Weaver said nothing. Only a smirk at the mention of that insignificant British investment bank.

'Do you know why he left your firm's London office?'

'I think I recall that he resigned.'

'Are you sure?'

'Yes.'

This was monosyllabic conversation at its worst. Time to go for the killer blow.

'I understand that Mitchells fired Schneider.'

'Who told you that?'

'Brad Franklin told me over the phone last week.'

'I think Franklin must be mistaken. He's managed a lot of dealers over the years.'

Mark wasn't giving up yet.

'I understand that at the time you personally confirmed to the NASD that Schneider had been fired?'

'Who told you that?'

'It's on their files,' Mark lied.

'I don't recall that. In any case it would be off the record.'

'Precisely. I need to know, too. Off the record again, if you like.'

'I can't comment off the record with you.'

Silence. Ominous. Weaver rose.

'I have a Board meeting in ten minutes' time.'

That was it. Weaver was succinct. Like Imperio had said.

'Good day to you, Mr Robinson.'

Mark needed much more. He had to know about Schneider's past.

'Look, that's not good enough for me.'

Weaver was visibly taken aback. He obviously wasn't used to such behaviour in rosy corporate America.

'What?'

'I don't mean to be rude but I have travelled six thousand miles to find out why Schneider was fired. I must know. You are in Legal & Compliance. I am in regulation. We're both in the same business.'

'We're not. You and your kind are out to get people like us.'

'I am about to charge Schneider with insider dealing and I need all the information I can get.'

Weaver gave him a look that halted him in his tracks.

'Good luck in your endeavours then.'

J. Edson Weaver motioned towards the door. Mark now knew what the initial stood for. Jerk.

Mark left livid. What a waste of time. Flushed with his earlier success at negotiating the transport system, he re-entered the subway at Broadway and made for the 6-train platform. He waited. Where the hell was the uptown train? The platform was packed. The heat in the tunnels was unbearable. Ninety plus for sure. The train arrived but was packed to capacity. He found himself pushed against unknown warm bodies as it moved off. Voices clamoured all around him, none of them in English. Rather Spanish, Russian, Portuguese, African, he didn't know exactly where. Enormous Afro-Americans and Arabs in all the gear backed into him. Jesus. It was so hot in here.

At the next stop school children clambered aboard. Three-thirty p.m. Schools out. Only these were New York kids, all six foot three sixteen year olds, kitted out in Hilfiger, Adidas and Mecca street gear, shaved heads, loud voices. Muther fucka this and muther fucka that. Elbows up against Mark. The heat. This bloody train. He could take no more and got off at the next stop, escaped to street level and hailed a cab up to midtown. To hell with the subway. Never again. New York had got to him in a day. The illusion was shattered.

Mark collapsed onto his hotel bed. There was no fatigue like walking in New York City in hottest August in a heavy winter suit, pounding the pavements and feeling the sweat progressively settle, layer upon layer. He called Norris in London to report on the lack of progress but only managed to get his secretary. Norris was off on sick leave. No word on Peter either. Mark was alone in New York. Very much so. What to do?

He was at a dead end and contemplated his predicament. There was no chance of getting any more information from Weaver. Imperio had told him all the NASD knew. Mark had started his American investigation, and possibly also concluded it, on the same day. He couldn't face Norris on that basis. He needed a break. Suddenly the telephone by the bed rang.

'Mark, hi. Herb here. How did it go with Weaver?'

'He was as bad as you said. Like getting blood from a stone. He told me nothing. I need hard evidence if I can progress this case.'

'Precisely. I did some work today. That clerk gave us the name of someone at the SEC who he advised of Schneider's sudden departure.'

'So the SEC were involved?'

'Yeah. Now you can see why Weaver was reluctant to talk. He may have something to hide.'

'What do the SEC know?'

'That's for you to find out. I lined you up to see a Laura Ziegler first thing on Wednesday morning. That's the earliest that she can do.'

'Fine. Where are they? Downtown as well?'

'No. Far more exotic than that. They're in Washington DC. I took the liberty of booking you a seat on the nine a.m. Delta shuttle out of La Guardia. You can pick up the ticket and pay for it on departure.'

Another location. Mark was impressed.

'So what should I do tomorrow. More research?'

'Mark, chill out, do what anyone else would do in your shoes, miles away from their boss.'

Mark waited for Imperio to impart his professional advice based on years of regulatory experience.

'Take the boat out to Liberty Island and climb the statue. Take the Staten Island ferry over and back for the view. Walk down Fifth Avenue and take it all in. Soak up some rays in Central Park. Go up the World Trade Centre or the Empire State building. See the Met or the Guggenheim. Catch a game in Madison Square Garden or Shea Stadium. New York is waiting.'

CHAPTER TWENTY-FOUR

BISHOPSGATE, LONDON EC2

They sat around the Special Situations desk waiting for the moment of truth. Ten minutes to go. The Companies Announcement department at the LSE said that Provident shares would be relisted at eight-thirty a.m. Old Nick had come out of his office and sat to the right of Greg. Few expected the share price to be anywhere near the ten-pound level at which they were suspended so suddenly.

It had been an appalling week for Provident. They made it to the BBC Nine O'Clock news on the day the story broke. The loan losses were estimated at almost a billion pounds, all due to errors in calculating estimates, deliberate under-provisions, over-valuation of properties, even non-existent properties in some cases, thousands of mortgages in arrears. Fingers were pointed at the guilty parties. Alexander Soames was criticised. Go ahead. Do speak ill of the dead.

CEO David Webster was next in the firing line. City pension funds and shareholder groups demanded his immediate resignation. Webster hadn't been seen for days in public although reporters and TV crews had been driving between his Highgate pad and Suffolk country house looking for him. Then they realised he was closeted with some City lawyers working out the best severance package from Provident. Typical.

Greg felt worse. At least two million in dealing profits foregone. A non-existent job offer. The rape of his girlfriend of a year. He knew it had been rape. He hadn't spoken to Barbara since. She had taken a week off work. Holidaying at her parents' place said her colleagues in research. Greg knew the real reason. He didn't know if he could face her again. He wondered if she had talked to anyone about it yet. To a girlfriend or to her mother or to someone at work like Crosswaithe. Or worse, to the police?

Then the return of the drinking problem that he had kicked years ago in the States. Old Nick was too close right now. Close enough soon to smell the Jack Daniel's on his breath. Weird sort of liquid breakfast in hindsight. Greg took another stick of spearmint chewing gum. That should work to camouflage his breath.

'A minute to go, guys. Watch the screens. Are we selling, Greg?' asked Chas from across the desk.

Crosswaithe responded on behalf of the Blakes Directors before Greg got a word in.

'You're bloody right we are.'

Old Nick's language was definitely deteriorating of late. The screens flashed. Provident was alive again. Roll the dice. The market makers had entered their opening morning bid prices. One or two delayed until the last possible moment, sizing up the opposition. They would bid low to avoid making the best first offer and being swamped with incoming telephone calls to buy up unwanted Provident stock. How low?

'The best offer is from Morgans. It's eight pounds ten pence,' announced Chas.

But not that low. Jesus. They were down two million quid from their original purchase. Greg's worst nightmare had come to pass.

'What are you waiting for, Greg?' prompted Crosswaithe to his left.

'We can't sell out at that sort of price. That's ridiculous. It's a damn fire sale. It's a rip off.'

Crosswaithe pulled his chair right up to the desk. He was beside Greg. Less than a foot between them. He inhaled, talking in the pseudo-alcoholic air. He wondered what the odour was.

'Greg. This Provident position has been a disaster. I am telling you now to sell the lot of them.'

'Down to eight pounds exactly. And falling,' offered Chas unhelpfully, finger on the trigger.

Greg threw another obstacle in Old Nick's path.

'We'll never shift a million shares now. The price will plummet.'

'I don't care, Greg. The Directors have spoken. Sell every fucking share. Now.'

Old Nick had never used a four-letter word on the dealing floor. He was serious. In that single moment Greg knew he was finished at Blakes. Crosswaithe was running the desk, making the call to sell. Chas, Jules and Henry knew it too. Greg's authority was gone forever. He stood up.

'Right. Sell them all in lots of fifty thousand. Offer them to every market maker on the screens.'

'Is there a limit on the price?' asked Jules naively.

'No. Get rid of them.'

They yelled into the phones. Greg didn't make any calls. He watched the share price over the next few minutes. Seven ninety pence. Seven eighty. Seven sixty. Seven fifty-five. Jesus. What a blood bath.

'All done,' shouted Chas.

'What's the average sale price?' ordered Greg.

A bit of hammering on a calculator. Then a swear word. Chas started again. This time he got it right.

'Seven sixty pence Greg. All done.'

Greg and Old Nick both did quick mental calculations.

Blakes had lost two and a half million quid on the position over two months, plus there was the cost of funding the position. Greg knew that many a dealer had been fired for far less in the past. Crosswaithe knew that too as he walked back to his office, slammed the door and called the other Directors to report on the morning's grim events.

Lenny called around for the rent. The bruises had healed nicely. Make-up helped too. He didn't ask any questions. She handed over the cash, trying to make the visit seem as routine as possible. Best not to give Lenny any hint of her impending flight to freedom once the new passport arrived. Pimps don't like losing their best girls. And if he was a pimp then that made her someone she no longer wanted to be. She could wave him goodbye but revenge was still uppermost in her mind. That bastard in the City who'd beaten her up. Lenny pocketed the envelope of cash. He turned to leave. She held him by the arm.

'Hold on, Lenny. Can you do me a favour?'

He seemed pleased at the prospect.

'Sure, doll. Just name it.'

It was a long shot but if anyone could help her, Lenny could.

'Could you get me into someone's flat? And make it look like I hadn't been there?'

He pondered the question for a few moments and shrugged.

'No, I couldn't do that.'

Pity.

'But Pug could.'

'Pug? Who's Pug?'

'He's my driver. He's sitting outside. Did three years at her Majesty's Pleasure for burglary, breaking and entering, amongst a few other alleged offences. There's no better man at getting inside someone's home. Ugly as sin but he has the best set of spare keys in London.'

'Does he have the keys with him now?'

'I'm sure he does.'

'Can we do a job?'

'Yes. Where is it? Local?'

'Near enough. It's in St John's Wood.'

'What do you want to do? Steal something?'

'No. Quite the opposite. I want to return something to its rightful owner.'

Sarah walked over to her favourite drawer. Lenny did his best to ignore the bundles of sterling inside but it was hard work. It was all he could see from where he stood. She took a plastic bag from ASDA and put her right hand into it. She carefully grasped the cover of a Sony CD 90X car stereo and reversed the bag inside out so that the noisy plastic enveloped the evidence. She never touched it. Lenny didn't see the contents. The less he saw the better for all concerned. Lenny was thinking ahead already.

'Have you been to this flat before?'

'No.'

'Are you sure of the address?'

'Yes. I looked it up in the telephone directory earlier. It's on Viceroy Terrace. Number 125.'

'One other thing, doll. Who lives there?'

'One guy.'

'Alone?'

'Think so.'

'Is he definitely out at work today?'

'I can check.'

She made for the phone and started to dial his number at Blakes. Lenny stopped her in time.

'No, don't use that. Use my mobile instead. He won't be able to identify the call so easily.'

She dialled on the proffered phone and asked for Greg. A voice answered. She knew that voice.

'Greg'.

He sounded pissed off. Good. Must be a bad day at work. She hit the end conversation button.

'He's definitely at work.'

'Then let's go.'

Pug greeted them in the Jaguar, surprised that his boss was bringing along staff. Lenny explained the job. Pug was still surprised. Imagine bringing a girl on a job. Lenny was going soft in his old age. Pug scared Sarah. He was a brute of a man; muscled, tattooed. Ugly too.

They drove along the Embankment, left off Parliament Square, past Victoria station and up to Hyde Park Corner. The traffic was murder but Pug proved himself to be a suitably aggressive driver. He lane changed and cut up lesser mortals whenever it was so required. The odd lewd hand gesture was part of his extensive repertoire. Up the Edgware Road and right into the monied suburbs of St John's Wood. Viceroy Terrace was a wide incline off the left, with soft-tops parked along the centre of the road in Westminster residents parking bays. Zone C perks. Red-brick three-storied mansion apartments lined the road. Number 125 was towards the end on the right. Pug did a reckless U-turn and pulled up.

Lenny turned to Sarah who sat alone in the back like a chauffeured passenger.

'I'll mind the car. We don't want a ticket from one of these wardens around here. You and Pug do the job. Don't be long.'

Pug stood before the communal hall door downstairs and surveyed the scene. Sarah watched him mentally debate the obstacle before them.

'How are we going to get in?' she asked.

She wondered if he was simply going to lean into the door and push it off its hinges. Should be quite easy for him. Pug was a step ahead of her. He put on a pair of leather gloves. Force of habit. A pro at work.

'These turn of the century mansion blocks used to have porters who came around every day to take out rubbish and deliver newspapers and coal and the like.'

'So?'

'So they have tradesmen's entrances. They have doorbells that let you inside at certain times of the day.'

Pug pushed the top bell. The one marked Tradesmen. Easy when you knew how. He pushed the door. They were into the downstairs hallway. All was quiet. No one around. One door down. One to go.

Number 125 was on the first floor. Pug examined the door closely. One mortice lock and one Yale lock. He took an enormous key ring from an inside pocket and fingered through them. He found one that looked well worn, tried it in the mortice lock, gently twisted it a few times, and they heard the lock open. Then he tried a selection of Yale keys. The fifth one worked. Sarah and Pug entered. He stood in the hallway while she quickly surveyed the various rooms in the apartment.

She needed the right place. Somewhere Greg wouldn't see it, yet a place where others might find it later if they were told to look in this particular apartment. The main bedroom contained a wall-to-wall wardrobe bulging with expensive suits, ironed shirts on hangers and rows of silk ties on rails. On the floor of the wardrobe were four cardboard boxes crammed with apparently unwanted household effects wrapped in newspaper. She rolled back the newspaper. Glasses, ornaments, statuettes, silver, the like. Perfect.

She took out the plastic bag from her pocket, moved a few items in the first box and placed the car stereo inside. Then she replaced the few items on top. Pug locked the door behind them and Lenny complimented their quick work. He was smart enough.

'So what's next in your master plan?'

'Leave that to me, Lenny. All in good time.'

A phone call to that cop in Harrow Road Police Station would suffice, but only when she was long gone. First though was a call to her account executive in Jersey, Sell, sell, sell.

* * *

Ted Hammond knew how much time it took to recover from the death of a spouse. Forever. He knew how Helen Soames felt. But a death lay unresolved and there had been no response to the TV appeal for information on the car stereo cover. The only alternative was to go back to the desolate home in Little Venice. He sat opposite Helen and dared to open the conversation. A hazard of his chosen vocation.

'I have some more information about the evening your husband was last seen.'

She feigned some token interest. Alexander was gone. No amount of information could bring back the father of her twins, the breadwinner of a family home in West London.

'Such as?'

Ted produced a pile of bank statements held together by a single green treasury tag.

'We discovered that he used two cash machines after he left the Dorchester Hotel.'

She sat up and leant forward. More interested.

'Cash machines?'

'Yes. He withdrew two hundred and fifty pounds from each.'

She was thinking about something. Ted pushed his luck further. No tears yet.

'I wondered why he might need a large amount of cash like that?' He paused before the next harsh two-liner. 'The money wasn't in his wallet when we found his body. The first thing that I thought of was drugs.'

She glared back at him and almost shouted.

'No, Alexander never did drugs. No way.'

He tried to calm her. With difficulty.

'OK. I understand. I'm sorry, but I have to ask these questions.'

She relaxed at the reassurance. Ted persevered.

'This wasn't a one off. There is a pattern to these cash withdrawals. He took out a few hundred pounds or more every few weeks or so over the past year. It's all in his bank account.'

'What bank account?'

Ted handed over the account statements for the past twelve months. Helen was puzzled.

'Whose account is this? I've never seen this before.'

He pointed to the name and address at the top.

'The statements were addressed to your husband at his office in the City. The account was credited with money from valid expense claims from his bank. If he went overseas on travel he bought items with his corporate credit card, reclaimed them from his Accounts department and lodged the cheques here.'

They were both thinking about what else a married man could spend money on. Ted had no choice. It was all about sex at the end of the day. He chose the words carefully. Less hurtful.

'If it wasn't drugs, I was wondering if he might have been unfaithful to you?'

Bad question. Ted saw the tears welling up. Helen wiped her eyes. This was difficult. Unfair too.

'No. Never. He was the perfect husband.' Almost. But Ted had sowed doubts.

Ted had said enough. He rose. She could think about it further in private.

'I'll leave the statements with you. If you remember anything please call me at the station.'

She hesitated. She was indeed remembering something else but no need to jump to conclusions yet. She could tell the police later if her suspicions were confirmed. She'd thought it was all over but now looking at the cash in those bank statements, she wasn't so sure. Ted remembered the phone call he'd received that morning.

'The pathologist phoned me to say that they have released the body for burial. You can arrange the funeral as soon as you like.'

She looked at him, eyes still wet. He had done the best he could in the circumstances. He had been there before himself and survived. His children had survived. She would survive too. Ted would help.

'Will you be there?' she asked.

She needed him to be there by her side on that most difficult of days. He remembered feeling so alone as he threw the first handful of clay onto the brass plate. Margaret Hammond RIP. There was a bond somewhere amidst all this grief. He had to help her anyway he could. And catch her husband's killer.

'If you want me to.'

'I do.'

He left. Helen was alone again with her thoughts and fears. Alexander didn't need five hundred pounds to be unfaithful, but certain services cost much more. Certain specialised services for the more upmarket gentleman. The twins were at the Montessori school. The au pair had left for the morning. Now was as good a time as any to ease her doubts.

Alexander was so reluctant to talk about it. She'd had to coax it out of him. He cried when he spoke about his childhood in a cold orphanage in rural Wales and the elderly nuns from a strict Catholic order who ran the place. The beatings. The cold dormitories. Didn't spare the rod. Locked him up for hours. Starved him. The gruel. The trauma when you are ten or eleven years old made a lasting impression. Alexander did his best, but since that day Helen knew a darker side lurked beneath his exterior City respectability.

She climbed the stairs to the master bedroom, thinking back to her accidental discovery years ago. The room overlooked the canal and sunlight streamed in through open sash windows onto an unmade four poster bed in the middle. One side of the bed was evidently slept in and the other untouched under the fine cotton sheets. A widow at home. Helen walked into the expansive wardrobe and reached up with some difficulty to the top shelf. She placed his small black case with the initials AS on the bed.

It was locked. She took a metal comb from the side table and rammed it into the underside of the lock. It was easy. She threw open the case on the bed and the contents lay there. She exhaled to herself alone.

'No.'

The case was full of contact magazines. She was stunned at the explicit shots. Ladies in thigh boots wielding bullwhips. Men in stocks or draped in chains. Women in cat suits with men on all fours following behind on leads. Some of the publications were in German and Dutch. The text was indecipherable but there was no doubt about the content. Hard core at its worst.

The filth was recent. The top magazine was dated from two months ago. There were scribblings in some of the magazines. She recognised Alexander's own handwriting. Wednesday 7 p.m. number 55. Two hundred and twenty five pounds. April 16th Gravesend Road, basement flat. Red-brick townhouse, number 32. He had lied to her for years. He had been seeing someone for what he so desperately craved.

She slumped onto the bed, lay momentarily beside the filth and then flung the material in all different directions about the bedroom in a violent rage. The evidence was rapidly disappearing. He had told her this was all over. Years ago. He'd lied. He said this case contained confidential business papers and the like. She was never to open it. He had the key to it at his office.

She didn't know enough but perhaps some unknown name written here in his own hand may have been the last person to see her Alexander alive. Before he had spent five hundred pounds for the last time in his life. No one else was in the frame according to Ted.

She stood by the window and looked out at his police car pulling away from the kerb. She thought about the twins, her relations and family friends and the adverse publicity.

She knew that she would have to tell Ted about her growing suspicions as to the death of her husband. Soon.

Sarah stepped off the morning flight from Heathrow and took a taxi into St Helier. She sat in the reception of Blakes for five minutes and idly paged through a prehistoric *Horse and Hound* magazine as the private clients were expected to do. Gabrielle brought her into Penelope Swales' office at the appointed time and she came face to face again with her account executive. They shook hands.

Sarah placed her new Samsonite vanity case on the floor, bought with a purpose in mind days ago on that trip to John Lewis. She sat in the comfortable leather chair, took in the harbour view for the last time and allowed Penelope to get into first gear of her autopilot sales mode.

'Ms Hart. I am so delighted to see you again. It's been a while,' she gushed.

Sarah had never liked Penelope. She'd learned long ago from the idle chit-chat in reception that all the staff here hated Penelope too. They had dropped enough hints in the past as to how she had charmed her way into her comfy executive position. Sales and missionary no doubt. Sarah knew that they were in the same basic line of business. One vocation was more legal than the other. You decide.

'You were last here in May according to my file,' Penelope stated the bleeding obvious.

Sarah didn't need a sociable conversation today. She was here on business and booked on a flight back in two hours' time. What she needed couldn't be entrusted to the Royal Mail. Penelope prattled on.

'It's two years since you opened your account with a mere ten thousand pounds. Your account has performed excellently in the meantime.' She glanced at a computer screen that was purposefully hidden from the view of the loaded clients who sat before her. 'Up to a net worth of six hundred thousand pounds now. I'm so pleased you chose Blakes.'

She had some nerve. Sarah made all the decisions. Penelope knew nothing in contrast and simply earned easy commission from her account for no work whatsoever. Sarah always settled her share deals on time and always had enough ready cash to buy whatever she wanted. Sarah gave her no trouble except the need to count all the wads of crisp notes she deposited offshore over time.

'I know that you sold most of your shares and gilts last week and are now holding nearly all cash. Do you know something about world equity markets that I don't?' cooed Penelope.

Of course Sarah knew more about equity markets than Penelope. That was the secret of her success.

'What do you mean, most of my shares? I told you to sell them all. What happened?'

Penelope tried to cover up her own involuntary gaffe.

'We sold your equities and gilts easily but we had some trouble with your Far East investment trust holdings. It's rather embarrassing since our own Hong Kong office manages these trusts in Singapore, Indonesia, Thailand and Malayasia. I'm sorry for the delay.'

'What's the problem?'

'The trust managers only facilitate new investments and disposals once a week, on a Monday. They need a week's notice of any disposals. We registered your wish to sell last week but they say that they never got the fax from Gabrielle and so we missed the most recent opportunity. It will be later this week before the sale happens. It will take a few more days to get the funds over to us here. So you actually have five hundred and eighty thousand pounds cash and twenty k in investments. So what do we do with the rest of your cash? Are you going back into the market today big time?' More commission here we come.

Time to drop the bombshell. Show me the money.

'No. I wish to close my account here and withdraw the proceeds in cash today.'

Penelope was gasping for breath. She couldn't believe it. She was losing this account?

'Really?'

'Yes.'

'All of it?'

'Yes.'

'All six hundred thousand pounds?'

'Every last penny. Or cent in fact. I want it all in US dollars.'

'A draft?'

'No. Cash. Large bills too. It has to fit into this case.'

Penelope played for time.

'I don't think we have that sort of cash here.'

'You must have. This is a bank, isn't it? You can get it from your dollar correspondent.'

Penelope caught the barbed comment. She was beginning to lose her patience.

'I'll see what I can do. We can ask Chase down the road to get dollars for us.'

Perfect. That was why Sarah had chosen Blakes. They never asked questions. Greg had told her that years ago. Their Compliance Department was a joke, he'd said. Run by some Dickensian guy in his fifties who didn't know what was happening in the London head office, let alone the overseas outposts like Jersey. Penelope stood up to leave. Sarah annoyed her further.

'And can you hurry up? I have a return flight to catch to London.'

Penelope hesitated by the door.

'It's a lot of cash to have on your person.'

'I know it is. But the customer is always right. Don't they tell you that?'

Penelope returned in forty minutes with a brown envelope from Chase. It looked about the right size. Sarah peeled back the brown paper to reveal bundles of notes. Each bundle contained fifty thousand dollars in hundred bills and a quick eyeball indicated that nineteen bundles lay before them on the desk, plus some small change. She was short?

'I thought there would be twenty? A million even? What rate did you get on the conversion?'

'We got 1.6850.'

Crap FX rate thought Sarah. Blakes had shafted her on the commission. Penelope probably took a cut of that too. Still a million was almost there. It would do. Sarah lifted the vanity case up on the desk and loaded in the cash. The lid snapped shut and she locked it with a small key. The deal was done.

'So what do we do with the last twenty thousand from the Far East fund? Will I mail you a cheque?' asked Penelope.

Jesus. Don't do that. No post ever to my home with a big shiny Blakes' Jersey envelope. Penelope must be stupid.

'Of course not. Haven't I made that clear to you before? I'll call you.'

Penelope was rebuffed and it hurt. She couldn't resist the challenge of some sparring.

'I hope you get as good a return on your investments elsewhere as you got at Blakes over the years.'

That was it. Sarah snapped. This woman had annoyed her sufficiently.

'Return? What do you mean return? Do you mean great investment ideas that made so much money?'

'Yes.'

'Really? You never gave me a single decent idea. I alone traded the account.'

'Well, yes, that's strictly true but I helped to buy and sell the shares.'

'Face the facts, you took telephone messages. I reckon Gabrielle outside could do that.'

Penelope wasn't beaten yet.

'I accepted all the cash you lodged here.'

'You sure did. And did you ever ask me where it all came from?'

Penelope hadn't. Something to do with rental property? She wasn't sure.

'You don't even know what I do for a living, do you?'

Penelope was lost again. She should have re-read the file before this meeting.

'It's common knowledge in this office how you got your job here. Do you want to know what I do? I'll tell you. It's an amazing coincidence but we both screw people for cash. Get it?'

Sarah turned and left. Penelope was livid. She stood in the top window and watched her former client descend the steps to an airport taxi. A million dollars in cash walked away down the steps too. Penelope would miss those sure-thing investment ideas.

Sarah's plane touched down at Heathrow in the early afternoon. None of the sleeping customs officers or immigration officials stopped the well-dressed lady with the laden vanity case. She took a black cab to the West End. Forty pounds to Central London but she could afford it. Still so much to do to escape.

First stop was Debenhams on Oxford Street. Full of uninformed tourists. Sarah had never darkened their unfashionable doors before. She bought the most awful blouse she could find in the alleged designer section. A gaudy floral thing with a knotted bow top. It was so unlike the old Sarah. Everything in her wardrobe was in muted colours, blacks, whites, greys, olives and charcoals. Timeless fashion statements that could be easily co-ordinated. Now she wanted to be different. She wore the blouse as she left the shop.

Then down to René, her lisping stylist in the little salon off Bond Street for her four o'clock appointment. She wanted something radical this time. He was all ideas. He suggested the chestnut dye and the short bob that came just below the ears with a straight fringe. So fashionable, he lisped into the wall to wall mirrors. Sarah thought it was great. It would be easy to live with in a tropical climate.

The final touch was the new glasses. She popped into the busiest Specsavers shop she could find, picked up a set of metal Armani frames and asked for clear lenses. She told the inquisitive shop assistant that it was a fashion statement. Not a disguise. She bought a new pair of sunglasses too. She'd need those soon.

Then time for the awful photographic evidence in the new blouse. She sat in a booth at Boots and was flashed at four times. She tried four different poses. Happy. Disinterested. Relaxed. Intense. It didn't work. The colour photos all looked the same. She took the first photo, put it into an envelope and caught another cab for the short trip to a side road off Whitehall. She waited as agreed.

At five-thirty precisely he appeared on the far side of the road, crossed the traffic and stood looking for someone. It was him. The Mandarin. Punctual as ever. He knew her. Or did he? This disguise was so good. She approached him but he seemed hesitant about acknowledging her presence. Always so shy.

'Sarah? Is that you?'

'Yes.'

He knew the accent at least.

'What a transformation.'

The image change was complete. No more the blonde femme fatale who attracted continuous unwanted glances from members of the opposite sex. Instead the prim Miss Anonymous looking to mind her own business in her search of complete anonymity in some foreign locale.

'Thanks. I used my imagination.'

'I'll take the photo if you have it? By the way, you still look great.'

Good to hear. He took the envelope and returned to his monolithic office. She left for home, knowing that the day had been a success. She felt free from the guilt of inadvertently causing a death. Free from the fear of meeting the detective from the Met, the one on that Sky TV news clip. Free from the LSE's investigations into Provident. Free from the presence of Lenny. Free from the abuse of Greg. Free at last.

CHAPTER TWENTY-FIVE

MANHATTAN, NEW YORK CITY

Getting up at six-thirty a.m. any time would normally require a superhuman effort on Mark's part but not this morning. It was already midday in deepest Battersea, SW1. This felt like a lie-in. He had scribbled six a.m. on the room service card he hung from the door last night and right on cue a cheery Hispanic waiter brought his monster breakfast. He could get used to this sort of jet-setting. After a day off work in NYC, he felt like a local. Almost.

He sat on the bed in a bath robe that he would dearly love to purloin, watched the early morning business news on CNBC and downed the chilled OJ, rye cereal, pungent coffee and strawberry pastries. No one would ever starve in New York. The Dow Jones was expected to open weaker following poor Asian and Japanese markets overnight. JGB yields had hit an all-time low. He wondered about Provident.

The NYI news forecast mid-eighties and high humidity today. Mark thought about the Wall Street citizens, getting up all over Manhattan, Queens, New Jersey, Staten Island and Brooklyn, setting off on their daily commute to the routine of work in whatever investment bank or brokerage they honoured with their services. Mark was flying to work in DC instead. No contest whatsoever.

The Lincoln town car with driver was waiting outside on 34th. Another good idea courtesy of the ever efficient concierge. They headed out through the lead oxide of the Midtown tunnel and then through a web of inter-linked freeways. All the time travelling against the incoming suburban swarm, occasionally overtaking cruising Carey airport buses. La Guardia was only half the distance of JFK from his hotel.

Once inside the cramped terminal, he sat with the assembled Suits at the departure gate. Rows of American corporate lawyers off to DC to sweet talk some government department or grease some politician's palm in a mutually beneficial deal. The Suits travelled in groups of three in a search for safety in numbers. The elder statesman Suit sat in the middle seat paging through the Business and Metro section of the *New York Times*. The young crew-cut beefcake followed lugging the compulsory laptop over his shoulder. The female sat to the left with carefully crossed legs, icy demeanour, yet perfect as porcelain.

Delta Shuttle 109 left on time. The forty-minute hop to the next major metropolis was punctuated by a mad rush as hassled air stewardesses dispensed sufficient quantities of coffee and enormous blueberry muffins to the Suits, still sitting three abreast in that same order. Then a swift descent to Washington National airport, a relic of the 1950s, quaint yet only suitable for short-haul inter-city flights.

The taxis were numerous outside. Mark clambered in and gave directions.

'The SEC, please.'

Washington was so unlike New York. So carefully co-ordinated. Perfect grids of streets devoid of garbage. Broad Avenues radiating like spokes from the White House and the Capitol. All lined with government buildings designed to impress. No skyscrapers. Too many parks, fountains and monuments.

Pedestrians who refused to jay walk. Traffic which even obeyed the red, amber and green.

The cab stopped at 540 West Street. Mark had to pass through a metal detector before he could tell the receptionist about his appointment. Top security in all federal buildings. He was advised that Laura Ziegler was running late and was asked to wait in a meeting room down the corridor. No windows, no air, no pictures, no ambience. Only a cheap Fed table on thin legs with four almost matching chairs.

The only distraction was a glossy brochure left on the table for those with time to kill. Mark paged through it in an attempt to glean as much information as he could in the short space of time available. The SEC didn't sell themselves short. The front type proclaimed them as the world's leading regulator of the securities industry. Mark was sure that Norris would have a word to say about that. They described themselves as an independent, non-partisan, quasi-judicial regulatory agency with responsibility for securities laws under the 1933 Act, and with too many adjectives in Mark's professional opinion.

He went straight to the most relevant page. Their Enforcement Division investigated federal securities law violations. There were glossy examples of recent trading suspensions, fraudulent stock offerings, price manipulation, broker disputes, investor alerts, litigation procedures, client complaints, disciplinary hearings, record dollar fines, time behind bars and potentially most relevant of all, insider dealing cases. The SEC paid a cash bounty to those who reported insider dealing. Perhaps a throwback to the Wild West of old, because sure as hell the cowboys were still out there. Mark might even be in line for a few bucks himself from the SEC if this went well. Or a pay rise from Norris.

The door opened abruptly and Division Director Laura Ziegler arrived decisively. She was in her early forties, well dressed in a flowing tan suit but she evidently had more important matters on her mind than a certain dealer called

Greg Schneider. She was heavily pregnant, dangerously so, thought Mark. He was obliged to ask about her recent maternal progress. She liked the common touch.

'I'm due in one month's time, Mr Robinson. Thank you for asking. You've timed your visit well. This is my last week at work for some time. Just as well. I need a break.'

Mark hoped that the conversation would be productive but not too stimulating. He couldn't run the risk of exciting Laura too much. She also seemed to appreciate the urgency of his day trip. Down to business.

'I did some research when Herb called me. We have an old file here on Schneider. Do you want to know about the background?'

'Sure.' Mark took out an A4 pad and scribbled notes as Laura summarised the file on the table.

'We took a call a few years ago from the NASD in New York. A clerk there said that one of the dealers, a guy called Schneider at Mitchells' Domestic Equity desk, had been fired but that he didn't really know why. As a matter of routine we asked Mitchells' Compliance Department what had happened to this dealer. A senior compliance guy there told us there'd been a misunderstanding on the telephone with the NASD and that the dealer had resigned and not been fired. They had notified the NASD of this in writing. So case closed. Smallest file in our history.'

Mark was partially familiar with the facts immediately.

'Was the senior person at Mitchells called Weaver?'

Laura paged on through the file and found a memorandum.

'Yes. He was. He runs Compliance now. How did you know that?'

'The NASD told me. I met him this week. Then what happened?'

Laura opened a few more pages in front of her.

'The file went cold for some months until we got a telephone call from a Katherine Gorin, a young corporate lawyer who worked in Mitchells' Mergers & Acquisitions Department in New York.'

Mark was impressed. M&A was where all the action happened and where a lot of price-sensitive information was held prior to corporate deals being announced. His hopes for a lead were rising.

'Gorin said she wanted to talk to an investigator here. She took the train one day and I met with her. She said she had evidence of insider dealing by a dealer in Mitchells, but that she was involved and she wanted full personal immunity before she would discuss it any further. We are always keen to know about events in the biggest investment bank on Wall Street so we immediately signed a waiver form for her. She named one Greg Schneider as the culprit. We re-opened this file.'

Mark was scribbling furiously. He hoped he could decipher this back in London next week.

'What were the allegations that she made against Schneider?'

'She said that he'd got information from her about impending mergers, takeovers, acquisitions and disposals. He traded in the stocks on the NYSE before the announcements were in the public domain. She said that all of his dealing profits came from these stocks and that otherwise he was a useless dealer.'

Mark could see a few initial obstacles.

'But it's impossible to get information from M&A, isn't it? M&A departments are always behind locked doors with coded security access. The staff do not talk about their work to any colleagues? How did he do it?'

'She said that she and Schneider were in a relationship for two years.'

Sex always complicated work matters. Mark needed to know more.

'So she gave him the confidential information?'

'No. He used her but she never knew until it was too late.'

'How did he do it?'

Ziegler found another page in the file.

'It's here in her draft statement. He got the information the easy way. Mitchells are advanced technologically. All the M&A types have ISDN telephone lines at home so they can dial into the office and work crazy unsociable hours from home if the need arises, particularly over the weekends. These big M&A deals are time critical with tight deadlines. Schneider hacked into her work PC from her home. Once he dialled up from there he could see all the shared Word files, the Excel spreadsheets and PowerPoint presentations on the M&A PC network. Gorin said that Schneider also read her personal e-mails.'

'How did he get past all the system passwords? They must have those in Mitchells?'

'They do. Gorin was at fault there. She admitted that she wrote her password down on the inside back page of her diary. She left it lying around frequently. I know it's stupid but it's what we all do, isn't it?'

Mark thought about his own ID and password to the LSE system. It was still written on a yellow post-it note and stuck on the back of his desk drawer which he never locked. Ziegler was right.

'So how did she find out that Schneider was hacking in?'

Ziegler paged onwards in the file.

'She got some cast iron evidence. She came in to work one Monday morning and a techie type from Mitchells' Systems Department called her to apologise about some emergency repair work that was done on the system. He said he had to log her out of the network without notice on Sunday evening at 7 p.m.'

'So?'

'So she wasn't on the PC or even at home. She was visiting her grandmother who was slowly dying of cancer in an upstate hospice. She visited every Sunday evening and it took hours to get up there and back. It was a regular journey. Schneider knew that and he had a key to her apartment. That was the firm evidence.'

'Firm evidence that someone had accessed her files, but was it actually Schneider?'

'Gorin wondered too. So the next Sunday she left her apartment at her usual time but went over the road to sink the first of many cappuccinos in a corner deli. She hadn't touched the froth on the second, she says, when Schneider appeared and crossed the road to her apartment block. One hour and three solitary cappuccinos later, he emerged and melted away into the subway. What hurt her most was that she missed the chance to visit her grandmother that night. She died two days later. She never saw her again.'

Mark didn't know Katherine Gorin but he sympathised with her.

'Why did Gorin wait so long to tell you about this?'

'She broke up with Schneider immediately, but he wouldn't leave her alone and wouldn't give her back her key to the apartment. She changed all her passwords and locks to stop him. She should have done more at the time but she was worried about her personal involvement. She had been at fault in making the access to the office systems so easy for Schneider. She thought she might be fired from Mitchells. Then an incident happened which made her mind up about telling us.'

There was more? This was getting better. Mark's right hand was sore from all the frantic scribbling.

'What happened?'

'Schneider was asked by his boss to move to the London office. She says that he was livid. He tried to get out of it, but no joy. If your boss in Mitchells asks you to move, then you sure as hell do it. I can see why he wasn't keen to move. Schneider was going to be a fish out of water, in a foreign land with no local M&A contacts and thus no inside information on which to trade. Schneider asked Gorin to move with him to London. He said he loved her and wanted them to live together. She hated him by then. She knew what he was doing and definitely didn't want to go to the UK. Schneider went wild when she told him she was definitely going to stay in New York. That's when she saw his darker side.'

'What do you mean?'

'Schneider met up with Gorin the first time he came back from London for a weekend in New York. She didn't want to go out, but he cornered her near her home. He attacked her outside a late bar in Murray Hill one night. He'd drunk an ocean of alcohol. He had a drink problem that he hid from colleagues at work. He couldn't get enough basically. He punched her around and cut her face with a broken bottle. She spent three days in hospital and reported the incident to the NYPD. They immediately went looking for Schneider only to find he'd taken United back to the safety of London the next day. The NYPD want to put him away for assault and battery. That's five years' mandatory jail time, and the correctional facilities over here are a lot tougher than any damn dealing floor.'

Mark stopped writing for a moment.

'Did you talk to Schneider about this at all?'

'He'd moved to Mitchells' London office. He was out of our jurisdiction. They fired him when Gorin told Weaver. Schneider knows we want to talk to him about this. Word spreads fast in Mitchells. We have his name on an immigration department blacklist. If he tries to enter the USA, whether it's at JFK or Newark or through the Canadian or Mexican border, the cops will pick him up immediately. That's why he hasn't been back here since all this happened. That must hurt.'

Laura winced too. A twinge. She shifted in her seat. Baby was apparently misbehaving.

'Why haven't you gone after Mitchells?'

'We hit a snag. Gorin withdrew her statement a month later. She said she'd made mistakes in it and that she wouldn't testify in court for us. She wouldn't talk but I think Weaver leaned on her. He threatened her about her job. Weaver is not keen on us ever getting to talk to Schneider. He's careful about safeguarding Mitchell's reputation. The last thing he wants is a scandal. He denies everything and makes sure that nothing leaks out of Mitchells. If I were you I'd be careful. I've heard he's a tough piece of work. His Compliance & Legal Department is also responsible for Security at Mitchells and he has some unsavoury contacts. Gorin told us that he's threatened to break Schneider's legs if he ever returns to the US or talks to us or the NASD or anyone else for that matter.'

It all explained Weaver's attitude yesterday. Mark had what he needed.

'That's very helpful. I'll have a look at this file. We'll do our best in London to nail this dealer for you.'

But where was the evidence? Laura was thinking the same.

'The only problem I have is the lack of evidence. Do you have any more on him in London?'

'Not enough. Yet. But I now have a few more ideas.'

Mark was beginning to see parallels. A dealer sitting at a desk with no original trading ideas finds a local girl who has the information he needs. He starts up a sham relationship to extract the information. He makes lots of loot. He becomes a star dealer and makes even more at year-end bonus time. There was definitely a parallel to Blakes in London. And then he remembered where he had first seen Schneider.

That day the couple met up on the steps of Broadgate. Mark had watched the dark wiry guy clambering all over the star research analyst. His gorgeous Barbara and the dealer in collusion. Such a pity but it seemed that Barbara was in this up to her eyes. Now Mark would eventually get to talk to her. About work alas.

The next stage was obvious. Get back to Manhattan. Find this Katherine Gorin. Talk to her about Schneider. Find more evidence to use against him. And maybe even confront Weaver again. Then home to London and a couple of arrests at Blakes once Norris agreed.

*　　*　　*

Mark went to the first pay phone in the arrivals area, looked up Mitchells' switchboard number in a tattered NYNEX phone book and dialled, optimistically.

'Katherine Gorin please.'

A pause as the tension built.

'Katherine speaking.'

'My name is Mark Robinson from the London Stock Exchange.'

'Yeah?'

'I got your name from Laura Ziegler at the SEC.'

'And?'

'I'd like to talk to you about . . .'

'Wait. Don't say anymore. These telephones are taped. I know what you mean. I can't talk.'

'Not now, but perhaps we could meet up face to face?'

'No. No way. I'm sorry. Bye.'

'Wait, please. I know what happened. I know what he did. We can get him in England. Make him pay.'

She was still on the line, weighing expediency over justice. Mark pushed her.

'I need to know more about him. It's important. I'm in New York now. Please make the effort.'

'All right. Off the record. Only you and me. The coffee shop on 3rd and 33rd at seven tonight.'

She was gone. Mark had the date. Now to beat the rush hour and get to midtown in time. The cab driver drove like a lunatic from La Guardia for an extra ten bucks tip. He pulled up outside Mark's hotel directly behind a dark sedan that was illegally parked. The cab driver pointed at the car ahead and mumbled something derogatory in some unknown Caribbean dialect. The only English word Mark could understand was asshole.

Mark wasn't bothered. He felt much more optimistic than yesterday as he paid the fare. Now he had definite incriminating information on Schneider. He gave the driver a generous tip, knowing that Norris back home would sign the expense claim. He was sure getting used to this lifestyle. Spend as much as you can and get reimbursed. Every day in New York was less time in Sainsburys and was saving him a fortune back home in his Barclays current account with the big red overdrawn balance.

A coloured man stepped out of the sedan ahead. A tall, stocky guy in a sharp dark suit built like a defensive lineman from the Giants. He arched his square shoulders and stood on the pavement, looking too deliberately at his watch. Mark assumed the guy was waiting for somebody. It was only a few short steps to the safety of the hotel lobby but Mark didn't make it. The man stood in his way.

'Robinson?'

Who the hell was this? Mark was curious.

'Yes.'

'This way.'

Mark had no choice. A firm hand was placed on his shoulder and he was bundled into the back seat of the sedan. The door was closed behind him and the man remained outside by the door. Mark wasn't alone inside. Apart from the driver in the front, there was someone else. That oily Mitchells' executive. Weaver sat beside him in the rear seat.

'Mr Robinson, I do apologise for this but I was curious about your visit here.'

Mark half thought about getting out of the car but knew that the circumstances did not permit such an easy escape route. Defensive linemen are used to big hits. Escape wasn't in Weaver's immediate plans.

'What the hell is going on here?'

'Relax, Mr Robinson, I want to talk to you about where you were today?'

'That's none of your damn business.'

'But you see it is. Just tell me. It will be easier for all concerned.'

Fuck Weaver and his cronies in their sharp suits.

'I was uptown doing some shopping.'

'Really, Mr Robinson, and where is the evidence? Do you have any Macys, Saks or Bloomingdales carrier bags? I think not.'

One nil to Weaver.

'I was window shopping.'

Weaver inched closer and Mark could smell the expensive aftershave and the bad breath. And the danger.

'Robinson, you are out of your depth here. You are dealing with Security from one of America's biggest corporates and we won't let an English shit like you damage our firm. I know that you left here in a town car this morning at 7.12 a.m. and that you headed out to the Midtown Tunnel towards the airports. We lost you in the tunnel but your hired driver was delighted to tell us later for fifty bucks that he dropped you off at the Delta Shuttle terminal for Washington DC? Isn't that so?'

What the hell. There was no point in denying anything. Weaver knew it all anyway. Mark nodded.

'And what did you do in Washington?'

Time to give Weaver a decent shock. Take back the initiative.

'I visited the SEC Enforcement Division.'

Weaver was taken aback. Annoyed too.

'And what the hell did you discuss there?'

'I looked at a big juicy file they have on Greg Schneider. All about insider dealing and a cover up by Mitchells when the facts broke in the firm a few years ago.'

Weaver debated the information and then took an instant decision. He rolled down the smoked glass partition and instructed the driver.

'Right. Let's go.'

The three-litre engine started immediately. Mark made to get out. The door was opened momentarily as the lineman climbed in and sat beside Mark. No way to leave now. They pulled out into the traffic on East 34th, Mark wondering if this was going to be his last trip for some time. Forever?

'Where are we going?'

'Shut up.'

Mark entered the Midtown Tunnel for the second time that day. Were they going to some quite part of the city where the worst could happen? Down to the docks where the murky depths might beckon for the unfortunate few? He feared the worst. Then he saw the freeway signs he recognised. JFK in the left lane. The Van Wyck Expressway. They were going to the airport? Sure enough they pulled up outside Terminal 6, right where Mark had alighted a mere three days ago. Weaver turned to Mark.

'You're going home right now to London. You are going to stay there for the foreseeable future. If I hear that you are in New York again then you'll be going home on crutches. And that's a promise.'

Mark could see more immediate problems.

'You can't throw me out of the country. I haven't even got a passport or a ticket.'

Weaver took Mark out of the car and around to the trunk. He opened it. Mark's luggage lay inside.

'You'd be surprised what a hotel valet will do for a few bucks. There's your flight bag, flexible ticket and passport. Now get the fuck out of here and check in. My colleague here will make sure you do.'

Mark felt like an errant child as he was frog-marched over to the BA check-in desk and stood in line. He was in a daze, his attention distracted by so many around him in the airport. Couples with more luggage than they could use in a year. Pilots walked by as if they were God's gift to the world. Porters looked for the best tip they could get for the least amount of work. Air stewards ambled with a bit too much spring in their step. Tourists tried to steer luggage trolleys with minds of their own. Backpackers huddled together for mutual protection. His turn came and the crony stepped forward.

'My colleague here urgently needs to be on this evening's flight to Heathrow.'

'No problem, sir.'

Mark handed over his documents in return for a boarding pass that he definitely didn't want. He had no choice at all as the lineman watched his every move.

'You're in seat 7F, sir. Have a nice day.'

Too late for that. Mark was further marched over to the departures. The crony was inches away.

'And don't even think about coming back. We will be watching. Mr Weaver wouldn't like that at all.'

Mark waited in the BA business lounge, still dazed. Life carried on around him. Solo business passengers in Dockers chinos and loafers sipped spicy Tomato juices and G&Ts while they digested the nibbles. Lone single girls in hugging black Levis stood by the complimentary drinks bar, simultaneously eyed up by the men with wedding rings and modest aspirations. Husbands used credit cards to call wives, girlfriends, or both on the AT&T telephones to state the bleeding obvious. 'Hi, I'm at JFK.' Others watched the airplanes taxiing outside in the massive car park that essentially is JFK.

A large TV screen in the lounge blared out twenty-four hour Eyewitness news. The Newscopter, only in America, showed live aerial pictures of a car smash on the BQE. Then exclusive reports about the gang rape of a seventy-year-old woman and the veteran high school principal who kept dodgy photographs of male pupils at his home. And of course the odd murder or four. None of the locals stirred from their freebie reading material as the gory details of death were imparted. Hardly a news event in New York at all.

Mark could see the headline already. English visitor dies in car accident. Missing London businessman found in Hudson River. Tourist murdered by drug gang in Central Park. Jesus.

It would all be so easy for Weaver and his security colleagues.

They left the soft tarmac shortly after seven and Mark wound his watch onwards by five hours. He remembered his missed appointment. Somewhere down below in the metropolis a young female M&A executive from the nation's largest investment bank sipped a cold coffee on 3rd and 33rd and wondered who the hell had telephoned her at work today? And, more importantly, where was he now?

CHAPTER TWENTY-SIX

OLD BROAD STREET, LONDON EC2

Mark was completing the world's largest US dollar expense claim when his boss arrived at the LSE. He went into Norris's office immediately.

'You'll never believe it. I've got to tell you about Mitchells. They ran me out of town. Like a John Wayne movie.'

Norris wasn't interested in Mark's bizarre return. His mind was on something else.

'We can talk about New York later, Mark. First I have to tell you something. I didn't want to worry you in the States, there was nothing you could do. It's about Peter.'

Mark felt guilty. He had only managed one phone call last week.

'I was going to ask you. How is Pete? I didn't get a chance to visit him over the weekend. I was jet-lagged and slept most of yesterday.'

Norris stared at the floor for a moment and slowly returned his gaze to Mark.

'Peter's condition deteriorated in the early hours of Friday morning. The doctors put him on a life support machine around lunchtime. He got worse. They tried everything. His parents agreed on Friday night to let nature take its course. Peter passed away at 5.20 on Saturday morning. I'm so sorry. I know you two got on well. It's so hard to believe that we could lose someone just like that.'

Not hard. Impossible in such a short space of time. Sitting across the desk, playing his Walkman, out having a laugh at the talent in the City at lunchtime, then suddenly no more. Mark slumped into a seat.

'Take it easy, Mark. Take some time off today. Go home. Forget about work.'

Tempting. It was the easier option. This was personal now. Peter's mugging was no accident. There had been too many threats of late. The assault of a colleague. That Jaguar at the traffic lights. The one way trip to JFK in Weaver's sedan. Too much fear going down. Mark decided there and then. To hell with the threats, he owed it to Peter. This case had to be closed and he would do it alone if necessary.

'No. I'm staying here today. I've got work to do.'

Norris saw there was no point arguing.

'It's your call, Mark.' He waited a polite moment. 'So what did you learn about Schneider?'

Mark had incriminating evidence but was it enough? He threw some photocopied pages on the desk. Gorin's typed up statement to the SEC.

'Schneider was insider trading in the US. The SEC have proof from a former M&A colleague at Mitchells. But when the news broke, he'd left US jurisdiction. Mitchells fired him and covered up the facts from the US regulators. Their Head of Compliance doesn't want any of this to be investigated and told me so as he forced me to leave New York. They don't want adverse publicity. Schneider hasn't been back to the US.'

They both knew that while the US authorities might serve an extradition warrant on an Arab terrorist or a serial murderer who fled to the UK, they would not do the same for a suspected dealer.

'So he has a history of insider dealing. What's his modus operandi?'

'He finds a girl who has market information. He chases her until he gets close enough. She falls for some of his alleged exterior charms but he uses her for dealing ideas. I even have an idea of who he may have targeted as his girl in Blakes. I saw them together one day in Broadgate. But it's only a hunch.'

Norris didn't hang about when making crucial decisions. He was a changed man.

'Let's go down to Blakes' dealing floor this morning and pick up our dealer for questioning.'

This all seemed rather sudden to Mark.

'Are you sure? What exactly are we going to question him about?'

'His dealings, his great profits, his contact with Sarah Hart.'

'But don't we need more evidence first?'

'We might get it later today.'

'How?'

'Schneider may wilt under the pressure in the interview room. I've seen some big names crack in the past once they're stuck in a windowless room with only the company of a PC and a plastic coffee cup for six hours. You can also make a search of his desk in Blakes. Talk to this girl you suspect is involved. Search his home afterwards. That's where the evidence will be. All we need is some incriminating letters or faxes or lists and we'll have him over a barrel.'

'So the police will be involved?'

'Sure. They'll come with us to Blakes.'

'Is that necessary? It's not going to get ugly, is it?'

Norris shrugged his shoulders.

'You'd be amazed at the effect that a uniformed City of London policeman in a crested helmet has on a bank dealing floor. The whole place goes quiet. I've never had any problems in the past. If Schneider gets difficult with us

then we'll cuff him at his desk and drag him out screaming.'

Handcuffs? This was getting serious.

'We'll need a warrant, won't we?'

'I'll get one in the next hour from a magistrate I know well.
He never refuses to help.'

Mark was surprised at the speed of the developments.

'What do we do about Sarah Hart? Pick her up as well?

'Later. One at a time. We'll get Schneider first. Make sure
he talks to no one when you and I arrest him.'

'You mean that *I* will be there for the arrest?'

'Sure. It's good practice for you. After today you'll be well
and truly blooded.'

Ted sat at his desk with a partially read *Daily Mail* and a
half-finished cup of coffee, watching the clock on the wall.
Ten past nine. Fifty minutes to go to until his appointment.
He wanted to convey some positive news but he felt utterly
useless. He had checked all the personal telephone calls on
Alexander Soames's mobile and work number. He had recalled
every cheque from Soames's current account and gone though the
payee details. He had been through his American Express bills
for the past three years courtesy of some mammoth computer
in Brighton. Nothing. Zilch.

Ted felt guilty that he had spent so many weeks with so
few leads. He still wasn't sure that Helen Soames had told him
everything she could about her husband but he couldn't push
her too hard. He needed a break in this investigation and he
was sure that it wasn't going to come at a funeral in deepest
Acton. He knotted his dark tie. His funeral tie. The one that
he instinctively wore almost every day.

After the service at ten, the mourners went on immediately
to the nearby graveyard in a small convoy. It was not merely
a family affair, rather a corporate outing. David Webster had
dragged along rows of Suits who emerged from the polished

black company saloons and stood in line to mourn their departed colleague. Their drivers hadn't even the common decency to show some respect and leant against car bonnets in the sunshine reading the lewd tabloids and looking on at the grieving family.

Helen stood with the twins, one on each side, hand in hand, as the vicar read the last rites for the late Alexander Soames. Other family members huddled close by offering support. Ted took his cue and stood off to the right, partially hidden by leafy trees and low bushes. He knew how Helen felt. Memories of that smash on the A12 flooded back. No amount of familial support could ease her pain.

The oak coffin disappeared into mother earth and Helen cast a single rose into the grave. The mourners departed. The Suits headed back to the air con of their Granadas and Lexuses, glancing at watches and wondering how much time they had spent away from their desks to grieve at the loss of the one man who had fought the takeover and cooked their books since the public flotation.

Family members drifted away too in clusters of threes and fours. A woman, possibly a sister of Helen's from her appearance, took the twins in hand and returned them to the Volvo estate. That Volvo. Such memories. Helen was alone, looking down into the grave, that dark void that was her life. Ted turned to leave, but stopped and looked back at the solitary figure in black. Helen needed someone right now. He emerged from the cover of the foliage and walked towards her.

'Thanks for coming, Ted.'

'I had to. I wanted to. I know how you feel.'

'Yes. I think you do. You're one of the few who does.'

Neither of them saw the friend in the new sunglasses and the chestnut bob who melted away into the greenery. She had seen the death notice in *The Times* and had felt compelled to pay her last respects.

*   *   *

The doorbell rang at midday precisely. Sarah opened the door to a dapper man in a dark suit with oiled hair with an indentation where his peaked cap usually sat. He held it under his arm in deference.

'Your car, madam. Are you ready?'

Ready as she ever would be. The Mandarin had insisted. It was his last chance to thank her. Sarah looked out at the polished Bentley and marvelled at how many strings her former client could pull in Whitehall.

'Yes thank you, I'm ready.'

He pointed at the two labelled and locked Samsonites in the hallway, sitting beside the vanity case.

'Shall I put these into the car?'

So civilised.

'What about the small case? Shall I take that too?'

'No,' she interjected, 'I'll take it with me.'

Especially with a million dollars in cash inside. She wasn't letting the case out of her sight until she got to the next semi-respectable offshore bank. He struggled with the weight of the cases.

'Pardon me for saying so, but you must have your life's possessions here?'

Exactly. All in a mere two suitcases. Lucky she was a light traveller. He took out an envelope.

'The principal-secretary asked me to give you this, Miss Carter.'

She opened the envelope and took out the burgundy-coloured passport. It was Euro style, no longer the traditional British version. So that was her new name. Sarah Carter. Perfect. Unassuming. And he had even kept her first name. So confusing to live life on a day to day basis under a complete alias.

'Thanks. Just in time.'

He saw her hesitation in leaving the townhouse. It had been her home for the past four years but now she stood with the keys in her hand and no one to give them to. Lenny would be livid when he found out but who cares now? Pug would break in easily enough. She left the keys on the hall table. She needed one last look around. Not for the memories, rather to check there were no clues left behind.

'Give me a few minutes and I'll be out to join you.'

He obliged tactfully. She wandered alone back into the kitchen and stared out at the grey Thames flowing outside. The burial place of her one fatality. The stainless steel sink and marble worktops did not impress her today. They were dirty. Pity that the Mandarin himself hadn't come around also today to wipe the surfaces down for the last time. But he had provided the passport to freedom and the vital piece of information on Provident Bank's demise. She could forgive him.

The townhouse was stripped bare. The furniture had been taken away yesterday by Eddie, the dodgiest second-hand furniture dealer in south east London. The alcove by the kitchen where her PC used to sit was empty. The computer went too once all the personal investment files had been wiped clean from the C:drive. The main living room had a gaping empty space where the pine table used to rest, the same table that Greg threw the cash onto whenever he slumped into her couch. Sarah ensured the much-used top drawer was empty before Eddie and a shaved UB40 mate dragged it off into their decrepit van. No car stereo covers here anymore either. Nice to know that.

She didn't wish to check anywhere else but there was no choice. That was where the incriminating evidence was most likely to be. She descended those wrought iron stairs into the dark basement for the millionth time. A flick of the light switch revealed a perfectly normal residential garage with smooth concrete floors and finely pointed red brick walls. She ran her manicured fingers over the brickwork for the last time, ensuring that the various metal screws, hooks and rawl plugs had been removed. A few small holes remained in straight lines at regular intervals but who would ever notice them?

No item of physical restraint nor any implement of correction remained. She had sold everything to a fellow professional whom she had met at a Soho party a few months ago. The young runaway girl from the Midlands was starting out in the business and needed all the help she could get. Sarah knew how she felt. A job lot for a grand in cash. It was a bargain but Sarah would have paid to get rid of the artefacts you couldn't shift in a small advert in *Loot* magazine, especially that fatal bench. That damn item upon which it all happened down here one clammy July night.

She inhaled. The atmosphere still felt bad here. An odour of leather, rubber, PVC, raw wood, sweat, tears and pain. It didn't smell like a normal garage. No oil, petrol or diesel fumes. She had tried to air the place in the past few days but it would take a lot more time to erase the memories of four years of intensive and abnormal usage.

The basement was as normal as any scene of death could be. Sarah was finally satisfied. She lingered in the hallway upstairs and picked up the vanity case from the floor. It was heavy. A million bucks was a lot of paper and the extra weight of the aerosol cans, perfumes and soaps on top were a necessary disguise.

She took one last glance in the hall mirror. The bruising on her cheek was gone. She gathered the still novel chestnut bob under her favourite canvas baseball cap and pulled the peak down low over her eyes. She decisively closed the hall door behind on her prior life. Outside the sun blazed down relentlessly on Docklands. She was going to enjoy getting used to heat like this in the near future.

She slipped on her shades as she walked to the Bentley. The V6 engine was already running smoothly. She noticed the small metal pennant holder on the front right hand side of the car where a Union Jack or diplomatic flag might fly. He had the sense to remove any flag today. Anonymity was good. Her man dutifully got out and opened the rear door for her. Once inside he swivelled around in the front seat and smiled at her.

'Where to madam?'

'Heathrow. Terminal 4 please.'

Must fly. Courtesy of Her Majesty's Government.

It was the afternoon lull in Blakes, that dark time of the day when the punting was done and everyone watched the array of international wall clocks before departing at a semi-respectable hour. The dealers totted up their trades, worked out the buys and sells and the daily profit and loss. It was mostly profits today and the general mood was bullish. The FTSE was up sixty points on sustained institutional buying in size and on a continental European surge in the DAX and CAC. Only Greg wasn't smiling today.

Nothing was going right. He sat at his dealing desk but it was a pointless activity. The Directors had pulled his dealing limits with immediate effect. Old Nick was in his office on call with the Directors to try and restore his limits and obtain funding from the treasury department. He had warned Greg that it could take days. Until then he was a poker player with no chips, a race goer without a damn cent to bet.

He didn't know if he could ever re-establish his reputation at Blakes. All the profitable trades over the years had been erased by one monumental high-profile loss on that Provident position. He feared for his job and wondered if he could find another in the City. Would Blakes even give him a reference when they turfed him out? He would have to fake another one, to lie again. Life really sucked. It couldn't get much worse.

Suddenly there was a commotion by the escalator that brought staff up to the dealing floor. A few dealers and salesmen stood up and stared at the group of visitors who had arrived. Four to be precise. Greg was so bored that he too took a look over the rows of heads and screens. A bemused, pensionable Blakes' security guard stood there looking surplus to requirements.

Greg saw some old serious guy in a suit striding purposefully down the floor, looking as if he was enjoying himself. Then a young guy beside him. Jesus. That same guy from the LSE. Robinson was back in town and he was coming in this direction. Greg started to sweat, heartbeat racing. Then he saw the third man walking behind the two suits. A tall policeman, the suspended glaring lights on the dealing floor reflecting off the polished crest on his peaked helmet. Shit. Cops in the building. This was serious.

Nick too heard the rising voices, hung up on his bosses upstairs and came out of his office. He almost collided with Norris.

'What's going on here? Who are you?'

The policeman stood with hands clasped behind his back. Norris flashed his LSE identity card.

'We're from the LSE. We are looking for Greg Schneider. Where is he?'

Nick was speechless. He went a shade of pale white. Mark raised a pointed finger towards the crowd.

'That's him over there.'

The policeman moved to stand directly behind Greg. He laid a hand on Greg's arm. Politely yet securely. Norris stood a few feet from Greg and read him the party line.

'Greg Schneider, I am arresting you for suspected insider dealing. You don't have to say anything, but anything you do say may be later used in a court of law against you. Do you understand?'

Greg muttered something that sounded like a yes. Sort of. The dealers and salesmen were silent. Chas and the others moved away from him. The policeman produced the handcuffs.

'Shit,' uttered Old Nick in the background.

Greg walked with the policeman along the dealing floor, head lowered, avoiding eye contact with his ex-colleagues who stared back at him. Best to say nothing. It was the longest walk of his life. Norris ambled a few steps behind. Mark followed the party down the escalator and out into the plaza. A few press photographers flashed cameras aggressively at them as Greg sat in the Rover saloon with the red City of London police crest on the door. Norris reached in and frisked Greg briefly, found what he wanted and extracted a set of house keys that he passed to Mark.

'Check his desk and box all the contents. Find out where he lives and take the second car around there. Search his home. Then get back to the station so that we can grill him face to face.'

'OK. Will do. But how the hell did the press know all about this?'

Norris winked back at Mark.

'I guess word must have somehow leaked out. Still, it will be a good reminder to the others in the City to play by the rules. Every little helps to keep them on the straight and narrow. Don't you think?'

CHAPTER TWENTY-SEVEN

BISHOPSGATE, LONDON EC2

Mark wasted an hour going through Greg's drawers. He examined the contents page by page and felt the hostile glares of the others at the Special Situations desk. Not so special now. The fat bloke swore under his breath. The leggy one took great pleasure in glaring at him. Others mumbled in the background. Mark knew they resented his presence and the arrest of their former star dealer.

He stored the dealing blotters with their lists of past purchases and sales in a banker's box. Then three notebooks full of manic scribbling to be read later back at base. He even took the personal effects as well. Pens, staplers, post-it notes, Bic disposable razors, a few spare Barneys ties and boxes of chewing gum. As he carried the single box towards the exit, he passed an executive office.

'That was well out of order,' said Crosswaithe as he motioned Mark into his office like an errant pupil.

'We do what we have to do.' It wasn't an apology but it was all he was going to get from Mark.

'There's a right and a wrong way to arrest someone. Doing it here on my dealing floor is not the right way. You should have arrested him at his home or outside the building, if indeed you even had to do it at all.'

Mark put his box of evidence down on the floor. It might be worth annoying this Director.

'We couldn't take the risk of losing Schneider. It had to be done here and now.' Norris had wanted it done in public for all to learn the lesson, but Nick didn't need to know that. Don't mess with the LSE.

Crosswaithe still fumed, growing ruddier with every exasperating moment.

'It's a trumped up charge anyhow. There is no basis to it whatsoever.'

'I'm not so sure.'

'You don't actually have any evidence on Schneider?'

Close enough to the truth. Mark didn't want to say too much. Just enough to score a point.

'Did you know that he was fired from Mitchells' New York office for insider dealing?'

'What?'

Evidently a revelation. LSE one, Blakes nil. Crosswaithe slumped into his chair.

'And did you know that he faked his reference when he applied to Blakes?'

'No!' Two nil. Then a pause. 'I suspected something was going on. Tell me, how did Schneider get his inside information when he was in Mitchells New York?'

Mark sat down, giving the overt signal that he was ready to talk.

'He charmed a girl in the office who had the inside track on corporate activity there.'

'Jesus. I should have seen it coming. So that's how he does it.'

Mark's suspicions about one particular research analyst were worsening by the minute.

'Do you want to expand on that? Did Schneider have any good contacts in Blakes?'

Crosswaithe mumbled distractedly.

'I found out a few weeks ago that he's been seeing a leading light in our Equity Research Department here. He never told me about the relationship. She knows what's happening in many listed companies. There is a Chinese Wall between our Dealing and Research Departments but it's damn hard to enforce it in the bedroom after work.'

So it was true. Mark sensed the lead that he so badly needed. Was it her?

'Who's the research girl?'

'Barbara Ashby, our Head of Equity Research.'

Damn. Looking guiltier by the minute. Mark needed to know.

'Is she here? Can I talk to her?'

Crosswaithe cast a glance out over the shell-shocked dealing floor. Others stared back at them, wondering who was next perhaps.

'No. She's busy right now.'

'I'll rephrase that. I'd very much like to talk to her right now.'

'No way.'

'Then I'll be back in an hour with a warrant and she can join your dealer down at the station. Your call?'

Crosswaithe relented, realising the superior forces of the law were against him. He stood up.

'I'll send her in to you.'

Mark waited alone, expectations rising by the minute. It almost felt like a first date. Nerves. Would she be as great in the real world as she was on television? Did she even exist or was she simply a product of Sky TV?

'Mark?'

He turned to greet her. Wow. Everything on his JVC wide screen and so much more. She radiated effervescence and personality. They enjoyed a firm handshake. She faked an easy smile.

'Hello, Barbara. I'm from the LSE.'

She sat opposite and leant forward towards Mark's chair, apparently intent on their conversation.

'I know. I've seen you on the dealing floor here a few times in the past few weeks.'

She actually remembered his visits. Slow down. Take this easy. Focus clearly. Work first.

'We've taken in Greg Schneider today on suspicion of insider dealing.'

Good riddance. She nodded but said nothing. Her smile was gone. Mark couldn't see any concern about her boyfriend's arrest.

'Investigating people's private affairs is unfortunately sometimes a hazard of my job. Crosswaithe says that you and Schneider are presently in a relationship.'

She shook her head vehemently. Her voice rose in anger. Some raw nerves there.

'No. He's wrong. Greg and I are finished. Permanently.'

Dead-end? Mark tried another tack.

'Can I ask you about your relationship?'

She nodded reluctantly. Then loosely folded her arms. Defence mode. Something was wrong here.

'Did Schneider ever ask you about your equity research work?'

'No.'

'Did he ever visit you at home?'

A loaded question in hindsight. Casting aspersions on her lifestyle. She was so edgy. She fidgeted with her nails, peeling back some skin along the cuticle so that the blood almost ran. She looked up at him and something sparkled in her eyes. Mark thought he could see tears there.

'Sometimes. But more often I visited him at his home.'

Think back to the NASD.

'Do you keep any confidential information on corporates at your home?'

'No. It's all in the office, locked away at night or secure on my PC.'

Another dead-end? One last try.

'Do you ever dial in from home to your work PC? Say for example over the weekends?'

She tried to laugh off the question. Great pearly white teeth. The humour didn't work. She was acting.

'You must be joking. At Blakes? I can hardly log into my PC while I am at my desk here, never mind from home by some minor miracle of twentieth-century remote engineering.'

A good command of the English language too. Well educated? He pushed his luck.

'Can I ask why the two of you broke up then?'

'It's nothing to do with you.'

He watched her eyes up close. Another potential tear welled up in one corner. She was uncomfortable. Her voice was weak. He thought back to the SEC. That fight at the bar. The alcohol. That other girlfriend's pain.

'I'm sorry. One last question. Did Schneider ever hurt you at all?'

She stared back at Mark. He knew. Somehow he had deduced those awful events in the NW8 bedroom. Was he someone she could at last open up to and share the pain? Someone who read the signs that Old Nick couldn't see. No. Second thoughts. Best not talk about it to a total stranger.

Mark was about to ask the next question but held back. Her body language was so different now. She had retreated into the depths of the leather chair. Somehow diminished as she folded her arms more tightly, across her chest. He saw pain and regret in her vulnerable posture and knew it would be wrong to pursue this line of questioning.

'I'm sorry if I asked too much today. Maybe we can talk about this some other time?'

She looked back at him, held his stare for slightly too long and knew that he meant well. This guardian of the City from the LSE had walked in and removed the cause of her pain and humiliation in a pair of handcuffs. She owed him something for that.

'Maybe.'

Barbara withdrew gracefully. Mark watched her sit back at a desk and pick up a telephone with perfectly extended fingers. The camera doesn't lie. He was smitten. He would definitely have to ask her more questions. He recalled her parting line. It sounded like she would talk to him again.

This was the good life. Sarah rolled over on the sun lounger and re-adjusted her bikini top to some degree of respectability. She had fallen asleep, easy enough to do in the late afternoon when the only sounds were the ebbing water in the azure pool, the muffled Salsa music on the hotel system and the far away sound of a million dollars earning daily interest at five point three per cent annualised.

'Your drink, Ms Carter.'

Ms Carter? Oh yes. That was her. The waiter in the crisp white shirt handed her the fruit punch, topped with a small umbrella of assorted tropical fruit. The glass was cold to the touch. She let the base of it sit momentarily on her chest and admired the modest tan from a mere three days in eighty-five degrees of most excellent sun. She enjoyed the almost decadent chilled sensation. All was going to plan.

Seat 3A in BA Club World on the way to the Caribbean had been ideal. The upper deck cabin was full of patently monied types on their way to an overseas summer break. She blended in amazingly well with the others. Rugged yachting types with perma-tans and hardened hands from chasing uncoiled ropes on deck. Silver haired middle-aged professional types in dark blazers, pink Ralph Lauren open neck shirts and ironed khaki chinos. Greying ladies with more jewellery on one hand than Tiffany's had in their window. Lithe things in their mid-twenties going to meet their sugar daddies in their villa.

She had enjoyed the company of Mr 3B, a leathery South African divorcé called Rich on his way to join a party on his yacht in an outlying island. He talked non-stop yet made the seven hours fly by. Literally. He had travelled so much, experienced so much, knew so much. A good catch. Hard to believe he was now available again. So handsome. And wealthy too. They had so much in common. Rich indeed.

They had reluctantly parted company when they touched down at Grantley Adams International Airport. Then she took a clapped out taxi along the coast to Worthing, the lack of air con made up for by the sea breeze through the open car windows. She checked into the most expensive hotel on the island, The Dunes Resort, near St Lawrence Gap. She stored her vanity case in the hotel safe for one night. She paid in advance for two weeks in the penthouse suite as pre-arranged by email from the Isle of Dogs. She paid cash up front in crisp hundred dollar bills. What else? The view from the top floor was worth the four hundred bucks a night. It was a luxury for one single occupant.

She took another cab ride on the first morning into the centre of Bridgetown. A walk down the main street with her loaded vanity case in one hand, eyeing up the various bank offices along the waterfront, all competing for her business. All the big banks were Canadian, they were the big players in the local market. She chose Canada Trust bank simply because she liked the cool modern décor of the lobby. She spent forty minutes with a deputy manager called Winston Farley explaining her fortuitous inheritance from her wealthy mother and her need for utmost secrecy and confidentiality. He nodded in sympathy and then his eyes glazed over when she opened her vanity case. All those greenbacks.

She had made only one error. It sort of came out. Farley immediately tried to interest her in some mutual funds. She was not keen. She had no information here on the overseas markets. Without her inside track and her PC she was like any other investor. She wanted to stay liquid. He insisted. She mentioned the last problem she had with Blakes in Jersey. They had screwed up and she was still down 20k sterling in some investment trusts that had proven difficult to sell. Pity in hindsight. She didn't need to mention Blakes or their funds. It was a minor indiscretion in an otherwise perfect game plan.

She applied some more Ambre-Solaire factor four and faced into the rays again. The fruit punch had refreshed her. The past was behind her. Her only thoughts were of ten minutes in the power shower when the sun went in and a pre-dinner cocktail in the hotel bar with Rich. He had been so keen to delay his yachting trip that she didn't like to say no. Then dinner at The Cliff, the exclusive restaurant he knew from prior visits. And finally there would be some excellent sex in the queen size in the penthouse.

The coup de grace had been yesterday's *Daily Express* that she had bought on the news-stand in the hotel shop. Three Barbadian bucks fifty for an English paper overseas but worth every last cent of it for the news it held. It was force of habit for her to read the inside business pages although she had no need anymore to watch the fluctuating fortunes of Provident Bank, Sportsworld or County Beverages. The lead story in the business section caught her immediate attention. LSE Arrest Blakes' Dealer. The photograph taken on the kerbside in Broadgate was convincing evidence that Greg was under lock and key. Nice.

Justice had been swift in coming. So fast that there was no need now to make that call to the TV copper in Harrow Road. Insider dealing carried a heavy penalty and that bastard deserved every year of the sentence he would surely get from an Old Bailey judge. Case closed. Roll on life in retirement.

The police Rover 400 pulled up outside 125 Viceroy Terrace, St John's Wood. Mark enjoyed being chauffeured by the City of London police. Most convenient and far better than the nightmare of catching buses and taxis from Battersea. The disinterested driver sat on in the front seat. Mark needed his help.

'Can you come inside too? Two of us will do the work in half the time.'

The driver reluctantly got out and shrugged his shoulders.

'What are we looking for anyway?'

Mark opened the communal hall door with a key from Schneider's key ring and stepped inside.

'We're looking for any paperwork about shares. Evidence with figures and names of companies. Personal bank statements or broker confirmations. Anything that you think might be out of the ordinary.'

The PC wasn't enthused.

'I'm no expert on this type of thing. It's out of my league.'

'Make the effort.'

Mark opened the upstairs door to the apartment and was immediately impressed. If this was the way star investment bankers lived then perhaps he could handle the lifestyle after all. The apartment was enormous, all stripped Junkers maple floors, expensive yet subtle Persian rugs, wrought iron curtain rails with tie-backs, flashy Shaker kitchen units with chrome utensils and implements hanging from the ceiling, giant beds in giant bedrooms. The contents here were worth more than the entire flat Mark currently inhabited. He decided to make the search easier for both of them.

'You do the bedrooms. I'll do the lounge, kitchen and study. What we're looking for is most likely to be in the study.'

They spent the next forty minutes covering every nook and cranny in the extensive apartment. It must be two thousand square foot minimum. Mark had to admire Schneider's taste. Good CDs and well-thumbed books. Evidence of travel all over the world. A well-stocked fridge with chilled bubbly, French cheeses and Scottish salmon. Fresh fruit on the kitchen table. Good modern art on the walls. The surroundings almost distracted him from his endeavours.

Despair soon set in. There were no files hidden in drawers, no scribblings in the study, no marked up papers or computer printouts, no letters or faxes. Not even a PC. Absolutely nothing with which to incriminate a City of London dealer. How would he break the news to Norris? Schneider was surely going to walk.

'Have you found anything in the bedrooms?'

The PC reappeared in the corridor.

'Nothing that I can see. It all looks normal.'

Mark couldn't take any chances. He had to be sure. He went into the master bedroom and eyed the enormous bed, knowing that sometime in the recent past, the chances were that Schneider had taken that gorgeous research girl down on these sheets and enjoyed what Mark would have died for. These City guys had it all. And more. Until now that is. Mark opened the wall to wall wardrobe and admired the rows of suits and shirts, and then down below, the rows of polished shoes and the ties that hung on two rails.

Four boxes lay along the floor of the wardrobe. They looked like they contained old household effects, the sort of place you put things that you didn't really want. He turned to the PC.

'Have you looked in these?'

'Sort of.'

'What does sort of mean?'

'Not really.'

'Yes or no?'

'No.'

If you wanted a job done properly, then you had to do it yourself. Mark delved into the boxes, not knowing what he was looking for at all, just hoping for some evidence. But it was all rubbish from the past. Ornaments that were just plain tacky. Sporting trophies from a stellar high school past. Memories of a well-travelled life. And a small plastic bag from Asda with something black inside. Mark was curious. Surely Schneider wasn't the sort to frequent Asda? He was more of a Waitrose or Harvey Nicks type. This was carefully wrapped. Whatever it was. He took it out of the box and stood up.

'What's this?'

'Dunno.'

Mark unwound the plastic bag to reveal a piece of Japanese consumer electronics. It looked like a cover from a car stereo. He stared at it momentarily. So did the PC. Mark thought back to something someone had said at work. Or was it something he saw in Jersey or in New York or DC or somewhere else? It was somehow familiar. The brand model was a Sony CD 90X. Definitely familiar. The PC saw the dawn too, remembered a flyer on the notice board back in the nick and awoke.

'Guv, that's been in the news, hasn't it? Someone in Harrow Road Station, I think.'

That was it. Sky News. The copper in Harrow Road station with the evidence. The missing stereo from Alexander Soame's Volvo in Stratford. Surely not? Impossible. How could it be in Schneider's home?

The PC was of the same mind. They needed proof. There must be thousands of these in London. It was a hell of a coincidence. There was one sure way to check if this belonged to the dealer currently sitting in a Bishopsgate Police station cell, waiting to be grilled by the LSE. Mark took out Schneider's key ring and scanned the keys. One of them was a solid looking rubber-topped key with a distinctive Mercedes star on top. Schneider's car? Typical. Time to see if this stereo fitted his car.

They left the flat and stood by the police saloon looking up and down the road for Schneider's car. Totally impossible. The place was wall to wall Mercs. Like a bloody West End showroom. Estates, saloons, A-classes, convertibles, coupes, the lot. The PC finally regained some initiative.

'Hit the alarm button and watch for some flashing indicator lights.'

Mark held up the key and pushed. A nearby SLK flashed

back at him. Speed, lightness and comfort all in German of course. They walked to the car and opened the solid driver's side door. Mark was madly envious. This motor was gorgeous and the black leather seats invited him to rest a while amongst the luxurious interior fittings. Miles better than a Mark one Golf with a grey plume. The car stereo made the biggest impression on the two men. It was a Mercedes own model, welded into the dashboard so that no Luton louts could nick it over night on a London thieving spree.

Mark stared at the Sony model in the plastic Asda bag. It was definitely not from his car. Was it the vital evidence that the DI was looking for? Norris would indeed be interested.

Winston Farley, deputy manager of the Barbados branch of Canada Trust Bank, was efficient. Not for him the *manana* attitude of some of his local colleagues at the quaint head office building in Bridgetown. Service mattered to him and the bigger the client, the more he wanted to do for them.

Take for example that lovely English lady who had opened that big dollar account this week. Ms Carter had mentioned a bad experience she'd had with some Blakes funds in the Far East. Twenty thousand sterling was a lot to forego and his first thoughts were to do whatever he could to recoup her loss.

And so it was that he reached for his set of Bankers Almanac books first thing in the morning, knowing that it was still early afternoon in sleepy St Helier. The books listed the names and telephone numbers of all the banks in the world. Blakes in Jersey was easy to find. The next stage was to talk to the right person.

'I'm ringing from Canada Trust. I would like to speak to someone who dealt with Ms Carter's account.'

Gabrielle at the private client's reception desk was puzzled. She thought she knew all the private clients, but evidently not this one. Must be a new client or one of the less active, perhaps. She searched the desk-top client database. No sign of any Ms

Carter there. She told the polite Caribbean gentleman that there was no client of that name. Must be some mistake on his part? But he insisted.

'She told me that she had an account with you. She had some Far East investment trusts which settled late and she is still missing twenty thousand pounds.'

Gabrielle was thinking fast. That late trade rang a bell. One of Penelope's clients had a problem there. Hart? She'd seen a memorandum about it and she had recently typed a few stroppy faxes to the lazy operations manager of their Hong Kong back office. But this guy on the phone had the wrong client name.

'I think you have the wrong name.'

'No. You must be mistaken. It's definitely Ms Carter.'

Gabrielle was in two minds. To hang up on this guy? But the facts he mentioned were correct. Maybe Carter was her married name? Or else maiden. Though she hadn't exactly looked the sort. Gabrielle put him through to Penelope Swales.

'Penny, I have a Canada Trust banker on the line who I think is enquiring about Sarah Hart.'

Penelope took the call, regretting yet again the loss of her much-treasured former client.

'Hello, this is Winston Farley calling from Canada Trust. I believe that you are dealing with a delayed settlement in Far East trusts for a mutual client of ours? She wants her twenty thousand pounds sale proceeds as soon as possible.'

'Hold on.'

Penelope moved the rubbish on her desk and found what she was looking for. A cheque for twenty-one thousand five hundred quid from Blakes Hong Kong. It had arrived two days ago in the ever-efficient inter-office mail. She hadn't known what to do with it until now. She had no idea where Hart was, no forwarding address. She had been about to lodge the cheque to the bank's own suspense account and let it sit there for all eternity along with the hundreds of thousands that already lay there unclaimed.

'I now have those funds.' She was curious. 'Are you in Canada somewhere?'

'Goodness, no. I'm in Barbados. Please mail the cheque to me at our head office in Bridgetown.'

'I'll do that.'

'Ms Carter will be most appreciative.' And then he hung up.

Penelope was puzzled. Ms Carter? Who the hell was she? On second thoughts she couldn't send the cheque to a total stranger. She needed specific written instructions from Hart before any £20k plus left the office. That was the procedure and she would follow procedure.

She filled out a lodgement slip for the bank's own internal suspense account. To hell with that pushy banker from Barbados, she thought, with just a hint of envy. And to hell with Hart who had left her with a million bucks less to manage. To hell with both of them.

CHAPTER TWENTY-EIGHT

CENTRAL LONDON, WI

Mark sank into the front passenger seat and called a certain DI in Harrow Road station. The direct police radio link got him straight into the pre-fab communications room in W9. He waited for the connection as the screeching saloon took the sharp bends around Hyde Park Corner. The skilled driver evidently now felt some sense of urgency as he transported a passenger with a clue to a high profile murder investigation, rather than a mere civil service investigator as previously believed.

'DI Hammond speaking.'

'Mark Robinson from the London Stock Exchange here.'

A pause. Ted had no idea who he was talking to.

'Are you still looking for that Sony car stereo in the Alexander Soames investigation?'

'Yeah. What do you know about it?'

'I found one like it thirty minutes ago in the home of a City dealer.'

Ted was silently evaluating the new information as Mark hit a traffic tailback near Victoria. The driver took the law into his own hands. It was his prerogative. He flicked a switch on the dashboard and the siren and roof lights swung into bright and deafening action. Ted was ever more puzzled.

'Where are you calling me from, Mark?'

'I'm in a police car going down the Embankment to Bishopsgate Police station. We have this City dealer in custody and we are about to interview him about insider dealing charges. Do you want to come down too and check out this stereo cover at the same time?'

'What's this guy's name?'

'Greg Schneider. He works at a Special Situations desk at Blake Brothers. He's an American.'

'Never heard of him.'

Ted instantly decided that if this LSE man was being driven to the station in a screaming panda car then there had to be some substance to his inside track on this baffling murder. No time waster here.

'I'll be there in twenty minutes. Do me a favour. Don't talk to your suspect about this until I get there.'

Mark handed the radio mike back to his driver. They took a sharp left before Tower Hill and in a few minutes pulled up by Bishopsgate nick. Three or four idle journalists loitered outside. One of them recognised Mark from the earlier impromptu press show outside Blakes and came up to him.

'What's the news on the Blakes' dealer?'

'No comment.'

Norris was waiting alone in an anteroom inside, cheap Styrofoam cup of coffee in hand, a worried look on his ageing face, still keen for any news from St John's Wood.

'Mark, did you get anything?'

'Yes and no. I've got nothing at all to use as evidence for insider dealing. My only hope is to root through some banker's boxes of stuff but it doesn't look hopeful.'

'Damn.'

'But I found something that may tie Schneider to a far more serious crime, to the death of that Provident Bank director, Alexander Soames.'

'You gotta be joking. What on earth could Schneider have to do with that?'

'I dunno yet. Time will tell.'

'Time is the one thing we haven't got. Forget about murder and all that. Schneider is our man and we want to do him for insider dealing. We only have twenty-four hours to nail him. Either we formally charge him with insider dealing or he walks back his dealing desk in Blakes and we get a large amount of egg on our face.'

'So what do we do?'

Norris paced the small room anxiously.

'We do what we have to do. Make him think we have some evidence on him. Get him worried. See his reaction. Try our luck. Let's go.'

'No. Let's wait for the DI investigating Soames's murder. I said we would.'

Norris wasn't persuaded. He picked up the case files on Schneider and made for the door.

'That's got nothing to do with us. We want to get this guy before someone else charges him.'

Mark was about to have a stand-up row with his boss when the door swung open and a panting middle-aged guy in a brown suit and dark tie entered. Ted made the mistake of going to Norris first, right hand outstretched, to greet his saviour in a pig of a murder investigation.

'Mark Robinson?'

Norris pointed to Mark. Ted turned to him, thinking this guy was too young.

'Mark, thanks for the call. Can I see it?'

Mark reached into the inside pocket of his suit and produced the ASDA bag. He laid it on the cheap wooden table and began to unwrap it deliberately. Ted was worried.

'Have you handled this yourself?'

'No.'

'Then don't touch it. Fingerprints could be vital.'

Mark already knew that. There it was in all its glory. A Sony CD 90X model, brand new, not a scratch on the front. Ted was starting to get excited. He knew the serial number of Soames's stereo off by heart at this stage. He turned the cover over with a Bic pen and read the black ink by the bar-coded label. XX5657769473ZS. Incredible. This guy from the LSE had delivered the goods out of the blue.

'Jesus. This is it. Your City dealer is connected to Soames's murder. I need to be sure.'

Mark sensed some hesitation and knew the next step. Definite proof was required. Ted was first.

'We need to check for fingerprints. Mark, do you have any prints yet from Schneider?'

Norris cut in.

'No. We don't yet.'

Mark was a step ahead, doing a bit of lateral thinking.

'We do have a set of prints. They were taken six years ago but prints are prints forever, aren't they?'

Norris was lost. So was Ted. Mark obliged.

'You have our Provident Bank case file here. And that includes the NASD files on Schneider. All dealers are fingerprinted for Series 7 exams in the USA. Herb showed me them. Let's use those.'

'Bloody brilliant', exclaimed Ted, whose only prior experience of a Series 7 came from his days on the stolen car squad in the East End. So they had fingerprints at work in the US. Trust the Americans.

'Hang on,' observed Norris. 'We can't use fingerprints taken in the US in a court of law over here.'

'It's OK,' assured Ted. 'We will use them for identification. We'll take a new set afterwards if they prove to be a good match.'

The duty PC at the station dusted the cover in minutes, placed pieces of clear tape over the front and removed them one by one, evaluating the subtle pattern that was emerging. He looked unhappy.

'This ain't going to be easy at all. There are lots of prints here. I'll go for the freshest ones first. That should be our best bet.'

He took Mark's page from the NASD, pondered for a moment about what all the registration details meant and then placed the bottom corner under a microscope. He examined the recently taken prints, one by one. The others waited, unwilling to speak or shatter the man's total concentration. He took one print back and looked at it again. A sigh. Then another print. An intake of breath. He stood up.

'I'd say this single print is a match. Damn near perfect.'

Ted was beside himself at this stage. The DI would be delighted. So would Helen. He turned to Mark.

'You may have accidentally stumbled upon the man who murdered Alexander Soames. Well done.'

Greg was pissed off. He sat in the windowless interview room across a narrow wood effect table that was last in fashion in the early Seventies. The three stooges sat opposite. That asshole from the LSE who had pored over his share dealing for weeks, the old guy in the waistcoat who had invaded his office today and some grand daddy of a DI. He rolled up his sleeves, ran his hands through his sweaty hair and prepared for the bout of his life.

Greg only had his fighting instinct and his stuck-up attorney, a West End solicitor with a sharp suit and a two hundred quid an hour charge out rate. Justice didn't come cheap these days. The attorney had duly done his briefing. Greg was to say zilch. He had always been careful never to leave any dealing records at home. Everything had been destroyed as he bought and sold those profitable shares, including the damning tapes. There were none lying around when he had last looked around the hi-fi system, although he thought he might have had one on

Sportsworld? But definitely no tapes left in view. No little black book of deals, no printouts, no files saved on magnetic disks anywhere. It was all in his head. There was nothing they could pin on him. He was safe.

'We are recording this interview,' said Norris.

Greg didn't care. He was going to say either yes or no. And mostly nos at that. So said the attorney.

'We wish to ask you about your recent share dealing.'

Go ahead. Greg shrugged disinterestedly. Norris started.

'You have made sustained dealing profits in a number of highly speculative stocks. You bought these shares before significant price sensitive information was released to the wider market. We believe you knew about this corporate news in advance and that you traded on that inside information contrary to the provisions of the Financial Services Act 1986. Do you wish to make a statement or any admission to us? It would save us all a lot of time.'

Sure it would. Your time. Taxpayers' time. No way in hell.

'No. I don't.'

'Why did you invest in County Beverages shares?'

Careful here. Choose the words carefully. Give them some City bullshit. Shovels full of the stuff.

'I was of the opinion that it was a worthwhile medium-term investment.'

The attorney smiled. Perfectly vague. The American client was good.

'You made a hundred k plus on County in a single day.'

Greg sat back in his chair and folded his arms. This was going so much better than he'd expected.

'Is that a question or are you telling me something I already know?'

The authorities were unimpressed. Visibly. Mark shifted in his seat and cut in.

'And you almost made two million quid on Provident.

You had a million of the stock and needed that takeover deal to go through. At any cost. The Provident board were going to do the deal. And then the loan book went sour and the deal collapsed. What went so wrong there then, Greg? Didn't you see that coming?'

That hurt, the bastard mentioning that loss. That was the day it had all started to go belly-up.

'It proves I am not always right. Remember what it says on your pension statements about the value of securities. They can go down as well as up. Past performance is no guarantee of future performance.'

The attorney didn't like the involuntary social conversation. It wasn't what they'd agreed in their hour-long private conference. He didn't know if his client had anything to hide but he could see that he was beginning to get rattled. Deny everything. Follow his advice. Norris saw that Mark was making better progress. Schneider had shown his potentially vulnerable side. He gave Mark the nod to continue alone.

'Greg, why did you leave the employment of Mitchell Leonberg Inc?'

'I wanted to work in Blakes.'

'I don't believe you. You were fired, weren't you?'

'No.'

'The files in the NASD and the SEC say that you were suspected of insider dealing, so they fired you.'

Shit. He knew about the past. What else did he know?

'No. I left there on good terms. I got a good reference from my boss.'

'You wrote it yourself. I asked Brad Franklin. He's never seen the reference, let alone signed it.'

Greg winced. Those names from the past. A killer blow to the solar plexus.

'Do you know a Katherine Gorin from the M&A department in Mitchells in New York?'

They knew about her. Sweet, trusting Katherine. He never

meant to hurt her. Like Barbara. Something deep inside made him do it. Spur of the moment. The demon drink. The liquor shots. The pressure of making millions of bucks. The darker side. He said nothing.

'We'll ask you again. Have you been insider dealing?'

'No.'

'Greg, a leopard never changes its spots.'

'Prove it then.'

Mark would prove it in time. Somehow. First he needed a break. He tried a change of tack.

'Did anyone tell you in advance about the proposed takeover of Provident Bank?'

'No'

This annoying asshole was getting warm. Too warm.

'Did Barbara Ashby tell you about it?' Worth a try at least, thought Mark.

'No.'

Way off base man.

'Do you know a Sarah Hart who lives in the Isle of Dogs?'

Jesus. They knew about her too. Greg wondered if his facial reaction gave it away? Best to lie. Why change the habit of a lifetime now? He was wondering if they had spoken with Sarah. What would she say? She'd deny it all too. Hopefully. She was in it up to her neck. She'd never talk to the police. He was still safe.

'No, I don't know her.'

A pause. They all evaluated the situation. Mark wrapped up.

'Then that's all for now from me. We will continue later.'

Greg smiled. Fatal. The old copper looked like he wanted to speak for the first time. The others deferred to him.

'Mr Schneider, I on the other hand am investigating a recent death.'

Greg relaxed. What was this old guy on about? What planet was he on?

'Yeah? So?'

'Did you know Alexander Soames?'

The attorney shifted beside him. They hadn't discussed any guy called Soames. He was unprepared.

'No. Not really.'

'Meaning what?'

'I mean I've heard of him. He worked for Provident Bank.'

'And you know that he was killed a few weeks ago?'

'Yeah. I heard about that. It was all on Reuters and Bloomberg.'

Greg rarely read the better newspapers, never watched the news. Everything he needed to know was in a tabloid or on the screens. He was thinking about Sarah. What the hell had happened in that townhouse with Soames?

'We've been looking for a vital clue for many weeks.' Ted put the stereo cover in its plastic bag on the table and unwrapped it. 'This item was taken from Soames's Volvo and we found it this morning.'

Greg looked at it hard and knew the awful truth. It had been in Sarah's house. It was the clue that linked Soames to her. Soames had been in that basement on his last day on God's earth. She had done it.

'So what's that got to do with me?'

'Mark here found it in your flat in St John's Wood.'

'Get the fuck out of here.'

The attorney didn't like this turn of events. He hadn't planned to discuss a murder investigation and it wasn't his chosen field of legal expertise. He raised a hand in protest. The others ignored him.

'So how do you explain that, Greg?'

'I've never seen that stereo before. You guys planted it in my flat.'

Mark interjected.

'I have another witness from this station who was with me when I found it this morning.'

'It's a set up.'

Greg stared at it and then involuntarily put a hand on the table, so near to the evidence but yet so far. He was thinking back to that last visit to that awful basement. He had found it in the corner of the garage. He had picked it up and left it on the table upstairs. Did she ever hold it? He wasn't sure.

'Be careful, Greg. You don't want to touch it now, do you?' asked Ted.

'No, I don't.'

'Especially when your fingerprints are already on it. It wouldn't look good when we get to court.'

Greg knew they were bluffing. They couldn't be so sure.

'You're joking. You haven't even taken my fingerprints yet.'

Ted leant over the table, coming closer to Greg and to the evidence.

'The NASD have had your fingerprints on their files for six years. They match those on the stereo perfectly.'

Greg hadn't given up hope yet.

'You've got no damn motive. Why the hell would I want to kill Soames? There's nothing in it for me.'

Ted had thought about this already. Conversations with others came flooding back to him.

'I've spoken at length with David Webster, the Provident CEO, about the takeover deal. Some people knew that Soames was against the deal and was urging the board to reject the offer. If so the share price falls and you lose. Were you aware that Soames felt that way?'

Sure Greg knew that. It had been on those tapes. In so many words. He said nothing.

'And Mark said that you were sitting on a paper profit of two million quid. It was your biggest killing for some time, if you don't mind me using that phrase. Could you afford to let Soames have his way? Did the deal mean that much to you? Did the deal have to happen? Was he someone in the way?'

Greg was seeing the dreaded word. Motive. So was Ted.

'So we have incontrovertible evidence and motive in millions. What about opportunity, Greg?'

He had decided to say absolutely zilch. This was no longer an interview. It was an inquisition. Ted had seen the light when the Yank had first run his hands through his dark, wiry hair and uttered the first words in his American drawl. This guy was quite good looking. Rita at the Dorchester hotel would ID him for sure.

'We know that Soames disappeared on a Wednesday six weeks ago from his West End hotel. Where were you that evening?'

'I have no idea.'

'Think hard. It's important.'

Easy. It must have been the same as any day after work. Drinks and sex.

'I was probably with my colleagues after work for drinks and I was with my girlfriend all night in my flat.'

Ted wasn't giving up yet.

'What time did you leave work?'

'At six o'clock, I guess.'

'What time did you go for a drink?'

'I can't remember.'

But he could. The night Soames had been last seen alive, Greg had been late meeting up with Barbara. He had been down at the Dorchester. He had a missing hour or more. Potentially fatal. He was lying. They would check out his alibi with Barbara. This was all going wrong. Ted pushed him further.

'Did you go anywhere else that evening? At around six o'clock?'

'Like where?'

'Like the Dorchester Hotel?'

Shit. The cop knew.

'I've spoken to reception staff there. Someone matching your description tried to deliver a package to the Provident Bank meeting. Only the CEO says there never was such a delivery. We found an envelope hidden in a pot plant. Mark says you work for a Special Situations desk. Those are the words on a newspaper inside. We can get fingerprints from it.'

'Nothing to do with me.'

If there had been a lie detector in use, it would now have been off the far end of the Richter scale.

'Did you go for a spin in a borrowed Volvo in the East End and stop off by the Thames afterwards?'

That was a fucking loaded question. Greg suddenly rose from his seat and lunged at Ted. He caught him in his rib cage. It hurt. The others rose and subdued Greg. He suddenly knew that he needed a drink.

'I didn't kill Soames. No goddamn way. You'll never make that stick.'

The attorney had seen enough. This was looking like a lost case already. He made it clear that he needed to confer with his client. They left the suspect and attorney alone. Greg wasn't listening anymore.

He was shell-shocked. This was his worst fucking nightmare. Being pulled by the cops for insider dealing was bad enough but it was beginning to look like the lesser of two evils. He sure as hell wasn't being done for the murder of that guy Soames. One person in the Isle of Dogs did know the truth about that stereo cover She had surely planted the evidence in his flat. Sarah had killed Soames. The police would have to interview her about the deceased but to point them in that particular direction, Greg would have to admit knowing her and her assorted vices.

But they'd find the tapes, search her basement den, interview her clients and look at her personal dealing in Jersey. All the evidence about his inspired dealing would come to light. Greg's life as a dealer would be over. He could never work anywhere in the City again. He'd be done for insider dealing and do serious time in the UK.

He couldn't see any way out of the dilemma. Mission Impossible. And he was no Tom Cruise.

Ted needed to be sure. He took a diversion off the Edgware Road and pulled into Regents Drive. The Volvo estate was parked two cars away in a residents bay. Helen answered the door immediately.

'Is there any news, Ted?'

'Not really. I need to check one more thing in your car. Do you mind?'

'Sure, no problem.'

She took a set of keys from the hall table and made for the steps to the pavement.

'Don't bother. I'll do it myself.' No need to set her mind racing.

'OK, will you be long?'

'Five minutes maximum.'

'Good. Come in for a cup of tea afterwards. I've got some hot scones out of the Aga.'

'Thanks. I will.' Nice invite. Helen smiled. She must be in recovery mode at last. He made off down the steps alone. She called out to him.

'Be careful. The car alarm's on. We don't want someone calling the police, do we?'

Definitely in recovery mode. He smiled back at her. The car doors opened as he hit the sonic alarm button on the key ring. He sat into the plush driver's seat, momentarily admired the Swedish leather interior and firmly closed the door. A glance back to the house confirmed Helen had returned inside. He took out a pair of white latex gloves and put them on with some difficulty. The wrong damn size he guessed. He had nicked them from Beath's morgue on his last trip there. Beath must have small hands.

He took the plastic evidence bag from the inside of his jacket and carefully removed the stereo cover. Sure, the serial numbers matched perfectly but he wanted definite proof. The manager in the Sony warehouse said the odds of the cover working in a different base unit were a million to one against. Ted had to know. He'd look a right fool in court in a few months time when some legal brief legged him over.

He placed the cover flush against the base unit and eased it into position with an extended thumb and forefinger. The key turned in the ignition and he saw the lights flash on the dash. He dared to press the power button with the nib of a Bic pen and saw the liquid crystal display power up immediately. Capital 95.8 FM was visible. Probably the last radio station Alexander Soames ever listened to in his life.

Some anonymous dance track emanated from the quadraphonic speakers. A regurgitated 1980s soul classic with added bass and repetitive sampling. High on plagiarism, low on creativity. It was truly awful. Ted sat back into the leather seat. The stereo bloody well worked. Schneider did it. Music to his ears.

CHAPTER TWENTY-NINE

OLD BROAD STREET, LONDON EC2

Mark sat at his barren desk contemplating the fruitless events of the prior day. This had not gone to plan. He had tried to reel in an insider dealer but had inadvertently landed a murderer instead. That opportunistic detective had stolen his big fish for a far greater crime and there was no point in pursuing any insider dealing charges against Schneider. The penalty for murder was far greater than anything that the Enforcement Department could throw at a guilty as hell dealer. Case closed.

Norris's secretary approached Mark in the morning lull, that precious time between the first coffee and a read of the days *FT* and the second coffee with the early morning edition of the *Evening Standard*.

'You've got a visitor.'

'Who is it?'

'Some girl. Nice looking too. Barbara somebody or other.'

And there she was. Right in his office. Barbara Ashby in the flesh. A wonderful thought. Mark hardly recognised her out of her City uniform. She was different today. No power dressing suits, sheer tights, gathered hair or carefully applied make up. The real Barbara away from the TV screen.

Her long hair hung onto a loose denim shirt, worn with a

pair of dark tailored culottes topped by a perfectly weathered leather belt. Her shirt had a discreet logo on the pocket. Her clothes were co-ordinated for what the American investment banks call the smart casual look. Many banks had a dress down day during the week. Mark was too distracted to speak.

'Hello, Mark. Can we talk somewhere private?'

'Sure.'

Mark looked around. The one meeting room was empty but was a mess. The ugly remains of a half-eaten team breakfast meeting lay on the table, empty coffee-pot and crushed croissants, stained cups and the smell of stale cigarettes in the still air. Norris had left the office earlier at short notice, looking a bit grey. A chest pain of some sort according to his secretary. Had to see the Doc. Mark ushered Barbara inside the vacant office and closed the door, despite glares from the secretary. He sat into his boss's easy chair. Comfy. He could get used to the chair of the Director of the Enforcement department. Dream on.

'Is it casual day at Blakes today?'

She laughed. That laugh. She was better up close. Perfect skin even without the Max Factor. She oozed latent sensuality as she crossed her legs and tilted her head to one side. Mark was almost salivating.

'A casual day at Blakes? God no, Mark. We're still stuck firmly in the nineteenth century. That's the way Old Nick likes it. Traditional. He requires a smart suit everyday. It's only in places like Goldmans that you can go casual on a Friday. It spilled over from their US head office. I'm on a day off.'

She paused, thinking about something or other. She had used his forename again. Always a good sign. Personal. He could sit here and gaze at her all day but that would be rude. They were past the social pleasantries stage. He debated about asking her more about her relationship with Schneider who must have used her for information on hot stocks. Barbara had indeed come with a purpose and evidently it wasn't to ask Mark out on the date of his life.

'I want to talk to you about Greg Schneider, Mark.'

Good. Mark nodded, still distracted. He would never miss another Sky Business Report again. No way.

'How's your investigation into his dealing going?'

Mark regretted the question. Not because of the lack of progress in the case, nor his growing jealousy of Hammond's success, but also because he could tell her nothing. Confidentiality reasons forbade it.

'I can't talk to you about that. It's work in progress.'

Bad move? She shifted in her seat. Was she going to leave? He needed her to stay. He did his best to prolong the conversation, lest she walk out of his life again. Her charms were breaking down the barriers.

'I'll make an exception here. What do you want to know, Barbara?'

'Do you have any incriminating evidence on him?'

Mark debated. She saw the hesitation. He had plenty of evidence of murder but damn all on insider dealing. He thought back to Schneider's alleged alibi for the night of Soames's disappearance.

'Schneider says you met him on the evening that Soames disappeared and that you spent the night with him?'

It hurt him to ask about that night. How the hell did a tosser like Schneider ever lure someone as perfect as this? It must have been the flash job, the ample cash, the Merc and the ego. It couldn't have been personality and charm. Barbara looked down, her enthusiasm evaporating for the first time that morning.

'Yes, that's probably true.' She'd spent too many nights at his place.

It hurt her to say it. That rapist. She had talked to no one about it. Not even her mother back home during her week off work. She wanted so much so tell someone about it. Maybe even someone like Mark right now, or ask him to get one of his police contacts to help. She still couldn't face the public knowledge, the questions, the sympathy, and the inquisition into what happened in the king size in St John's Wood.

'Did you spend the whole night together?'

'Yes. But he was late getting to the pub that evening. I don't know where he was.'

'How late?'

'An hour or two.'

Enough time to meet someone and kill them? Barbara was still providing vital information.

'I remember that week well. Earlier I was out of the office at an AGM in the Dorchester and I telephoned in to the Special Situations desk. I remember chatting to him. That was a weird day in hindsight. I saw him in the hotel that day.'

'Who? Schneider?'

'No. Soames. The Provident Bank Director who was killed.'

'Did you tell Schneider that Soames was there in the hotel?'

'Yeah, I did. Anything wrong with that?'

She didn't yet know that her ex was a murderer.

'Nothing.'

Mark had found Hammond another witness who would confirm that Schneider knew of Soames's whereabouts. That supposition by Hammond, the drive to some East End location in a borrowed Volvo, looked a dead cert. But Barbara wasn't interested in dead Directors. She wanted revenge against Greg.

'This isn't what I came to talk about. What about his dealing?'

'I think he's guilty as hell but I can't prove it.'

'Maybe I can.'

'How?'

She shifted again, pulled a single cassette tape from the top breast pocket of her denim shirt and handed it over to Mark. He looked at the pocket for too long, then shifted his gaze.

'I found this in Greg's apartment a while ago. It has conversations between two people about a company deal on it. I think he was somehow getting this information and dealing in it at work.'

The insider dealing charge was looking unlikely but Mark was nevertheless getting excited. Maybe there was more to this. Two people? There could be some extra mileage left in this case after all.

'Would you testify that you found the tape in his apartment?'

'For you? Of course I would.'

Nice touch. Subtle signals.

'And Schneider's voice is on the tape?'

'No, it isn't. I've listened to it a few times and I have no idea who the people on the tape are, but it's definitely incriminating. Have you got a tape recorder? Play it and see if you agree with me.'

Mark rushed out of the office and looked in vain for a recorder of any sort. No joy. It wasn't standard LSE operating equipment. Then remembrance of a former colleague. He opened Peter's old desk drawer, took out that much-used Walkman and returned to Norris's office.

'We don't have any speakers. I need to use the earpiece instead. Let me listen first.'

'Let's listen together.'

'I've only got the one set of earphones.'

'That's OK. We can share them.'

Barbara got up and leant on the edge of the desk. She took the left earpiece, pulled back those long locks and was ready to listen. Mark took the right earpiece. They sat on the desk, only a foot apart. The perfume, the aroma, the body scent, the pheremones, whatever it was, were truly overpowering. He was so close to her, as close as he had been to any girl he had fancied this much in months. As close as lying side by side in bed. He didn't have the energy to press the play button. He fumbled.

393

She obliged, their hands touching momentarily as she did the necessary. Play time indeed.

Mark was puzzled. This conversation was weird. Some woman with a great accent taking to a guy about his work as a lawyer on a deal. Then sounds as if she struck him. He cries out in anger and agony. All the noise echoed back at them, as if in some empty hollow room. He mentions the takeover by Sportsworld of their high street competitor. The tape ended as suddenly as it began.

'What the hell was that all about?'

She illuminated Mark.

'I think she's beating him to get the information.'

'But it sounds like he enjoys the beating. Weird?'

But there was something else that jarred. That accent. It wasn't any old voice.

'Play it again, Barbara.'

Eat your heart out, Bogey. Second time around, Mark was starting to get definite ideas. Third time around he was a hundred per cent certain.

'I know that voice.'

'The guy? Who is he?'

'No. Her. I know who she is.'

Memories of a trip to the Isle of Dogs returned. That accent. Sarah Hart without a doubt. Reality dawned for Mark. Schneider wasn't getting information from Barbara Ashby or anyone else at Blakes. Hart was the missing link. She was the one getting the information from lawyers, bankers and others. They didn't need this evidence anymore against Schneider, but it was the first evidence against Hart. And it meant that Barbara was not involved. Just as he'd hoped and prayed.

Time to pick up a second suspect in the investigation into what really happened in Provident Bank shares. Barbara left but she had made a great impression. Her parting words encouraged Mark.

'Let me know if you need to see me again.'

He would.

Mark stood alone at Bank, the busiest intersection in the City. Twenty minutes or so he had been told over the telephone to wait. True to his word the Rover stopped by the kerb and Ted rolled down the front passenger window with a puzzled look.

'So why do you need my help? Who's this Barbara Ashby?'

'She works at the same bank as your murderer.'

Evidently Ted didn't follow the markets that closely or watch Sky at 8.30 every Wednesday. Mark climbed in, slammed the door and pointed to the road ahead. Ted persevered in his quest to know more.

'Who's this Sarah Hart?'

'She may be insider dealing. I've been to her place before. I thought you should come along too. We may need a policeman to make an arrest today. It might be connected to your guy Schneider.'

It suited Mark to get a free ride and some police protection at that townhouse. Much better than the Docklands Light Railway and he didn't know who or what he might find there.

'Sure. Wouldn't miss it. Where are we going?'

'Isle of Dogs.'

Mark offered Hammond another juicy morsel. This was becoming a habit.

'Barbara Ashby will testify that she told Schneider that Soames was in the Dorchester on the last day he was seen alive. So he knew where to go to find him.'

'Blinding. That guy is as guilty as hell. All we need is a confession to make the court case less work for all of us.'

They arrived in Thames View and parked beside number 32. They tried everything for ten minutes, rang the doorbell in vain, peered though the cracks in the closed curtains at the windows, and looked into the hall via the brass letterbox. Post had been left unopened on the floor. Mark was worried. He couldn't remember exactly what had been inside before but he was rapidly forming the impression that the house was too sparsely furnished.

'This ain't looking good. She ain't here.'

Ted wasn't so discouraged. Mark was suddenly glad that he had requested his company. The policeman was resourceful.

'Let's push in the hall door and have a look.'

'Can we do that?'

'Of course. This is linked to a murder investigation. Gimme a hand.'

They both put their shoulders against the wood and heard the Yale lock crack under the pressure.

'Easy does it.'

The door still didn't budge. Even the cop was beaten.

'Shit. There's two mortice locks here. Top and bottom. Five lever, I'd say. This is bloody Fort Knox. She must be obsessed with security. What's she got to hide? We'll never get inside this way.'

Ted walked to a corner window, gave it the once over, took a large stone from the small garden and smashed it through the glass. Within a minute he had opened the biggest window and they were inside. The place was eerily quiet and devoid of any personal artefacts. Any furniture come to that. This was a house, not a home.

'We've missed her. She's gone.'

Ted gave his professional opinion.

'Looks like it.'

Mark recalled his one previous visit. He should have been more thorough last time. Pity now.

'Last time I was here Hart had bruises on her face; she also had some new suitcases. She must have been in trouble or must have known something was going to happen to Schneider.'

Ted wasn't so downbeat.

'We can track her down. Use the local police. Circulate her details. Check with airports.'

Mark didn't hold out much hope. Hart seemed to be a step

ahead of him. He cursed the day that he'd visited her. That must have been the tip-off she'd needed to move on. He had lost his second decent insider dealing suspect in as many days. This was a truly disastrous investigation and could set back his alleged career in the LSE by years. Norris would not be impressed at all. Ted was more optimistic.

'Let's have a look around anyway. I'll take upstairs, you do down here.'

Mark pointlessly picked around the remains of the townhouse for ten minutes. There wasn't one single clue as to Hart's whereabouts. No rubbish in the kitchen bin. No letters or cards on the mantelpiece. No answering machine with incoming calls. No bloody telephone in fact. Hart had left the light bulbs and plugs and that was about all. Mark lastly decided to check out the garage and descended the stairs.

It was a strange garage. Absolutely pristine, perfect concrete floor with not one oil stain on it. It didn't even smell like a garage, no petrol fumes. The garage door looked brand new, almost untouched. Must have been rarely used for the Beamer outside. Wherever that was now. He shouted up to Ted.

'Have a look at this garage.'

As soon as he spoke aloud he realised where exactly he was standing. That familiar echo came back to him, just like on the tape he had listened to less than an hour ago with Barbara across the desk. The tape had been recorded here. This was where that bizarre interrogation had taken place. He shouted again to be sure and Ted scrambled down the wrought-iron stairs. Yes. Mark was sure. Ted was expecting more.

'What did you find?'

Mark was examining the garage wall. There were marks along the brickwork. Rows of them in straight lines. Then holes from where rawl plugs had been fixed into the mortar. Bigger holes where hooks must have been. Some marks on the floor too. Candle wax in one corner. One big hook in the darkened corner of the roof. The ever-careful Hart must have missed them. A hole in the roof in another corner. Mark was thinking about how the tape recordings had been made and where that hole led to upstairs. 'This is where she got her information. She took guys down here, beat the living daylights out of them for information and then dealt in Jersey. Shit. I really fucked this case up. It was all so simple.'

'Never mind. Your boss need never know. Maybe you'll get a break somewhere else.'

Mark didn't share Ted's optimism. The two men walked back to the car just as. A creaky hall door opened across the road and a little old lady in a pink floral cardigan approached them.

'It's about time,' as she pointed to the police car.

'I'm sorry?' replied Mark. What was she on about?

'You ought to be an' all. For over a year I've been telling you something was going on in that house. All those men coming and going at all hours of the day. All those big cars parked near my home, blocking my view. I told your station so many times but they did nothing about it.'

Ted apologised on behalf of the entire Metropolitan Police Force.

'I'm sorry about that. Anyway, we're here now, madam.'

'It's too late. The lady who lived in 32. She's gone for good.'

'What makes you so sure?'

'A van came to take away some of her furniture last week. There were some strange pieces. All heavy wood and metal covered in sheets, but the sheets fell off and I saw it all. Then a big car came for her with a chauffeur. One of those black ones with the little flag pole on the bonnet. The chauffeur helped her with her things. She had her suitcases packed. Vanity case too. I'd say she was heading off for good.'

Gone. For good. Mark hated those words.

'Anything else you want to tell us?'

'Well, you're not the first people to come looking for her.

There were two other men here They had a key. They went into the house and came out looking very unhappy.'

Mark's curiosity was instantly aroused.

'Two men? What were they like?'

'Nasty looking. One big ugly man and one smaller man in a suit. They were in a Jaguar.'

A Jag? Two men?

'Was it a maroon Jaguar?'

'Yes, it was. So you know about them then?'

Memories of an abortive shopping expedition.

'Sort of. Did you get the registration number of the car?'

'No.'

'Pity.'

'But I have got a photo of them. I take lots of them. They're up to no good in that house.'

They already knew that.

'Have you got the photo handy?'

'No. I'm only on number four in the film. Twenty more to go before I get it developed.'

Mark looked at Ted and raised an eyebrow.

'You've been very helpful. We'll send someone down to talk to you later today,' he reassured her.

The old lady was satisfied. She had done her bit for the authorities. About time they came she thought. Mark sat in the police car as Ted revved the engine unnecessarily. Mark was still frustrated.

'How the hell am I going to find Sarah Hart?'

Mark and Ted sat with Schneider in the interview room. The twenty-four-hour holding period was almost up. They had to make a decision on whether to charge their suspect. And with what? Murder or insider dealing. Ted wanted the former. Mark still hoped in vain for the latter.

Greg was shattered. His eyes were a give away. Bloodshot. He hadn't slept. He missed his power shower and Gillette contour blade in St John's Wood. The night in the cell on a damp mattress without his belt, cuff links, tie and shoelaces had softened the suspect. But he had come to a definite decision. An insider-dealing rap was preferable to being tried for murder.

'Ok, guys. I'll do a deal with you. I'll trade information.'

'About what? asked Mark.

'About the murder?' chipped in Ted. 'You want to make a confession about Soames's killing?'

Greg recoiled in his chair.

'Jesus, no. I've told you before, I didn't touch him. I'm talking about admitting to insider dealing.'

'Go on,' prompted Mark.

'I got inside information from that Sarah Hart in Docklands. She beat it out of her clients and recorded it all on tape for me. I used the tapes to make decisions on buying and selling. It was fool proof until Sportsworld and Provident Bank. Now it's over. That's my confession. I'm guilty.'

Ted wasn't impressed.

'That's pathetic. Is that the best you can do?'

'It's the goddamn truth.'

'You're only telling us that to get charged with insider dealing. What about the murder?'

'You've got the wrong person for that and I can prove it. I know who did it. Sarah Hart.'

'And how did she do that then?'

'I don't know exactly but Soames was a client of hers. She often tied him up, but this one time I guess she strangled him or choked him or something like that. She's the one you want, not me.'

Ted wasn't impressed.

'How come we found his car stereo in your apartment then?'

'She must have planted it there. Maybe it's not even the one from his car?'

'It is. I tried it. It works. And what about your fingerprints being found on it?'

'I found the stereo in her basement. I picked it up. That was where Soames left it when he came for a visit. She wanted to get back at me.'

'Why?'

'We fell out. We had a row.'

'And you beat her up?'

'Sort of.'

'So, do you have a history of violence?'

'Jesus. No, I don't. It's not like that. It's a set up, guys. Can't you see it?'

Ted wasn't convinced at all.

'She did a damn good job of framing you then. So what's her motive? What's in it for her?'

'That's the whole point. I'm sure she didn't mean to kill him. It was an accident. There's no motive.'

'So what proof do you have about all this?'

'Just ask Hart about it. She'll fold when you grill her. She's my alibi.'

'So you do think you need an alibi? Interesting.'

Schneider was adamant.

'I was nowhere near Soames.'

Mark enlightened Greg about his recent visitor from Blakes.

'We have a colleague of yours from Blakes who says she told you Soames was in the Dorchester that evening.'

Greg saw the light. He had been at the Dorchester. This was looking bad. He said nothing.

'We'd have to find Hart first to talk to her about all this, wouldn't we?'

Greg had an answer for almost every obstacle that his adversaries put in his way.

'Sure, it's not a problem. I know where she lives. You can pick her up right now.'

Ted smiled back at him across the table.

'Really? Thirty-two Thames View? We've just been there. She's long gone. Packed her bags and took off in some chauffeured limo. Convenient, isn't it?'

Greg needed her so badly. She was a witness, an alibi, a dealer, a murderer all rolled into one.

'She can't be gone. You've got to find her.'

Mark was just as keen to locate his other insider-dealing suspect.

'Do you have any idea where she might have gone?'

Greg was stumped. He knew so little about Sarah's private life. She was still a mystery to him, someone he hadn't even deigned to consider seriously except on his brief visits to get the tapes and pay the money.

'No. I have no idea but you must find her. You've got the wrong person. Do me for insider dealing but not for murder. Shit. There's no motive for me, guys. Think about it.'

'We have a motive. Soames wanted to can the deal. You needed it to happen.'

Ted had made a decision on behalf of the CPS. He stood up and recited the usual caution.

'Greg Schneider, I am charging you with the murder of Alexander Soames. You do not have to say anything but anything that you do say may be later used against you in a court of law.'

Mark had indeed lost his man. Ted had his. Greg rose up from the table, fists clenched, blood rising.

'No fucking way. You won't fucking pin this on me, you bastards.'

Ted stared back at him, pencil in hand, equally certain of the facts before them.

'I'll make a note of your comments for the trial.'

Mark was a beaten man. He was back in the office alone. Norris was at the doctor again. More severe chest pains. The Provident Bank file lay untouched. What an utter waste of time. His quarry had fled. Norris's secretary noticed his despondency and tried to cheer him up.

'There was a call for you while you were at the police station. Penelope Swales from Blakes in Jersey. She wants you to call her back as soon as possible.'

That woman who had churned and burned him in Le Meridien hotel. Used him for one night. He wasn't cheered by the news. He had no desire to call her. But ten minutes later his direct line rang and without thinking he picked up the receiver.

'Hi, Mark. It's Penny here.'

He mumbled a muted acknowledgement of sorts. What did she want? Was she in town and alone again? No surprise. He hated that affected accent. It did absolutely nothing for him. He made a token effort.

'Penny, what can I do for you?'

'You know what this is all about. I see you're famous now. I never realised that your visit to me in Jersey was so important. It's all over Blakes in London and the newspapers here. I'd never have believed that Schneider was insider dealing. Thank God he only opened a small deposit account with me. Otherwise you'd have to come out here and visit me again.'

Some minor celebrity hunting? So this was purely a social call. One that Mark didn't need.

'Don't believe everything you read in the newspapers, Penny.'

'What? So he didn't do it?'

'He did but it doesn't matter anymore. He's also a murderer. That criminal charge takes precedence.'

'What?'

'It'll be in the papers tomorrow. He killed that Provident Bank director, Soames. There's lots of evidence, opportunity and a motive.'

'Jesus. And to think that I sat alone with him in my office.'

Penny was truly living life on the edge in her mock regency office with its harbour view. Mark decided it was time to knock the stuffing out of this pushy woman.

'By the way, you also had another client who was insider dealing.'

'What? Who?'

'Sarah Hart. She was getting information from men in the City.'

'I should have guessed. How?'

'You don't want to know.'

Penny loathed former clients on principle, but Sarah Hart especially for what she had said.

'That bitch. She closed her share account with us a week ago. Took all her money out.'

It was as Mark had expected. Hart was gone for good. He tried one last vain hope.

'I don't suppose you've heard from her again?'

'No. Not a word.'

'Any idea where she might be?'

'No. And you?'

'No. She's disappeared.'

If in doubt, follow the money. It was Mark's only hope.

'Where did you wire her money to?'

'We didn't. She took it out in cash. A million dollars left here in her vanity case. Some hand luggage.'

Mark knew that vanity case. It had matched the rest of the Samsonite luggage. Hart had been light years ahead of him. His only lead had disappeared. This call was going nowhere fast.

'If you hear anything about her, let me know immediately.'

He was about to hang up. Penny held on the line, contemplating recent events.

'Well, I do know something else; I got a telephone call this week. A bank manager rang me looking for some late sterling sale proceeds that are due to someone called Carter. I think he meant Hart. He wanted me to send the funds on to him but I refused to do it. We need explicit client authorisation before paying funds to third parties.'

Mark sensed an escape clause.

'Do you know this bank manager?'

'Not personally. But he was called Farley and he works for Canada Trust.'

Canada? What the hell was Hart doing in Canada?

'Where in Canada? Toronto, Montreal?'

'No. That's what I thought too at first. He's in Bridgetown. Barbados.'

Mark smiled. Exactly where he'd go if he'd a million dollars to spend on the good life.

Helen had lost count of the number of times Ted had visited her at her home. Each visit became more special but this would be different to all others before. Her husband's black leather briefcase from the wardrobe upstairs could not be ignored any longer. She had carefully replaced the sordid contents. She had thought about nothing else for days, delaying the inevitable moment of disclosure. There must be some connection to her husband's death. She could trust Ted to be discreet.

He had called her an hour ago to advise that there had been a significant development in the murder investigation. In the past he had given her information. Now she was one who could enlighten him about Alexander's dark and sad childhood. Mercifully Ted arrived before the twins had returned home from school. He sat opposite Helen in one of the deep cream sofas and updated her on the case.

'We had some big news today.'

'Me too,' she said slowly. 'I have something that may help you.' She recalled those scribbled names, addresses and telephone numbers. Ted could make the sordid follow-up calls.

'Today we charged a man with your husband's murder.'

Ted was surprised at her reaction. Helen seemed amazed rather than relieved or even pleased.

'Really? Who?'

'A dealer in the City. The guy was about to make millions on the Provident takeover deal. He knew Alexander was fighting the deal and a receptionist at the hotel saw him in the Dorchester on the day your husband was last seen alive. We found the missing car stereo in his flat yesterday.'

Helen still wasn't convinced.

'Are you sure he's the right person?'

'Yeah. The stereo we found plays in your car. That's why I was here yesterday. Thanks for the scones again. This guy's fingerprints are all over the stereo. He has no alibi for part of the night of Alexander's disappearance. He was going to lose millions if this deal didn't happen.'

That's far more convincing, she thought. She'd been wrong all along. This had nothing to do with Alexander's dirty secrets at all. She had jumped to too many conclusions too fast. The twins would be spared. Ted was surprised by her level-headed reaction.

'So you said you also have something to tell me?'

She thought about the briefcase upstairs.

'It doesn't really matter now.'

Ted was impressed by her composure. She had taken the news well. They stood close together in the hall. He liked that. She stared at the dark tie he always wore.

'Hold on a minute, Ted. Don't go yet.'

She went upstairs, opened her husband's wardrobe and returned to the hallway with something hidden behind her back. He was puzzled. She stood close to him and reached out to his shirt collar.

'You know, I've grown fond of you but this tie is depressing me. Do you mind?'

He evidently didn't. She unknotted the tie, rolled it up neatly and placed it into his suit pocket. She produced a blue silk tie with a tasteful subdued animal pattern.

'Time heals all wounds, Ted. I've started to learn that. You must too. I bought this for Alex when we were in Milan for a weekend last April. He never got a chance to wear it. You can have it if you like it.'

She knotted the tie expertly for him. Ted ran his hands over it. He would never have bought a tie like this, much as he admired it. It was good Italian silk and it was truly a perfect knot. He felt like a new man.

'Thanks. I like it. You've got good taste.'

'I'm starting to know what I like. Keep in touch, Ted.'

CHAPTER THIRTY

GATWICK AIRPORT, LONDON

Mark awoke at six a.m. He barely had enough time to gulp down breakfast before the mini cab arrived for the short hop to Victoria Station. He only just made the six-thirty a.m. express train from platform fifteen. All for the ridiculously early two-hour check in time for the scheduled Britannia departure at nine o'clock. He met Ted as agreed and gave him the ticket courtesy of the LSE. He'd need a cop to make the arrest.

Gatwick this time. Hell on earth. Wall to wall with backpacking students, parties of wandering school children, hostile parents and lost foreign tourists. The queues for check-in had the sort of travellers who finally got to the front of the queue after forty minutes and look blankly at the check-in staff when asked for their passports and tickets. Then a five-minute rummage, several minutes of communal anxiety and success as some tattered envelope from their travel agent was discovered amongst the latest *Hello* magazine, the Grisham paperbacks and the Thomas Cook travellers cheques.

The scheduled departure time was a mere aspiration. They took off at ten-thirty after sitting in a queue of eight planes on one niner waiting to get airborne. Mark and Ted got two middle seats miles apart from each other and between hyper holidaymakers. Incessant cabin noise for eight hours while they travelled westwards. Harassed plastic airline staff pushed plastic trays of plastic food at them, handed out sick bags and sold duty free like it was going out of fashion.

Salvation at last. The plane began to descend from its cruising altitude. Mark peered over the chubby mass beside him and caught his first aerial view of the shimmering sea. And there a few hundred miles away, a row of sparkling dotted islands, nestling in outlying coral formations, surrounded by gleaming sandy beaches mixed with golf courses and dense lush undergrowth. Mark didn't know which was the most easterly island, but he knew that one of them must be Barbados.

This was going to be easy. Mark's telephone call on the first morning to Farley at Canada Trust in Bridgetown confirmed that he had opened an account for a wealthy English lady called Carter. Once Mark got the Blakes Jersey connection established he was sure that Carter and Hart were one and the same person. Carter had given an address at the Dunes resort outside town. They would all be on the next flight home in a day and Mark wouldn't even get the chance to enjoy this tropical paradise.

He hired a car while Ted went to sweet talk the local police. The choice of hire cars in the car park was limited but Mark knew that he wanted the tornado red jeep. He paid the deposit, flashed his UK licence, rolled back the soft canvas roof, put on his shades, found the local soul station on the crackly stereo and cruised down to meet Ted in the city centre. And the LSE paid him to do this? Ted wasn't impressed.

'Do you think you could have hired something less obvious? If we have to find Hart, then we might as well try to blend in with the locals.'

'We are blending in with the locals. Local tourists. What's wrong with that?'

Ted's morning had been more successful. He met the local Inspector of Police and used his connections to get written authority to arrest Hart on sight. The under-utilised Inspector got overly excited at the thought of a celebrated international financial criminal at large on his home patch. The entire Barbadian force was at their disposal. Both of them. Ted assured him that the arrest was a mere formality. The portly Inspector in the gold braided uniform waved them off from the whitewashed steps of his sleepy station.

They hit the first snag. The duty manager at the Dunes recognised the name of his affluent guest but was obstructive to the point of open hostility until Ted produced the typed letter signed by the Inspector. He reluctantly escorted them up to the top floor of the hotel. The suite was devoid of guests, the bed evidently unused for the night. They checked the closet and bathroom. Some clothes and toiletries were still there. Mark recognised the luggage. The vanity case was empty. Hart should still be around. The duty manager wondered who the hell forked out four hundred bucks for a room and never used it. Mark wondered where his quarry was. So near. So far.

Ted won the toss and paced the grounds of the hotel, checking the public areas, restaurants, car park, poolside and health club. Mark lost and so spent the rest of the day sitting in the darkened lobby killing time. So frustrating to watch the sunshine outside from the wrong side of the main door. He sat behind a copy of the riveting *Barbadian Times* and digested the news of the day. Brian Lara flies in with stunning girlfriend. Goat escapes from farm. Thefts of coconuts in the high street. Major news items.

He eyed up the talent that entered by the main revolving doors. Unbelievable guests passed before his eyes. Bronzed pseudo-athletes in navy Yankees baseball caps, cut away Reebok Lycra halter-tops and figure hugging Speedo shorts. They made him think of Barbara back in the City. He missed her. He toyed with the idea of buying her a postcard at reception, writing her some lines care of Blakes and telling her that he would like to meet her again. Work or pleasure. It didn't matter. On the upside the activity would kill ten minutes of boredom. On the downside she might think it was a stupid thing to do.

Despite staring hard at every resident who came down to the lobby for her room key, a certain Sarah Hart never showed. They left the Dunes at midnight in their Day-Glo jeep without their suspect. The night manager obliged them with a telephone call at the crack of dawn. Still no sign of Hart.

The pensionable porter opened the main doors of Canada Trust Bank at nine-thirty a.m. sharp every day. But his first visitors today were not customers of the bank and never would be. They hadn't the cash. Mark and Ted sat again in Winston Farley's corner office under a revolving fan. Mark tried another angle.

'Has Hart, or Carter as you know her, given you any other address?'

'No.'

'Do you have any idea where she might be?'

'No.'

'Did she mention going anywhere else while she was on the island?'

'No.'

Farley grinned.

'Hey. She's gotta come back here.'

'Why's that?'

'We got her million bucks.'

Mark's imagination took over. He was wondering if he would find Hart alive. Perhaps she would wash up on a deserted beach on the other side of the island in a few days time, be found in some mangled road accident or attacked by some anonymous hired locals downtown. He didn't know exactly what had happened over the past few months in London and New York and the uncertainty of the present sewed more doubts.

The battered telephone on Farley's desk rang. They evidently didn't object to a break in the conversation so he took the call while his English visitors silently pondered their predicament.

'Hello. Yes. Certainly. Tomorrow. Fine. See you then.'

Winston placed the telephone back down and smiled at his guests. A gleaming row of molars and gold fillings were on display. He was enjoying the moment of power.

'Well gentlemen, guess who that was?'

Mark and Ted looked at each other. They hoped for the best.

'You don't mean ... it was her?'

'Precisely.'

'And?'

'She is going to visit this branch tomorrow morning.'

'No. Why?'

Those teeth flashed back at Mark and Ted. Colgate eat your heart out.

'Last week we ordered her a new credit card and cash card for the ATMs here. She has to come in to pick them up this week.' He held up a white envelope.' 'I guess that's why she's coming.'

At last the frustrating search was nearly over.

They sat by the rear window of a small beachside apartment block, the curtains partly drawn over the window that faced out across the quiet street. Mark lay on the bed taking his turn at a break. Ted crouched by the window with a pair of binoculars borrowed from the helpful Inspector. He stared through the lens at the Canada Trust Bank and fumed.

'Jesus. It's almost midday and she still hasn't turned up. Where is she?'

Mark stretched and yawned. Either delayed jet-lag or sheer boredom.

'Relax. Take it easy. We're in the Caribbean, remember.'

'What does she look like again? Maybe I've missed her?'

'I told you before, she's about thirty-five, slim, five nine or thereabouts, and her most distinctive feature is a shock of blonde hair, probably tied up in a ponytail. She's not exactly one of your regular bank customers. She'll stick out a mile when she turns up.'

All Ted could see were a local couple parking outside the bank and going inside. Then some tourists emerged, looking at local bank notes, trying to work out much to the US dollar. Then a husband and wife getting out of a taxi. Promising at first but not his quarry. The woman had short reddish hair and stylish glasses. The husband was tall and good-looking in navy Bermuda shorts and a smart yachting jacket. He carried a hold-all. Mark got up.

'What time is it?'

Ted averted his eyes to his wristwatch.

'Ten to twelve. I hate these bloody stakeouts. Hungry at all?'

'Yeah.'

'Then go and get us something to eat. I need some chocolate. Sweet tooth and all that.'

Mark needed a break too. He checked his wallet for his wad of Barbadian dollars and closed the apartment door behind him. He descended the battered wooden steps at the front and looked at the other view. Not the damn bank. The beach, pearly white and almost deserted. The clear skies above. Catamarans moored offshore. Solo skiers passing by at speed. White water breaking over the coral. A few torsos of swimmers visible. Children tip-toeing gingerly across the burning sand. Water lapping against the ankles of lazy holidaying paddlers. That's where he'd much prefer to be today. What a waste of a day.

The Seven-Eleven store in the Shell garage at the corner sold coffee and sandwiches. Anything would do. He cast one lingering look back at the bank just as Winston Farley appeared at the door. He saw Mark and waved. Waved again quite animatedly. What the hell was he doing? That was one way to scare off Sarah Hart. Winston crossed the road, dodging some determined traffic, and yelled.

'What are you doing? Why didn't you get her when she left?'

'Hart? When?'

'Just five minutes ago in a taxi.'

Ted had seen the commotion from his vantage point and ran down to them. Mark broke the news.

'We missed her. No, you missed her. She left five minutes ago.'

'No way. I was watching everything. Five minutes ago?' He remembered the last departing customers. 'The only person who left was a white woman with short reddish hair with a man.'

Winston waved his arms again. 'That was her, mon. What's wrong with you? She was with a man.'

'What man?'

'I dunno. He didn't talk much. South African accent. Well dressed. Tall.'

'Shit.'

Mark still wasn't so sure.

'No, you're wrong. I met Hart in London. She has long blonde hair.'

Winston wasn't convinced. 'No. She has dark reddish hair. Look. This is a copy of her passport.'

Mark stared at the photocopy. It was a good enough copy. Definitely short and dark.

'Fuck. She's changed it. She's too damn smart.'

He sat down on a low concrete wall by the shop and instantly forgot about his hunger pangs.

'So now we have to wait around to catch her some other time?'

Ted was more hopeful.

'She has new credit cards and an ATM card. We can see where she uses them and trace her that way.'

'No,' advised Winston. 'I was wrong. She didn't take the new cards with her. We cut them up in my office.'

'Shit. She'll be back here, though.'

'No, I don't think she will.'

'Course she will. You still have her million bucks.'

'That's just it. We don't anymore. She withdrew it all in cash in a hold all.'

Mark jumped to his feet.

'Why the hell did you let her do that? That money was our only lead.'

'I was waiting for you guys to pick her up outside. I never thought you'd miss her. This ain't such a busy bank, you know. And she said she'd checked out of the Dunes.'

Mark was almost goaded into a bitter riposte. Winston gave him a big smile. Nothing fazed the man.

'Don't worry. I know where she went. She was late and in a hurry. She was going to the airport.'

'Jesus, not another trip. Norris will go ballistic at these airfares.'

Ted threw him the set of keys to the jeep.

'You drive. Let's get to the airport and catch her there. Now at least we know what she looks like.'

Mark drove like a lunatic back to Grantley Adams airport. As they pulled up by the perimeter buildings a single LIAT turbo-prop accelerated down the runway and rose into the cloudless sky. He swore.

'I know she's going to be on that fucking plane.'

Airport security were helpful once they saw the Inspector's letter. A passenger called Carter was indeed on the LI 434 which had left five minutes ago. The destination was St Lucia.

'Where's that? How far away is it?' Mark pressed them.

'It's a twenty-minute flight, mon.'

'When's the next flight?'

'In two hours' time.'

'We'll take two seats on it.'

Ted was not so optimistic.

'How the hell are you going to find her in St Lucia?'

'We'll work that out when we get there.'

Mark and Ted took a chance and entrusted their lives to Leeward Islands Air Transport, or LIAT as the locals knew it. Its reputation for tardiness was legendary. Known fondly as Leaving Island Any Time. They weren't the best with the baggage either. Luggage In Another Terminal more often than not.

The 37-seater De Havilland Dash 8-100 plane was tiny. Mark could only crouch inside amidst the 1980s velour interior. They were both grateful that it only took twenty-two minutes to cover the fifty nautical miles to St Lucia. They touched down at a small airstrip and walked across the melting tarmac to the much-needed shelter of the single airport building.

All Mark knew about St Lucia was what he had recently read in the LIAT Islander in-flight magazine. He was on a former plantation island that had survived the colonial struggles between the French and the British. There were eight onward flight connections including Caracas. Great for escapees. The currency was the EC dollar. The island population had been precisely measured at 138,150 inhabitants. How to find one person? Ted loitered by the Hertz desk.

'How do we find her on this island? Do we hire a car and drive around all day hoping for a break?'

Mark stood at the taxi rank and looked around for inspiration. And there it was in front of him. A row of four damaged but usable local taxis, all Nissan Hi-Aces. He walked up to the first cabbie leaning against his rusted bonnet, smoking some dubious-looking weed and tried to stay upwind to avoid inhaling.

'How many taxis are there on the island?'

'About fifty on a good day. Ten on a bad day. If the cricket is on.'

'Were any of you guys here earlier this morning? Did anyone pick up a tourist couple, a woman with short dark red hair and a tall South African guy? They would have arrived here about two hours ago.'

A driver at the end of the queue got out and approached them.

'What's it worth to you?'

Ted took out his letter from the Inspector.

'We're here on official business. We need to know.'

The driver gave him a scathing look.

'That's from Barbados. That don't mean nothing here in St Lucia.'

Mark knew what the driver meant. He took out his wallet.

'It's worth fifty dollars.'

'US or EC dollars?'

'OK. US it is. So you do remember them?'

'Yeah. I took them to Rodney Bay.'

'Where's that?'

'It's a yachting marina over the other side of the island. Lots of tourists go there.'

Hart and her male companion were heading for a yacht. They could be gone already.

'Take us there. And there's another twenty in it if you break the speed limit.'

The cabbie took Mark at his word and in ten minutes they had crossed the island roads amongst palm trees, lush rain forests and banana and sugar cane plantations, overtaking struggling lorries and honking ambling drivers. Mark was dismayed. The marina was enormous. Hundreds of yachts, cruisers and gin palaces were lined up along wooden berths and piers. It was needle in a haystack time. The cabbie left them as they walked towards the bobbing boats.

'So what next, Mark? Which boat do we want? Or are they gone already?' Ted said dubiously.

'They must be somewhere. Give me a minute to think.'

He needed a vantage point. He climbed the steps to the second floor of a row of souvenir, food shops and yacht charter companies and looked out over the mass of gleaming white and blue hulls reflecting the sunlight. They all looked bloody identical. The only real colour out there in his eyeline were the rows of international flags fluttering at the rear of the boats. Every nationality seemed to be here. Barbadian, St Lucian, American, British, Grenadian, French, Trinidadian. That was it.

'Ted, take a look at the flags.'

'What? All very nice and that but so what?'

'Think of the BBC news and those shots of Mandela and the national flag. Gold and red and blue diagonals. Take a hard look. Do you see any South African flags at all?'

Ted knew what he meant. They scanned the horizon. They both saw it at the same time. Way down the end of one of the berths to the left-hand side. A small pennant on a mast. ANC colours and all.

'That's gotta be it.'

Mark could hear the sound of voices as they approached the fifty footer at the end of the pier. A good sign. The boat was occupied. Sound of laughter too. Mark wondered if Hart would have much to laugh about soon. Five middle-aged people sat at the rear of the boat holding flutes of champagne as smooth reggae music emanated from inside the main cabin. One tall man in shorts and a garish polo shirt stood up as Mark stopped by the boat.

'Can we help you at all?'

That was all Mark needed. The accent was definitely South African. The description was close enough to the one Winston had given earlier that morning. This had to be the right boat.

'We're looking for a Sarah Hart.'

The mariner shrugged his shoulders, almost spilling some precious champagne overboard.

'There's no one here by that name. Sorry, guys.'

'You might know her by her alias, Sarah Carter. Mid-thirties? Short dark red hair? English?'

'No. Still never heard of her.'

Ted took out the warrant and the letter again. This time to more effect.

'We're from the Metropolitan Police in England. We are here to arrest her on charges of insider dealing.'

'I'm telling you, she's not here.'

Ted brushed past the mariner and his bemused guests and gave the boat the once over in five minutes dead. Mark stood embarrassed on the aft, hoping Ted would deliver the goods. Pity.

'He's right. She ain't here.'

Mark persevered. 'Were you on a LIAT flight from Barbados this morning?'

The mariner squared up to him.

'It's none of your damn business what I did this morning, but to get rid of you I'll tell you I was here all day and have been all this week. I never left St Lucia.'

'OK. Calm down. But you are South African, aren't you?'

'There's no law against that so far as I'm aware.' The mariner waited and then offered some assistance for the first time since the mini-invasion of his yacht. 'You probably want the other South African boat.'

Mark sensed a break for the first time that day.

'Where is it?'

The mariner swivelled around, walked up to the front of the boat and pointed off to starboard.

'Oh. It was tied up there a few hours ago. It must have left.'

'Any idea where it might have gone?'

'No idea. I never spoke to the guy. I don't even know the name of his yacht.'

'You must have some idea where it went. Where would you go if you were on the run from the law?'

'On the run? I guess I'd find a quiet inlet off some deserted island and moor up till the heat was off.'

Ted pushed his way forward to the bow of the boat.

'And how many deserted islands are there around here?'

The mariner grinned, enjoying the brief moment of revenge.

'I'd say no more than a few hundred at least. Good luck in your search.'

The clock at sea and to muster about three than the
muster.

Any conversation avoiding religious today?

Ranks were otherwise recognised. Why, was it about the
English school. There is a nature behind the good school
system will work hoping to get home and enjoy it as
soon as possible all agreed no matches and close shop.

Not, we... Well be seen together.

CHAPTER THIRTY-ONE

GRANTLEY ADAMS INTERNATIONAL AIRPORT, BARBADOS

The check-in girl in departures tried in vain to attract Mark's attention.

'Are you gentlemen travelling together today?'

Mark was otherwise occupied. What was it about the English abroad? They stood in line behind the pink Anglo-Saxons who were looking to get home and out this heat as soon as possible. All dressed in singlets and cheap shorts, perfectly suitable for an evening departure from the tropics but they were going to freeze to death at six a.m. in LGW. Disgruntled children wore assorted t-shirts from Antigua, St Lucia and Grenada as they sat on the marble tiles in floods of tears for some unknown reason.

Ted was first to react and handed over their passports and tickets. Mark wished they were three today.

'Yes, we are. We'd like seats together.'

Mark's gaze still wandered around the area. English middle management with beery paunches, knee-length white socks and open-toed sandals gave the children grief as they listened to unintelligible announcements on the Tannoy. Wives with sun-damaged hair sat protectively upon their collection of accumulated luggage, wondered where the hell the trolleys were hidden in this airport and prayed that the announcements confirmed that Britannia were on time today. Rastafarians with dreadlocks under berets stood ready to return to their digs in Brixton and Peckham. Bob Marley was alive and well and still jammin'.

'That's twenty-five dollars departure tax each please.'

Ted handed over the fifty bucks on their behalf. It should have been seventy-five. It would have been a small price to pay to transport Hart back to London. If only. Mark took his boarding pass and saw that Ted had been allocated the prime window seat. It was that sort of day.

Mark rummaged in his pocket. Even after the tax, he still had a few Barbadian dollars left. No use to him back in the UK. Might as well spend it now on something that might realise a long-term investment. He went over to the souvenir shop, avoiding the tacky Caribbean reminders of his five-day stay and opting instead for a standard postcard and a stamp for Europe. He sat in the check-in area and pondered his words.

'Greetings from Barbados where I am for a few days – work unfortunately. I enjoyed meeting you. Could we meet up again? You have my work number. Regards, Mark.' That would do. He scribbled the address on the other side. Barbara Ashby, Blake Brothers & Co Ltd, Bishopsgate, London EC2, England. The postcard would definitely get there but what would she make of it? She might throw it in the bin. She might call him. Time would tell. Nothing to lose.

He took one last look at the picture on the other side of the postcard. It looked like paradise on earth. A small bay, white beaches and tilting palm trees with fronds hanging into the water. The small print on the other side named it as Marigot Bay, somewhere on one of the other islands in the Caribbean. It was a slightly misleading impression of Barbados but Barbara would never know. Like a scene from South Pacific, he thought.

He dropped the card into the postbox, knowing his hopes

were also accompanying it on its way to a leading City research analyst. Barbara might be impressed that he was now a jet setting international investigator not a mere civil servant crony. Dream on.

Sarah sat at the best corner table of Dolittles restaurant staring out at that gorgeous flash yacht. The aptly named Krugerand bobbed in the lapping water of the sheltered bay. One of the eager crew washed down the deck with a yard brush while another took laundry back from a girl in a rowing boat. In the background the lush hills were fronted by neat rows of palm trees lined up along the shore, all leaning at the required forty five-degree angle towards the water. Like a scene from South Pacific, she thought.

Some less fortunate visitors on charter yachts promenaded along the shore between the laid-back customs office, the mini-market, the diesel depot and the ice machines. Essential for keeping the Piton lager six-packs chilled at the correct temperature. A pontoon boat enthusiastically shuttled between the two sides of the inner harbour. Two boys played with a tyre hanging on a rope from one palm tree, taking turns to launch themselves from on high and swim back to shore for the next turn. Their occasional splash was the only sound that carried over the water in the warm evening atmosphere.

The open-air restaurant in the bay was also appropriately named. It was just about the best place to relax in the world. When God made time, he made plenty of it here. No hurry, mon. The staff waited upon tables set on a wooden platform where the sea glistened below through the gaps in the old beams. The rattan furniture blended with tropical décor and humming overhead fans. Soft music emanated from a subtle sound system. A waft of the barbecuing catch of the day drifted past to tantalise the elite diners. Sarah turned to her host as he downed the frothy remnants of his third Pina Colada.

'So where exactly are we, Rich?'

'We're on the southern tip of St Lucia.'

'We haven't even left the island then?'

He nodded and thought about ordering a fourth Pina.

'Specifically, where are we?'

'Dolittles,' as he hand-signalled to the waiter.

She smiled back. 'Even I know that. Come on.'

The South African ran a weather-beaten hand along his jawbone and looked deep into her eyes.

'This is Marigot Bay. It's one of the best-kept secrets in the entire Caribbean. Centuries ago an entire English fleet hid in this bay while being pursued by the French. They disguised their masts and rigging with coconut palm fronds. It's a very safe location.' Sarah already knew that. It was perfect for her needs. 'And more recently the musical of the same name was made here with Rex Harrison as the good Doctor. I thought you might like it here. Nothing but the best is good enough for you.'

The plate of seafood arrived, overtly piled high with lobster, crayfish, giant prawns and shrimp.

'So what have you got planned for me next, Rich?'

He placed a tanned hand upon hers. Not a bad comparison at all. Her own tan was improving rapidly.

'You and I are going back to the Krugerand to spend another night alone in the rear cabin.'

'Suits me. And afterwards?'

'We are going to do some liming for the next few days.' He noticed her blank stare. 'Liming is what the locals call doing absolutely nothing.'

Sarah looked out over the fleshy lobster claws, past the still mast of the Krugerand, past the inclined palm trees and out into the wide-open spaces of the Caribbean Sea.

'Perfect.'

EPILOGUE

CITY MURDER TRIAL OPENS IN OLD BAILEY

A major murder trial began yesterday in the Old Bailey following recent events that have gripped the City of London for weeks. American Greg Schneider, 33, a former equity dealer at City investment bank Blake Brothers & Co., is charged with the murder of Alexander Soames, Finance Director of Provident Bank. Soames's body was found last July in the Thames at Greenwich two weeks after he disappeared from a top-level board meeting in the West End. A post mortem revealed that he had been tightly bound before he died from a heart attack.

Schneider held a large dealing position in Provident shares at the time and was about to make a profit of over two million pounds if a planned takeover deal had gone ahead. Schneider yesterday pleaded not guilty to a charge of murdering Soames at a place and time unknown. Helen Soames, the deceased's wife, was in court for the case but left mid-morning visibly distressed.

The Independent

Surprise Departure Of Leading City Regulator

City bankers and regulators alike expressed surprise at the sudden departure of Clive Norris from his position as Director of Enforcement at the London Stock Exchange. Norris, 55, had been at the helm for the past twelve years. He is believed to have been in poor health recently and will take an early retirement deal from the Exchange.

The Board of the LSE acknowledged Norris's contribution to regulation of the City last night. In his time at the Enforcement Department, he has led a number of high profile and successful investigations, including those into the SIMEX futures dealing at Baring Brothers, unlisted offshore investments at Deutsche Morgan Grenfell Asset Management and currency options trading at Nat West Markets. More recently Norris led an insider dealing investigation at Blake Brothers which inadvertently also uncovered the alleged murderer of a director of Provident Bank.

Sources inside the LSE say that this time the Exchange may choose his successor from outside in order to bring some industry expertise to the existing team. Others suggest that there are several good internal candidates for the vacancy. An announcement is expected shortly.

Financial Times

TAKE THE MONEY AND RUN

Institutional shareholders in Provident Bank have been through the mill over the past six months as the share price has gyrated wildly. Few can now recall the heady days of last July when Provident shares hit twelve pounds after the unexpected takeover bid from British Commercial Bank. Since the subsequent discovery of the billions of unreported loan losses in the due diligence process and the acrimonious departure of former highflying CEO, David Webster, Provident has floundered in a sea of negative publicity and severe hits to the bottom line.

Kapital Bank's takeover bid is timely. Their decision to come back to the table is as much a leap of faith as it is a sign of their utter desperation to enter the lucrative UK banking market. They are buying into a black hole at present and the not inconsiderable risk remains that other loan losses will be uncovered in due course. Kapital's revised takeover price of seven pounds thirty pence may seem meagre in comparison to the glory days of Provident but in our opinion it's the only thing that's keeping the Provident share price afloat at present.

Our recommendation: Take the 730p from Kapital.

> Barbara Ashby – Blake Brothers'
> Weekly UK Equity Bulletin

Regulators Set To Question Jersey Banker

Officials from Jersey State's Banking Supervision Department are set to question an employee of Blake Brothers in St Helier next Monday. Penelope Swales, 27, worked as a private client account executive until her sudden suspension from the bank last week. A terse press statement issued by Blakes confirmed that an internal investigation is to be launched into her dealings with certain clients.

Sources inside Blakes office confirmed to the Herald that Swales dealt personally with the financial affairs of a number of high net-worth clients. These are believed to include the account of Sarah Hart, a London-based investor recently sought by UK authorities in connection with suspected insider dealing. The Blakes source indicated that recent share dealing in Ms Swales' own personal account at the bank had followed an identical and equally profitable pattern to that of Ms Hart.

Banking Supervision staff also confirmed that the island's banking regulations require each bank to know their client and to establish the source of funds which they accept. Blakes was recently embarrassed when further facts in the Hart case came to light in London. Ms Hart had apparently worked as a high-class call girl, meeting the sometimes bizarre needs of affluent City executives.

Ms Swales is well known amongst St Helier's banking community but has not been seen in public for weeks.

Jersey Herald

MITCHELL LEONBERG ACCUSED OF
INSIDER DEALING COVER UP

Pressure was growing yesterday for Mitchell Leonberg Inc. to make a formal statement about revelations disclosed in a murder case in London, England. Prosecution lawyers at the Old Bailey on Friday questioned Greg M. Schneider, a former Mitchells' securities dealer in New York, regarding his dismissal from Mitchells four years ago.

Under searching examination, Schneider admitted that he was fired for soliciting price-sensitive securities information on hot stocks from a girlfriend who worked at the time in Mitchells' Mergers & Acquisitions Department. She in turn advised the SEC. Laura Ziegler of the SEC in Washington, DC said that the allegations were formally denied at the time by J. Edson Weaver of Mitchells and no further action was taken. However NASD regulators in New York have now alleged a cover-up.

Weaver has since risen to become Head of Compliance and Legal at Mitchells. On Friday, Schneider named Weaver as the Director who had specifically ordered his firing from Mitchells. Weaver could not be contacted at his Upper East Side brownstone this weekend but if the facts prove to be true, his senior position in the US's leading investment bank is likely to become untenable.

The New York Times

STAFF ANNOUNCEMENT

Following an internal investigation the Board of Directors have decided to cease equity dealing at the Special Situations desk until further notice. Consequently, the desk personnel, Charles Wilson, Julia Anson and Henry Smythe, have left the employment of the Bank with immediate effect.

Personnel Department –
Blake Brothers & Co.

EXCLUSIVE: WE NAME CITY GENTS WHO VISITED EAST END DEN OF VICE

Today your *News of the World* names the sick perverts who visited the den of vice in London's Docklands referred to in a City murder case. Details emerged in court this week about those who visited the Madam of Pain to receive punishment in steamy sex sessions.

Our sensational photo scoop comes courtesy of an elderly neighbour who lives in Thames View, the location of these sickening events. She was concerned at the number of men who regularly visited quiet number 32 across the road. She took Polaroid photographs of those who came and went. Her many complaints to local police went unanswered.

We can reveal that amongst those who visited were Sir Gordon Harvey, the fifty-five-year-old head of giant consumer goods company County Beverages. Harvey's company limo was often seen parked nearby. He even made his company chauffeur wait while he went inside number 32 for up to three hours at a time. Harvey was knighted two years ago by the Queen for his charitable work for under-privileged children but was unavailable for comment this weekend.

Our chief political reporter at the *World* recognised another sick client from a colour photo. Jeffrey Simpson is a senior civil servant in a Whitehall government department. He was once photographed leaving the vice den carrying cleaning utensils and a pair of rubber gloves.

Also seen regularly was Simon Fry, a partner in the City's largest legal firm, Speake Windsor & Co. Fry, 36, earns hundreds of thousands of pounds a year so the exorbitant sex fees charged by the mysterious Lady of the Whip were no problem for him. He was photographed getting out of a black cab near Thames View. When we telephoned his Chelsea home last night, his wife was stunned by our revelations.

News of the World

POLICE SWOOP ON LOCAL VILLAINS

South London police yesterday arrested two suspected local gangsters in Bermondsey on charges of threatening behaviour and intent to cause serious injury. Leonard Riggs, 52 and Sidney 'Pug' Wickes, 35, both of Rotherhithe, were taken to Croydon Central police station to be questioned about a bizarre incident last August. A motorist alleges that the two men threatened him with a gun while he sat in his car at a set of traffic lights in Wandsworth. A maroon Jaguar saloon was traced to Riggs having been inadvertently photographed at a townhouse in the Isle of Dogs.

Police sources said that the two men are known to them due to a string of previous convictions for theft, fraud and extortion. They also intend to investigate possible criminal business dealings, including a number of central London rental properties recently bought for cash with the suspected proceeds of drug trafficking. There is also speculation that Wickes will be questioned about the mugging and subsequent death of a London Stock Exchange employee outside his East London home this summer.

South London Gazette

CROSSWAITHE TO RETIRE FROM BLAKE BROTHERS

Nicholas Crosswaithe today confirmed he would retire at
the end of the year from his current position as Director
of Dealing at Blake Brothers, London. He has worked at
Blakes for twenty-nine years and was one of the senior
partners who took the second-tier firm into new markets
and business in recent years.

Crosswaithe refused to comment on whether his departure was due to the allegations of insider dealing at Blakes'
Special Situations desk. Questions have been asked about
management control at Blakes over the dealing activities
of Greg Schneider, the former employee at the centre of
the current Old Bailey murder trial. Crosswaithe said he
would now spend more time on personal matters, including
his membership of the Board of the Royal Opera House,
his chairmanship of the MCC and his National Trust
directorship.

Also retiring at the end of the year is James Ingrams,
Director of Compliance at Blakes.

Bloomberg News Wire

WIDOW OF CITY BANKER WINS
OUT OF COURT SETTLEMENT

The widow of a murdered City banker won her long
running legal battle against Kapital Bank AG yesterday
when the defendant agreed to an out of court cash
settlement, believed to be in excess of £1.3 million.
Helen Soames's late husband, Alexander, was Finance
Director of Provident Bank before the takeover by Kapital.
Major accounting irregularities were later discovered at
Provident but the acquisition was nevertheless completed
last month.

Mrs Soames' lawyers argued that her late husband had
an employment contract with Provident that guaranteed
compensation to her husband, and thus both herself and
her children, in the event of a takeover. Kapital Bank had
argued that her husband, murdered and dumped into the
Thames during the bidding war, was not a Director at
the time of the acquisition and was thus not entitled to
any compensation. However the bank were not prepared
to continue the case in court next week and offered the
settlement to Mrs Soames's legal team. Mrs Soames has
been accompanied in court by DI Edward Hammond of the
Metropolitan Police, the man responsible for identifying
and charging her husband's alleged killer.

The Guardian

HIGH SOCIETY ATTENDS CAPETOWN'S WEDDING OF THE YEAR

Capetown's finest were out in force yesterday for the society wedding of the year. Multi-millionaire Richard Weinberg tied the knot at the City Cathedral with Sarah Carter, his beautiful English bride. The bride wore a Givenchy strapless cream dress with pearl inlay especially created in Paris and complemented by stunning diamond earrings.

The couple met only seven months ago on the Club World deck of a British Airways flight out of London. Weinberg had completed a landmark property deal in the West End and was off for a break in the Caribbean. Carter too was on holiday. Close friends say that it was love at first sight at 38,000 feet and they have been inseparable since time spent together in the exclusive St Lawrence Gap resort in Barbados.

Weinberg, 42, made his money in commercial property development in the central business district of Johannesburg before branching out into retail and residential property. Last year he publicly split from his long-time wife Heidi following revelations about her extra-marital affair with a government minister. Ms Carter, 34, is an English heiress who recently inherited the bulk of her mother's investments.

The newly weds wouldn't say where they were heading off to on their honeymoon but friends hinted that they were immediately flying to join the Krugerand, Weinberg's yacht, currently moored in the Seychelles.

The Capetown Times

JUDGE HANDS DOWN SENTENCE
TO FORMER DEALER

The long running Alexander Soames murder trial came to a conclusion today when Lord Justice Hartley passed sentence on former Blakes' dealer Greg Schneider. The jury had earlier thrown out the murder charge following the sometimes contradictory expert medical evidence about Soames's health and the exact cause of his death. However they did reach a unanimous manslaughter verdict after three further hours of deliberations. In his summing up the judge said that the evidence against the defendant meant that he had no choice but to pass a six-year sentence. Schneider had pleaded his innocence to the charge during the trial.

Daily Mail

THE ODD COUPLE AT LARGE

Who'd have guessed the identity of Barbara Ashby's mysterious escort at the Institutional Investor awards bash at the Grosvenor House hotel last night? Envious comments were discreetly whispered about the dashing gentleman who accompanied Ashby, formerly of Sky TV fame, to the exclusive top table. Imagine the surprise when her new beau was later revealed to be Mark Robinson of the LSE Enforcement Department. Talk about the sheep running with the wolves. Whatever next? Nick Leeson popping in for Sunday lunch with the Baring family? Ashby won the coveted top equity analyst award for her work at Blake Brothers. She was headhunted last month to become Senior Vice President of Equity Research at Mitchell Leonberg's London office. Robinson, 30, was the recent surprise choice to take over as Head of Enforcement at the London Stock Exchange.

City People – *Business Supplement*
Evening Standard

The author may be contacted by e-mail at

paulkilduff@eircom.net

PAUL KILDUFF

SQUARE MILE

6.25 a.m. Monday, 18 March: Jeremy Walker, a director of the City of London's most respected global investment bank, Steen Odenberg & Co, is discovered in his luxury Wapping penthouse, strangled with his own silk Hermes tie.

Anthony Carlton, a young colleague, is reluctantly drawn into the subsequent police investigation, only to learn that his initial enquiries lead to EPIC, the mysterious multi-million dollar property fund recently launched by the bank.

As Anthony follows the trail of mounting evidence to Europe and on to the Far East, he becomes enmeshed in an international scandal of intricate and horrifying proportions. As he attempts to unravel this finely-woven and ever-expanding web of greed and deceit, Anthony begins to fear for his career, his livelihood and the safety of those he cares about.

HODDER AND STOUGHTON PAPERBACKS

A selection of bestsellers from
Hodder & Stoughton

All Hodder & Stoughton books are available at your local bookshop or newsagent, or can be ordered direct from the publisher. Just tick the titles you want and fill in the form below. Prices and availability subject to change without notice.

Hodder & Stoughton Books, Cash Sales Department, Bookpoint, 39 Milton Park, Abingdon, OXON, OX14 4TD, UK. E-mail address: order@bookpoint.co.uk. If you have a credit card you may order by telephone – (01235) 400414.

Please enclose a cheque or postal order made payable to Bookpoint Ltd to the value of the cover price and allow the following for postage and packing:
UK & BFPO – £1.00 for the first book, 50p for the second book, and 30p for each additional book ordered up to a maximum charge of £3.00.
OVERSEAS & EIRE – £2.00 for the first book, £1.00 for the second book, and 50p for each additional book

Name _____

Address _____

_____

_____

If you would prefer to pay by credit card, please complete:
Please debit my Visa/Access/Diner's Card/American Express (delete as applicable) card no:

☐☐☐☐☐☐☐☐☐☐☐☐☐☐☐☐☐☐☐

Signature _____

Expiry Date _____

If you would NOT like to receive further information on our products please tick the box. ☐